LOUDER THAN WORDS

ALSO BY LISA ELLIOT

Dancing It Out
The Light in You
Up Against Her

Louder Than Words

~

Lisa Elliot

Copyright © 2022 Lisa Elliot

The moral right of the author has been asserted.

All rights reserved.

Edited by Gia Darwin

Cover design by Eve A. Hard

ISBN: 9798843771188

This is a work of fiction. All characters and events in this publication, other than those clearly in the public domain, are fictitious and any resemblance to real persons, living or dead, is purely coincidental.

For all the wounded inner childs

One

Gripping both ends of the gold Christmas cracker, I pulled them apart and did not flinch. I took out the green paper hat and carefully placed it on my head. The smooth feel of it sliding over my ears was strangely comforting. Christmas songs boomed out of my radio on the kitchen windowsill. Taking a sip of red wine, I gazed at the table I'd set with red tartan place mats, napkins and the Christmas dinner I'd cooked for myself. My plate was filled with turkey, roast potatoes, parsnips, sprouts, gravy, and cranberry sauce. The works. The meal itself would last for a few days. Leftover roast potatoes were such a treat. I was always the one who did the cooking growing up. My mother was never one for spending time in the kitchen.

After my feast I decamped to the sofa with my wine and put on a Christmas film. Resting my legs on the footrest, wrapped up in my cheetah onesie, I relaxed into the sofa and the black and white film. My favourite cinnamon Christmas candle flickered next to the television.

I needed this film today, even if I didn't like to admit it. As usual, I cried a bit at the end despite having seen it more times than I could remember. I switched off the television and got out my laptop, opening a folder titled 'mother'. I hadn't looked in here in years. I clicked on a video I took of her on her last Christmas before she passed away. My chest tightened as she ripped open her presents. We'd had such a great Christmas that year.

My phone flashed up. Rebecca, my flatmate, had gone to her parents' house for Christmas with her boyfriend.

Rebecca: *Happy Christmas!! How's your day been?*

> **Myla:** *Happy Christmas to you too!! How's the family?*
>
> **Rebecca:** *They're good, thanks. No drama this year. You should have come with us! I hate to think of you on your own today…*

I wasn't fond of displays of sympathy towards me like this. I was fine. Being on my own at Christmas was normal for me. I'd told Rebecca countless times that I could handle being on my own. It was just another day, after all.

> **Myla:** *I'm fine. Seriously, you don't need to worry. How many Baileys have you had?*
>
> **Rebecca:** *Bottles or glasses?*
>
> **Myla:** *My point exactly. Glad you're having a good Christmas. Please note, I am too.*
>
> **Rebecca:** *Note taken. You opened your Baileys yet?*
>
> **Myla:** *Getting it now. Btw, would you like me to water your plants while you're away?*
>
> **Rebecca:** *Yes please! I totally forgot. You're a good flatmate, Murray.*

We messaged for a while longer, which was nice. Rebecca left to say goodbye to her grandparents, and I poured myself a generous amount of the Baileys I'd splashed out on. Yes, it was just another day, but that didn't stop me from wanting to enjoy it. As I contemplated which Christmas film to put on next, half looking at the paused laptop screen of my mother smiling, my phone went again, this time a picture of Cara, my mother's best friend, stared up at me. I accepted the call, instinctively.

Louder Than Words

"Hey." I went through to my bedroom, which had better reception. I stood by the window in the darkness to save money on electricity. The only light came from the streetlights.

"Hi," Cara said. "Can you hear me?" Cara's London accent was loud and clear in my tiny bedroom. I smiled at hearing her familiar voice. Normally we spoke earlier on Christmas day.

"Yep, I can hear you. Happy Christmas, Cara!"

"Happy Christmas! Sorry I didn't call before now. It's been manic here. How are you doing?" There was real concern in her voice. I wasn't sure why.

"I'm good. I've had a lovely and relaxing day. Can't complain."

"Nice." There was silence on the line. "When are you coming down to visit? We'd love to see you."

I'd politely declined to spend Christmas with Cara and her wife Kay for two years running. They were brilliant, but I'd wanted my own space again this year. I'd needed it. "Soon, yeah. I need to save up some money for the train ticket, but once I do I'll come down."

"Nonsense! We'll pay! You don't have to worry about money."

Since I'd moved up to Scotland, Cara and Kay had often paid for my visits to London. Cara knew I was uncomfortable about this. I didn't have it in me to fight her on it today though. "Okay, thank you. We'll make plans in the new year."

"Great. You should bring your guitar with you. Kay keeps asking me when you're going to teach her."

I glanced up at my guitar case collecting dust on top of the wardrobe. "Sure, I'd be happy to."

Cara went quiet again. "You know I still think about her," Cara said. "About your mum. She used to love Christmas."

"She did."

We hadn't spoken about my mother in a while. The conversation jarred at first, then it settled between us like familiar territory.

Cara's voice softened. "Do you think you'll move back to London one day?"

"I like it here. I like my flat. I like my job. I'm settled."

"As long as you're happy."

I didn't answer that. Instead, I asked about their Christmas and listened as Cara filled me in on the intricacies of their day: who had come to visit and what had been eaten. I sipped my Baileys. Cara's voice was so soothing. I'd spent many a Christmas with Cara and Kay in their London townhouse in the west end so I could imagine their day vividly. They tended to have lots of visitors and lots of fun. I would hide in the bathroom to take breathers from the non-stop socialising.

When we hung up, I stayed in the darkness scanning the street for signs of life. A family was leaving a house across the street. The grandmother waved from the doorstep as her daughter and grandchild moved towards their car.

I ached to know what it would be like to have three generations of family around me. That sense of unconditional love, connection and belonging was alien to me. It was all I'd ever wanted. I longed for it. I hadn't found the right person to build a life with yet, and it was hard not to look back and think about everything that I'd lost or missed out on and what most people took for granted. I hadn't found my people. Rebecca and Michelle were my world here in Edinburgh, but I wasn't the main person in theirs by far. Cara and Kay were the closest thing I had to family, and I wasn't the centre of their universes either. They each had their own main family and friends, which was wonderful for them. I, on the other hand, was very much an outsider, even with the people I spent most of my time with.

The way the grandmother lingered on her doorstep as the car pulled around the corner and out of sight gave me a lump in my throat. I swallowed heavily and shut the curtains. This day always got to me in the end.

***

I was glad to be back at work. I'd spent way too much time wallowing in self-pity over Christmas. I needed to get out of this funk and back to being positive again. The smell from the oven wafted up from the basement kitchen, giving the whole café its warm and soothing vibe that I loved. I'd power-walked here in the pitch black this morning because I'd agreed to take the early shift. But I'd managed to get the baked goods in the oven by seven so I could have a latte and a blueberry muffin before we opened at eight. Hardly any customers came in, so I was able to enjoy absent-mindedly scrolling on my phone and sipping coffee.

"Busy, I see?" Michelle said, appearing after nine. Michelle, the owner, was a married lesbian in her late forties and had a cracking sense of humour. "I guess people must still be sleeping off their hangovers."

"We've had one customer," I said, placing my phone face-down on the table. I'd worked here for four years, and we were friends, but I didn't want to take the piss. She was my boss after all. "Four large lattes. Never seen her before."

Michelle shrugged. Her red hair swung in its high ponytail and her trademark long black dress and big dark boots were in fine form. "Hopefully brunch will be busier."

It was early January and the flow of customers could be unpredictable. But a steady brunch turned into a busy lunch, and we were run off our feet for the rest of the afternoon. By three it calmed down, and Michelle and I took an uncharacteristic break together after clearing up. I was scrolling through Tinder, wondering if this was the only way to find a date these days.

"What the internet should have been invented for." Michelle held her phone out towards me as a bunch of golden retrievers jumped into a sunny garden swimming pool and swam around together, living their best life.

"Oh my god I want them *all*."

An unrecognised number flashed up on my phone. I let it ring out, turning my attention back to Michelle, who was typing on her laptop now. It rang again. Same number. That was odd. Didn't random call centres move on after a missed call? I ignored it again. It rang one more petulant time before leaving us in peace.

Michelle was intrigued, looking over her laptop at me. "They're a bit keen, aren't they?"

"And now a voicemail. Let's see what they're selling." I tapped on the notification and put the voicemail on speaker. The voice that boomed out was not what I expected. It was an older man's voice, and somewhat authoritative.

"Good afternoon. This is Graeme Henderson from HLD Solicitors. I'm calling to speak with Ms Myla Murray regarding some family matters. Please can you call me back on this number as soon as you can. I look forward to hearing from you."

I was confused. I didn't have any family. I was on my own after my mother died. I shifted in my seat. "That's a scam, right?"

"I don't know. It's hard to tell. He sounded pretty legit. Do you know what it could be about?"

"No idea. I don't have any family."

I'd mentioned this to Michelle once or twice before when the topic of family came up. It wasn't something I talked about with anyone, but I'd worked here for so long and become friends with Michelle, so it had been unavoidable to not tell her something. But I kept it light. The truth was too bleak.

"You could look him up?"

"Already googling him."

I found the website for HLD Solicitors within seconds. They were based in the Scottish Highlands. His profile as one of the partners of the firm seemed real. The practice was established in eighteen-ninety. Why would he be contacting me? I didn't have any siblings or cousins. I'd never known my dad. My mother grew up in Scotland but as far as I was aware we didn't have any family. "They seem pretty above board?"

Michelle sat forward. "Are you going to call him back?"

"How did he get my contact details? Why is he calling me?"

"You'll never know unless you call back."

I took a deep breath, considering it. It couldn't hurt to find out, could it? "If it's a scam, I'm hanging up."

"Good plan. I'll be here if you need me."

I tapped his number. The call picked up after only a couple of rings. "Hi, my name is Myla Murray and I'm returning a call from a Graeme Henderson?"

"Thank you for calling back, Ms Murray."

His voice was deep and trustworthy, but I wasn't going to fall for this that easily. "I don't mean to be rude but how did you get my number? How do you know my name?"

"I appreciate this is quite out-of-the-blue. However, I'm calling on behalf of your great-aunt, Margaret McCallister, who sadly passed away a few weeks ago."

What? That didn't make any sense.

"She has named you in her last will and testament."

What a cruel thing to do to someone who was on their own in life, and especially so soon after Christmas. "I think you have the wrong Myla Murray."

"I'm assured you're the right one. Your great-aunt has been attempting to find you and your mother Sarah for some time. More recently, she hired a private investigator, who finally found you."

My insides twisted. How did he know about my mother? This was too much. Michelle looked concerned and put the closed sign on the door.

"It would be more appropriate to discuss this matter face to face. Is there a good time and place we can meet?"

My alarm bells were ringing now. This was crazy. I had a great-aunt who had been trying to find me and my mother?

"I can come to you. You are in Edinburgh, yes?"

I was wary about saying anything further to him at this point. "I need to think about it. Can you call me back in a few minutes?"

"Certainly, Ms Murray."

Why couldn't he tell me what was going on over the phone? Why did he want to meet in person? Was he a serial killer? I looked up at Michelle. "It can't be true."

"But what if it is? Aren't you curious? It could be a chance to learn more about your roots?"

I knew very little about my roots. If he had something to share with me, and there was even the slightest chance of finding out more about where I came from could I seriously *not* take this opportunity? No. "True. I should hear him out. Would you mind if I met him here in case he's a nutcase and his website is fake or something?"

"Of course not. Meet him here and I'll keep an eye on you."

My phone buzzed and we shared a look of *why not?* I made arrangements to meet Graeme in the café in two days. With a tremble in my hand, I hung up. "It's done."

I spent the next two days thinking about little else. Had I really had a great-aunt? It stirred something deep inside of me. A longing for something I never even knew I had. Was there any more family? What was in the will? Why was I named in it? Why hadn't my mother told me about my great-aunt? It brought up uncomfortable feelings that I hadn't felt in a long time about my mother's unusual attitude towards her own past, and the lack of information she'd been willing to share with me before she died.

The little I knew was that my mother was from the Highlands and had moved to London when she was pregnant with me at eighteen and never returned. My mother didn't know my dad's name or how to get in touch with him. They were students at the time and had met at a party. My mother had refused to tell me anything about her own parents, her childhood, and where she was from. When I was little, I used to beg for her to tell me something more. But she never did. So, in the end, I gave up. I could have explored it for myself after my mother passed, but the thought of finding family at that point in my life was too painful and I hadn't wanted to go there. I still didn't. I was fine on my own. It was what I knew. It was safe.

"Today's the day!" Rebecca said, standing in the doorway to my bedroom as I got ready for work. Rebecca had been amazed to hear that I'd been contacted by the solicitor of a late great-aunt in the Highlands and was probably more excited than me. I'd asked her to join me, for moral support, and was touched that she'd said yes. "You could be a millionaire!"

I paused brushing my hair and gave Rebecca a sceptical look. "Nah. I don't think so. It'd be good to find out anything about my family background, but there won't be any money."

Rebecca crossed her arms and sighed, then leant against the doorframe. Rebecca was so tall she filled the doorway, even when leaning to the side a bit. "I'm just saying it could be on the cards. She went out of her way to find you. How many people at the end of their life have the need to hire a private investigator?"

"I guess we'll find out. And thanks for coming with me today."

"That's what friends are for, right?" Rebecca pushed herself off the doorframe, making a *cha-ching* sound as she walked away. I laughed and resumed brushing my hair.

The meeting was arranged for five. Work passed slowly. Twice I thought the clock needed a new battery. Rebecca came in around four thirty, demolished a slice of cake and sat there on a sugar high glancing at the door. Not long after I sat down next to her, the café door opened and a well-dressed older man walked in. He had on a tweed jacket and carried a worn leather briefcase. His shoes were gleaming. This was a man who came from another world, a world where money and ownership of land, buildings and assets were likely the norm. Why was he here talking to me?

I stood and waved, gesturing for him to come over to our table. When he recognised me, his expression softened, and he smiled with his eyes. Perhaps he was legit after all.

"Ms Murray," he held out his hand. "So pleased to finally meet you."

We shook hands and I introduced Rebecca.

"I'm sure you're wondering what this is about, Ms Murray. I apologise again for the manner in which I got in touch with you, but I'm delighted that we have been able to meet." He sat down, with his jacket still on, and got out a file with the HLD Solicitors logo on it and an expensive looking fountain pen.

Rebecca and I shared a quick glance. Rebecca stiffened up, as if she was in trouble with the headteacher at school. Michelle gave me a relaxed smile and thumbs up from behind the counter. The idea of this man being dodgy no longer seemed likely. He seemed like a well-meaning old lawyer with something to tell me about my past. I crossed my arms, feeling less comfortable by the second, sensing that whatever this man was about to say was going to affect my life in some way. Rebecca gave the back of my hand a quick squeeze.

"Ms Murray. As I said on the telephone, your late great-aunt, Margaret McAllister, has sadly passed away. She was eighty. She was your maternal grandmother's sister."

He placed a thick letterhead piece of paper on the table between us with a family tree on it. My eyes widened. These were my relatives? This was so weird. And so few children.

"Margaret and her husband didn't have any children. There are no other living relatives on Margaret or her late husband James' side."

I gripped my wrist, and nervously twisted my hand around it. I glanced down at the small treble clef tattoo on the inside of my wrist, which gave me a momentary sense of calm. "I wasn't aware of any of this. My mother never spoke about where she came from."

"We thought as much. Ms Murray—"

"Myla. You can call me Myla."

He cleared his throat. "Yes, of course, Myla." He paused. "Your mother's family has been looking for you for a very long time."

This brought a lump to my throat, and an unwanted glaze stole across my eyes. I looked away from them both, to conceal it.

He continued, more gently this time, "Margaret sadly passed away shortly after finding you. She used the time she had left to ensure that you were named in her will. She wanted you to know that she was very much in her right mind when she named you in it."

My chest tightened. That was so sad. I could have had a chance to know a long-lost relative, but that chance was gone. They were all gone.

"Myla. Your great-aunt has left her entire estate to you." He placed another piece of paper on the table. "This includes the family home, Glenbuinidh House, a substantial amount of land, and full ownership of the family business – one of the world's most recognisable whisky brands – Glenbuinidh. There are other assets too, but we can cover that another time."

My jaw hung loosely as I sought reality and grounding from Rebecca, but her face reflected mine, so did Michelle's. This couldn't be true. It could *not* be true.

"Margaret wanted to make sure that the estate stayed within the family. Your mother's family comes from a long line of landowners. It was Margaret's last wish on this earth that you received the estate, and I promised her that I would personally deliver this news to you myself."

"I… I don't know what to say."

"Legally, it's all yours now. All the documentation is in this file, which I will leave with you to read through at your own convenience. I would also advise you to find a good financial adviser. I'd be happy to recommend one or two, if you like."

The words he used were strange to me, yet I hung onto every single one.

"There was one other thing," he pulled out an envelope and slid it across the table to me. "Margaret wrote a letter to you."

I rested my eyes on the envelope as if it were a window to another life, a life where I had a family and I knew who I was and where I came from. Where I wasn't alone in this world.

"Margaret wanted me to tell you that you were always in their thoughts and that you were always loved."

I closed my eyes. Tears threatened to form and then one or two bubbled over onto my cheeks. When I opened my eyes he and Rebecca were sitting quietly. "Sorry," I murmured, wiping my face with the back of my sleeve.

Rebecca squeezed my hand.

"It's quite all right." Graeme said.

"How did Margaret pass away?"

"Cancer."

"Oh." I nodded, feeling completely overwhelmed. I touched the envelope with my fingertips as if I was reaching back through time. I had so many unanswered questions. Why did my mother leave her family so young? What were my grandparents like? What was this about a family whisky distillery? Hopefully this letter would contain everything I needed to know.

I looked up at Graeme. "Did you know my grandparents?"

"I did, yes. Your grandfather, William Murray, was a GP and your grandmother, Hazel, looked after the home. They were a big part of the local community."

"And you said it was a family whisky business?"

"Yes, the distillery has been in your maternal family line for generations. Your great-aunt and her husband made it an international success. They handed the day to day running of it over to someone else in the town when they retired. They never really let go, of course. Margaret was still involved right up until the end." Graeme paused, as if sensing this was a lot of information. "The town is Balbuinidh. Have you been before?"

"No. Not that I'm aware of."

"I would encourage you to visit the house, the area, and perhaps even the distillery. It might help this make more sense."

"I will." I had more questions but needed to pace myself. My head was spinning.

Graeme looked between Rebecca and me with a kindness that I appreciated. "Thank you for your time today, Myla. I'll leave you this file and here is my business card."

"Thanks for travelling all the way down to see me in person like this. I really appreciate it."

"You're very welcome. As I said, I knew your family and this was very important to them."

Once the solicitor had left, I finally took a deep breath and sank into my chair. I'd been so tense the entire time.

Rebecca gave a nervous laugh. "What the actual fuck just happened?"

I was frozen. I couldn't take it in. "I don't know."

Michelle joined us. "Are you okay?"

"Aye, she's fine," Rebecca said. "She's landed gentry now!"

I glanced at the file sitting innocently on the table as if it wasn't the bombshell that it was. When my mother was alive, we'd been comfortable. We lived in north London, and I was sent to boarding school. My mother carved out a good career for herself in journalism after she went back to university and got her degree. Before that, we'd lived off her savings. Savings from where, I never knew. I never asked. My mother wasn't good with money, however – she was chaotic like that, and the savings ran out. She didn't have life insurance or anything either. Since she passed away, I'd been scraping by in various low-paid jobs. This was one of the biggest things that had ever happened to me. I was no longer poor. The concept was hard to get my head around. "I'm okay, thanks. Shocked but okay."

"I'm not sure what to say because of the family revelations but, uh, congratulations!" Michelle said. "You've just won the lottery!"

"Yeah! Congratulations! This is so crazy. I called it! Millionaire! You've got to celebrate!" Rebecca squealed, bursting with the appropriate amount of enthusiasm.

My reactions to good things weren't normal. I *should* be overjoyed about this, I should be going crazy with glee, but I didn't feel like that. I felt... numb. Off. "I don't feel like celebrating."

Michelle gave me a quizzical look.

"Why not?" Rebecca frowned.

I shifted in my seat. While I was friends with Rebecca and Michelle, I still felt like they didn't really know me. It was my fault. I didn't open up much, and especially not about my past or my mother. I'd been on my own for so long it was second nature to me. I was fine that way. I had to answer this though. "I am thrilled and excited about the money. I mean, who wouldn't be? But I need to process. I'm disappointed I never got to meet my great-aunt, that I never got to meet any of them." I ran a finger over the small family tree, unable to prevent the words that were spilling out of my mouth. "I don't know why my mother never told me any of this. I feel so betrayed."

Michelle sat down. "That's understandable. Take your time. Let it sink in."

"She never told you she was from a rich family," Rebecca said, matter-of-factly. "And you have no idea why she might have kept that from you?"

Rebecca was never one to skirt around an issue. I liked her directness and how authentic she was, even if it cut a little close sometimes. "I don't. And I don't think I'll ever know."

"That's rough. Hard to understand. Seriously though, when you feel up to it, we should totally go out and celebrate this. You deserve some good news. And this is incredible, so yes, we are definitely celebrating this for you. And not in the flat. I mean out out."

Louder Than Words

Michelle nodded. "Rebecca's right. You should enjoy this. It's life changing."

"I know." I could see my whole life opening up and expanding in ways I never thought possible. I knew I wouldn't quite believe the whole family thing until I went to the Highlands and saw it for myself. Until I was ready for that, I could at least let this ridiculously good fortune be what it was and enjoy it. I didn't have to face the past right away, and the idea of indulging in the money first was way more appealing. "You're both right. And I will. Once I recover from the shock, the drinks will definitely be on me. The lottery winner! Can you believe it?"

Two

Kelly used to love going to gigs. She needed a blow-out tonight after a busy day of meetings with the marketing agency about a new advertising campaign for her new single malt. She was exhausted but not tired enough to prevent her from making the most of her time down in the city. Tonight's gig was an American band fronted by two very *celesbians*. Kelly was there with her friend Anna who had organised the tickets. Anna had seen two exes at the gig already. Quite possibly every sapphic woman in the country was here tonight.

The venue was large, packed, and the floor was sticky. Anticipation was building for the main act. Excitable chatter could be heard even above the pre-band music. There was nothing like being around a bunch of zoomers her siblings' age to make her feel like she didn't belong in places like this any more. These days, she increasingly stayed at home with a cup of tea, TV, her emails, and her dog Barley. She hadn't expected her life to turn out this boring and predictable.

While she was comfortable in her picturesque Highland hometown, the buzz and excitement of city life had been feeling very enticing lately. Sometimes she toyed with the idea of moving back to a big city. Maybe she could have more nights out like this if she lived closer?

She hadn't had a drink yet despite talking about alcohol all day. Like most days. At the bar, someone beside her ordered two double Glenbuinidhs. In the noisy venue it had been difficult to hear, but not impossible. The young woman was well-spoken with a refined English accent. The way she spoke caught Kelly's attention – softly, hesitantly, and with a layer of meaning when she said Glenbuinidh that Kelly couldn't place. It was Kelly's drink. Her distillery. Her focus for the last seven years. Hearing it out in the wild never got old. Seeing it ordered by a young woman was a touch unusual, especially in places like this where most people were drinking lukewarm pints of lager from plastic cups.

Kelly looked over again at the young woman's profile and watched as she hovered her card over the machine. She was attractive. Kelly's eyes raked over her shoulder length blonde hair, elegant neckline and plain white v-neck t-shirt. She had a tattoo of a treble clef on the inside of her wrist. But it was the way she held herself that drew Kelly to her the most. She had an ethereal quality that was nothing short of magnetic. Before she could disappear, Kelly was compelled to say something. Anything. She hadn't chatted up a woman at a bar in a *long* time, but she remembered the basics and quickly decided to take a chance.

"Hey. I like your taste."

The young woman flinched at being spoken to. She turned her head towards Kelly with her brow furrowed, looking annoyed. "Excuse me?" She shot back with.

Kelly nodded at the small plastic cups in the younger women's hands. "Your drink. I'm a big fan." The double whisky drinker blushed fiercely and smiled, shyly, suggesting her head had gone to another place entirely. Kelly laughed, amused at the blushing. "What did you think I meant?" This was fun. Harmless flirting was okay, right? "It's a sexy drink. It suits you."

The beautiful girl froze for a split second and then regained her composure, which excited Kelly immensely. A few beats went by, as they caught each other's eyes as people jostled beside them at the bar. Her eyes were blue and steady, and held a maturity in them beyond her years. Kelly's breath caught.

"Thank you. You might want to work on those chat up lines though. Enjoy the gig."

The younger woman bit her bottom lip and moved away, cup of whisky in each hand. Kelly inhaled. Heat spread through her body. Her head turned involuntarily to watch her make her way through the crowd. Kelly's eyes dropped to the slender back and sexy body which was suggested through the young woman's t-shirt and jeans as she wove in and out of the crowd as the lights dimmed and the band neared the stage. Something about the way she moved had Kelly transfixed. When she came to a stop next to a taller girl and handed her one of the cups, Kelly registered that her staring was becoming creepy and turned back around to face the bar.

Finding Anna in the centre of the audience towards the back was a relief. They both liked a bit of space at gigs and to see the crowd's reaction to the band. The front was for the super fans and the kids. Kelly handed Anna a pint of beer.

"Cheers. Seriously, have you ever seen this many lesbians in one place before? The sapphic vibes are off the charts!" Anna said, before taking a sip.

"Not recently."

Kelly took to scanning the backs of people's heads around the spot she'd last seen the woman she'd met at the bar. Disappointed at not being able to find her, she knew that she had to let it go. Random strangers came and went all the time; it was silly to expect to see her feisty whisky drinker again.

The band were met with riotous applause when they came onstage. It was like seeing lesbian royalty in the flesh. "We're so happy to be here, Glasgow. Thank you for having us." The crowd roared. "We flew in today from California and we love it here already. You guys have such cute accents!" This was from the most famous lesbian of the band. The audience purred in response.

Kelly lost track of time listening to the set as song after song eclipsed the one before it, transporting her to a pure moment where nothing else existed but this band and this crowd. Just when she thought they couldn't take it any higher or hit her any harder with their expansive sound and emotional lyrics, they did. And then some. The music was pure energy, pulsating from their hands, falling into the hearts of the people in front of them. Life had gotten so monotonous lately. She'd needed this. To escape. To breathe.

To feel something.

A gap opened up a few metres to Kelly's left, offering her a glimpse of that same white t-shirt and shoulder length blonde hair. Kelly's breath caught. The woman was swaying gently to the music, nodding her head slightly, as if pondering something deep and meaningful about the song. Sometimes she sang along, seemingly knowing the lyrics. Her eyes closed every now and again. Kelly really wanted to know what she was thinking about.

The song, one of Kelly's favourites, finished to thunderous applause. Kelly's awareness never left the silhouette of the young woman only a few metres away. When her head turned briefly in Kelly's direction, their eyes met, before the young woman turned away again.

Kelly watched her try to pretend she hadn't seen her, intrigued by the look she'd found in those eyes and the sensation in her body compelling her to keep looking over. When a slow tilt of the head very definitely made its way in Kelly's direction again and they held three seconds of pure eye contact, a jolt of electricity shot right through to her core. Now that was a look. Excitement coursed through her veins. Stealing glances across crowded rooms was something that happened only in movies and romance novels, not in sweaty gigs in Glasgow, right?

For the rest of the gig, it was safe to say that the band wasn't the only thing occupying Kelly's attention. It was a great gig, and in normal circumstances she'd be glued to them and the finale, but tonight she had other things on her mind. She watched as the young woman raised her hands in the air and cheered and clapped as the band made their way offstage.

When the lights came on, Kelly realised her stolen glances would have to stop. With a sigh, she shook her head and told herself to snap out of it. Yes, watching the hot young woman had been the most exciting thing to happen to her in a while, but it was over now. She'd be back to the humdrum of adulting tomorrow. As people shuffled out, she and Anna joined the herd and waded through the sea of empty cups on the floor.

"That was immense. Best gig I've been to this year," Anna said, enthusiastically. "You still up for going to the gay club next door?"

"Definitely."

Kelly was buzzing, and if there was even the slightest possibility the hot young woman would be there too, and they might happen to bump into each other, she was in.

An hour or so after they'd been in the club, Kelly was about ready to leave. The dancing was fun, and Anna was great to be around. Anna had got talking to some people and they hung out with them for a bit. It reminded Kelly why she liked Anna so much and how lucky they were to have her manage the bar at Glenbuinidh. For a gay club, however, no one had caught Kelly's attention as much as the woman at the gig had.

Until she spotted her again.

She was standing next to her tall friend in a group of people. Kelly was sitting down, and she was directly in her line of sight. When they saw each other again, Kelly smiled, causing a slow and endearingly shy smile to creep onto the gorgeous young woman's face. That was it. She absolutely had to go and talk to her. When she went to the bar on her own, Kelly forced herself to go for it. Feeling strangely nervous, she followed her to the bar and stood beside her.

"Do you come here often?" She couldn't hide the smirk on her face as she said the line. Thankfully, her whisky drinker seemed to get the joke because her eyes lit up at her.

"I see you have improved your repertoire then."

"Can I buy you a drink?" Kelly put a hand on the bar, trying to find something to say to her.

She regarded Kelly carefully, and her expression softened after a few beats. "Sure."

"What's your name?"

"Myla. And yours?"

"Kelly. It's nice to meet you, Myla. Another Glenbuinidh?"

"Just a beer, thanks. The whisky is too strong. I'm already feeling it."

"Are your friends okay for drinks? Were you getting a round in?"

"No, um… they're fine. I was just getting some water for myself, but a beer is good." There was a sparkle in her eyes along with that shyness that Kelly found magnetic.

Kelly ordered two bottles of beer and two waters. Myla drank the water immediately, while Kelly took a token sip. They stayed standing at the side of the bar. It was packed, so they ended up unusually close together, not that Kelly minded. Myla seemed a little awkward, so she decided to tread lightly. "Did you enjoy the gig?"

Myla's eyes lit up again. Her whole expression opened up. It was quite beautiful. "I loved it. Their music sounds much better live, I think."

"You think so?" Kelly was intrigued and found Myla's posh voice really quite sexy.

"You feel the music from each part of the band more. You feel their energy. Like in the way they link the music between songs sometimes and the songs they choose to play and in what order. It sucks they'll probably not be back for years." Myla spoke quickly, almost rambling, and mostly to the floor, but when she looked up and their eyes locked a warmth spread through Kelly's chest. "And you?" Myla swallowed. "Did you enjoy the gig?"

She had. She also enjoyed how passionate Myla was about it. That youthful exuberance. It was mesmerising. Myla was mesmerising. Realising she was taking ages to answer, she quickly found some words. "Yeah, I loved it too. It was great. The crowd was amazing too." Myla was gazing at her now. Her features were bright and delicate, and held a natural beauty. She could look at this stranger's face all day. "And I met someone at the bar. Someone very pretty. I thought I'd never see her again but…" Myla

Louder Than Words

blushed, though didn't look away. Kelly took a deep breath and stepped a little closer. "But I did."

Myla was visibly flustered, but still didn't make any moves to leave. Gently, she cleared her throat. "And now that you've met her again?" There was a challenge in her voice that excited Kelly. It contrasted with her obviously quiet and soft-spoken nature.

"We dance?" Kelly held out her hand. Myla smiled and took it with less resistance than Kelly expected. As their hands made contact and their fingers entwined, Kelly gasped. It was electric.

Kelly slowly detached her fingers from Myla's as they began to dance and blend in with the rest of the people around them, moving to the beat. This was so unlike Kelly these days. Dancing with strangers in clubs wasn't the sort of thing she did any more. She was the CEO of a major international business. She was thirty-seven and getting too old for this, right? She used to be much more adventurous than she was in her life now. She used to party all night and say yes to new things. What a contrast she'd become to her younger, wilder self. Simply being out this late felt a bit daring.

Her old confidence gently kicked into gear as they danced and stole furtive glances at each other. She'd missed this. She was thirsty for this sort of thing in her life again. Clearly, she needed to get out more.

Myla moved so easily and so freely and was just so damn sexy. Something about the way she danced spoke to Kelly. They were on the same wavelength, that was for sure. That was all she could think of to describe this insane connection she felt. She could not take her eyes off this stunningly attractive and interesting person who seemed to have a lot going on behind those deep blue eyes. Myla sipped from her beer bottle every now and again. Kelly finished hers quickly and placed it on a shelf beside the dance floor. Myla wasn't exactly hiding the fact that she was interested in Kelly either as her eyes raked *all over* Kelly's body and especially her mouth. The dim lighting and anonymity of their encounter gave Kelly that final push to make a move. She placed a hand on Myla's waist, as they grinded to the beat together. When no look of confusion or boundary came up, Kelly inhaled, and placed her other hand on Myla's waist. She could feel the gentle jut of Myla's hip bone and the sexy indent of her waist. Kelly's heart rate spiked as they met each other's eyes and didn't look away. Kelly swallowed hard, feeling an intoxicating mixture of desire, excitement and genuine interest.

The *look* Myla gave her as Kelly tucked a finger in the loop of Myla's jeans made her wet. She'd forgotten how thrilling this could be. Swaying to the music now, more than dancing, Kelly led them over to some free seats.

Their thighs brushed as they sat down. Kelly crossed her legs, resting her foot against Myla's and her hand on Myla's thigh. Myla inhaled sharply, so responsive to Kelly's touch.

"Am I making you nervous?"

"A little. But in a good way."

Their heads moved closer together. The rest of the club paled away. Kelly dropped her gaze to Myla's mouth before finding Myla's eyes again. "How about now?"

"Now's good." Myla gave her that look again, dropping her eyes to Kelly's mouth and subtly licking her lips. Their heads drifted closer together still, as the energy between them fizzed. Kelly leaned in pausing once to check Myla definitely wanted this too. Since Myla's lips were parted, ready for her, and her pupils were dilated, Kelly took it as a yes. Their lips met. Kelly marvelled at the fullness of Myla's lips and her sweet taste mixed with the faint hint of alcohol. There was no hesitancy from Myla, who quickly deepened the kiss, parting Kelly's lips. When their tongues met, a wave of electricity rushed between Kelly's legs. Adrenaline coursed through her. The kiss was both urgent and gentle, taking and giving. Kelly was surprised at how confident Myla was in the kiss, and she liked that a lot. Kelly stroked Myla's cheek as she got lost in the moment. She wanted to kiss Myla like this all night long, but they were in the wrong place for that. She pulled back, finding Myla's eyes, which were dark and full of desire.

Kelly smiled. "Wow."

Myla nodded, eyes hazy and hooded, looking like she wanted more kissing and less talking.

"Would you like to come back to my hotel for a drink?"

Myla's eyes regained focus. "You don't live here?"

"I'm in town for work. I'm staying in a hotel around the corner. You should see it."

Myla raised an eyebrow. "Should I?"

"You should. It has a very luxurious bed."

"A luxurious bed."

"Yeah."

Myla ran her hands through her own hair, as if deciding, and then blew out a breath. "Okay."

Kelly could hardly believe her own ears. "Okay to coming back with me?"

"Yes." Myla gulped, nodding. The slow smile that spread across Myla's face made this feel somehow less crazy than it actually was.

Kelly found Myla's hand and leaned into her ear, lightly brushing her lips against Myla's earlobe. "I want to fuck you so hard."

Myla blushed. Even in the dim lighting of the club Kelly could see the redness spread across her face and neck. "I can't wait. I just need to go to the bathroom first and tell my friends where I'm going. Could I meet you at the door in like five minutes?"

"Yeah, sure. I'll meet you there."

Kelly watched Myla walk away. She had a certain aura about her which Kelly was completely transfixed by. She was so taken with this perfect stranger, and not just in a physical way. She was drawn to her. Kelly had been oblivious to their surroundings until now. They had been quite visible, in fact, but she didn't care. No one knew her down here anyway. She found Anna chatting with a few gay guys and let her know she was heading home, *with someone.* Anna raised her eyebrows and gave her a look of approval.

"Still got it, Kel."

Kelly rolled her eyes, moving away. "I'll text you tomorrow. Have a good night."

She waited inside the entrance to the club as it was freezing outside. After a while, she glanced at her watch. It had been more than ten minutes now. After fifteen minutes, she was concerned she was being stood up. Where was she? She considered going back to look for Myla, but Kelly wasn't one for searching a club for the person she was supposed to be leaving with. She settled on checking the toilets in case Myla wasn't okay. She wasn't there. She peeked into the main area of the club not wanting to be seen. She didn't want to bump into Anna, either. The thought of finding Myla there with her friends laughing at the zealous older woman who had no business being here made Kelly shudder. She was only thirty-seven but already felt past her peak from the lens of someone in their twenties.

The doubts ran riot in her head as she waited outside the club in the cold now. It was now more than twenty minutes since they'd parted. Had Myla had second thoughts? She'd seemed like she wanted to come back with her. Perhaps Kelly had come on too strong? Couldn't she have settled for talking to her and getting her number? Myla didn't seem like the one-night stand sort of person and must have got spooked. Kelly wasn't either, any more, she just really wanted to have sex with Myla because of that kiss.

Kelly sighed, roughly. What was she doing here waiting like this? She was too old for this nonsense. Myla was too young for her. There was clearly an age gap. Kelly already knew she couldn't be bothered with the immaturity of a twenty-something, even if they did come across as wiser beyond their years. She hated drama. The disappointment at being ditched like this was huge, and surprised Kelly a lot. On the face of it, this was simply a one-time hook-up situation. So why did she feel like this was such a loss? And such a blow to her ego? With still no sign of Myla, Kelly decided to call it quits and headed back to her hotel room, alone.

Three

I got out of the car at my great-aunt's house unable to believe this was my life now. I'd been putting off coming up here for nearly two months. It had taken me a while to process the initial shock of it all. But it was time to face the music. More money than I ever thought I would see in my lifetime was transferred into my account the day after I signed the paperwork with Graeme. I still hadn't come back down to earth.

Cara was overjoyed when I'd told her over the phone and as in the dark as I was about this mysterious family estate in the Highlands. At least I wasn't alone on that front. Although everyone had had a normal reaction to the inheritance except me. It was like I didn't know how to respond to something so positive. I was blocked. I wasn't used to it.

I'd indulged in a very practical spending spree that would confuse most people. I got things I was needing but hadn't been able to afford lately: new clothes, ethical toiletries, good make-up, and things for the flat such as plants, paintings and new technology. I'd rocked up to a car dealership and bought the latest top-of-the-range SUV, although I didn't need such luxury. The drive up to the Highlands had been like something out of a fancy car commercial.

The whole situation so far had been like a dream and standing on the precipice of the next stage like this was unreal. I kept thinking someone was going to pinch me and tell me it was a joke. This kind of luck didn't come to someone like me.

The house – Glenbuinidh House – was *huge*, standing three stories high and flanked with smaller adjoining buildings, some of which looked like garages. It was *grand*. Nestled inside a lengthy drive into its land, the house itself could not be seen from the road. Graeme had offered to show me the house himself, but I'd declined. I wanted to be alone to really take this in. To feel this. The only thing he had insisted on was accompanying me to the whisky distillery. I agreed to meet him there on Thursday. I'd given myself four days to get a feel for the house and the small town of Balbuinidh, and then I would get back to my life in Edinburgh. This was just a temporary visit.

I paused outside the stately front door. This was it. Taking a deep breath, I unlocked it and went through. The door was heavy. The entrance was a large open-plan hallway leading up to a grand staircase. The house was freezing and eerily quiet. It was littered with oversized and traditional furniture. There were ornaments everywhere telling a story of their own. I wandered around, finding the massive house a bit of a maze. The kitchen was huge, with a large wooden table in the centre. The place needed updating, that was for sure. But it was homely, in its own way. It spoke of a time gone by, full of traditions and meaning. One in which I would never fully understand, probably. There were many pieces of art of the walls. Of landscapes and nature, but not many of people. This was someone else's home. I was nothing more than a trespasser.

At least I'd got here before sunset so I could find my bearings. Arriving in the dark would have bordered on creepy haunted house territory. I'd packed as if I was going camping, anticipating an inhospitable, empty and cold house and brought all the sleeping gear and food that I would need. I'd only been camping once and didn't have any equipment, so I'd visited an outdoors shop and bought half of it. Like with the new car, being unconcerned about cost was such a strange feeling. I'd watched as piles of equipment were put through the checkout, mesmerised by this new life I'd been so lucky to receive.

After getting my luggage and groceries out of the car, I dumped the bags in one of the many large square bedrooms and took off my jacket finally. I changed into jogging bottoms and put on a second oversized fleece and thick socks with faux-fur-lined slipper boots. I found the mains electricity box and turned it on. It was clunky and less modern but seemed to work as the house lit up from the overhead light in the hall. Thankfully, there was central heating and it was easy to use. As the heating clinked into gear, hot water filling up the radiators, I put the kettle on for a cup of tea with the teabags and cup I'd brought up with me to feel more at home. I used cleaning wipes on everything, taking care to wipe handles and surfaces in the kitchen.

Taking my cup of steaming hot tea into the main lounge I turned on the old-fashioned light switch and several floor-standing lamps. The room was even more charming in the evening light. There were logs and kindling beside the stone fireplace. Damn. I didn't know how to start a fire.

I leant against the radiator to try to get warm. There were many picture frames with people in them in this room. Scanning them, Margaret had had a variety of dogs over the years, which I totally approved of. I couldn't work out who anyone was, except for what must have been

Louder Than Words

Margaret and her husband, based on the grander portrait in the hall. Margaret was petite and had soft blue eyes, James had broad shoulders and a square jaw. I would have liked to have known them.

And then, my eyes fell on a picture of my mother as a child, all gangly legs and arms, perhaps around nine or ten, next to a woman with blonde hair standing in a garden in full bloom. It was her eyes that told me this was my grandmother. They were blue and resembled my own, and my mother's. I stared and stared at the picture. It was so strange seeing someone else who looked like me besides my mother. They were smiling. I loved that they looked happy. This was the first time I'd seen a picture of my mother as a child, too. It meant everything.

But I had *so many* unanswered questions. Who were my grandparents and what were they like? What had made my mother the person she was – eccentric, stubborn, brilliant, magnetic? Why had she left this town and cut off her parents?

What the fuck happened?

Margaret's letter lay unopened in my bag upstairs. I hadn't been ready to discover what it might say before. My world had been shaken and I was still reeling from it. What if the letter unearthed a truth I couldn't reconcile with, like finding out my mother wasn't my mother? Or some other awful truth. My mind had taken me in all sorts of directions, and nothing seemed real until now, in this house, looking at these pictures on the wall in a place that should have felt familiar to me, but didn't. I fetched the letter and went back to the sitting room, taking a seat on the deceptively comfortable wing-back chair beside the cold, empty fireplace. My hands trembled as I opened it, but I forced myself to continue.

Dearest Myla,

Words can't express the happiness and relief that have come to me since finding you. Please know that we looked for you both for so long, my dear Myla.

I am so sorry to learn that your mother passed away. We were not aware, and I will take the shame of this to my grave. I cannot imagine the life you must have lived as I know nothing of it, but I want you to understand that we never stopped loving Sarah or you, and we always prayed for your safe return home.

Hazel and William, your grandparents, were heartbroken when Sarah left, and they never fully recovered. Sadly, they are both gone now. By the time you read this letter I will be gone, too. My deepest regret is that we will never meet, but I have peace knowing that you will receive the estate.

My husband James and I lived a good life. We worked hard and built a wonderful business around the family distillery. I hope you will give the house, the distillery and the local area a chance. It brought us much happiness and I hope it can offer you something too. This is your home now. Please take of it and from it what you want. It would make me so happy if you stayed in the house and looked in on the distillery from time to time. The whisky and the estate have been in the family for hundreds of years, and it is my dearest wish that you keep them both in the family line. Your family, Myla. I wish you a lifetime of joy, happiness and peace. May your future bring you all that your heart desires.

With my deepest love,
Margaret

I swallowed hard, tilting my head back on the chair as my eyes glazed over. My head was spinning with even more questions now, and my chest was heavy from the lack of answers in this letter, but also the kindness.

I gripped the letter even harder. Why my mother had cut off her family had always eaten away at me. But I'd given up asking a long time ago. My mother and I had been alone for so many years. It was all I knew. My mother had flat-out refused to talk about her past. She could be so elusive when it came to certain topics such as money and family. It made sense, somehow, that she abandoned her family, because she was always so ready to abandon me. She could be so indifferent to what I was doing, sometimes. I could have become a concert level pianist and it wouldn't have been enough to hold her attention for long.

Was it not selfish and downright abusive to deny her daughter access to extended family? If she were here, I'd tell her as much. But she wasn't here. Sighing, I felt a blanket of sadness envelop me. A familiar melancholy that felt like home. No one knew what this was like. This unique brand of isolation. No matter what I did or who I was with, nothing had ever been able to take this pain away. Nothing.

Not even coming here.

Never having to worry about money again for the rest of my life was the best thing that had ever happened to me. Words couldn't do justice to the gratitude I felt to Margaret and the investigator who'd found me, whoever that was. They'd given me the freedom to live the life that most could only dream of. Maybe one day it would sink in how incredibly lucky I was, but right now, cold and alone in this big and empty house, I felt only abandonment and loss.

I thought I'd got over the loss of my mother. I no longer got that stabbing pain whenever I thought of her. I'd grieved her for years. I didn't want to drag that up again because of this inheritance. No, I wanted to enjoy the money and never look back, aside from a little snoop around this house and town in person. I'd researched it online, but that could only tell you so much. There was no substitute for visiting a place in person. I was dying to learn about my mother's roots, which were technically mine. I wanted the truth.

Unable to sit still now, I wandered about the house again searching for anything I could find that would give me some answers.

Margaret had wanted to know me and had always loved my mother, and me, apparently. Which was Margaret's bedroom? They all looked the same. There were no personal items lying around. Presumably, Graeme had had the house tidied up after she'd died. The particulars were left for him to sort out. He'd said that towards the end she had nurses and carers coming in around the clock. I would have wanted to have been there for her. To have helped. To care for her and look after her. But I wasn't. I'd been elsewhere and out in the dark.

The story of my life.

Climbing onto my blow-up mattress later that night in a bedroom facing east for some nice morning sunlight, I zipped up my sleeping bag feeling a mixture of conflicting emotions – pain and loss, and excitement and curiosity. I put on my hat and hoped my nose wasn't going to freeze off overnight. This place was full of the ghosts of people

I'd never known. There was nothing keeping me here except a ton of unanswered questions.

Where was the comfort in that?

***

The distillery was on the outer edges of the estate and a short drive away. I'd explored some of the land but hadn't made it over this far yet. It was like having a whole part of the Highlands to myself. I hadn't seen anyone except for some deer and red squirrels. For some reason, be it the remote location, lack of people, or general safe vibe of the place, I'd stayed out after the sun had set, and made my way back to the house in darkness last night using the torch on my phone. I'd found a beautiful spot near a stream with a view down towards the glen. The estate had hills and woods and a small river ran through it. It was pure heaven. Next time, I'd find a way to make a campfire and sit out until I saw the stars.

I'd never been to a distillery before. It was the smell that hit me first. Thick wafts struck my nose as soon as I got out of the car. Scrunching up my face to appease the smell, I walked quickly towards the entrance. Leading down from the car park, the site was very spread out. There were multiple old stone buildings making up the distillery, and two pagoda-shaped things on the roof. A newer building with huge windows instead of walls was merged with an older one to form the main entrance. The old and the new merged together was impressive. It was much bigger than I was expecting. The place was clearly set up for tourists in addition to being a working distillery. The entrance courtyard included a landscaped greenspace leading up to the visitor centre. Barrels were laid out in the middle of the courtyard with letters on each one spelling out 'welcome to Glenbuinidh'. The whole area had a sense of purpose and class.

Graeme was waiting for me at reception. As always, he was smartly dressed. Today he sported a dark green tartan flat cap, which I enjoyed.

"Good morning, Myla. Did you find the house okay? I hope everything is all right?"

The days had flown past. I was excited to see the distillery, but more from a tourist perspective if I was being honest. I wasn't sure what anyone wanted from me today. I was a trespasser in someone else's world again, only this time, there were people involved and legal things or something or other. "Yep, fine thanks. I got into the house. Settled in."

"That's good. If you ever need anything do let me or anyone at the office know. It's a tight-knit community and we'll be happy to help make you feel at home."

Home. Why did he think this was my home? Home for a short visit? When I thought of home, I thought of the flats I grew up in with my mother in London. I had zero emotional attachment to this place other than disappointment and loss. It was full of history, but not my home. Wherever that was now. "Thanks, Graeme. I'll be leaving tomorrow to go back to Edinburgh, but I appreciate your offer."

"So soon? You just got here?"

"I have things to get back to. My job." In truth, that was pretty much the only thing. It gave me a purpose and I wasn't going to give that up because of the inheritance. That café was my world.

"At the café?"

I shifted on my feet, hearing how odd it sounded now that I had money. "Yes."

Graeme considered this for a few moments and then conceded, respectfully. "In that case, could you come by my office before you leave? We'll need to discuss what you plan on doing with the distillery."

"Okay. But I don't know if it'll be worth meeting just now. I need time to figure things out."

"That's fine. We can do it at a later date. There's no great rush. But the distillery will want to know if anything is going to change. You might want to factor them into your deliberations."

I didn't want to cause any concern, especially since I didn't plan on getting involved with the distillery in any meaningful way. "Of course. I don't see why I'd need to get involved."

"That's entirely your choice. The opposite is also true. You could take over if you like."

"I'm sure the staff would love that."

"Or you could sell it. As someone who has lived in this community his entire life, I'd hate to see that happen, but as your solicitor, I'd be remiss not to let you know it is an option. I'd recommend you speak to an independent financial adviser either way."

Selling up? That seemed drastic, and not what Margaret wanted. This inheritance was still blowing my mind. It was far more complicated than winning the lottery. The house, the land, and now this. It was hard to think straight. "Thank you for letting me know my options. I plan on taking my time over this though, if that's okay."

"That sounds sensible." Graeme gestured to the door and held it open for me. "You might get more clarity once our meeting is over. I think you'll find the distillery quite interesting."

The reception was bright and airy. The smell from outside had gone, which was a relief. A giant rug of the whisky label sat in the centre of the atrium, beside a sleek and modern welcome area. Glass cabinets containing multiple variations of the Glenbuinidh bottle lined one wall. There were barrels stacked in the rafters above an enticing gift shop.

A young woman with red hair sat behind the reception desk, looking up as soon as we both entered. "Hi. Welcome to Glenbuinidh." The name on her badge was Lucy.

We introduced ourselves and Lucy picked up a phone, balancing it on her shoulder as she typed something into the computer. "Hey. Your guests are here."

Graeme waited by the reception, and I wandered over to the glass cabinets. I took an interest in one of the finest bottles. The labelling was full of intrigue. It was a forty-year-old Glenbuinidh priced at four thousand nine hundred pounds. How much distinction could there really be between the different ages? I liked the Glenbuinidh that I'd had at the gig a couple of months ago, but I wouldn't pay nearly five thousand pounds for it.

"Hello," said a woman behind me. The voice was assertive, clear, and distinctly Scottish. It sounded familiar. I turned around.

Oh my god.

My breath caught. It was the hot woman from the gig I'd wanted to go home with but got stuck in the fire exit. She must have thought I'd stood her up. I froze, sure the blood was draining from my already pale face. When our eyes met there was a flicker of recognition, but it quickly disappeared from Kelly's face and was replaced with something harder. Kelly – yes, I remembered her name, I remembered everything about that night – adapted faster than I did to the situation. She was even more beautiful in the day than in the dim lighting that night. She was dressed in an elegant long-sleeved blouse, grey pencil skirt, and sexy-as-hell high heels making her even taller than she already was. Her wavy brown hair fell onto her shoulders, and her eye make-up was nothing short of smouldering. She had such warm brown eyes and I remembered how they had looked at me that night with such *want*. My cheeks burned hot, unable to hide my embarrassment and discomfort upon seeing this gorgeous and very sexy older woman standing in front of me again, someone I had for sure already *met*.

"Ms MacGregor. Thank you for meeting with us today. This is Myla Murray. Myla is the great-niece of Margaret, and now the legal owner of Glenbuinidh. Myla, this is Kelly MacGregor. Ms MacGregor runs the distillery."

Kelly had been so different then. Free, untamed. Now, she was more guarded, professional. She regarded me coolly.

"Pleasure to meet you. I'm the Chief Executive of the distillery." Not acknowledging that we'd already met, Kelly offered her hand and I took it, causing a spark of electricity in me akin to the night we first met. The physical contact, the soft skin of her hands and the memory of our kiss took my breath away.

Why did I have to blush like this?

"Hello."

There was an awkward silence. I remembered kissing those lips as if it were yesterday. We'd been so close to going back to Kelly's hotel room. And now I was face to face with her once more, but under very different circumstances.

Kelly's expression was still cool. "I'm sorry about your great-aunt. She was a wonderful person. I liked her a lot."

I didn't know what to do with that. I'd never met the woman. "Um… thank you. She seemed great."

Kelly kept a straight face. "So, Margaret left everything to you?"

"That's what we are here to discuss with you, Ms MacGregor. Is there somewhere we can go?" Graeme said.

"Of course. Let me take you through."

My insides twisted and my mind raced as we followed Kelly into the distillery. Who asks someone if they inherited a fortune like that? It wasn't as if I had any say in it. Kelly's demeanour was standoffish, especially compared to her previous disposition. No doubt, Kelly must have thought I'd ditched her. That I'd lied about wanting to go home with her and had essentially run out on her. Ever since it had happened, I'd been plagued with guilt and winced whenever I thought about it.

Today, on the least expected of days, we were now reconnected. How could it be that she was the CEO of Glenbuinidh? What were the chances? When we got into a spacious room with four deep lounge chairs and a circular coffee table, Kelly closed the door and gestured for us to take a seat. In my old and faded jeans, black hoody and Vans trainers, I was painfully underdressed for this meeting.

"Can I get either of you anything to drink?"

"Nothing for me, thanks," Graeme said.

That night, Kelly had been so bold and confident, and so… *sexy*. Today Kelly was the epitome of polite and professional. I found her even sexier in her business attire and heels, which did nothing for my heart rate. She was powerful and confident and well, *hot*. The gig didn't seem like a place someone like Kelly would be at. I was grateful she was, of course. Kelly waited for my response, not giving anything away. "Um, no thanks. I'm fine. Thank you."

She nodded. Graeme informed Kelly of the situation, talking at length about the legal side of things. While I fidgeted, Kelly sat quite still as she took it in. I tried hard not to stare and found myself biting my lower lip far too much. There was a barrier between us now. Would it ever come down again? Were we some sort of colleagues now?

This was crazy.

When Graeme was done, Kelly took a deep breath. She caught my eyes and we looked at each other for a couple of seconds longer than necessary, I suppose. I squirmed, feeling hot and bothered from simple eye contact.

"Do you have any questions, Ms MacGregor?"

Kelly cleared her throat. "We've all been wondering what would come of Margaret's passing and the future of the distillery. Including a lot of potential buyers in the industry. They've been keeping a close eye on us, and on Margaret's health for years. I haven't cared for their attention."

"This is a world-famous brand. It would be unusual if it had not been receiving any interest for future ownership," Graeme said.

Kelly frowned. "They've been circling like birds of prey."

"I'm sorry to hear that," I said.

Kelly found my eyes and held them again. "Do you know what you want to do with the business, Myla?

The way she said my name at the end made my insides melt. Instantly, I flashbacked to when we were kissing and

Kelly's hand was sliding up my thigh. My cheeks started to burn again. Damn it. "Um, well. I'm not sure yet."

"Right."

I could tell Kelly wasn't satisfied by my response, but I was grateful she didn't overtly show any signs of irritation or disgust at my complete ineptitude.

"As I've stated, Ms Murray has several options available to her. We wanted to make you and the staff aware that there may be changes ahead." Graeme paused, glancing in my direction. "In order for Ms Murray to consider her options, she will need a full breakdown of the distillery's financial position. Its incomings, outgoings, and everything else in between. Is that something you can provide?"

Kelly was quiet. Her tone sharpened when she spoke next. "I'll have it with you by the end of the day. A lot of people in Balbuinidh depend on this distillery. They work here or have a family member who works here. It's one of the main employers in the area and has been for a very long time, as you know." Kelly shot Graeme a look. Turning to me, she continued, but less sharply now. "It's been a family-run and then locally run business for years. It's a household name. We get an influx of visitors wanting a slice of the magic we bottle and sell. To say this is a beloved business to the people of this wee town is an understatement. I'd rather not worry people unnecessarily, until we know more."

That my situation would cause people to worry was highly troubling to me. "Thank you for telling me that. I had no idea. I don't want anyone to worry."

This elicited a small and polite smile from Kelly, which I took as a victory. "That's good to know."

"Do you live locally?"

"Yes. Born and raised."

Our eyes caught again, causing a flutter of butterflies to sweep through my stomach. "I've only been here for a few days. It's lovely."

"Are you staying long?"

"I'm leaving tomorrow."

"And you haven't decided what you want to do with the distillery yet." Kelly's tone found its sharpness.

I scratched my ear. "I'm sorry. I haven't. But I'll do my best to figure it out soon."

Kelly's exasperation slipped out from her cool exterior as she looked away and sighed under her breath.

"I understand this is very uncertain, Ms MacGregor, but Ms Murray does require more time and more information to determine her next steps. We wanted to keep you in the loop. It's up to you whether you want to tell anyone in the meantime."

Kelly held Graeme's eye. "Yes. It is."

"I think that we've covered everything for now, Ms MacGregor. If you could send over the requested information," he handed Kelly his business card, "we'll be most grateful. We will then get back to you as soon as we can."

To her credit Kelly was gracious as she saw us out. The walk back to reception was deadly quiet, however. I already regretted not getting a chance to say anything to Kelly that wasn't taking-over-the-distillery-related. My own quietness and awkwardness in this encounter grated on me. Why couldn't I think on my feet quicker?

The next day started slowly. I was supposed to be packing up and driving back to the city, but it wasn't happening. All I did was make coffee after coffee from the wonderous machine that I'd bought and sit in the bay window looking out towards the land like a pensive

Victorian royal. Seeing Kelly again had really thrown me. I kept thinking about the meeting yesterday, the distillery, and what she'd said about Balbuinidh. But mostly, I kept seeing those warm brown eyes and how they'd searched mine.

What I knew for sure was that I wanted to speak to her again without Graeme. About what, however, I was less sure of. Based on Kelly's icy reception, my position as the new owner of the distillery was not welcome news. I'd wanted to know more about the distillery, but Kelly hadn't exactly seemed open to showing me around. I'd left with Graeme instead, too stressed to linger. At worst, she probably thought I wasn't interested in the distillery or the local area. Neither of which was true.

The house itself had grown on me. Yes it was draughty and had more fireplaces than I knew what to do with, but I was finding it comforting to a certain extent. I had to admit having such a huge space all to myself was appealing. I could move about so freely, make as much noise as I cared to, and feel what true silence felt like for the first time. I'd be lying if I said I hadn't been eyeing up different rooms and spaces in the house and thinking how I could use the space differently and redecorate.

Part of me *still* kept waiting for someone to walk into the house and tell me to get out. These mixed feelings about the house and my place in it, meeting Kelly again, and the new information about the distillery and the community kept me rooted to the spot.

Was it not a sign that I'd met Kelly before? The chances of such a thing had to be slim. It couldn't be ignored.

But Michelle was expecting me back tomorrow. I'd worked there ever since moving up from London.

Michelle, the regulars, and the local area had become my new home. The thought of upping and leaving made me feel anxious. Where would I go? Certainly not back to London, even though being closer to Cara and Kay would be nice. I could move up here and live. But I didn't know anyone. I had a life in the city. My life was fine.

I didn't want to let Michelle down. It had been just me and Michelle in the café for ages. On the other hand, I *was* enjoying having all this time to myself – stress free, notwithstanding the decisions I needed to make on where to put the inheritance and what to do with the distillery. Maybe a few more days wouldn't hurt? I decided to text Michelle to test the waters.

> **Myla:** *Hi Michelle, how are things at the café? All's well up here. It's pretty incredible, actually. I've got a few more things to sort out. Would it be okay if I took another few days off? Sorry, I know that's super short notice!*
>
> **Michelle:** *I'm glad things are going well! All good here. Honestly Myla, you can take the next three months off if you like. Whatever you need. You must have a lot to deal with up there. I've got some students covering your shifts so please don't worry. Your job will be here for you whenever you want it again. Keep me updated xxx*

That was unexpected. I thanked Michelle and agreed to the three months off and put my phone down instantly feeling as if a heavy weight had been lifted from my shoulders. I didn't have to leave the house or the area just yet. I could try and speak to Kelly again. That was exciting. I could find out more about my mother's past and my family background.

Maybe I could stay here and *be* for a little while.

My shoulders relaxed. I took a mid-morning bath and then sank into the sofa with a good book. There was no need to rush any more.

Four

As Kelly closed the boot with one hand, Barley, her golden retriever, pulled in the opposite direction nearly yanking her shoulder out of its socket.

"Come on then," she looked down at Barley who was already panting with excitement.

The cold air bit her cheeks, and she was glad she had remembered her beanie. It was a dull day with a grey sky, and it looked like it might rain at some point. On Saturday mornings, this car park in the centre of town was the epicentre of Balbuinidh and about as exciting as it got in the area. They made their way towards the start of their six-mile walk along the loch flanked by snow-topped mountains, Barley pulling the whole time. It was the perfect walk but having done it countless times before the novelty had most definitely worn off.

Once they joined the start of the path, she unclipped his lead from his collar, and he bolted away to the nearest smell. She got her walk on and tried to zone out and enjoy the nature around her, but it was hard not to think. It had been a stressful week, one that threatened the future of the distillery and many people in the town. It was unclear how it was going to play out. Kelly hadn't told Georgia, the manager of Glenbuinidh, as she didn't want to worry her, or any of her colleagues. Georgia lived and breathed her job at Glenbuinidh, had two kids at home and was a single mum. The last thing she needed was the stress of this.

The young woman who'd stood her up a couple of months ago in the club was *absurdly* now the new owner of

Glenbuinidh. When Myla had turned around in reception, Kelly had been so mortified inside, but professional mode kicked in and she was sure it wouldn't have shown. Her neutral professional face was well-practised. Myla was quiet and blushed often, causing Kelly to think she was somewhat embarrassed about the whole thing too. Kelly had done her best to forget about meeting Myla, so when she saw her in real life again, it shook her. It also reminded Kelly of how attracted she was to her, their instant chemistry, that kiss… Not that any of that mattered any more given who Myla was. Kissing the new owner of the distillery did *not* seem like a good idea.

A cold chill ran through her. Would their prior meeting influence Myla in her decision over the future of the distillery? Kelly had been very forward and then Myla had ditched her. It didn't bode well. The one time Kelly had let loose and expressed that side of herself this happens. Myla had seemed to like it though… until she'd disappeared. She'd been ruminating like this since Thursday, not getting anywhere at all.

Walking briskly, she reminded herself that this was her time to connect with Barley and take a break from it all. Stopping beside a little bay, Barley sprinted into the water and splashed around as if it weren't close to freezing. The look of pure joy on his face made her smile.

"Let's go, silly puppy," she said, walking away from him as this was the only thing that got him out of the water. He wasn't budging. He put his head under the water and fished out a stick then lay down on the bank to chew it. "Byyyyyeeeeee," she called, getting further away from him. He would always wait until she was *just* out of eyeshot and then come sprinting. There was no point in trying to fight his little quirks like this. It was his personality and she loved him for it. Kelly power walked the rest of the circuit and felt great by the time they'd got back to the car.

Crouching down to dry Barley with a towel she glanced up as a figure walked past. It was Myla. Her heart started beating faster and she stopped drying Barley.

Fuck, fuck, fuck.

Again, the sheer humiliation of coming on so strong to this young woman that night came flooding back. So strong, and so misjudged, that Myla had been forced to ditch her. To think that a hot young thing like this would be interested in her had clearly been absurd.

Myla spotted her too and she stopped dead in her tracks as if she'd seen a ghost. Myla's face turned even paler for a second and then a deep crimson blush spread across her skin, much like it had the other day in the distillery.

"Hi," Kelly said, standing up, recovering quickly. "You're still here? I thought you were leaving yesterday." Shit. That sounded colder than she'd intended. "I'm glad you decided to stick around."

"I wasn't quite ready to leave yet."

Kelly noticed her trolley full of groceries, logs and kindling. The tips of some wine bottles protruding from a bag made her chuckle. "Getting in some supplies?"

Myla glanced down at the trolley as well, and her blush deepened. "Um, yeah."

There was an awkward silence until Barley registered an opportunity to socialise and went over to Myla. He wiggled around her knees, demanding some attention. Myla bent down and patted Barley's head.

"Who's this?"

"This is Barley."

"Ha! Great name," she looked into his eyes and he gazed into hers. "Hi Barley, you're such a sweetheart aren't you."

He wagged, nuzzling into her legs, resting on her feet, claiming Myla as his new friend. He was such a charmer. Myla let him rest on her. He only did this with certain people and Kelly took it as a seal of approval from her most trusted four-legged wee pal.

"He's friendly, isn't he?"

"Sorry. Barley, come here."

"No, no. It's good. I wasn't saying to get him."

He obeyed anyway, freeing Myla's legs. Kelly put him in the boot and closed the door.

Myla straightened up and cleared her throat. "Um, I'm sorry we didn't get a chance to talk the other day. Would you like to go for a coffee sometime?"

Their eyes met. The rejection from that night still stung. "Sure."

"Are you free now? I know you must have other things on since it's a Saturday and all, but it would be really great to talk. Or another time is fine too, it doesn't have to be now."

"I could do now."

What was she doing?

Myla beamed. Her eyes sparkled and Kelly couldn't help but smile back at her. Myla wasn't acting like someone who ditched her. She was as warm now as she had been that night.

"Perfect. I'll get this shopping in my car then. You'll know where's good around here so just wherever you want to go is fine by me."

Myla was no shrinking violet, that was for sure. There was a toughness in her that Kelly liked.

Kelly opened the door of the boot again. The visitor centre had a great café and was dog friendly so they would go there. And it was right across the car park. Barley jumped out again with the same enthusiasm as before his walk. Kelly tried so hard to tire him out, but he had boundless energy, one of the many things she loved about him.

Myla's car was a whopper. A new-looking and very impressive black SUV glistened in the cool winter sunlight. Myla came back towards her once she'd finished putting her things away. Kelly found it hard not to watch her every movement, and barely resisted staring at the beautiful woman in front of her.

"Nice wheels."

"It was the inheritance."

"You chose well."

Kelly held the door open for Myla as they entered the café. Myla thanked her quietly as she passed. Barley bounded past them. She was pulled up to the counter that Barley knew so well as Myla watched all this with an amused smile tugging at her lips. Barley did his best sitting while waiting for a treat to magically appear from the counter.

"What would you like?" As Kelly asked this of Myla, echoes of the night they met entered her head, but she pushed them aside. This was a totally different situation now and that was firmly in the past.

"A flat white, please."

"Hi, Kelly. Hello there, *Barley*," said Jenny, the owner of the café coming out from the back. "Look at that gorgeous little face. Can he have a biscuit?" Jenny looked at Kelly for permission knowing full well that it was coming. Kelly nodded and thanked her. His eyes were like saucers, and he took the biscuit out of Jenny's hand way less gently than Kelly would have liked. "There you go, good boy," Jenny said.

Barley wasn't satisfied with only one and pressed for more, but Jenny turned her attention to Kelly. "How're your parents liking their new extension? Jack said it was a tough build what with all that bad weather we've had. Got there in the end though, I hope."

"They love it, thanks." Jenny's husband Jack ran a building services company in the area. They generally knew everything about everyone. "Jack and his team have outdone themselves this time."

"Took them long enough!"

Kelly shrugged. The new wing to her parents' house had gone two months over. Still, her parents were happy with it in the end so that was what mattered. Jenny leant on the counter, looking between Kelly and Myla. Kelly didn't quite know how to introduce Myla right now and in her hesitation the moment passed.

"What can I get for you ladies?"

Kelly ordered two flat whites and they waited for them. Kelly was oddly self-conscious next to Myla. She seemed to observe everything. She had this invisible pull, quietly telling you that she was there, and she was taking everything in.

"Enjoy your drinks, ladies. Hope to see you again soon," said Jenny, who had now moved on to greeting the next customers.

Myla carried their mugs to a table as Kelly navigated with Barley. He lurched around sniffing under tables until they found one and Barley rested at Kelly's feet.

"Everyone is so friendly here," Myla said.

"It's a good place. Everyone looks out for one another. Everyone knows each other's business, too."

"I've never lived in a place like that."

Kelly wondered again what age Myla was. She looked about twenty-two. Far, far too young for her. "Do you live in Glasgow?"

Myla shook her head. "No. I live in Edinburgh. I'm from London, originally."

She had a refined accent suggesting she was from a posh part of London but other than that, Kelly found it hard to place Myla. She seemed so mysterious. Elusive. Soft-spoken yet steely. Untouchable, even. Her blue eyes spoke of a depth Kelly found mesmerising. "You like it here then, in Scotland?"

"I love it here. I work in a café in one the most beautiful cities in the UK." She shrugged. "Life is fine."

"So, you're a city girl."

Myla shrugged again and took a sip of coffee. Their eyes met as her lips met the cup. The intensity of the connection hit Kelly. Kelly would be lying if she said she hadn't thought about that night more than once. She'd fantasised about it pretty much constantly, even through the cold sting of being stood up so brutally.

Myla put her cup down. "Kelly, I want to apologise for what happened when we first met. I got trapped in the fire exit looking for the bathroom. I banged on the door for ages but no one heard. Eventually, I followed the corridor and exited the back of the building. But then I got lost in the old alleyways and had to walk all the way around the block to get back. When I finally made it back to the club, I couldn't find you." Kelly let the words hit her, stunned at how direct Myla was and that they were so quickly discussing *that night*. Myla hadn't rejected her after all. Wow.

"I'm sorry you must have thought I had led you on."

"I assumed you had changed your mind."

"Um, nope. I very much wanted to go home with you that night."

I very much wanted to go home with you that night.

Kelly's breath caught. Images of what she'd wanted to do with Myla raced through her mind. About a minute passed in silence. Myla fiddled with her earlobe, looking off to the side. Kelly gazed at her, probably too openly, feeling that same blistering attraction she'd felt when they'd first met. It had been one of the best kisses she'd ever had, and she'd had a lot of good kisses in her life.

She took a deep breath to steady the fire burning within her. "And now you're here," Kelly smiled. Their eyes met again and this time the air felt thicker. Myla let out a smile that reached her eyes. The smile was definitely something she 'let out' rather than gave away for free. It was a privilege to see it.

"I know. It's so weird. I'd just found out about Margaret and her passing, and I was out celebrating with my flatmate. Wait, that doesn't sound right. I didn't know of her or my grandparents before finding out what she left to me. It was a shock."

Kelly hadn't realised Myla hadn't known her family here. "It must have been."

"Still is. And the first time I ever drank Glenbuinidh was at that gig."

"When I rocked up beside you?" Kelly shook her head. "What are the chances?"

Myla nodded. A shared understanding passed between them. "It *was* the centre of the known sapphic universe in Scotland that night."

Kelly laughed, feeling slightly easier around her now. It was nice. "True."

Myla continued. "I've been trying to get my head around the inheritance and everything. I found out that my mother grew up here. She passed away when I was nineteen, eight years ago. I've been pretty much on my own ever since. I never met my dad. I don't have any siblings. Inheriting all this has come out of the blue. It's been crazy."

That made Myla twenty-seven. Kelly was rubbish at guessing ages. To lose her mum at such a young age and to have no family, and then find out she'd inherited a fortune was a lot. Was she going through this major life changing experience alone or did she have someone to support her? "It must be."

"I've been burying my head in the sand since finding out, I guess. I work in a café and live in a tiny two-bedroom flat with a friend who's a student. I don't feel like I deserve any of this. I don't have the first idea about your distillery."

Kelly took some coffee as she contemplated this new information, and the sheer honesty. Myla was so naturally good, honest and gentle. Delicate, even. It both put her at ease and energised her. Her world was all go, go, go, but Myla seemed to take life a little slower, yet, she had this intoxicating *something* as well, something Kelly couldn't put her finger on but was very drawn to. The more she studied Myla's face, the more she saw that complexity in Myla's eyes and the youthfulness of her features. It was such a contrast.

While Myla was still a threat to the distillery, and by extension the whole of Balbuinidh, Kelly only saw the human being sitting with her right now. It sounded like Myla was going through this mostly alone. Part of Kelly wanted to wrap Myla up in a big hug and help her navigate this strange new world she had found herself in. In another life, she would have liked to have seen where things might have led had they not been so needlessly kept apart that fateful night and now through this inheritance. It was a shame Myla had got lost that night. Kelly would have loved to have taken her back to her hotel room. But things were different now. Myla was the new owner of Glenbuinidh, with the power to do with it as she pleased. Even sell it. She'd discovered a family and a past she knew nothing about. She had enough to be dealing with without a horny older woman with a crush on getting in the way. No. A romantic connection was out of the question now. They could be friends, though, right? She could help Myla get to know more about her ancestral town, and the distillery. It was the decent thing to do.

"It's your birthright. You may as well own it. Accept it."

Myla smiled.

"Would you like a tour of the distillery sometime? I should have suggested it on Thursday. It was rude of me not to. I apologise."

"I'd like that. But only if you have time, I don't want you to go out of your way or anything."

Myla took a sip of her coffee, and Kelly again found it difficult not to stare at the full and pink lips she'd so much enjoyed kissing.

"I have time." This wasn't strictly true, but she would make time for Myla. "It would be my pleasure."

They caught eyes at the last part of Kelly's sentence and Kelly felt her cheeks redden. Defiantly, she pushed through and ignored it, and since when did people make her blush? "If we swap numbers we can message about when you want to come in?" The hope in Kelly's voice wasn't lost on her and clearly not on Myla, either, who bit down on her lip and then smiled.

"Sure."

Kelly handed over her phone and they swapped numbers, as Kelly reminded herself this was for professional reasons only. Barley stirred at her feet, probably uncomfortable on the hard floor. She reached down to pat his head. "You're such a good boy." He shot her a look and settled again.

"Balbuinidh seems so steeped in history. I can't wait to learn more about it."

Myla's interest in Balbuinidh was oddly satisfying. Kelly was proud of her hometown, even if she had had itchy feet lately. "There's an old slate mine around the corner hence why everyone has a slate sign outside their front door."

"That's so cool. I love learning random facts like that. See, I'd never have known that had I not chatted with a local."

"I'll have to brush up on my local facts then."

Myla laughed. It was warm and classy. And cute. "There must be lots of walks around here with all the mountains so close by. I bet Barley takes you up a fair few?"

"He does love to bag a Munro. These days I'm either working or I'm walking in the hills. I used to be cool once. Now, not so much."

Myla laughed again. It would be nice to have a new friend in the area.

"That doesn't sound so bad. Being cool is overrated."

"Or maybe I meant wild. I was wild once, and then I became a CEO at thirty and now all I do is work and recover from it."

"That's quite young for a position like that, isn't it? You must be very intelligent."

"I'm afraid it was pure nepotism. Seven years ago my dad wanted to step down from running the distillery, so he put me in charge instead. I'd been working in the City, in London, living in the corporate jungle. Hence, the wild."

Myla smiled, warmly. "I know the type."

"You do?"

"Yeah. I see them in the café all the time. And growing up in London, let's just say I know you city types," Myla said, eyes sparkling. "So he gave you the job?"

"Yes. It was a great opportunity and I'm glad I took it. Whatever the circumstance it arose from."

"Does your dad still work at the distillery?"

"No. He's retired. Although he likes to offer me unsolicited advice and think he's still pulling strings in some way."

"That must be annoying."

"It can be. I let him think he's helping, mostly. I prefer to keep the peace and focus on getting the job done."

"How's that going?"

"It's the path of least resistance. It works, kind of."

"You don't strike me as someone who likes taking orders. Aren't you the boss?"

Kelly inhaled, picking up on a slight undertone of flirting in the way Myla said that. Myla, who was her actual boss now. "Anyway," Kelly flashed a quick smile. "I came home to take over the distillery. The two big cities are within reach. So is Europe. I travel a lot for work. That keeps me busy," she shrugged, knowing that she wasn't being entirely honest. She'd been less happy here for a while. She was bored. Bumping into Myla, the hot girl from the gig, was one of the most exciting things to have happened to her in a long time.

"Did you know my mother?"

"A wee bit. She seemed very glamourous. She left town when I was still quite young."

Myla nodded, absorbing Kelly's words.

"She seemed like a great person. But she was an adult to me, really. One time, she bought me and a friend some ice cream from the shop in town. I liked her." Kelly hoped her fond memories of Myla's mum were coming across well. She couldn't imagine the pain of losing a parent.

Myla took a sip of coffee. "I'm glad."

Barley sighed, loudly. He wasn't shy to let her know he had missed a meal. "I'd better get this one back for his post-workout snack. Unlike with my dad, I don't mind being bossed about by him."

Myla spoke to Barley. "Do you keep a strict schedule for your mummy?"

Barley bounced up and wagged his tail, knowing they were talking about him.

Kelly smiled. "Of course. He has a whole crew. My mum looks after him during the day a lot and he has a dog walker. *The Woof Pack*."

"I love that."

Back at the cars, they hovered before saying goodbye. Kelly had enjoyed their chat. Plus, it was such a relief to find out, for her ego, that she hadn't in fact been rejected that night.

"Hey Myla."

"Yes."

"Thanks for today. I'm glad we got a chance to have this chat."

Myla's face lit up. "Me too."

***

Later that afternoon Kelly was having afternoon tea with her parents at their house. The weather was howling outside, and a storm was coming in, so they kept warm in the sitting room beside the wood-burning stove. Kelly sat across from her parents on a two-seater sofa. Barley took the corner nearest to the fire. It crackled and popped and was almost loud enough to be heard over Barley's snoring. She filled her parents in on the headline news at the distillery. She also told them that Myla had no family. She did not tell them about their prior meeting in Glasgow, however.

"That's right. Sarah left and never came back. We never knew why." Her mum spoke while looking off to the side as if remembering the past. "Your gran was friends with Myla's grandmother, Hazel, years ago. Sarah was a troubled young woman. She went to London, I think. Everyone was worried sick about her and the baby. Such a tragedy, the whole thing."

Kelly tried to reconcile this story with the mild-mannered person she'd met on three occasions now. There must be more to it. "You never mentioned it before."

"It never came up." Her mum sighed, wearily. "And now Myla has finally made it back and she's all alone up in that big house by herself." Her mum paused, looking distraught. "We'll invite her around for supper one night and give her a good welcome. I'd love to meet her."

"That's a nice idea, Eilidh." Her dad nodded.

Kelly shifted in her seat. "I don't know how long she's planning on staying but I will see if she's interested."

"You should," Kelly's mum said.

Kelly hoped her *interest* in Myla over and above the situation wasn't obvious.

"She sounds vulnerable," Kelly's dad said. He was very colourful tonight in his golden corduroys and red woolly jumper. "It might be wise for you to keep an eye on her. Make sure she doesn't make any rash decisions, if you know what I mean."

"Malcolm!"

Kelly narrowed her eyes at him. "To what end?"

He tilted his head, the way he always did when he was explaining things in that patronising way. Usually, she found it endearing or funny, but today, she was already annoyed at what she thought he was going to say next.

"In case she hands over the keys to the distillery to some large corporation that no doubt has their eyes on her. One word from her and the distillery is gone."

Kelly scoffed. "That's ridiculous. No one has their eyes on her." Barley opened his eyes, momentarily stirring at Kelly raising her voice. She patted his back a couple of times and lowered her voice. "Sorry, pal. Go back to sleep," she looked up at her dad. "You think she's some sort of target then?"

"Might be. We know that the future ownership of the distillery has been drawing attention for quite some time now. We haven't been too impressed at some of their tactics so far. Prying into Margaret's illness, bullying a dying woman like that. Who's to say they won't try and pick off a defenceless lamb for the slaughter, so to speak."

Some dodgy looking men had been staying in the area, asking questions and generally being shifty. The whole community had been nervous about it. "Ew, gross, Dad. And she's not a defenceless lamb. She's sensible."

"That's good," her dad's voice was kind. "I know this is unpleasant. I'm only saying this so you can be aware of what might be happening and prepare for it. It's good she trusts you. We can work with that."

"I will not engage with Myla in any other way than total honesty. I don't do games, you know that. Also, there's nothing to prepare for, it's Myla's decision."

"She's right, Malcolm. There's no need to go down that road. The poor girl should be enjoying her new-found money and freedom. She won't want to know anything about a stuffy old whisky distillery."

Both Kelly and her dad looked at her mum in confusion.

"It's one of the most successful businesses in Britain. How could she not be interested?"

Kelly agreed with her dad's point. Myla was already interested. She was coming in for a tour.

"You should be guiding her to the right decision, Kelly."

"I'm not going to do that."

He took a deep breath, then finished his tea. "I'm sorry. I'm just worried about this getting out of hand. I don't think this Myla knows what she's got herself in to."

"She hasn't got herself into anything. She inherited it, remember?"

"Just keep her close. Get to know her. For her own sake as well as the distillery's. She needs help."

"She has Graeme."

"His role will come to an end soon, if it hasn't already."

Kelly clenched her jaw and glared at him. Her dad wasn't giving Myla any credit. Hopefully Myla would decide to keep things as they were and let them get on with it. And by getting on with it, Kelly meant continuing to make the business an ongoing local, national, and international success – for everyone. But if Myla had other plans, there was nothing Kelly could do about it, besides give her a good tour of the distillery, sing its praises and start working on a new CV.

"Come on now, you two, everything's going to be fine," Kelly's mum said. Kelly and her dad were quiet after that. It took the sting out of their heated conversation. Her mum was usually the one to make everyone feel better, even when things were uncertain. Her dad said he missed the routine of working but not the stress. At times like these, Kelly understood exactly where he was coming from.

Five

Crouching in front of the fireplace, I scratched a match across the box and held the flame to the newspaper under the kindling. It gradually took light. I threw the match into the fire and sat back, still amazed that I now knew how to make fires. I liked being able to figure things out like this, even if it took me a while and I'd used 'how to' videos on YouTube. It was an achievement. The fire spread quickly, and its heat soon reached my face. I closed my eyes and listened to the soft crackle of the fire in the glorious silence this house offered. From growing up in London and living in cities all my life, I would never tire of this peace.

Compared to when I'd met Kelly at the distillery, today had gone well. We'd had a proper conversation and I'd enjoyed talking to her very much. I kept seeing her tuck some hair behind her ear or lick her lips unconsciously. Thinking of Kelly comforted me, much like this fire. Seeing Kelly in her walking clothes, all natural and down to earth had sent my pulse racing. That Kelly was so warm and friendly, coupled with the knowledge of how impressive she was in other areas, sent my hormones raging. And the fact Kelly was a bit older only added to my attraction to her. I had a thing for older women, especially women like Kelly who oozed confidence. She had this unmistakable sexual energy that I couldn't not see, especially since I'd had a taste of it in the club.

I'd thought about kissing Kelly pretty much the whole time we were in the café. Hopefully she hadn't picked up on how ridiculously attracted to her I was. The chances of us meeting again like this were so small. Surely it was worth pursuing given our instant connection. Trying to seduce a sexy older woman seemed like a pretty good way to spend the next few months.

However, there was one slight problem. Compared to the sparks that were flying when we'd first met, Kelly was different now. Guarded. She'd acted polite and professional, but that was about it. Owning the distillery and coming to her workplace probably didn't do it for her, so I'd have to tread lightly. Hopefully it wasn't a lost cause. At the very least, Kelly would make an awesome friend to have up here.

I texted Rebecca to fill her in. Rebecca replied with a series of escalating emojis ending in a number of flames and a GIF of two women kissing.

> **Rebecca:** *I want your lucky charm, Murray. First the inheritance lottery and now you get to hang out with the hot woman from the gig. Fuck me! Tell your fairy godmother to drop in on me next.*
>
> **Myla:** *Ha!*
>
> **Rebecca:** *Has she made another move on you yet?*
>
> **Myla:** *No. She didn't acknowledge it. I had to bring it up. There're solicitors involved and everything. Bit of a cold-shower I think – for her. For me, I'm dying. She's even hotter in real life.*
>
> **Rebecca:** *OMG. Are you going to ask her out? See if she's still interested?*
>
> **Myla:** *I'd like to. Don't know if I will actually go through with it though.*

Rebecca: *Ask her out! If you don't, you'll never know. Keep me posted!*

Myla: *Will do.*

Rebecca: *What's the house like?*

Myla: *It's a mansion. Our whole flat would fit in one room.*

Rebecca: *Wow. Nice. Found out anything about your family? How are you feeling?*

Myla: *A bit. Been looking through some old photos and snooping around the house. It's so surreal. The history goes way back. I'm going to go all* Who Do You Think You Are? *on it when I feel up to it.*

Rebecca: *Take your time. Then you can sell your story to Hollywood :D*

I laughed. There was a knock at the door. The knock was quiet, slight. It happened again. I left my phone on the hearth and dashed through to see who it was, adrenaline coursing through me. Looking through the rusted peephole, there was a small figure standing there. Not a threat. Phew. I cleared my throat and opened the heavy door. A little old lady peered back at me. She stared at me for a few moments, as I did to her. After a while, she spoke.

"Hello Myla. I'm Hilary. I was a friend of your family for many years, and I wanted to come and introduce myself and welcome you home."

"Oh! Thank you. Would you like to come in?" I held the door as she stepped inside. She had the air of someone who knew this place better than I did. She didn't look around or make small talk, which lowered my defences, ironically. She stared at me with a mixture of expressions on her face – curiosity, approval, and... sadness. She kept staring. It was getting a bit weird now. "What can I help you with?"

"Excuse me. I apologise. You are the spitting image of your grandmother. She was a dear friend of mine."

I'd noticed this on the photographs. Still, it came as a surprise to hear someone say it.

Hilary continued. "I still miss her very much. And now Margaret, too. Death creeps up so fast." She paused, with a faraway look in her eyes. "We were friends for over seventy years. She was so happy to have finally found you and very much wished to meet you. Sadly, she was very frail towards the end and passed away not long after."

I nodded, wanting to know more. Anything, really, that this tiny old lady who was friends with my grandmother and great-aunt could tell me. "Would you like to sit down? Can I get you anything? Tea?"

"I wouldn't say no to a wee sherry if there's still some in your sideboard."

I showed her through to the warm sitting room, grateful that I had the fire going and looked like someone who knew how to run a house like this, because I really did not. Hilary gazed around the room, with a solemn look on her face. Losing a lifelong friend must not be easy.

"Which is the one you like?"

Hilary opened the cabinet and pulled out a new bottle. "One of these would be lovely." She gently placed her fingertips on a half-empty crystal decanter. "I'm afraid this will have gone off by now." She seemed sad, but not about the expired sherry. She looked so small and fragile.

"Would you like to sit down, and I'll find a glass." I looked at a cabinet full of glasses.

"Thank you. Middle shelf on the right, the wee ones." She sat in one of the huge chairs by the fire. There was a gentleness about her that put me at ease.

Hilary studied me intently as I carried over our sherries.

"It's so lovely," Hilary said, "to finally meet you."

Her words carried a hint of emotion, loaded with decades of meaning. I made Hilary out to be in her eighties. She had a slight stoop and deep wrinkles on her face, but there was a beauty to Hilary that time could not erase.

"It's nice to meet you, too. Thank you for coming around to visit me."

"Where have you come from, pet?"

"Edinburgh. Before that I lived in London, with my mother."

At the mention of my mother, Hilary tensed up a little. It was only slight, but I saw it.

"Did you know about your family up here?"

"No. My mother never told me about them."

"I see."

Hilary continued to regard me carefully, as I got settled in the chair opposite her. "You have your mum's eyes, too, and her smile. She must have been delighted with you."

I smiled but didn't want to confirm or deny such a bold statement from a practical stranger. Hilary took a sip of her sherry. I took a sip too, unsure whether I was going to like it, but I did.

"Did you know my mother?"

"I did."

"What do you remember about her?"

Hilary considered her answer, which I appreciated. "She was a spirited young woman with big dreams. She wanted to explore the world. Balbuinidh was always too small for her, that's for sure. A very headstrong person. Stubborn. She drove your grandparents mad with worry sometimes. She would go out to parties and come back in the early hours of the morning. Lovely girl though. Always very polite to me."

"Yep, that sounds like her." For someone who knew my mother decades ago, she was spot on. I used to worry about the exact same things. My mother treated me more like a friend, and she was a bad friend to me. We became like sisters as I got older. I was often the one to take care of her. She would go out partying and come home drunk or high in the middle of the night while I stayed up and waited for her. She could be very charming when she wanted to be. She told me all her problems and I was the one to support her, not the other way around. She was a bit shit, actually.

"How are you finding the house? Is it what you expected?"

I puffed out my cheeks. "It's... much grander than I thought it was going to be, I guess. I don't really know what I'm doing here."

Hilary found my eyes and held them. There was such an openness in her watery brown eyes. And a fierce intelligence. "You will, pet."

"Did my grandmother ever live here?"

"Yes, she and Margaret grew up here."

"And Margaret, she never had children?"

Hilary shook her head. "No. She and James wanted to focus on the distillery. You would have liked them. And Hazel. They were wonderful people and the best of friends."

"Where do you live?"

"Across town. On the other side of the river. I've lived there my whole life; can you believe it?"

"I can. I love the Highlands. I can see why you haven't wanted to go anywhere else."

"It's a special place. If you give it a chance, you might want to stay." Hilary took a sip from the delicate glass, as if lost in thought. "Your mum never talked about where she came from?"

"No. She never mentioned it. I've always been drawn to Scotland though."

Hilary listened. A soft glaze appeared in her eyes. Had I said something to upset her? "I'm sorry to hear that."

I took a gulp of sherry.

"Was your mum... well?"

That was an odd question. What was she getting at? "She functioned." I didn't sound convincing at all. I could hear it in my voice.

"What did she do for work?"

"She was a journalist."

"Oh, how exciting. That would have suited her."

"She was passionate about finding truth."

"That makes sense for her."

"She worked a lot. She had a busy social life. She was well connected. Her mental health wasn't always the best, but she got on with it. She had her good and her bad days." I looked away, remembering the chaos that my mother created. It had been exhausting. I didn't know how to handle her. Some days she would be as high as a kite and then the next day or week, she was... blank, depressed, as though she was empty behind the eyes. I felt like the grown-up in the household half the time. The other half, I felt like a burden, like her life would be so much better if she didn't have me in it. I knew this from a young age. I'd curtailed her. "I don't know how much exploring of the world she got to do. Having me kind of held her back. I killed her dreams."

Hilary frowned. "Oh, Myla, I'm so sorry. Do you have anyone? A partner? Friends?"

I gulped. Here was where I came off sounding like a freak. Everyone else seemed to have a lot of family and friends in their life but I seemed to drift around on the outside, alone and unattached. I'd lost touch with some people, too. "Yeah, I have some friends in Edinburgh. I keep in touch with some of my mother's friends down in London."

Hilary put down her sherry, held out her arms and stood. "Come here, sweet pea."

Before I knew it, I was enveloped in the frail arms of this stranger who smelled like a bouquet of flowers, yet she wasn't a stranger at all. She felt so safe, and of a different time. Her warmth seeped into my bones. "You've been through a lot." She patted my head. I felt like I was five and needed this. I did.

I pulled away from the hug and gave a small smile. We chatted for a while afterwards and it was so lovely. She told me all about her life and how she'd brought up four children and now had eight grandchildren. Finding out about Hilary's life was surprisingly insightful into my family. She talked about the laughs she, Margaret, and my grandmother Hazel used to have when they were younger. They used to go dancing on a Saturday night, and that's how my grandmother met my grandfather. My mother loved dancing. I guess she had to get it from somewhere.

"You know," Hilary cleared her throat. It was adorable in its lack of bite. "Margaret was able to pass over in peace knowing that the estate would stay in the family. It gave her great comfort, at the end."

"I'm glad about that."

"Your family has been in this town for hundreds of years, back when it was a tiny village. Your ancestors owned most of the surrounding land, but they sold it off over the years."

"How did Hazel and Margaret inherit it all? Didn't everything go to men back in those days?"

"Not always, but if they'd had a brother, he would have inherited it. They were always a tight family. Margaret chose to take on the estate and the distillery. Hazel didn't want the hassle. She was happy to let Margaret and James run it. And they made it such a success."

We finished our sherry, chatting more about the house and its quirks. Hilary knew a lot. Like when Margaret had a new spa-like bathroom installed and the get-togethers Margaret used to host. Like how Margaret had employed different contractors to help with the running and upkeep of the house: cleaners, gardeners, window cleaners. I'd seen some business cards in the kitchen, but I wasn't ready for all that yet. I kept that to myself as Hilary continued. She told me how Hazel used to love taking her and Margaret out on a boat on the loch and how they were all members of the Girl Guides for most of their lives. Margaret had looked up to her big sister. They both did. She commented on how Hazel was blessed with good looks, but that she never let them go to her head.

Learning all this was so unreal. It meant the world to me.

In a very civilised manner pertaining to ladies of a certain generation, Hilary didn't overstay. I helped her to the front door, holding the arm that she gave me.

"Do come over and see me whenever you like. I'd love to chat with you again. My door is always open to you, Myla." She looked me squarely in the eyes. "Anything else you want to know about the past, just ask."

With the oracle of truth standing before me, I realised I didn't know if I could handle hearing the answers to the hard questions yet, but I was grateful for Hilary's gesture. "I'd like that. I will. Thank you."

After meeting with Hilary and listening to her stories I couldn't shake the feeling that I *was* somehow connected to this place and this town. To the past. And closer to my mother, in a strange way. It was a side of her I had no idea about. I hadn't realised how much I'd needed someone like Hilary to offer me a friendly welcome until now. The picture of the past that Hilary had painted seemed so idyllic. So why did my mother leave this lovely little place and never come back? What had she kept from me?

***

Although a destination for tourists, I knew next to nothing about Balbuinidh. From my internet research, aside from its whisky, Balbuinidh was famous for its shinty team, and called itself the walking centre of Scotland given the variety of walking opportunities it offered locally. I decided to leave the car and walk in, to get a feel for it. Much of the walk was on my own land. *My own land.* Those words would never not amaze me.

I walked along the river until I reached the edges of the picturesque and proud little town. It was cloudy today, which was a shame. I bet the area looked magnificent when the sun was shining. The houses were beautiful, all unique and set in sprawling gardens with well-established trees. The river walk led into a well-maintained public park with yet more gorgeous trees peppering the space. Walking through, I wondered if my mother ever came here. Did she hang out here with her friends? Did she take the same route? I'd probably never know.

I let google maps tell me where my grandparents' house was. Strolling up to the gate of a huge townhouse near the centre, I gazed at the traditional stonework and how well-maintained it was. Someone was clearly looking after it. There were window ledges with flowerpots hanging off them and a small garden at the front. It looked like it stretched back at the rear, probably to a nice greenspace. The house wasn't what I was expecting at all – compared to Margaret's, it was relatively normal. To think that my mother, who used to tell me so much about herself, albeit not about her childhood, had never thought to tell me this. I didn't let myself feel anything while standing at the gate looking up at the house like a calculating burglar. I had no emotional attachment to this building, and I was going to keep it that way.

The town centre was busier than I expected as I wandered around. It consisted of a thriving main street full of local businesses and not too many chains, with a few busier streets running off it. There was a town-hall, a library, an old church which dominated the skyline, a fish and chip shop, a famous cheesemaker, shops selling art and pottery and homemade soaps, and a gorgeous lochside promenade filled with hotels, restaurants, and cafés. Beyond that there was the visitor centre and main supermarket, where I'd been before. I even saw a brown tourist sign for Glenbuinidh Distillery. God, the distillery was so official looking.

I bought the local paper and found a bakery and sat on a stool at the window, people-watching while sipping some coffee and eating a pastry. I read an article in the paper about the local school and the new sports hall they were having built. I would have to find out if that was the school my mother had gone to. It was nice here. People weren't rushing about like crazy. But it still had life about it: parents pushing prams, delivery drivers unloading vans, elderly people stopping to chat with friends. I liked it. It felt so... normal. Homely.

I had a meeting with the independent financial adviser that Graeme had recommended. I didn't want to go. What to do with the money felt like an important thing to sort out though. My old student current account didn't seem like the right place. I found the premises for my appointment in between an artisan deli and an arts and crafts shop. The sign read: NS Independent Financial Advice.

"Hello, come in, come in." I was met at the door and gestured inside to a small office. The man seemed out of breath, with a slight shine to his shaved head. His drooling gaze wasn't lost on me. I hated it when men looked at me like that. "I'm Nigel. It's Myla, isn't it?"

I nodded, keeping a straight face. "Yes."

"Graeme gave me a quick briefing on your situation, if you don't mind me saying so." I imagined Nigel's eyes lighting up in pound signs, much as they were right now. He continued. "Where I come in is in helping you with what to do next. To put it in the simplest way possible, I can help you keep your assets safe, and I can help you grow the funds you already have."

It was unlikely this man could help me with what to do next and I didn't need things put in simple terms. I *hated* being underestimated. He probably thought I would be easy to manipulate. I'd done a bit of research online. I knew I had to be sensible with the money. I'd already blown loads in the first couple of months. I'd hoped that meeting with an IFA would help me with it. But I wasn't sure about this guy. I'd probably go to a firm in Edinburgh instead, when I went back.

Once we got chatting, however, I had to admit that some of what he said sounded good. He said that if I were his daughter, he'd want to make sure the money was safely invested somewhere first, and then I could enjoy it knowing that I had an income for life. However, I left with a brochure and papers with Nigel's handwritten sums on them more confused than when I'd gone in. This wasn't fun.

I walked without direction for a few minutes then headed towards the lochside. As I turned the corner, I was nearly blown over by a biting wind blowing off the loch. Most of the lochside places were empty, but it was clearly a lovely place for people to come and enjoy. Summer strolls along this promenade would be so nice, with views of the surrounding hills reflected back off the loch. Did my mother ever come here? How could my mother have preferred London to this?

I didn't feel right. I was supposed to be enjoying my time here, but I wasn't. I was stuck in a past I didn't even recognise and not making use of my new-found freedom. Where was all the free spending, the champagne, and the indulgence? Screw what Nigel said. I knew that most people would be living it up right now, but here I was sensibly trying to work out where to invest it. A lot of my purchases had been such *practical* buys. That had to change. Why couldn't I be more carefree? I walked back up to the main street looking for places to spend some money. When I spotted a camera shop, I crossed the pedestrianised street lined with planters. The bell chimed as I went in.

A guy in his mid-thirties, probably, looked up from behind the counter. "Can I help you?"

The shop was the opposite of Nigel's. It looked expensive with the latest top of the range cameras proudly displayed around the store. Not that I knew what the latest tech was in the world of taking pictures. The only camera I had was a two-year-old iPhone.

"What's your best camera for taking pictures of the landscape? I like the mountains and I like people. Can you get one that does both well?"

The same pound signs I'd imagined in Nigel's eyes now appeared in this man's. Or they did so in my imagination, anyway.

"Certainly."

He showed me various models, each one ascending in price and specification quality. Clearly he didn't believe I could afford the real deal. Before long, he pointed out the most advanced camera, which also happened to be not too bulky and heavy like the other ones and handed it to me as if it were a newborn baby.

"This one is for the professionals."

I turned it around in my hands taking a good look at it while listening to him reel off further impressive specifications. It was perfect. "I'll take it."

"Are you sure?"

I frowned. Was I going to have to beg this guy to let me buy this thing? "Yes. What extras does it need?"

By the time I left the shop I'd cleared the wall of things to accompany the camera: a case, a large tripod, a small tripod, and different lenses. I'd always had an interest in photography but never the time or money or enough of an inclination to explore it fully. But I did now. It was thrilling spending money like this. I needed another hit. Music. A rush of adrenaline shot through me. I could buy all the instruments I wanted. Yes. I'd build a studio and start playing and writing music again. With that thought, I headed home to continue my retail therapy online, regretting not bringing the car – camera equipment was ridiculously heavy.

***

Kelly took a sip of their signature twelve-year at the bar, which was free of customers for the moment. The drink burned in all the right places before its warming layers took over. It was exactly what she needed after a hard day. All the paperwork and politics were getting her down. And it didn't help not knowing what was going to happen with Myla's ownership. Sometimes she needed to remind herself what it was all about in the end: just a drink. Nothing more, nothing less.

Anna, the Whisky Tasting Experience Manager, or 'the glorified bar manager' as Anna would say, was restocking one of the fridges behind the bar. She was a fellow queer and very hardworking. They had become good friends since Anna moved up here to take the job five years ago. If she didn't have Anna to decompress with, she didn't know if she could stay in such a small town, even if it was her hometown. Most of her friends from school had either moved away or were very tied up with young families, although Anna was always out running or in the gym these days.

"When is your Loch Ness Marathon again?"

"Four weeks." Anna stood, closed the fridge, and leant on the bar towards Kelly.

"How're you feeling about it?"

"I can't wait! I've always wanted to run a marathon. Tick it off the bucket list and all that."

"I love that. And you're doing it right by training properly for it. It's going to be great."

"It better be. I run in my dreams now, too."

"That's committed."

"Or crazy."

"It's looking great in here, by the way."

"Thanks. A big group has just left. Pretty much a whole tour bus."

"What were they like?"

"Keen. They burned a hole in the till trying to save their pockets."

Kelly held up her dram and tilted it towards her fit friend before taking another sip.

"There is something I have to update you on." Anna said.

"Sure. What's that?"

"Some staffing issues."

"What's up?"

"Magda and Tom are leaving. They've got new jobs in a hotel on the Isle of Lewis. They always said they wanted to work their way around Scotland," Anna shrugged. "It's to be expected."

Kelly sighed, resting her elbows on the bar and clasping her hands in front of her. Magda and Tom, a young couple from Poland, had been excellent. They had every right to suit themselves, but it meant they'd have to recruit and train new staff. They needed people who cared about whisky and who cared about this place. It wasn't an easy thing to find. Anna herself was a pure diamond: passionate about whisky, happy in Balbuinidh, good with people, and very organised.

"I'm already on it. Don't worry."

Kelly smiled. She knew Anna would sort it out. "Thanks for letting me know. If you want any support from the management team let Georgia know."

Anna nodded, then shot her a dubious look. "What's up?"

"Sorry?"

"You only come in here during the week if there's something on your mind. What's up?"

Kelly scratched her ear. "To be perfectly honest I'm worried about the future of the distillery."

"Why?"

"We've got a new owner."

"Who?"

"Myla Murray. Margaret's great-niece."

"Shit. Really?"

"Yes. She's coming in for a tour tomorrow at four-thirty. I'm doing it. Could you set us up with the full set, our finest range?"

Anna's eyes popped out of her head. "Yeah, sure. No pressure then."

"Don't worry. She's lovely. You'll like her."

"You know her?"

Kelly puffed out her cheeks and let a slow breath out. "A bit."

Anna eyed her closely. "You are not telling me something. What is going on?"

"Nothing. I don't really know her. I've only met her a few times."

Anna raised an eyebrow. "A few times? When? You never said anything."

Kelly shook her head, indicating she would go no further on the line of questioning.

"Margaret's great-niece. How old is she?"

"Twenty-seven."

Anna leant over the bar, concern etched across her face. "That's young. And she completely owns the distillery now?"

Kelly exhaled, feeling more worried by the second. A young and unpredictable owner didn't sound good, and this was without the additional information about their first meeting and undeniable chemistry. "Margaret wanted to keep it in her family, understandably. It makes sense."

"Well. I can't wait to meet her."

Kelly was apprehensive about Myla coming in tomorrow. It had to go well. There was to be no more underlying tension and thoughts about exploring her soft lips again. It had to stop. This was serious. Myla could change the future of this entire town on a whim, if she liked. Kelly didn't think she would be that callous, she didn't seem the type, but after that conversation with her dad, Kelly hadn't been able to fully relax. The idea of new buyers ingratiating themselves with Myla made her shudder.

Anna walked around the bar and took a seat next to her. "Is there something else?"

Kelly looked down at her glass and then finished the rest of her whisky. Maybe telling Anna would help. She knew the secret would be safe with her. Kelly took a deep breath, then ventured forward with the truth. "I met Myla before I found out she was the new owner."

"Where? When?"

"At the gig in Glasgow in January."

"And?"

"We met at the bar. Got talking. I saw her in the club at the after party and we ended up kissing. She was the one who did a runner."

Anna's mouth fell open. "Oh my god, you pulled the new owner of the distillery?"

"It would seem that way."

"Is she a lesbian?"

"Maybe. Sapphic, for sure."

"She stood you up, though."

"Apparently it was by mistake."

"You've spoken about it?"

"We had coffee."

"You're dating?"

"No. Absolutely not."

"Right. Because she's your boss now."

Kelly gave her a look.

"You like her, don't you?"

Kelly gave her an even sterner look.

"Oh shit. You're in trouble."

"It's fine. It's not like that any more. I'm one hundred percent focused on the distillery."

Anna's face softened while simultaneously registering the situation and Kelly's predicament. "I know you are. You love this place more than anything."

"I'm hoping she'll fall in love with the distillery, too, and will want to keep it."

"It sounds like you've given this a lot of thought."

"I just want it to go well tomorrow."

Anna nodded. "Are you sure you don't want to explore anything with Myla? It sounds like there's something between the two of you."

"Besides a ten-year age gap? What would a hot young woman want with me? I'm hitting forty soon, a workaholic, and boring. She could do so much better."

"Hey," Anna's tone was gently scolding. "Don't talk about my pal like that. You're great."

Kelly sighed. "What happened in the club is history. The only thing that matters now is making sure Myla keeps the distillery and working out a way for her to be involved that suits everyone. She could just as easily want to take over and change everything. I don't know. I just don't know, and I hate not being in control."

"Ah," Anna said. "The real problem."

Kelly eyed up another dram and went behind the bar to pour it. Anna watched on, thankfully not pushing the topic further. Kelly came back with two glasses and placed one in front of Anna. "This is what I get for reliving my youth and pulling some girl in a club. When will I learn to act my age?"

Anna threw her head back, laughing. "Never, hopefully! Oh Kelly, you are so entertaining."

Kelly laughed, not meaning to. "Well at least someone's enjoying this."

Six

The distillery was unnervingly quiet. It was half four in the afternoon and gloomy outside. Kelly had asked me to come in at this time, for the last tour of the day. I hadn't been able to think about much else since she texted me. Her text had been a bit formal and brief, however, which was less promising. I re-read it:

> **Kelly:** *Hi Myla. For your tour, could you come to the distillery on Thursday at 4.30pm? Many thanks, Kelly.*

No one else was waiting for the tour to start. Lucy greeted me at the reception with an easy, friendly smile. I found the glass cabinet I'd scanned the last time I was here. My reflection startled me. I was so pale.

"You made it." Kelly came striding into reception, smiling broadly. She was wearing an oversized wax jacket, jeans and boots. She had her hair down and it was styled poker straight – the only giveaway that she was a professional type. Her outfit was the opposite of what I might have expected her to be in.

"Hey. Do CEOs usually dress like that up here?"

"Are you thinking of introducing a dress code already?" The teasing look on Kelly's face made me hot and bothered. "I'm giving you a private tour among the mash tuns, so I need to dress for it. Also, my heels tend to get caught in the metal grid walkways, so the boots are practical."

"You're giving me a private tour?" I choked.

"Nothing but the best for our VIP," she paused. "Also, we usually close early on Thursdays in the winter so there shouldn't be any other tours on."

"Great." I couldn't quite hide the smile that formed at my lips. The idea of being alone with her made my head spin. "I've been looking forward to this. I know nothing about whisky. I'm keen to learn what you do here."

"Open-minded, I like that."

I knew she wasn't, but it *felt* like she was flirting with me. I followed Kelly through to the older wing of the distillery, and into a dark room. I didn't know what this was, but I was here for it.

"This is where the tour starts," Kelly said, as if answering the question in my head. "If you'd like to take a seat."

I sat down in the front row of a small, cave-like cinema room. Kelly stood at the front next to the screen. She pointed a laser at it, and it fired up, blasting bagpipes and scenes of rugged hills and barley rustling in the wind. The music quietened down.

"That's my cue to start. I'll do the intro, so you get a feel for what we offer to visitors. Although I won't do the jokes that the guides come out with. They're way funnier than I am. They like to get a few laughs in, you know. Give the visitors a slice of some Scottish humour."

"No jokes, I understand."

Kelly looked at me again, a little longer than necessary, before steadying herself with a deep breath. Was she nervous, too? The thought really surprised me. It was likely Kelly was on edge due to my role as the new owner. This must be hard for her.

"Welcome to Glenbuinidh Distillery, where the past comes to life through our unique single malt. Local landowner William Gordon started making whisky here in eighteen-twenty-four and we've been making that signature single malt here ever since. What makes Glenbuinidh unique is that it has been a family-run business for most of that time, and to this day it is a huge part of the local community. Our local freshwater, barley, climate, and even the shape of our stills combined with some of the finest casks in the world is what gives our whisky its own special character. So, how do we do it? There are six distinct stages to how whisky is made in Scotland: preparation, malting, mashing, fermentation, distillation, maturation and bottling. Next, I'll take you through the distillery giving you a feel for what goes on at each stage, and maybe a little insight into this wonderful area and what makes our whisky so special. You will also get an opportunity to sample some of our finest malts at the end of our tour in our world-renowned living bar."

"Ooh. There's a bar?"

"Patience." Kelly mock scolded. "You have to see the tour first."

"I'm here for it."

A smile tugged at Kelly's mouth.

A wave of heat shot through my lower body. Kelly was ridiculously hot and being friendlier today. Even the slightest hint of her flirting with me was enough to send a gentle throb down low in my body.

Bagpipes came on again, before going into a short video about the history of the distillery. The land, the people, and the brand itself. It was fascinating. To think that this was in my background was remarkable. That it kept going in the family for so many generations was the stuff of fairy tales. There was no way I could sell up, right?

Why was that even presented to me as an option? It was unthinkable.

The video faded to black, and the music switched to fiddle-led folk. Kelly took me through to a noisy room. The smell hit my nostrils again. It was warm. Despite the enormous space filled with interesting objects all I could focus on as we walked into the working distillery was the back of Kelly and her tall slender frame. I forced my attention on the space instead. It was very industrial with dials and switches and pipes everywhere.

Kelly came to a stop. "Scottish whisky is made from three basic ingredients: barley, yeast and water…"

Kelly certainly knew how whisky was made. I was amazed she knew the script and could reel it off, since she wasn't a tour guide.

"…The kiln's traditional pagoda-shaped chimney is the distinctive hallmark of a Scottish distillery."

"Oh yeah, I saw them on the way in. I wondered what they were."

"Our kilns are among the oldest and largest in Scotland, much like this distillery."

We walked on high grid walkways among a dozen or more giant tubs. This place was legit. I felt the invisible pressure of hundreds of years of history bearing down on me. Part of me still couldn't believe this was my family's business.

Kelly spun around to face me. "Want to know something off script?"

"Uh, yeah. I expect full insider knowledge."

"One time, one of our whisky makers opened up to find an owl sitting on the edge of one of these bad boys." Kelly tapped another huge structure. "No one knows how it got in. One theory is that it came in through the vents," she pointed to the ceiling.

The machinery was so loud. I stepped a bit closer to her. She didn't falter. We had been closer once before, so this felt almost natural. It would be so easy to lean in and kiss her lips again. I inhaled the spicy fruitiness of her perfume. It took me right back to the club when it had filled my senses. I hadn't washed my top for days afterwards trying to preserve it.

"We had to get someone out to help it escape. Poor thing."

"I hope it was okay."

"It was fine. It was probably looking for a warm bed for the night."

"I don't blame it. Though, perhaps it'll choose somewhere less noisy next time."

Our eyes met and a wave of electricity rushed through me. "So, on with the tour?" Kelly said.

"Uh huh."

"The dry barley gets milled and mixed with hot water in these mash tuns, to create wort…"

I followed Kelly through to another vast room. Huge copper structures that looked like giant kettles sat majestically in the centre. She was good at projecting her voice over the machinery, and I enjoyed watching her mouth under the guise of lip-reading.

"The wash traditionally gets distilled in two large distinctive copper stills…"

I took a picture of the stills, in awe, despite not fully absorbing what Kelly was saying.

"Here, would you like me to take your picture?"

"Sure."

I handed her my phone and our fingers brushed. A jolt of electricity ran through me at her touch. I stood beside the railing. Kelly's eyes flitted from me and back to the screen several times as she tapped away. I was getting overheated by her undivided attention. The giant kettles weren't helping either.

She then led me down a long ramp to a strange device that looked like something out of a seaside amusement park.

"This is the spirit safe. The liquid runs off from the second still, into here. It's always kept locked, courtesy of Her Majesty's Customs and Excise, to make sure every ounce of whisky distilled is taxed."

"How much whisky do you make?"

"We make six million litres a year. We're one of the largest whisky distilleries in Scotland."

"That's huge."

We chatted for a while longer at the spirit safe. I was beginning to understand just how big of a deal Glenbuinidh was. Kelly told me about some of the challenges they were facing when it came to keeping up with global demand. In full tour guide mode, Kelly led me through to a dark and enormous room full of casks. Here, the smell was more refined, and thick with alcohol. The casks were stacked high into the air, like a never-ending bookcase of whisky. The walkway was lit up atmospherically.

"Once distilling is complete, the new spirit is poured into casks, and the waiting game begins. That's the maturation stage. We use bourbon and sherry oak casks mostly from Spain or America. It must be matured for a minimum of three years before it can legally be called Scotch. We have some casks in here which were distilled decades ago. It's kept dark and damp for a reason. The local weather helps with that too. Over the years, the wood of the casks and the surrounding atmosphere gives the whisky its colour, character and some its natural flavours."

It was so quiet. I nodded along, taking in her words better in the dark and more intimate space. We strolled among the casks, not going anywhere in particular it seemed.

"I hope that's given you a *flavour* for the distillery and the tours we offer." Kelly laughed at her own joke.

Oh my god, she was such a dork. "Yep, you seem like a fully-fledged tour guide to me, complete with corny puns."

"Hey, only barley puns allowed in here. Yeah, I've done a ton of these tours with a million different visitors. I could talk about whisky in my sleep at this point. I probably do."

I pictured Kelly sleeping. In bed. Snuggled up under a warm duvet. Naked under the covers…

"I hadn't realised it was such a visitor attraction, but I get it now. There's something magical about it."

"It's one of the most visited visitor attractions in the whole region. We're part whisky producer, part tourist destination."

We were quiet with each other as we wandered around the darkened warehouse. I ran my hand along the casks as we passed. "The water of life."

Kelly glanced over at me, approvingly. "That it is."

"There's something primal about whisky. There's this connection to our ancestors through it. Like with bread. You know what I mean?"

Another approving glance and this time a smile from Kelly. "I know exactly what you mean. That's one of the reasons I love working here. The history."

"What is it like working here?"

"It's good. We've got some wonderful people."

"Do you pay people well?"

"I think so. We have a high retention rate. It's usually the bottlers and the bar staff that are more seasonal as the work comes and goes depending on the maturation cycles and the seasons."

"Who buys the whisky?"

"We export to nearly every country in the world. Some of the biggest importers are the US, India, Brazil, France and Germany... It's big business."

"People love it."

"They do. And they will spend. Just last month we had an American lady visiting Scotland for her fiftieth birthday. She bought a bottle of our fifty-year-old on sale for nineteen thousand five hundred pounds. She was treating herself, and why not? She was so happy."

"What happens to the profits?"

Kelly narrowed her eyes for a second. "They went to Margaret. And now to you."

"That seems excessive."

Kelly held her tongue. I could tell she had more thoughts on the matter. "It is what it is."

We exited through another door which took us outside. What I saw next took my breath away.

"I give you the famous Glenbuinidh Living Bar," Kelly said, eyes twinkling in the fading light.

I shivered from the cold and the excitement of going into a building built into the land itself. It looked out over the glen, with sophisticated floor to ceiling windows lining the hillside.

"Wow. I've never seen anything like this before."

"Come on, I'll show you inside."

Kelly led the way across a manicured lawn with whisky casks as planters lining the path to the entrance. Kelly held the door open for me. I scanned the bar. The lighting was soft, and everything felt cosy and warm. Casks acted as tables interspersed with a couple of long tables, probably for bigger groups. Leather sofas and deep comfortable-looking chairs peppered the places by the windows with low tables in between them. You wouldn't know you were inside a mountain. "This place is so cool."

Someone came out from behind the well-stocked bar and walked towards us smiling. "Hello. Welcome. Please come in," she said loudly in a lovely Glaswegian accent.

"Myla, this is Anna, our Whisky Tasting Experience Manager. Anna this is Myla. Myla is the new owner of Glenbuinidh."

Anna had short, curly hair, shaved on one side. It suited her. She also had a sleeve of tattoos and a strong, steady presence. She *must* be a lesbian.

Anna's eyes were wide as she took me in. I got the feeling she knew I was coming already. Perhaps I wasn't what she pictured when she thought of the new owner.

"It's a pleasure to meet you, Myla."

I smiled, broadly. "It's lovely to meet you, too."

"Are you enjoying your tour?"

I glanced at Kelly, whose stance was rigid. "I am. Kelly has been telling me so many fascinating things, part of me wanted to take out a notebook and write it all down."

Anna's smile was genuine. I got a good feeling from her. "I'm sure she'd be happy to go over it again with you. Kelly knows everything about this place, and this town. She's a true believer in Glenbuinidh. Heart of gold."

Wow. That was quite the endorsement. Was she trying a little too hard to big Kelly up? Why would that be?

"I've laid out our sampling whiskies on the table by the window. Our best table. I think Kelly is going to personally go through them with you, but if you need anything please give me a shout. I'll be right over here."

"Thanks, Anna," Kelly said, shooting Anna a look I couldn't quite place.

I sank into the deep brown leather sofa, feeling instantly relaxed and comfortable, and ready to sample the line of whiskies before me. All this talk about how it was made had whetted my appetite for it. Unfortunately, Kelly took a seat across from me, much further away than I would have liked. Kelly was at work, I reminded myself, feeling disappointed this wasn't real drinks.

"Anna has prepared a selection of our finest single malts for you to sample. They're about half a dram each. You don't have to drink them all, sips are fine, or you can just smell them. Then again, you're very welcome to finish them if you like. We have a taxi service for that."

"Thanks. I'll see how I go."

"You'll notice they are slightly different colours." Kelly pointed at various shades of whisky. "Here, have a taste. It's the best way to understand."

I nodded. Our fingers brushed as Kelly passed a tiny glass with a small amount of amber liquid towards me, sending a gentle throb low down in my body. This was insane. I'd never had this level of outright sexual attraction to someone before. I raised the glass, and Kelly picked up one too, from her matching set across the table. I liked that she was drinking with me.

"Some people take their whisky with a dash of water or ice cubes. There's no right or wrong way to drink it. It depends on how you like it. I like to smell the whisky before I sip." I watched transfixed as she slightly parted her lips and inhaled, imagining her doing that to me. I couldn't help it; my mind just went there. "I like to know what I'm getting myself in for." Kelly tilted her glass towards me. "Slàinte mhath. That's how we say cheers in Scotland. It means good health." She took a sip then put her glass down. "You try."

Oh my god. I was getting wet. Her eyes were on me as I brought the glass up to my nose and gently inhaled. "Slanja va?" I brought the liquid to my lips and took a drink, after a valiant attempt at the Scottish way to say cheers. It stung at first, almost burning my tongue and throat, but then soft tones spread through my mouth. It ended with a satisfying and not too harsh bite as I swallowed. I let it simmer for a few seconds.

"That was really good."

"What were you getting from it? Was it sweet? Or Spicy? Creamy?"

"Creamy. With a hint of vanilla."

"Very good. It has." Kelly nodded. "Not many people are so accurate right away."

"It'll be a fluke." I finished the rest. "I'd better try another."

I wasn't sure what the next one tasted like, or the one after that, but they were good. Kelly was so invested so I didn't want to say they tasted like alcohol and not much else.

"A droplet or two of water can help bring out the flavours."

I added two drops from the pasteur pipette that was in a little jar and took another sip. My mouth was warm and my lips were pulsating. "Much better. It's quite spicy, this one. I like it. I'm loving these whiskies, they're so good."

"You have good taste."

My breath caught. The way Kelly said the words reminded me of the way she'd spoken to me that night at the gig. Very direct, in a tone or two lower. I'd replayed that night over and over in my head. Even now in her jeans and boots and jumper, she was so hot. The way her smooth brown hair fell forwards and brought out the depths in her eyes. I was so turned on by how much more experienced she was than me. I inhaled, smelling the whisky on my breath. We held each other's eyes for a few beats, and I yearned for this to go back in the direction of the first time we met, but Kelly broke the connection, sat back, and glanced up at Anna. "You must have the best. You should take a bottle home with you."

"Thank you." We held eyes again. Thoughts of going home with Kelly filled my brain. I wanted to keep talking to her and see if this barrier of hers would come down. "So, Ms Whisky Connoisseur, which is your favourite?"

"That's a tough one. But if I had to choose, I'd say it's our newest whisky I've got maturing across the way called Queen of Spirits. I had the first batches made twelve years ago, and we've kept it going since. My dad was trying to get me involved early on in my career, as he was always hopeful I'd take over one day. It's based on Scots Gaelic folklore and embodies the best of what we make here already. It's a smooth flavour with fruity tones – citrus, peach and spice. It's also organic."

Kelly smelled like that. I was intrigued that she'd made a whisky out of the same tones. "Sounds amazing. What is the folklore?"

Kelly leant forward. "Legend has it there was a Gaelic Goddess, Neachneohain, who was a warrior and fierce protector of nature. She was never afraid to walk her own path and was known as a quiet rebel. Sir Walter Scott even wrote about her. I try to follow her ethos in everything we do here at Glenbuinidh. I would like to launch it as our next big single malt. The first batches are ready and would be sold to independent spirit retailers, luxury retail as well as craft food and drink festivals. I'm currently debating whether or not it's the right time to launch it though. Not everyone is on board with the idea."

"Well, she sounds incredible, this goddess. You should totally go for it. You have my support, if that means anything. I am well aware that it doesn't, but I'd like to give it nonetheless."

Kelly's eyes lit up and there was genuine gratitude in them. "Your support does matter, Myla. Thank you."

"I'd like to try it sometime."

Kelly's shoulders relaxed and her face softened. It was nice to see. "It's not out yet. We don't keep any in this bar. I can let you have a taste from my personal collection sometime though."

I gulped. Everything she said to me was tinged with an intense sexual energy. It was almost tangible. "I can't wait."

"In the meantime, here, try another." Kelly passed me the lightest dram. "This one is our softest single malt."

It went down easily, and the aftertaste was pleasant. "Nice."

We then discussed the remaining whiskies on the table as I tasted them. I drank them all.

"Most people are surprised when they find out that despite our locally sourced ingredients, the climate here, our unique distillation practices and so forth, it's the casks that really make the difference. They make up about sixty percent of the final taste."

"That is surprising."

"The whisky is in there for years, soaking in the oak and hints of what the cask had in it before. Talk about environmental influences…"

"Makes sense. We're all products of our environments."

"True."

As Kelly talked, I realised I could listen to her for hours. Her passion for the topic, the tone of her voice and her delicious Highland accent held me enthralled. The way she held eye contact with me as she elucidated was simply causing me to ruin my panties.

"You are so passionate about this place."

Kelly smiled. "Yeah. I am. I'm very fortunate. I love working here."

There was also something else in Kelly's eyes, as if she wanted to say more but held back. I looked around the bar. It was magical. "I can see why."

Kelly cleared her throat. "I was going to ask you something. Please, feel free to say no, it is kind of unusual. My parents wanted to invite you over for supper sometime. They'd love to meet you. Totally no pressure to accept. My mum is basically a massive extrovert and is dying to get to know you. Be warned, though, she is very inquisitive."

I did a double-take. The invitation caught me by surprise. Kelly didn't seem overly keen on the idea. It was an invite from her parents, not her, obviously. Just thinking about going to dinner with her parents made me feel awkward, but then, it *would* be good to meet more people from the town. Kelly's dad had, after all, run this place before. "Sure. Okay. I'd love to."

"It will be just the four of us. Would two weeks on Friday work for you? They're not free until then and I'm not sure if you're still going to be here but if you are then they'd love to meet you."

"That's fine. I'll be around."

"Great."

There was *something* between us. But how did Kelly feel about it? Where was the Kelly I first met? My spirits sank as I faced the truth. Kelly wasn't interested in me romantically any more, whether she was going to admit it or not, and part of me couldn't blame her. I now owned her company, and she must feel pretty uncertain about that. I understood her predicament. Me being the new owner of her distillery was a bit intense. The distillery meant a lot to her.

"I'm really sorry," Kelly said in those dulcet tones of hers, "but I'm going to have to get going. Barley is waiting for me at home."

"Yeah, sure, of course," I said, trying to hide my disappointment, how much of an effect Kelly was having on me and how drunk I was.

Anna came over. Only empty glasses remained on my side of the table. Shit. Had I really drunk them all? Come to think of it, the bottles stacked behind the bar were a bit blurry. I swayed involuntarily, trying to focus on Kelly, whose cheeks were rosy and whose gaze had settled on me. Yep, I was drunk.

"Everything okay over here?" Anna said, hands resting casually on her hips.

"Everything was perfect, Anna. Thank you." I gazed at Kelly. She had such a good nature about her. God, she was attractive.

Anna grinned, cheekily. "Excellent."

Kelly reached for her wax jacket. "We were just leaving, actually." Kelly looked out of the window and frowned.

"It's snowing?" I hadn't noticed it was snowing either. Kelly's expression turned serious as she looked at me. "Normally we suggest our taxi service for guests who have had a few but I'd be happy to drive you home tonight myself. I don't think it's fair to get Tony out in this, it looks like it's settling quite heavy and fast. Would you like a lift home?"

Oh my god. The idea of leaving together was too much. It was like that night. We'd been so hot for each other. Fuck, I was still hot for her. I had to calm down.

"It's not far. I could walk."

"It's far enough. The car is safer."

"Okay, thank you. I can pick my car up tomorrow." I was mortified. I'd sat here getting drunk while Kelly had infused me with her whisky knowledge and shared her thoughts on the different tastes and smells. It had nearly been too much given my attraction to her. I didn't often drink much, well, except in social settings to calm my nerves and give me a boost in confidence.

I faced Anna. "And thanks for letting me loose on your nice whiskies. I seem to have drunk them all."

Anna laughed, kindly. "You certainly know how to enjoy yourself." She started walking back to the bar. "Come back soon."

I turned to Kelly who was looking at me with gooey eyes. What did that mean? "Sorry I got carried away. I hadn't realised I'd drunk so much."

Kelly shook her head, waved me away and regained her composure. "It happens. Trust me, we've seen it all."

Even while a bit tipsy I could tell Kelly was enjoying my company. Enjoying it too much though?

"Oh wait. I was going to send you home with a bottle," Kelly said. "Anna," she called out. "Could you get us a bottle of the twenty-one for Myla please?"

"Will do, boss."

A few moments later Anna reappeared with a cylindrical box of whisky.

"Enjoy." Anna handed me the bottle.

It had the most gorgeous blue and gold colouring, with ornate, enticing writing. I carefully placed it on the table, worried I might drop it. "Thanks! Um, I'm happy to pay for this. Here," I dug out my bank card.

"Uh, no," Kelly said, firmly. "There's no point. It's your distillery, remember?"

I shook my head.

Your distillery.

This place. All of it. It was mindboggling. My life had completely transformed in such a small amount of time. Being here, in the Highlands, with these people – it was crazy, but it was real. Maybe I *could* move up here and live in the big house? Maybe I *could* redecorate and fill it with a music studio? It would be good to have more time to explore the place that had shaped my mother. Michelle would let me go back to the café again if I wanted. Staying here for longer *felt* right. When my intuition whispered to me like this, I tried to listen. It had served me well in the past. Like when I'd had the strong urge to leave London and move up to Edinburgh while knowing no one there. Staying in Balbuinidh for longer felt more like a shout and I had received the message loud and clear. I would stay here for a couple of months and see how I felt. Decision made.

Kelly was still waiting for me to put my card away. "Okay." I slid it back into my purse. "Thank you so much. I will cherish it."

Kelly took a deep breath. Her whole body rose and fell with it. "Right. Let's get you home." Kelly stood.

"Yes ma'am." I caught the eyes that Kelly narrowed at me in a somewhat flirty undertone as I stood and picked up the bottle.

"Safety first."

"Keep me safe, Kelly."

Kelly bit her lower lip and furrowed her brow. I loved that I was having any effect on her at all. She was so lovely, and clever and kind. And hot.

Stepping out into the night air I was met with thick snowflakes on my cheeks and lips. The distillery grounds were white. The snow crunched underfoot. Glancing over at Kelly walking beside me I was super glad of the ride home because treacherous drives along country roads in thick snow did not count among my skillset even when sober. Neither did navigating three miles of unmarked countryside on foot in the dark over snow. Kelly looked very sexy in that wax jacket. She suited the country look. Then again, she suited every look I'd seen her in so far: dance floor, corporate, and her dog-walking finest. No doubt naked would be her utmost finest look. God, I was so sexually charged around her.

We walked in a not so comfortable silence through the snow and across the grounds towards the car park. Kelly's car was already covered in snow.

Kelly held open the door for me and I got in, less gracefully than I would have liked. She shut the passenger door with an amused grin. The next thing I knew Kelly was turning on the engine while standing next to the car and scraping snow off the windows as the air from the heater blasted into my face. I blew on my hands. It was quite cold. Finally, Kelly got in her side, shut the door with a thud and put her seatbelt on. Snowflakes had settled in her hair and her cheeks were adorably rosy. She smiled over at me and all I could do was gaze back at her like the hopeless romantic that I was.

"Balbuinidh gets very pretty covered in white; it can be dangerous once the snow ices over."

"I think it's beautiful with and without the snow. I like it up here."

Kelly gave me another strange look but this one was more curious than anything else. "I've only had a unit so I'm fine to drive but bear with me, this is a bit tricky."

"I trust you."

Seven

The drive back to Myla's was quiet and very white. The snow had settled fast making the countryside visible in the darkness. Neither of them said much. Kelly hoped this tension between them would dissipate soon. She couldn't go there again with Myla. Not with everything that was happening with the future of the distillery. Not with someone this young and who was going through so much. She just couldn't.

"It's right along here." Myla pointed.

Kelly knew exactly where the house was but didn't say anything.

"The big empty house." Myla murmured.

She parked outside the main door and the lights came on inside the car, illuminating them both in a way that made the huge car seem very small. Kelly just sat there, trying to think of what to say. Not many people made her speechless.

Myla shifted in her seat towards her. "Do you want to come inside and see how shockingly large this house is for one person?" Myla's eyes sparkled. It was lovely to see, and frustratingly attractive. Kelly took a steadying breath. She did want to see how Myla was getting on in the house. As a friend though, only. "I can't stay long, because of Barley and the snow but okay."

Myla nodded. "Awesome."

Snow fell as they approached the house. Myla fumbled for her keys and then let them in. To be fair, the house was far too big for one person. She couldn't image living here on her own. It must be so strange. It had even been a bit strange when Margaret lived here on her own, although she seemed to fill the house with her presence and always had lots of people coming in and out. The house was exactly as Kelly remembered it. But there were boxes scattered around that looked recently delivered and unopened. Kelly shivered. The house was cold. Myla carefully placed the vintage bottle of whisky on the sideboard with both hands, which Kelly secretly approved of. They went through to the sitting room with their jackets and shoes still on. Myla took a seat on the massive tartan sofa, shrugging off her jacket as she did so. Kelly sat at the opposite end from Myla, with her jacket still on.

"Thank you for driving me back. You're good at driving in snow."

Interesting that she didn't use the word 'home'. "Thanks. You're welcome. It was nothing."

Myla frowned, then got up towards the fireplace. Kelly watched as she knelt in front of it. Her frame was small next to the huge fireplace. Myla got the logs burning, sending orange flames flickering up the chimney. Myla sat back down in the middle of the sofa, closer to her than would be strictly platonic, which made Kelly both excited and uncomfortable. Myla's cheeks were flushed red from the heat of the fire, or perhaps something else, Kelly couldn't be sure.

"I am a little tipsy. I missed lunch and haven't eaten since this morning. That's probably why I got so drunk so easily."

"That would do it. Also, you had about seven units in about an hour…"

Myla turned towards her, moving that little bit closer to her. Kelly was reminded of the night they first met and the undeniable chemistry between them. Myla rested her elbow on the back of the sofa and her head in her hand. She looked right into Kelly's eyes and Kelly couldn't bring herself to look away, even though she should.

"I am sorry I got drunk. That was so crass of me."

Kelly laughed softly. "I don't think you have a crass bone in your body. You were fine. Like I said, we've seen a *lot* worse in the bar after tours. People pretend to be all cultured and sophisticated, but in the end they just want to drink it. You at least listened to my lecture."

This elicited a huge smile from Myla. "I enjoyed listening to you. You speak with such passion about it all."

A shot of pride rushed through Kelly's chest. She loved that Myla perceived her as passionate.

"And your jokes *were* good."

"Now I know you're just flattering me."

"What would be wrong with that?"

"Nothing, I guess."

Myla spoke quietly. "Because you're awesome. I'm really enjoying getting to know you."

"And I'm enjoying getting to know you." She wanted to say more about how lovely she thought Myla was, about how her whole body came alive whenever she was with her, but that was a terrible idea. This urge to touch her could go nowhere. There was a long pause. Kelly could do nothing else but gaze back into Myla's eyes. Her heart rate picked up, and her breathing felt shallow. The moment noticeably stretched on, and then she forced herself to look away and break the connection, and then got up and stood by the fire.

This wasn't happening. Not now, not ever.

Myla scratched her head. After a few moments, she spoke again, as if nothing had just happened. "Do you want that tour of the house? It's only fair since you showed me around the distillery in such depth." Myla's words said one thing, but her energy said another. She seemed deflated.

Kelly was disappointed too. She was attracted to Myla. Very attracted. But nothing could come of it. She was happy to be her friend but nothing more. Myla continued looking at her, and Kelly realised she'd forgotten the question. "Sorry?"

Myla smiled. "A tour. Do you want to see the house?"

"Yes please. I've never seen the whole house. I only ever saw this room when I visited Margaret. I used to feel like the Prime Minister visiting the Queen for a chat over tea."

"Oh. I didn't know you'd been here before." Myla shrugged. "But of course you have. That's cool."

Kelly missed Margaret. She'd looked up to her. Her counsel had always been spot on when they met for their monthly meetings. In recent years, when her health started to fade, they met less frequently, but Kelly always enjoyed her company.

Myla showed her around the various rooms on the ground floor – various sitting rooms, an empty room, the kitchen, the dining room and a rather rundown conservatory facing the grounds to the back of the house. The house was filled with antiques and giant persian rugs.

"It's very old," Myla said, stopping at the foot of the stairs. "It needs done up."

Did she want to stay in it and make it her own? She didn't want to pry but was also dying to know.

"Upstairs is basically a ton of empty bedrooms and bathrooms, and a library. I mean, a study."

"I'd like to see."

They walked up the stairs side by side as the staircase was that wide. As they walked along the hallway and peered into various rooms, Kelly could see what she meant. The rooms were square in shape, about the same size, with a huge bed in the middle of one wall.

"Which one do you sleep in?"

"In here," Myla said. She took her to the next bedroom and held the door open.

Kelly looked inside at the empty four-poster bed and separate blow-up mattress and a sleeping bag on the floor.

"Um, don't you like sleeping in beds? What's with all the camping equipment?"

"To be honest I don't know which bed my aunt died in. The rooms look the same. I'm going to buy new beds for every room, but I haven't got around to it yet."

Kelly burst out laughing. "Sorry, I just... that's so unusual. But I can see what you mean. I wouldn't like that either."

"I have to go furniture shopping. Not that I'm ungrateful or anything – it's just a bit creepy."

"You'll feel better about being here once you do. It's amazing what a bit of paint and your own belongings can do to make you feel more at home."

"That's true. Oh, I nearly forgot. Wait until you see this, it's like something out of a historical drama."

Myla was right. The walls were lined with floor to ceiling bookcases and ancient looking books. A massive desk sat in the middle of the room. Two leather chairs sat either side of another fireplace with a stag's head hanging from the wall above it. Kelly's parents had a similar room but not on the same scale and it was more like a reading nook. She loved sitting in there with them, reading, and chatting next to the fire. "I think this is my favourite room, apart from the dead animal on the wall."

Myla smiled. "Yeah, that's got to go. My favourite room is the empty one downstairs. I'm going to build a music studio."

"I didn't know you were a musician."

"I'm not. I play a few instruments. I used to write some songs. It's just a hobby."

Kelly was intrigued but decided to leave that topic for now. Myla led them back into the room with the fire going. They stood, hovering by the fireplace and its warmth. It cast a lovely glow over Myla's face. Staring down at the flickering hot flames, Myla looked thoughtful.

She really did have to get back to Barley. However, one question tugged at her. "Are you going to live in the house? Sell it? Start a hotel?" Kelly knew her questions were loaded with connotations about the distillery and Myla's hold over it, but in that moment she just wanted to know about Myla and her life.

"I've decided to stay for a little while. I'm going to do the house up and look after it. I like the area. I liked finding out more about the distillery today. I think some time up here will do me good."

Kelly found herself smiling broadly. It made her happy to think that Myla was going to stay for longer. She wanted to be part of her time spent up here in some way, but not in a romantic way, obviously.

"Margaret's friend Hilary popped in last weekend. It was extraordinary to meet someone who knew my family."

"That's great. Hilary is so sweet. I see her on my walks with Barley sometimes. She has tea with my mum every now and again. And she was friends with my gran, before she passed. She knows everything about this place."

Myla smiled. "Yep, she was the sweetest. I love how close people are up here. It's so different to anything I'm used to."

Kelly couldn't stop smiling. She liked seeing things from Myla's perspective. It gave her a fresh take on the benefits of living in this place. "I guess it is quite comforting knowing people are looking out for each other. There's a strong community spirit here. It's a bit quiet right now because it's winter. The local pub is where it's at." Kelly paused. "We should totally go to the pub sometime soon. I'll point out all the characters and introduce you to them." Hopefully she was interested in being friends.

"I'd love that, thanks." Myla paused. "Also, I wanted to let you know before you leave that I've decided not to sell the distillery."

Kelly froze.

Myla continued. "I want to honour my great-aunt's wishes. I'll need to talk to Graeme before I can make it official and confirm it with the distillery, but I've made up my mind. I won't touch it. I wanted to let you know as early as possible."

Kelly was again speechless. After a few long moments, she finally found words. "Myla – thank you so much. You've no idea how much this will mean to everyone."

"It's the right thing to do. I'm sorry it took me so long to decide. I guess I was going off the initial advice of Graeme and this rubbishy financial adviser. Now that I've made it up here and I've got an understanding of this place and my family history and the distillery, especially after your *thorough* tour, it's a no brainer." Myla smiled. "It clearly means a lot to people. So, it's staying put."

"I'm so happy to hear that." The ease with which this young woman talked about the future of the distillery and how she had come to her decision was remarkable. Such honesty and directness was refreshing. The way Myla was thinking of others instead of herself made Kelly feel safe with her. She wondered who Myla had gone to for financial advice but parked that thought for a later date. Hopefully not Nigel from the high street. There were rumours he had taken bribes in the past. Kelly had an uneasy feeling that the sharks circling the distillery might have made contact with Nigel regarding Myla's inheritance. The thought made her shudder but then the resoluteness of Myla's decision reassured her. "You didn't take too long. You were just figuring it out."

"I'm happy to do the same as what Margaret did, more or less, which was to basically leave you to it, right? But that's not to say I'm not interested in it. I am. I might be keen to get a bit more involved at some point but it's not something I'm expecting in any way."

Margaret really had left her to it for years. As long as they were hitting the sales numbers, growing year on year, and continuing the good name of Glenbuinidh she was happy. Kelly wasn't sure what *a bit more involved* was going to look like but they would figure it out. Myla had to have a role if this was going to work. "You'd be more than welcome to get involved in some way. I'd be happy to chat more about it at any time."

"Cool. Well, I'm in no rush and like I said it's not something I'm expecting. You guys are the experts. I'm not. I still have a lot to figure out here like where to put the money and how to run this house."

"Rich people problems, Myla. You can't complain about those." Kelly heard the judgement in her own voice and scolded herself for it. She shook her head. "Sorry. I can appreciate how overwhelming it must be."

"You'd think they make it complicated on purpose, to confuse people out of money."

Kelly laughed, softly. "You might be right about that."

"I might just ignore it all. That's my very mature response to the situation."

"I know of a really good IFA. She's helped my parents, too. I'm sure she'd break it down for you and take the stress out of it all. We trust her. She's a pro."

"Um, yeah. That would be great. Thanks."

"I'll send you a link to her website if you want."

"Yes please." Myla smiled, shyly, and ran her hands through her blonde hair. She was a bit of an enigma. One moment Myla could be bold and sexy, and the next, shy and sweet like this. The combination drew Kelly dangerously close to wanting to take this further again. *Must. Not. Go. There.*

"In case it isn't obvious, I'm extremely grateful about this dream come true. I'm still on cloud nine."

"It's obvious. Enjoy it."

They stood there, smiling at each other, but Kelly had left Barley longer than normal today. "I do really need to get going. Barley will be waiting for his dinner."

Myla nodded, looking more relaxed now. Maybe being friends would work out, after all? On her way out, Kelly spotted a professional looking camera in the entrance hallway surrounded by bits of kit. "Are you a photographer as well as a musician?"

"Oh, no. I just bought it recently. I want to take pictures of the landscape up here. I want to explore the Munros and maybe catch a sunset or two."

"I'd be happy to show you some nice walks. We've got some beautiful mountains in this area alone, so you don't have to go far to catch some gorgeous views. I know a few spots if you want me to show you them?"

"You had me at nice walks."

"Brilliant." Why did it feel like she was having to drag herself away?

"Are you sure you're going to be okay driving in the snow?"

"I'll be okay, thanks. The Land Rover can handle it."

Myla stood in her doorway watching Kelly head to her car. "Drive safe."

Kelly did one final wave before she headed down the drive. In the rear-view mirror, Myla stayed in the doorway, leaning against the side, arms folded over her chest as Kelly got further and further away. The solitary image of Myla standing there alone on the doorstep to that giant house burned into Kelly's head and heart and refused to leave.

***

Pulling into work the next day and seeing Myla's car still there made everything feel more real. It hadn't been a dream. Myla wasn't going to sell them out. Kelly hadn't told anyone yet, not even her parents. That Myla had confided in her before talking to the lawyers meant a lot, and she wasn't going to betray her trust. This was for Myla to announce. Kelly turned the engine off. The truth was she'd wanted something to happen last night. Kelly had struggled to forget their first kiss, especially now that she was actively *trying* to forget it. She'd vowed to keep things strictly platonic from now on. But Myla's confidence and candour mixed with that natural shyness had been a huge turn on nonetheless. Sleeping together would be a huge

Louder Than Words

mistake and would only further complicate matters. Saying that didn't make her feelings disappear, however.

In a meeting with Georgia about their yeast supplier, Kelly was finding it difficult to concentrate. She hadn't told Georgia about who Myla was yet and that she was keeping the distillery. The secret was killing her.

"Is everything okay?" Georgia's expression was curious. She was five or so years older than Kelly, had worked her way up, yet never seemed to hold a grudge that Kelly had been given this job. She would never not be grateful to her for that. "It's not like you to not have an opinion about supplier prices going up."

Kelly grimaced. "Sorry. I'm fine. Didn't sleep well."

"Shall we take a break and get some coffee?"

"Excellent idea."

By mid-afternoon Myla's car was *still* there. Kelly smiled to herself. Not promptly picking the car up made sense with Myla's easy-going and youthful nature. Kelly had meetings for the rest of the day, and by the time she came back to her car in the evening, Myla's car was gone. She hadn't popped in, which was a bit of a disappointment. Kelly shook her head. This was crazy. Having an ill-advised crush on her new boss was not a good idea.

After a short walk with Barley when she got home, she did a workout on her spin bike and then spoke with her younger sister, Nicole, on the phone. It was just a quick call, as Nicole was studying for an exam but needed a pep talk. After they caught up on their days and how they were glad it was the end of the week, Nicole asked Kelly if anything interesting had been happening. Like their dad, Nicole had an ear for any drama happening.

"Not really, no."

"That's not what Dad's been saying."

"What has Dad been saying?"

"That the distillery might be going up for sale."

"Oh for fuck's sake. He can be a right wee gossip sometimes."

"He likes to keep me up to date. I appreciate it."

"It won't happen."

"How do you know?"

Kelly hesitated. "I have a feeling."

"Okaaay. Hope you're right."

"How's the studying going?"

"Ugh. It's a lot. I knew my final year would be hard but this is something else."

"Physics at Cambridge was never going to be a walk in the park, Nic. But you can handle it."

"I hope so. I want to get a first."

Kelly sighed. "Is that necessary? Maybe you're putting too much pressure on yourself?"

"Pffft. Says you. You disappear into your work. And it paid off, right?"

It had paid off. Her job in London was an achievement. Being given a job by your father, was less so. "Just take it a bit easier, yeah. Take breaks. Go for a walk. It'll help."

"Thanks, Kelly. I'll try to."

"Will we be seeing you at Easter?"

"Sorry, no. Got to keep going towards May."

Nicole lived in Cambridge with two friends. She cycled to her college and met people from all over the world in seminars, coffee shops and house parties. Kelly wanted her to enjoy it for as long as possible. "That makes sense. What about Adam? Do you know when he'll be back? We haven't heard from him in a while."

Adam was Nicole's twin. They were twenty-two. "I think he's staying in Boston. Same reasons as me. Hasn't he told you all?"

"Nope." Nicole and Adam were close, which Kelly loved for them. "Doesn't matter. As long as he's happy."

"He's good. MIT is pushing him quite hard too."

They ended the call and promised to catch up soon. When a text came in from Myla, Kelly jumped out of her skin with excitement.

> **Myla:** *Hey! I picked up my car this afternoon. Thanks again for driving me home last night. I hope Barley was okay?*
>
> **Kelly:** *It was my pleasure. Barley was a bit grumpy but seems to have forgiven me.*
>
> **Myla:** *That's good. I bet it'd be hard to hold a grudge against you.*
>
> **Kelly:** *It's true. I have no known enemies. I melt the hardest of hearts.*
>
> **Myla:** *I assume you've broken one or two in your time, if someone like you is single :P*
>
> **Kelly:** *That's classified.*
>
> **Myla:** *Of course it is #heartbreaker*

After their texting Kelly still couldn't get Myla out of her mind. She kept thinking about her over in that big house all alone. She was about three miles away, give or take. What was she doing right now? Was she seeing anyone? Was she lonely?

The rest of the weekend was a bust as she would spend most of it on her work laptop. Her only joy was taking Barley on his walks. She was preparing for a trip to

Denmark to speak with buyers. Georgia had handled the travel logistics and background research, but Kelly had to prepare a tailored approach for the potential new buyers, hence why it spilled over into the weekend.

Her phone flashed up at her. It was a message from Myla. A photo. She tapped it open and her breath caught. She'd taken a selfie lying on a mattress in a store. She was smiling up into the camera but there was a look hidden just behind that smile that spoke to something deep inside Kelly. It stirred feelings that she was desperately trying to keep at bay.

> **Myla:** *This mattress is so luxurious. I think I've fallen in love.*

Was Myla trying to make this torture? Was she still thinking about that night? And if she hadn't been wondering what Myla would look like underneath her, she now had a visual and she knew it would never disappear from her mind. Kelly realised she'd been staring at the picture for a long time, and it was obvious she was still online and had seen the message. Quickly typing a reply, she vowed to be more careful next time.

> **Kelly:** *Then you should definitely buy it. You look very comfortable on it.*
>
> **Myla:** *I will. If I can muster the strength to get up.*
>
> **Kelly:** *The sooner you buy it, the sooner it will be in your bedroom and you can enjoy it.*

She hit send and then immediately regretted it. Damn. That was too flirty. It was hard not to be!

> **Myla:** *Good point… I wish I was there now.*

A short while later Myla texted again.

Louder Than Words

Myla: *I bought five of them!!*

Kelly wanted to text back but stopped herself. She considered talking to Myla about the fact that she thought they would be better just as friends, because it seemed like Myla was flirting with her, but the idea of facing it head on might jinx something. Kelly didn't want to burst this bubble.

A few days later Kelly was in Copenhagen airport waiting for her flight home. Her meeting had gone well. When she saw a message flash up on her phone resting on her lap her heart skipped a beat when she saw that it was from Myla and adrenaline coursed through her body. They were now texting every day. She tapped on the message which included another picture. Yep, Myla liked to send her pictures and she was just fine with that. Especially ones like she'd sent yesterday of her in a skimpy fitness top assembling furniture. Kelly had looked at that picture again and again alone in her hotel room. It was getting ridiculous.

Myla: *Sunset over the loch tonight. I love it here!*

It was indeed a beautiful picture and instantly made Kelly yearn for Balbuinidh. She hadn't had that feeling in a long time. Myla was part of it, somehow. Yet it wasn't clear how long Myla would be staying for. Either way, it was nice to hear from her again. She replied, just as her flight was boarding.

Kelly: *That's beautiful! You do take a good picture.*

Again, she hit send then realised how flirty that sounded.

Kelly: *I mean, the sunset. Not you.*

Shit! That was even worse!

Kelly: *You look good in a picture, don't get me wrong.*

Myla's reply consisted of nothing but a series of laughing emojis.

Kelly: *Ignore me.*

Kelly picked up her carry-on luggage and joined the queue, finding this line she was straddling with Myla not that easy.

Myla: *Never.*

Myla: *I hope your trip went well. Looking forward to seeing you tomorrow night and meeting your parents.*

Myla: *This is getting serious :D*

Kelly smiled. Myla was fun to talk to. She took a deep breath, inching forward in the long queue. They were seeing each other tomorrow night at Kelly's parents' house. It had been playing on her mind. Her fingers traced her phone again to reply. She had to rein this in as it was seriously getting harder and harder not to let herself go there. Because she desperately wanted to.

Kelly: *It went well. Yep, I'm looking forward to tomorrow night too.*

Myla: *Great. Hey, I was wondering if I could take you up on that offer to go walking? I'd love to get up there into the mountains and see Barley again. Maybe this Saturday if you're free?*

Kelly was nearly at the threshold to the plane. Making a new walking friend was too good an offer, and the thought of spending Saturday with Myla was too much of a pull that she could do nothing but say yes.

Kelly: *This Saturday would be perfect.*

Myla: *Yay!*

Kelly just smiled. Whatever this was, she was too tired to fight it.

Kelly: *Getting on the plane now. Have a lovely evening. Kx*

Myla: *Have a safe journey xx*

Kelly found her window seat after putting her carry-on luggage in the compartment above. She put on her wireless headphones and tilted her head against the side of the plane. Myla's smiling face among the sunset over the loch was all she could see as she closed her eyes.

Eight

Even in the darkness I could see that the MacGregor home was something else. I walked up the path to their home and took a quick moment to compose myself. This was way outside of my comfort zone, and I still didn't really know why they'd invited me around. I didn't know Mr and Mrs MacGregor. I was just getting to know Kelly. I wasn't part of this community.

There were two little dog statues either side of the door. Cute. And two chunky plant pots on the porch hosting spring flowers. I wasn't familiar with them, then again, I had a lot to learn about horticulture. I had a lot to learn about everything, come to think of it. My heart slammed in my chest. I pushed the doorbell and forced myself to take a deep breath, wondering if I actually had social anxiety. When a smiling Kelly opened the door my nerves subsided for a split-second then skyrocketed again.

Kelly was stunning. Had she got even more beautiful since the last time I'd seen her? It wasn't a formal dinner – I'd texted Kelly to ask – but Kelly still looked classy in her country-chic style with her Nordic jumper and casual trousers just above the ankle. Now Kelly had trendy to add to her many styles.

"Hey. Glad you could make it, come in."

"Hi." My throat was tight. The smell of home-cooking wafted towards me, as did a gust of warm air as I stepped inside and Kelly closed the door behind me. Barley came bounding through the hallway and zoomed around my legs like he was trying to start a tornado. He was so big and filled the space. I knelt on the floor revelling in his affection, momentarily forgetting where I was. He nearly knocked me over. This went on for some time, with Kelly telling him off and trying to keep him from me.

"Hello Barley," I said, a few times. "This is a lovely welcome. I'm happy to see you too." Barley calmed down after a while, as did Kelly.

"I'm sorry about this."

"No, I love it. He's adorable. Strong, but adorable." I stood up.

"You look lovely, Myla." Kelly's voice was smooth and sexy, if a little restrained.

"Thanks. So do you."

"Can I take your coat?" A comforting smile formed at Kelly's lips. Being all polite like this was going to be torture after the things I'd imagined us doing together. Torture. Hastily, I took it off and handed it to her, smelling those soft citrus and spicy notes of her perfume.

Similar to my great-aunt's house, Kelly's parents had a large entrance hallway with rooms leading off either side. But this home felt warm, lived in, and full of life. It was silly to show Kelly around my empty shell of a house when she came from something like this.

"It feels like ages since I've seen you," Kelly said, in her Highland accent, standing beside me now.

I loved the way she spoke. Sometimes I found myself listening to the melodic lilt of her voice rather than what she was actually saying. "Uh, huh." Kelly was a couple of inches taller than me and right now that height difference felt akin to the distance between us in terms of age and social skills. God, she was way out of my league.

She put her hand on my arm and squeezed it gently. "I'm happy you're here. It's all good." Her smooth voice was as light as a whisper, so that only I could possibly hear, which I was grateful for.

The kindness and warmth in Kelly's eyes and in her words dismantled my initial discomfort. I took a deep breath, reminding myself that I had wanted to do this and that I'd been looking forward to it all week. Kelly kept her hand on my arm, which was now causing a different type of discomfort, and tilted her head towards the delicious smells and smiled. "We're just through here."

"Hello!" said a woman with a round face and thick dark eye make-up. She smiled with her eyes and I instantly liked her. "Myla! It's *so* nice to finally meet you. I've heard so much about you; you're quite the talk of the town, young lady. I'm Eilidh. That's Malcolm."

Before I could process her comment or acknowledge Kelly's dad properly Eilidh had wrapped me up in a hug and squeezed me with a strength I didn't expect. She let me go after a moment or two and continued smiling at me, taking me in and generally giving off such strong maternal energy it nearly made me cry, which I was not expecting.

"Welcome," Malcolm said. He had the same look as Kelly, sharp jawline, strong cheekbones and wide brown eyes you could get lost in. But his demeanour was more reserved than either Kelly or Eilidh. He also looked a bit older than Eilidh. He would look the part in a flat cap and a tweed jacket out stalking deer with his buddies. "You came at a good time, we're just about to open the wine. Would you like any?"

"Hi. Yes please, wine would be great. Here," I held out my gift. "This is for you. Thanks for inviting me to your home. It's lovely to meet you both."

"Thank you very much. I'm just sorry it's taken us this long to have you over. It's been hectic around here but that's no excuse."

"Yes, Eilidh has been up to high-doh lately."

"Malcolm, really?"

Kelly's parents were fun. I instantly liked them. And I hadn't heard that saying in years. It was familiar. My mother used to say it all the time, particularly after she'd calmed down and was describing the manic state she'd been in before. I liked it because it was a metaphor using the musical scale.

"How are you enjoying the area?" Eilidh's eyes were open and expressive, eagerly awaiting my response.

"I love it. It's so beautiful. And everyone is so friendly."

"Och, that's what everyone says. How are you finding it really?"

I hesitated, caught off guard at her complete frankness. "It's a bit of an adjustment. I don't know anyone up here."

"That's understandable, sweetheart." She glanced at Kelly. "I hope this one has been making you feel welcome."

Kelly blushed. She *blushed*. It was adorable. What did it mean? I bet that didn't happen very often.

"Mum," Kelly said, once. Her tone was firm, fooling no one.

I smiled at Kelly, perhaps too broadly but I didn't care. "Yes, she's been very friendly." Oh god, now I felt like I was blushing. We were like two teenagers. I laughed, nervously, at the look of shock in Kelly's eyes. Eilidh looked between us, taking in our red faces and darting eyes.

Kelly and I weren't dating and this was *not* a meet the parents situation, yet I felt an element of it in the room.

Surely Kelly hadn't said anything about where we first met so it had to be something about the spark between us. It had to be.

"Good to hear it." She laughed, kindly. "People think coming to the Highlands is about getting away from people, to be on your own, but it's the opposite. Up here is like a goldfish bowl. It's the way it's always been."

Barley sat on my feet, leaning into my shins. "He likes you," Eilidh said.

Kelly was gazing at me, I could feel it, and the joyful stare of a wagging Barley was hard to miss.

"He does like you," Kelly said.

Our eyes met. I briefly caught a glimpse of the Kelly who I'd met that first time. I didn't want to look away as the air fizzed between us.

"So how about that wine?" Malcolm uncorked a bottle of white wine.

I thanked Malcolm for my glass and took a couple of large gulps. Shit. I should probably have waited for them before taking a drink. I lowered my glass hoping they hadn't seen. I clinked glasses with Malcolm and then Kelly, as Eilidh got something out of the oven. Kelly's eyes were as smouldering as ever, but I had to try and not focus on that right now. This was not the time for noticing how her eyes held mine and spoke of something richer and private between us.

No, this was not the time.

As Kelly and her parents attended to various things in the kitchen, all talking with the same lovely Scottish accent, I stood by the kitchen island not knowing what to do with myself. "Can I help with anything?"

"You're fine, hen." Eilidh said this to me while putting potatoes into a round dish as Kelly filled a carafe of water and Malcolm took the wine and a bowl of something into the dining room.

I took another large sip of wine, thinking about what it would be like to be here as Kelly's girlfriend. It was obvious Kelly didn't want anything to happen between us again. However, after a *lot* of thinking about the subject, I was hopeful that it wasn't off the table *completely*. I was already living out some sort of fantasy with this inheritance so getting the girl too didn't seem like a stretch too far. I used to think I was just an unlucky person, doomed to live on the fringes of society on my own. But what if that wasn't meant to be my story any more? Shouldn't I go for what I wanted? A part of me still felt that Kelly did want more; she was just holding back. I wanted to explore whatever this was between us. It was time to take a risk in that department. I'd enjoyed texting her these past couple of weeks. It was fun and refreshing and comforting to talk to Kelly at all hours of the day. I felt like we were making a real connection.

Taking it progressively flirtier happened naturally. It was so unlike me. Normally, I was quite shy with women, but with Kelly, I had this extra confidence, probably because of the way she so openly wanted me the first night we met. It was hard to believe that was completely in the past. And she'd been flirting back in her texts, too, there was that. But then she'd retreat, and I wouldn't push it. At the very least, I hoped we could be friends. Actually, it felt like we were already friends. I hoped we could keep whatever this was.

"Do you like salmon?" Malcolm said, interrupting my thoughts. He was cutting the largest salmon I'd ever seen on the kitchen island.

"Yes."

"He caught it last weekend himself."

"Wow, that's amazing."

Malcolm looked around as if embarrassed at the compliment from his wife and was searching for something to say to me. "Do you sail, Myla?" He said, after a few moments.

"Um, no." I smiled to myself that this was his question.

"Pity. There's much to be seen on the water."

"Myla plays music," Kelly said, interjecting. I almost forgot I'd shared that with her.

"Oh really? Which instrument?" Malcolm said.

"Instruments. Plural." Kelly said.

"Oh, do tell." Eilidh said.

"I play the guitar and the piano. And the drums, bass, and violin. I've been told I can sing but I don't really like the sound of my singing voice. I like to create music, but my favourite thing is to write lyrics because it's not that much different to poetry, at least for me."

Everyone was looking at me now. Even Barley. It was such a strange thing, having their attention like that. Kelly was staring at me intensely, with a look I couldn't quite place.

"How wonderful," Eilidh said. "What sort of music?"

I shook my head. I'd bigged this up more than I should have. I'd learnt most of the instruments at boarding school and taught myself the drums and the guitar while messing around. "I'm really not that good. It's just a hobby. But acoustic folk-like stuff, I guess. Some classical."

"Sounds very soulful," Kelly said, still watching me. "Creative."

My breath caught in my throat. She said I was soulful and creative. I loved the sound of that, but I didn't feel deserving of those terms. "I haven't written anything or played in a while. It's not a big deal."

Eilidh came right up to me, with a serious look on her face. "If you can play, you're a musician. End of. Have more belief in yourself, sweetheart. I hope to hear you perform sometime." She smiled, then returned to the food, and it infused me with a kind of confidence I hadn't known I was lacking.

Kelly smiled at me. "I would love to hear your music."

"I used to play the piano every now and again," Malcolm said. "I'm no Beethoven. I don't have the ear for it." He laughed at his own joke. "Eilidh plays quite well. The kids never took to it though. It just sits in the dining room collecting dust these days."

"I don't know, Dad. There's that one song you can play," Kelly said.

"Ouch," Malcolm said, pretending to be hurt.

"*À table*. Dinner's ready," called out Eilidh.

Their dining room was elegant and sophisticated. They had a modern yet traditional vibe going on. Much like their personalities. There was a record player in the corner beside lots of records stacked neatly on shelves. The upright piano doubled as a sideboard behind the dining table.

They'd made a wonderful meal of salmon, vegetables and potatoes with a white wine sauce and the most delicious smelling garlic bread. "*Bon appétit!*" Eilidh announced.

I was very aware of Kelly sitting next to me. Her hands kept drawing my attention. She had such long fingers. That bread was lucky.

"So, Myla. I just wanted to say I'm so sorry about Margaret's passing. We were all very fond of her. She was part of our lives," Eilidh said.

"She seemed like a great lady," I said, after tasting the most delicious salmon I'd ever had in my life.

"She was." Eilidh said. "A true character."

"What was it like working with Margaret and James?"

Kelly opened her mouth.

Malcolm answered first. "They were a great team. Real powerhouses. They had such vision for the distillery and the guts to expand at the right time. I considered them friends for many years. Mentors, if you will."

"They were really cool," Kelly said.

Eilidh looked at Kelly and Malcolm a little pointedly, and then back at me. "We were delighted to hear that you have decided to keep the distillery. It's wonderful news. Thank you."

I'd told Graeme a week ago and met with the financial advisor Kelly recommended. Graeme was very respectful and didn't comment on my decision, which I'd appreciated. He drew up the paperwork and sent it to Kelly and the distillery's lawyers. The fact that Kelly hadn't told her parents before it was made official gave me a good feeling. I could trust someone like that.

"No, no. You don't have to thank me. It had to stay within the community."

"That's very noble of you," Eilidh said. "I'm sure your family would be proud."

At this, I nearly teared up, but kept it at bay by sipping my wine. "Thanks for that IFA you recommended, Kelly. She was very helpful."

Kelly paused, mid-raising her fork to her mouth. "Yeah, sure. That's good she could help."

"Excellent," Eilidh said.

"Kelly told me you used to run Glenbuinidh?"

"I did, yes." Malcolm took a sip of wine. "Now I leave that in Kelly's capable hands. I spend most of my time fishing these days. Eilidh has a veterinary surgery in town."

"My mum is animal mad."

After dinner we had coffee in a lovely and cosy sitting room beside a gorgeous fireplace. It was in far better condition than the ones in Margaret's house. Kelly sat beside her dad on the opposite sofa with Barley resting his head on her lap. They all seemed so familiar and so at ease around each other. How would my life have been if I'd grown up with this? Would I have turned out to be the same person?

Eilidh was sitting next to me. I sensed a heart-to-heart chat coming on when she faced me squarely and stared at me.

"Myla." Eilidh paused, looking very concerned at me. "Kelly mentioned you never knew any of your family up here. You poor thing."

Her eyes were patient and kind. I could easily pour my heart out to this woman, but I was aware that everyone was listening, so I held back a bit. The truth was maybe a little too painful if I really thought about it, so I usually didn't.

Kelly spoke up. "I hope it's okay that I told them that?" Concern was etched across her face.

"Yes, it's fine. It's not a secret. If I'd known about Margaret, I would have wanted to meet her. I'd have wanted to meet all of them." I looked back at Eilidh, who had me locked in her sights. "I visited the library the other day. I enjoyed learning about the town's history. It's hard to believe my family had been here for so long." The library visit had been an eye-opener. My family line had had the run of this place for hundreds of years, back when there were clans and crofts.

"And still are." Eilidh's eyes were bright, urging me to go on. "How did that make you feel?"

"Um, kind of proud? It was nice."

"And your mum? How did she like London?"

I gave some basic details about my mother and where I grew up in London. I didn't want to bare my soul to these people on our first meeting. Or ever, really. That would be a bit much. Eilidh listened carefully and gave me a big hug when I finished with the news of the inheritance. Ah, fuck. I felt tears forming again and it took all of my willpower to force them down and regain my composure. And this was me keeping it light. Thank god it was dimly lit in here.

"Mum, back off a bit," Kelly said. "You're being too intense."

Eilidh looked over at her daughter. "Myla is part of this community. Her story is important," she looked back at me. "I'm so glad you found your way back home. Margaret was right to never give up on finding you."

I smiled, shyly.

Kelly and I were left alone as her parents moved around in the kitchen, tidying up. It had been such a lovely evening. I offered to help but Eilidh and Malcolm were having none of it.

"Your parents are awesome. Your mother is so lovely."

"I'm sorry she got so personal. You seem like a very private person, and she doesn't always have the best boundaries. She works with animals all day and I think sometimes she doesn't realise humans are different."

Kelly thought I was a private person? What else did she think about me? "It's fine. She's so warm and she's not put off by my quietness around new people. I can see her as a vet, she's very caring."

"She's also an artist. She paints."

"What does she paint?"

"Still life. Nudes. Landscapes."

"Cool. Does she sell them?"

"She does."

"I'd love to see them sometime."

"I'm sure she'd love to show you. Some are scattered around the house, one or two are in the studio in town, but most are in her studio upstairs. But be warned, once she starts talking about her art, there's no stopping her. If you show any enthusiasm she will talk the ear off you."

"Like van Gogh."

"Perhaps he talked his own ear off."

I laughed, softly. "She is very enthusiastic. I love it when people are passionate about things." There was a long silence after that. The room felt painfully small and I couldn't think of what to say next because all I could think about was that night in the club and how overwhelmingly attracted I was to Kelly. I wasn't sure I'd ever fully recovered from that night.

When her parents came back in, I announced my exit and stood. "Thank you for a lovely evening. It was great to meet you both." Eilidh came in for another tight hug, which was fast becoming my favourite thing. "You've to come back anytime. You're always welcome."

"I will, thank you." I realised they'd just wanted to meet me, and it had made me feel so welcome. I gave Barley a quick hug and waved awkwardly at Malcolm who did the same, then Kelly saw me to my car. Outside in the cold beside my car, Kelly stood with her hands in her pockets. She seemed hesitant as Barley wagged up at us.

"See you for our walk tomorrow then?" Kelly said, hopefully.

Her eyes locked onto mine in the orange glow of the front garden. It felt dizzying to be in their direct gaze.

"Yeah," I smiled, broadly, trying to cover up how my world was spinning from existing in this space with her right now. "Tomorrow."

As Kelly turned to go, I reached for her elbow. I leaned in and gave her a kiss on the cheek, then stood back and opened the car door. My senses barely had time to register it but her perfume lingered, as did the feeling of closeness that permeated the air between us.

Kelly bit down on her bottom lip and then took a deep breath. "Looking forward to it."

As I reversed out of the drive, we waved at each other. I looked back at her before my final turn out of the garden. She was still there and waved again. Driving along the dark country lane, I was so excited about tomorrow and the prospect of spending the day with Kelly just because we wanted to. If I hadn't been already completely infatuated with this hot, kind and successful older woman then I was now a lost cause. Tomorrow couldn't come fast enough.

***

While humming to myself locking the front door, my phone pinged. I was going to meet Kelly at ten by the visitor centre for our hike. Shit. It was a message from Kelly saying she had to cancel today because something had come up at work.

Deflated, I unlocked the door again and slumped at the kitchen table, re-reading the message. While I was disappointed not to see her today, her inclusion of several crying face emojis told me that she was bummed out about it too and would rather not be cancelling. Another message came in.

Kelly: *Ugh, I really am sorry. I was so looking forward to seeing you today. It's just there's been a mix up and I have to smooth over the situation and sort it out. Maybe another time?*

Myla: *Yeah, sure. Don't worry about it.*

Kelly started replying but then the three dots disappeared. I tried not to feel pathetic about this. Looking around the massive kitchen, I decided that since I was ready to go for a walk, hiking boots and waterproofs and all, I'd go myself. There were well marked forest trails up by the river that I hadn't tried, so I got in the car and made my way there. I was used to doing things on my own, anyway.

The walk was lined with ancient trees with their thick trunks and convoluted branches. Pine needles peppered the trail. The smell of Scots pine was strong and comforting. I loved that smell. It would have been so lovely if Kelly were here right now. The thought of getting her all to myself today had been heady. But she worked a lot. I wished I could see her more often than the once a fortnight of late.

I took lots of pictures with my fancy camera, still getting the hang of how to work it. When I captured two roe deer about fifty metres away, I couldn't believe it. They were in focus, and you could see their tough auburn fur and their spindly legs. The way up was challenging but worth it to breathe in the fresh air. Once I got up to the top, the break in the trees and the rolling hills was breathtaking. With mountain peaks still covered in snow to huge glens cutting through the land, it really was something special. I spent an age taking pictures from every angle until I was satisfied that I'd captured every inch of this view and of this feeling. Sitting down on a rock, I calmed down from the excitement of reaching the top. It was so quiet. Leaves rustled softly in the gentle breeze. I could get used to this. I got my phone out and took a selfie with the view in the background, then sent it to Kelly.

Myla: *Wish you were here. Hope work is going okay.*

Kelly: *You went on your own! Good for you. Believe me, I would far rather be there with you right now than sorting through this mess.*

She sent a picture of her office in the distillery, but I could only see a desk and the edge of another cabinet full of whisky bottles.

Myla: *I had to get out on a day like this. I hope you can get away soon. Have something of your weekend.*

Kelly: *Take care on the way down. If you're on the route I think you're on, the descent can get a little patchy in places.*

Myla: *Worrying about me?*

Kelly: *A little. Will you text me when you get back to your car?*

I took a sharp inhale of breath. She was worrying about me. It was of course *terrible* that I took any level of satisfaction in that, but also, it was kind of sweet that she was.

Myla: *I will.*

I put my phone away after that and put my beanie on. The wind had picked up and it was getting cold. It took longer than I expected to get back down. The path was well signposted though, so I felt completely safe the whole time. I wasn't sure which section Kelly thought would be patchy. I didn't come across a single person either. It was heaven. Excitedly, the first thing I did when I got back to the car was text Kelly.

> **Myla:** *Back safe. Legs are aching but my heart is happy. Sorry – that was so cheesy! You know what I mean though. Nature heals.*
>
> **Kelly:** *Yay! Yes, it does.*

I sat in the car for a few minutes looking at my phone for another message from Kelly, but none came. I wondered what I'd meant by saying nature heals. Heals from what? My stomach rumbled. It was hollow. There was something satisfying about driving away from the walk, like I'd achieved something and really experienced the area.

At the visitor centre I ordered a hot chocolate and a baked potato with cheese. The thought of getting two to takeaway and taking them to have with Kelly at the distillery crossed my mind. Had she eaten? I shrugged off the idea as I was just too damn shy to go through with it. I wanted to, though.

I was just about to pay when Jenny came through from the back. Her apron was dusty with what looked like flour and her smile was deep and unaffected.

"Hey Myla!"

"Hi Jenny," I said, feeling bad for not managing to match the same enthusiasm in my voice despite my fondness for her.

"Put that away. You eat for free here," her face was sincere.

"Um, pardon?"

"We heard the news that you're keeping the distillery. You've protected it from god knows what types of money-grabbing companies out there. Your lunch is on the house."

I was stunned.

Jenny stepped closer to the counter. "This is how we do it. You're one of us now. Please," she turned the card reader away from me, "enjoy your lunch."

I smiled. *You're one of us now.* I loved the sound of that. "Thank you, Jenny. You're too kind."

She asked me about my day, and I told her about my walk. Enthusiastically, she gave me the names of a few more walks that only the locals knew and directions to the starts of them. She was so well-intentioned, and I did my best to follow her directions but after a few sentences I already knew I wouldn't remember the way. I nodded politely, making a mental note to google them instead or ask Kelly.

I found a seat near the window. As I walked over, I swear random strangers were smiling at me. It was weird, but also kind of nice. There were a couple of families in and some pairs of friends. A few tourists. The usual café atmosphere but more relaxed. More homely. It made me think of Michelle and the café down in Edinburgh. I missed it. My phone buzzed on the table. A shot of adrenaline rushed through me at seeing Kelly's name.

> **Kelly:** *That's me done for the day. I think both sides are happy now. Sometimes I think I should join the UN.*

Myla: *Well done! But please don't leave for the UN. I've just got here!*

Kelly: *I'm not going anywhere. Believe me, I've tried. I always end up back in this place.*

Myla: *Don't you have staff you could delegate to on a Saturday?*

Kelly: *I do, but today was basic peacekeeping. I can't really ask that of my management team on a Saturday.*

Myla: *I don't think you're basic at anything.*

Kelly: *Wait until you see my cooking skills.*

I finished my hot chocolate, staring at my phone. After a few long minutes, another message came in.

Kelly: *What are you up to tonight? Would you like to come over to my place to hang out? I can cook and we can watch a film? I want to make it up to you after cancelling today. But expectations should be kept low re the food.*

My heart stopped beating for a moment. She wanted to see me tonight. She wanted to make it up to me. She wanted to *hang out*. That meant one thing, surely. *Finally!* I gulped, then forced myself to wait a whole minute before saying yes. She replied with a simple smiling hearts emoji.

Fucking hell, this was on.

We made the final arrangements and I zipped home to get ready. I showered, shaved, moisturised, and searched through my brand-new chest of drawers for any lingerie that was remotely sexy. I sighed. I didn't really have anything. I settled on a matching navy-blue set. Would she start acting like she had the first night we met again? Would she find me attractive?

I didn't have long before I needed to leave. I wasn't hungry having had such a late lunch, but this wasn't about food. Pruning myself had taken longer than expected. Nerves coursed through my body, but I didn't listen to them. I was having dinner with Kelly fucking MacGregor. Hottest woman I'd ever met. Sometimes I felt like this was the real jackpot I'd hit.

Nine

As I pulled into Kelly's driveway my mouth fell open. Her house was unlike anything I'd seen up in the Highlands. It stood alone, set back from the road, surrounded by trees. It was large, yes, like the others, but it was contemporary, with a mixture of old and modern, wooden beams and glass walls at the corners. This felt like the house of a grown up. And I was anything but a grown up. Imposter syndrome nudged at the edges of my self-esteem as I waited for her to answer the door. I'd made an effort with my appearance tonight, so that helped.

When she answered the door I just stood there staring at her, unable to speak. She was in a figure-hugging black t-shirt and lounge bottoms. Her skin didn't look like someone who'd been working all day. She seemed freshly showered and glowing. Totally relaxed and casual compared to my little black dress. Oh my god, I was so overdressed. Sheer mortification replaced my initial drooling. My cheeks burned.

"Hi," Kelly said, with a quizzical look on her face. "Come in?"

I looked at the ground, at a neat doormat with a faded rainbow on it. "Yes. Hi."

As I stepped inside, the first thing that struck me was the delicious smells of something in the kitchen and that her house was sexy. How could a house ooze sex? The sculpture of two women entangled in passion probably had something to do with it, as did a piece of lesbian art on the wall. Everything seemed pristine and classy while also being warm and cosy. She had thick cream carpets and modern oak furniture. Compared to my dusty old mansion this was a proper home. I took off my ankle boots and placed them neatly beside the door, feeling her eyes on me the entire time.

"You look really nice," Kelly said, raking her eyes over my body from head to toe. "I love your dress."

"It's a bit dressier than I'd meant," I stammered. "It was all I had." This was a lie, clearly. I cringed, hoping Kelly would overlook such foolishness. I'd worn it to get her attention and now I feared I'd made my unrequited intentions super obvious. Kelly was practically in her pyjamas.

"Barley is in the kitchen. He gets a little crazy when guests arrive, so I've banished him until you get in the door," she tilted her head good-naturedly, "last night's zoomies, for example."

"Poor Barley. I love his welcomes." My voice felt shaky, as did my hands. I put them behind my back to hide them.

Kelly studied me, it felt, and her smile was kind. It put me at ease. I took a deep breath, and bit my bottom lip, unable to focus on much else besides how hot she was.

"Ready?"

For you, completely.

"Sure."

Barley came rushing out of the kitchen towards me wriggling and wagging frantically. I knelt next to him again, patting his side as he settled against my legs, lapping up the attention. "He's such a sweetheart."

Kelly nodded and then crossed her arms over her chest and leant against the doorframe, looking on fondly. "He's my whole world."

Louder Than Words

"I've never had a dog. My mother said it wasn't fair to have a dog if you were never home. It's good Barley has your mum, too, and a dog walker. I love them. I've always wanted one."

"What's to stop you from getting one now?"

I looked up at her, realising that there was very little standing in my way any more from getting a dog. I couldn't believe I hadn't thought of it sooner.

"You're right. I could. I should."

"It's the best thing in the world having a dog, if you like dogs, that is."

Barley nuzzled into me. "I can see that. Your home is stunning by the way."

"Thank you."

There was a slight awkward silence, and I realised I'd forgot to bring wine or anything in my eagerness to get here. "Shit, I didn't bring anything over, I—"

"Don't be silly," Kelly shrugged. "I have everything. Wine, beer, and whisky of course."

"Great. Well, um, I wasn't going to drink any alcohol tonight."

"Oh, well in that case I don't have anything. Only kidding. What shall we have instead? I have loads of types of tea. It's probably what I drink most of." Kelly smiled. "You're looking at me like I've committed a crime."

I played with the seam of my dress, still feeling way overdressed and silly for not getting that this was just a friend thing. "It's probably not *officially* a crime, but have you come out at work... you know, as a *tea* drinker?"

Kelly touched my arm. "God, no, please don't tell a soul!"

My cheeks burned when she touched my bare skin. Great, I was blushing *again*. Her hand on my arm was causing fireworks inside me.

"My lips are sealed."

"I'll be back in a sec. Just going to get changed."

"For what?"

There was a pause. "For you."

My breath caught in my throat. I must have looked like a deer in the headlights because Kelly laughed gently, then disappeared. I took a seat in her dining room at the already made table. It was all very classy compared to the homes of the women, who were mostly students, I had previously dated. When she came back the sight of Kelly in her own little dress and casual slip-on shoes caused a sudden rush of pleasure between my legs. Kelly's dress didn't cover much of her legs and it was clear she wasn't wearing a bra. Concentration this evening was going to be a major struggle.

"Wow." My voice was shaky. "You didn't have to get changed. You look… great."

"Thanks. You inspired me."

As she took a dish out of the oven, her dress rode up dangerously high. Despite knowing that I should, I could *not* look away. When she turned around, I think she caught the tail end of my gaze leaving her. I ran my hands through my hair. "Do you need any help with anything?"

"No, I'm good thanks. I'll be right over."

Kelly was chaperoned by an interested Barley with his nose sniffing the air as the food was brought over. Kelly glided, it seemed, into her seat. "Help yourself."

At Kelly's suggestion I scooped some pasta onto my plate and took some salad, feeling like I was in a fancy restaurant. Kelly poured us both some water as I took a bite.

"This is delicious. What were you saying about your cooking?"

"It's one of the few meals I do. It's pretty basic."

"If you call this basic, I can't wait to see what you think you're good at." I held her gaze, hoping she'd see I was desperately trying to flirt with her.

Kelly didn't reply and instead changed the conversation and asked me about my life in Edinburgh. I talked about the café and Michelle, and Rebecca. I could hardly ask her anything about her life because she kept the focus squarely on me.

"What made you move up?"

"I've always felt this strong connection with Scotland. It's difficult to explain. I just feel at home here."

Kelly put her hand on mine, sending a jolt of electricity through my hand. "I'm glad you listened to that feeling."

"So am I."

She took her hand away. "What was it like growing up in London?"

"Good. Intense."

"And your mum, what did she do?"

"She was an investigative journalist."

"Wow. That's so cool."

"She had her moments."

"Did she travel a lot for that?"

"Sometimes. I was away a lot. I went to boarding school for most of the year." In truth, I felt like my mother had sent me away, so she could pretend like I didn't exist.

Kelly took a bite. "Did you like it?"

"Not really. I struggled to fit in. Felt like I had to be someone else. I left when I was sixteen and went to my local college. That pissed my mother off so much. In the end, I didn't fit in there either. Didn't really make any friends. My mother thought I was too quiet. Too boring. I spent most of my childhood feeling lonely. I went to uni and that was a bit better, but I dropped out when my mother died."

"I'm sorry to hear that."

"All I could get was café work. It's not what I wanted to do for the rest of my life, but it was fine. I got by."

"You're a survivor."

"Did you like school?"

"I went to a private school, too." Kelly hesitated. "I enjoyed it."

"That's great. A lot of people do. I don't know what was wrong with me."

"It's not for everyone, especially boarding. I was a weekly boarder, so got the weekends at home."

"I always felt like I had to hide the fact that I went to boarding school, because people assume you're rich and everything is perfect in your life. Did you ever find that?"

"Totally. No one cares about the rich girl. I get it."

"True."

"May I ask how your mum passed away?"

Ah. I knew this question had been coming. I could tell when people were building up to asking it. It was the way they asked around the question, getting closer and closer to it in a polite way. Some more polite than others. Kelly's approach was lovely.

"Bike accident. She was cycling and a car crashed into her. It happened at the junction just outside Kings Cross St Pancras."

Kelly's mouth opened slightly. "I'm so sorry, Myla." She reached over and placed her hand over my forearm this time, squeezing gently. I got goosebumps at her touch, but more from the show of kindness.

"It was eight years ago. I'm no longer actively grieving or anything. I nearly ruined my life afterwards but I'm fine now."

Kelly was quiet, her hand still on my arm. She stroked her thumb over my skin, unconsciously from the looks of it. "What happened after she died?"

I blew out a breath unsure of how much to share. I didn't want to put her off me. But then, if we were to be friends or whatever, I needed to be honest. "I went off the rails. Dropped out of university, got into debt, started taking drugs on nights out… dated the wrong people. At one point, I was practically homeless, sleeping on friends' sofas. My mother's friend Cara took me in. She and her wife Kay. They still live down in London."

"It's understandable you struggled. I'm glad you had people to support you."

"They were great. I needed too much from them."

"Even the most independent of people need help sometimes. Sometimes they need it most."

"And then I moved up to Edinburgh for a fresh start and to sort my life out. Things are pretty good now except I'm probably still carrying a shit-ton of emotional baggage I haven't dealt with yet." I half-laughed, half-cringed at my admission. I don't know why I'd just said that. Was I actively trying to put her off me?

Kelly sat back, removing her hand, as if only registering that it was still there. I missed it already and cursed my oversharing. She smiled warmly, putting me at ease in that way she did. "It sounds like you've had a lot to deal with. People can spend a lifetime trying to process their trauma. You seem to be doing really well, so don't beat yourself up about the things you might still be working on. You're still so young."

I appreciated that. Maybe this was another benefit of being with an older woman. "Thank you, wise one."

"Ha. I think you'll soon find out that I'm definitely not that wise. Would you like some dessert?"

"Uh, yeah. Please."

I was grateful for the reprieve. I loved that she wanted to know about my life but talking about my past wasn't how I wanted to spend this time with her. Kelly brought over two plates of sticky toffee pudding. The dessert was delicious.

"What about you? What was it like growing up in Balbuinidh?"

The skin around Kelly's eyes crinkled lightly as she smiled. It was so beautiful. "Idyllic. Safe. Boring. I was very lucky. I did have a lot of freedom, which was good. And I had a lot of fun breaking the rules, which was also good."

I laughed. "Then to London for some wild times?"

"After studying at Oxford and a spell interning in Melbourne."

"You must be super smart, then, and you've travelled."

"Not as much as I'd have liked to. I like to spend time living and working in a place to really get to know it."

"Where else would you like to live and work?"

"I don't know, maybe Amsterdam. I like their laid-back culture. Or Dublin."

"You said you had a younger brother and sister?"

"Yep. They're twenty-two, twins. My parents had them when I was fifteen, but they were good at not letting me become another parent to them. They're both away at university right now. My sister is at Cambridge and my brother is at MIT in the States."

"Are you close?"

"Yes. We're all quite close."

This gave me pause. My mother had me young, but it had been no fairy tale. She was on her own, and never contacted my dad. From what I knew now, my mother left a perfectly good family up here to live her life with me alone down in London. This had nothing to do with Kelly, I knew, but sometimes the contrast in life experience was hard to ignore. I *hated* this jealousy that gripped me from time to time. "That's great," I struggled to sound more enthusiastic, although I was happy to learn about her family. "Your parents are so lovely; I can imagine them being good with kids."

"Did you get on with your mum?"

For such a simple question, there wasn't a simple answer. "In some ways, yes. But we didn't always see eye to eye."

Kelly took a sip of water and shrugged. "Who does?"

"She worked a lot. She didn't take shit from anyone."

"She sounds great."

"Yeah. She was."

"When did you move up to Scotland?"

"Four years ago."

Kelly was quiet for a minute. "That means we would have been in London at the same time. I lived there for three years and moved back here seven years ago."

The fact that Kelly worked that out in her head made me smile. "So it does."

"Where did you live?"

"In Brixton."

"I dated a girl from Brixton for a while. We probably walked past each other on the street."

The shared experience made me feel even closer to Kelly although the thought of her dating someone was less pleasing. The subject area was an interesting one, however. "Are you seeing anyone at the moment?"

She put down her small fork, not quite having finished her dessert. "No."

I nodded, trying not to look *too* happy.

"Are you?"

For some reason, I hadn't expected her to ask me back. "No."

A short silence followed. I finished my water.

Kelly stood up. "It's more comfortable in the lounge. Want to watch a film?"

"Sure." I followed her and Barley down the hall, feeling silly in my dress but loving that Kelly had joined me in something similar. It was my faux pas and she made me feel better about it. Kind, as well as hot, really was an intoxicating mixture that I was finding it hard to come down from.

As she settled Barley on another sofa. I took a seat on the more luxurious one, and let my head fall back. "Fuck, this is so comfortable. How do you ever leave this thing?"

Kelly laughed. "This one," she nodded at Barley. "And running a distillery."

I got even comfier, stretching my arms along the back of it, hoping that it was drawing her attention, which it appeared to be from the dark look in her eyes that she was clearly trying to hide. "Let's just forget the world tonight. What do you say?"

Kelly sat down at the opposite end, which was a disappointment. "I'm up for that. Which film do you want to watch?"

"Um," I thought for a few seconds and then decided that this needed to go up a gear. "A romantic comedy? Preferably lesbian."

Kelly laughed softly, showing her elegance and sophistication in the face of my vulgar youth. I loved making her laugh. "Okay. Do you know of any new ones? I think I've seen them all. The good and the bad."

"I know what you mean. There is quite the range. I don't know if there are any new ones out though."

Kelly switched on the enormous flat screen mounted on the wall and scrolled through her streaming service.

"How about we watch that one." I interrupted her scrolling. "It's not my absolute favourite but it's fun and cute."

"Sure," Kelly hit play. "What is your absolute favourite lesbian film, out of interest?"

"A certain nineteen-fifties age-gap Christmas film based on a book." Kelly laughed softly again. Her dress was so revealing. Being close to her like this was thrilling. "What's yours?"

"Same."

Of course.

"Maybe we can watch it together sometime?" Kelly asked, casually.

It was nice. It felt so right to spend time with her, being free to be myself and just click with someone, even if there was this undercurrent of desire. "Sure," I said, doing my best to appear casual too.

As we watched our rom-com I was keenly aware of Kelly's presence next to me on the sofa. I kept looking at her out of the corner of my eye, wondering what her reactions were to the film, and trying desperately not to let my eyes linger on her legs. We talked a lot through it too, which was fun.

"Best line in the film," I said, in response to 'you're a wanker, number nine'.

Kelly laughed, less refined this time. I liked that laugh, too. "Totally. Dash to the airport. Classic."

When the two leads kissed, I felt Kelly take a sharp intake of breath next to me. I too tensed up at the scene of two attractive women really going for it. Memories of our kiss in the club came crashing back into my mind. Was Kelly thinking about that too? The feel of Kelly's lips against mine, the smell of her hair, the softness of her skin.

Kelly cleared her throat as the credits came up and had played for a few beats. "A feel-good. One of the best."

"Yeah. It's a good one." My throat felt tight.

Kelly stopped the film and there was that silence again. She hesitated enough for me to notice. "Would you like to watch our joint fave now? It's only," she checked her watch, "half past nine."

"Uh, *yeah*. I'd *love* to." I smiled, unable to hide my enthusiasm, hoping she wasn't going to change her mind.

Kelly smiled too. "Can I get you something else to drink? More water? Tea?"

"Um, could I change my mind and have a tiny drop of whisky with a little bit of water please?"

"Sure. I have just the one."

"Thanks."

"Here, can you find the film?" She handed me the remote. "I'll fetch the drinks and see to Barley. It's past his bedtime."

Kelly disappeared with Barley, and I found the film easily enough. While it wasn't exactly tearing my clothes off, that Kelly had asked me to stay longer had to be a good sign. For someone who was so forward in the club, her continued reluctance to openly flirt with me was a bit of a concern. I wasn't sure I had the confidence to make a move, or if I even should. There could be a real friendship here, did I want to risk that?

Fuck, this was terrifying.

"For you," Kelly put two glasses on the coffee table. My eyes moved from the drinks to her legs, and all the way up her body as she stood above me. "I give you Queen of Spirits from my personal bottle."

"Wow. I am privileged. Thank you." It was sweet she remembered I'd wanted to try it. Still standing up, she watched me closely as I cradled the glass in my hand, inhaled its intoxicating flavours, and tasted the amber liquid. The mixture of fruity spiciness was striking. "Delicious."

Kelly's face softened and she smiled. "You have no idea how much of a relief that is that you like it."

"I really like it. I want to savour it. Just sip it."

"Wetting your lips."

"Excuse me?"

"Seriously, it's a thing. I didn't make it up."

"I wouldn't have minded if you had."

Kelly took a long drink. I couldn't take all that whisky at once without wriggling around in agony afterwards. I patted the sofa next to me, taking a gamble and unsure if this would backfire. A few heightened seconds etched by after my blatant request.

Amazingly, Kelly sat down right next to me. My heart started racing. There was no way to avoid looking at her gorgeous and shapely legs now. Faintly taking in the smell of citrus with a touch of spice I now so associated with Kelly, and her new single malt, I crossed my own legs, grateful for some sort of friction to relieve some of this tension. In contrast to the earlier film, we watched this one in silence. I took little sips of my whisky trying to mask the tremble in my hand. When the sex scene happened, I held my breath uncomfortably. Kelly's legs were crossed towards me, and she had her hands in her lap. She'd barely moved the entire film, except to drink her whisky. Her body was as close to mine as it had been since that first night. I don't think I'd taken in less of a film before.

As the credits came up Kelly sat up and stretched her arms.

"So," I said, in a futile effort to break the tension. "Our joint favourite."

Kelly turned her head towards me a little. Her brown eyes searched mine and the *want* in them was easy to see. Why was she pushing so hard against this?

"Yeah."

"We need more happy endings like these for sapphic women in mainstream movies."

"Yeah. We do."

It was now or never. Taking a deep breath, I uncrossed my legs and turned my body towards her. Our thighs brushed and Kelly jolted. I spoke quietly. "I sometimes wonder what would have happened that night had we not got separated."

Kelly swallowed hard and looked away. "You do?"

"Often," my voice was shaky. "Do you ever… think about it?"

A period of silence stretched out between us. When she finally found my eyes again, she spoke softly. "Every day."

Oh my god.

"But then you turned up at the distillery. Things are different now."

"So you've kept your distance?"

"I thought being your friend was more important."

More important than what?

"That doesn't stop us from being attracted to each other." There it was. I'd said it. *Oh shit.* Hopefully the wanting in my voice wasn't too obvious. "Like when we first met."

Kelly looked at me tenderly. Her eyes were kind. "Myla," her voice was quiet. I knew that tone and the rejection coming. "I really like you and I am… attracted to you but I wonder if we are better just as friends. With the distillery now, and all that you're going through with discovering your roots. Plus, I'm a lot older than you—"

"What does me exploring my roots have to do with anything?"

Kelly hesitated. "You've just inherited a fortune and found out about a family you never knew. It's life changing. You need time to come to terms with it all, I would have thought."

"True. And I am staying up here for a few months to deal with it." I paused. "Thank you for being so sensitive to my situation but I don't see how any of that should come between us. Also, you're not that much older than me."

"It's just a lot. I'm enjoying getting to know you and I already value our friendship very much. I worry that anything more would complicate things. You're effectively my boss."

I sat with that for a while. I valued her friendship, too. I didn't feel like her boss. The distillery didn't feel like mine, and I had no intentions to interfere with it, didn't she know that? Instead, I blurted out the most base response. "Sleeping together doesn't have to complicate things." I didn't know if I wanted anything more with Kelly than sex and friendship at this point anyway, however perfect she was in my current state of infatuation. I wasn't necessarily looking for a relationship. All I knew was that I really wanted to finish what we started that night in the club. If only to complete my fantasy so that I could move on.

"I just think we should finish what we started that night. Get it out of our systems. I'm okay with just sex. I'd want to stay friends with you either way. We clearly have some chemistry and I think it would be fun. I promise not to go crazy and fall in love with you after one time. If we want, we could be friends who have sex every now and again, but only if that's something we're both up for. If not, we stay friends either way. What do you think?"

Kelly was quiet, and in the moments waiting for her to respond my embarrassment grew. I'd *never* been as bold putting myself out there like this in my whole life.

What the fuck was I doing?

"I don't know if it's a good idea."

"Oh." My whole body heated up and a wave of shame washed over me. She really did not want to fuck me, did she? I'd misread tonight. I'd completely thrown myself at her. Begged her, practically, to have sex with me. I drew back, scratching my head, humiliated. "I see."

Kelly grimaced. I so regretted saying anything now. I'd made this so weird, potentially ruining our friendship just as it was starting, despite what I'd said. "While I don't quite agree with your concerns, I'm not going to try any harder to convince you." I fixed down my dress, running my palms over it. Kelly bit down on her lip and avoided eye contact with me. "I'm really sorry I brought this up. I think I'm just going to go." I gave up hiding the tremble in my voice and went to stand up.

"Wait." Kelly put her hand on my knee. "Don't go." Her touch sent a wave of electricity right through me. She raised her eyes to mine and I held my breath. She moved closer, the side of her thigh pressing against my leg. "I didn't say it was a *bad* idea." The timbre of her voice was low and sexy, just like that night. *Yay!* "If we keep it simple."

"I like simple." I breathed.

"And if we make this a one-time thing only. No sleeping-over; no making things complicated."

"A one-time thing." I nodded, quickly, willing to agree to anything she said right now as long as it involved us fucking.

"We *should* finish what we started that night," Kelly lightly put her hand on my inner thigh, much higher than I was expecting. "To get it out of our systems."

"Yep. To get it out of our systems," I murmured, already completely done for.

Kelly stroked the sensitive skin on my inner thigh with her thumb, causing a contraction in my clit. My throat tightened. The prospect of having *just sex* with Kelly MacGregor was incredibly hot, even if we'd already started building an emotional connection.

"Are you sure you're okay with this?" Kelly asked.

"I'm sure."

She smiled with her eyes, causing that little crinkle again. "Good."

I'd fantasised about what could have gone down in that hotel room countless times, often during my extra special alone time. Knowing that Kelly had thought about it too was such an unbelievable turn on. I enjoyed pushing the boundaries with Kelly and getting her to face what was clearly between us. "What do you think would have happened... that night?"

"Well," Kelly stroked her thumb over my inner thigh. "Based on the way you were kissing me – so hungrily, so *demanding* – I think we would have fucked all night long. Which is exactly what I wanted."

I squirmed, feeling myself getting wet from her words alone. Her boldness was such a turn on. Kelly moved her hand up even higher, so close to my centre, and continued stroking the soft flesh of my inner thigh, her hand under the fabric of my dress. I could hardly move or breathe. Instead, I just sat there, desperate for her to continue.

"Until you disappeared," Kelly's voice was low and hungry with desire and frustration as my heart pounded in my chest. She traced a finger along my jawline, stopping under my chin, and tilted my face up to hers. We locked eyes and something shifted between us. Kelly leaned in so that our mouths were barely apart. "I would have done this again." Tilting my chin towards her, she leaned forward to my lips. A wave of heat rushed to my centre when our lips finally reconnected. We sank into a slow and passionate kiss. Kelly moaned into my mouth, causing another wave of electricity to course through me. This was like a dream. My hunger for her gripped at the corners of my decency as the wetness intensified between my legs. Kelly drew back and traced a finger over my bare collarbone and chest towards my breasts and then met my gaze. She seemed to know exactly what she wanted from me, and I would gladly give it, if she only asked. I followed her through her house, feeling the warmth of her hand in mine and her steady presence beside me.

"My bedroom," she closed the door behind us and pressed me into it. She rested her body flush with mine. I exhaled, already full of anticipation, still not able to believe we were actually doing this.

She whispered into my ear. "This is where we should have started that night." Resting her hands on my waist, Kelly kissed me again, but painfully slowly. I wanted everything she had to give, and I was done waiting. My head fell against the door as she planted kisses all over my neck and jaw. I got goosebumps when she moaned into my neck. Slowly, she inched my dress up my thighs, as my heart pounded. I'd thought about this moment so many times, but nothing compared to the real thing with Kelly. She'd hardly even touched me yet I was so turned on.

"Can I take your dress off?"

I raised my arms overhead and it was on the floor a second later. Kelly raked her breathtaking dark brown eyes over my body. Did she like what she saw? Perhaps it was the intense build up or the many reasons Kelly had given *not* to have sex with me that played on my mind. One false move could put an end to what we were doing here.

"Hey," Kelly took my hand, squeezing it gently. Her brown eyes were so open and kind, alongside a steady focus on the task at hand. "Shall we move to the bed instead?"

I nodded and refocused on the present. She guided me towards the bed. Kelly, in her skimpy dress, stepped closer, and my breath caught. She put her arms around my back, unclipped my bra and let if fall to the floor. She bit down on her lip as she hooked her thumbs into the sides of my panties. Tantalisingly, she kept her thumbs where they were, teasingly tugging on the fabric, as her gaze lingered on my naked breasts and travelled downwards. Kelly was a hot older woman who oozed experience and confidence. I *loved* it. I loved feeling under her control. Feeling like she wanted me like this.

I quivered when she finally slipped my panties down, fairly sure the wetness I'd caused in them was more than obvious. The air on my bare skin made me acutely aware of the arousal between my legs and the hardness of my nipples. Feeling more empowered by the minute with Kelly looking at me like this, I lay back on the bed and let my hand fall idle between my legs, noticing how sticky the sides of my thighs were. She smiled and slipped out of her dress. I gasped at the lack of panties and the immediate sight of her naked body. To think she had been sitting there half naked all night nearly ended me.

Kelly ran her hands through her long brown hair, and then took a hairband from her wrist and tied it up, elongating her body and baring her neck and chest to me in such a way that suggested she wanted my eyes to linger there – which they certainly did. She was so sexy, and her body was a mouth-watering mixture of slim and athletic. Her eyes were dark.

"To keep it out of the way."

Out of the way from what?

The answer to that question sent a wave of electricity through my body. I didn't know what I would do if she were to lick me between the legs. This *want* that I had for her was like nothing else.

Kelly knelt above me, straddling me. It was long enough since I'd been with someone – and given that this was Kelly, and she was being even more dominant and hot than I had been imagining – a new flush of wetness spread between my legs.

Louder Than Words

"Would you like me to touch you?" Kelly's voice was husky and her gaze never moved from my eyes.

"Uh-huh."

Kelly bit down on her lip and lowered her gaze, taking my nipple between her fingers. She put her other hand on the bed next to me and leant over me. I whimpered, not caring if she heard. When she started drawing circles around my puckered nipple I groaned again. I cried out when she switched to my right breast and took it fully in her mouth.

I ran my hands slowly up and down her smooth back. My hips lifted off the bed in a futile search for friction as she kissed my breasts. I *needed* her to move faster.

Kelly stopped and looked down at my frustrated body. "Are you looking for something, Myla?"

I couldn't speak, perhaps from lust, so I just nodded. She knew she was in control and torturing me with this slow build up.

"Patience," she said, and then kissed the side of my mouth, and then the other side, before indulgently finding my lips. We kissed deeply, with more intensity than I think Kelly had meant to let happen. Getting under the skin of someone so composed only heightened my already perilous state of arousal.

Pulling away, Kelly pinned my wrists above my head between the pillows. Had I known she was going to be this fucking sexy I might not have agreed we only sleep together this one time. I already knew I would crave this woman again and she hadn't even made me come yet. Who was I kidding? I had a crush on Kelly MacGregor – the hot as fuck woman from the gig – who was now firmly in my life in more ways than one.

"I think you like it when I take control." Kelly kissed my neck and then continued down to my breasts again.

"Uh-huh."

Full sentences were beyond me by this point. When she lowered herself between my legs, I whimpered, watching in wonder at the gorgeous woman on top of me who clearly knew what she was doing.

Her eyes drank me in as she spread my legs wide open. Her throat tightened. I gasped as she ran her hand along my inner thigh and brushed against my outer folds slick with anticipation. She lightly ran her hand over my clit, not quite making full contact but enough to let me know she was there. I had to force myself to breathe, and it came out shaky.

She ran her fingers up the entire length of me, stopping short of my clit and then back down. When she held the tip of her finger to my opening I nearly passed out, overwhelmed by how she was making me feel. I exhaled slowly as she added another finger and my hot juices engulfed her fingers.

Her eyes flashed up to mine. "You want this, don't you?" It wasn't a question.

I nodded, unable to form any words. I trembled when we locked eyes and involuntarily moaned when she lowered her mouth to me. I didn't care how utterly carnal it sounded. There was no use in being shy in a moment like this. I'd never slept with someone this confident before. She moved lightly, in no rush to give me what I wanted. She took her time to kiss every part of me, *except* directly on my clit. I'd never experienced anything like this level of pleasure, never felt this desired. I shuddered when she lightly ran the tip of her tongue over my clit, so lightly that my hips lifted the second it went away.

"Kelly, please."

Within seconds, her mouth was back and her fingers were inside me, fucking me as she pleased, probing to places that would surely render me hopelessly in love with this woman. Kelly groaned into me and swallowed. My legs began to shake uncontrollably. I'd never been so thoroughly *devoured* before. My body gave up and took over. I could no longer fight this. When she found a rhythm with her mouth and fingers that ignited me, I was done for. I gripped the sheets, holding onto something to ground me as Kelly played me to perfection. Wave after wave of intense pleasure ripped through me, in what was one of the most powerful orgasms I'd ever had.

"Oh my god," I said, touching her hair and pulling away from her, onto my side. I could hardly look at her exquisite face as she lifted her head, fingers still deeply inside me. I swallowed hard and forced myself to return her gaze.

She wiggled her fingers, causing me to shudder, with a triumphant smirk.

"I'm done," I breathed.

Her brow furrowed in such a sexy way. Holding my gaze she slowly curled her fingers towards her, repeating this again and again. For such a simple move, it had to be the sexiest thing that had ever happened to me. She was right, I still had more, much to my surprise. Her breasts bounced lightly as she expertly guided me towards another orgasm, her arm moved fast, working me up into a frenzy. I cried out her name when a fresh flood of wetness poured onto her hand as I came so hard. I had *never* had such a powerful whole-body orgasm before, well not since the one she'd just given me with her mouth.

As my muscles slowly and reluctantly relaxed around her fingers she caressed my thigh with her other hand in what felt like an overly affectionate gesture for someone who claimed to not want anything more from this.

"*Now* you're done."

My first instinct was to cuddle but I didn't want her to think I was making this about something more, so I smiled instead and asked her to sit on my face. Which was a far better solution in any case.

I got that she enjoyed being the dominant one, but I wanted to make her feel as good as she'd made me feel, but much quicker, if she'd allow me to.

Reaching between her legs, she touched herself without a hint of self-consciousness. "I'm extremely wet. Are you sure that's a good idea?"

I reached out my arms to beckon her up. I'd hardly touched her and now I thought I deserved to go for gold. She deserved as much. "I want all of you." Shit, that was too much. "I mean, I want to taste you."

A soft kiss on the lips ensued, where I could taste my own juices on her mouth. The kiss was deep and intense and gave me time to finally caress more of her body. I ran my fingers up the sides of her waist, part gesturing for her to rise up and give herself to me.

"Kelly, sit on my face."

The look she gave me spoke of pure desire as she made the decision to do it. I inhaled her delicious scent and slowly ran my tongue over her. She wasn't exaggerating about her wetness as her juices covered my mouth. Her whole body shook as I licked her all over, lightly at first and then firmer. I didn't hold back, driving my tongue inside her and reaching up to caress her breasts. They were so full and perfect. Our bodies moved as one as I played with her nipples and licked her until she came in my mouth somewhat unexpectedly, moaning loudly.

Louder Than Words

The sight of Kelly letting go on top of me like that would never leave my brain. Her body, her scent, her smile – she was perfect. Not until she was climbing off me and flopping onto the pillow next to me did I realise that it might be the last time I got to do that and I'd just squandered it by making her come so fast. We'd been clear: this was a one-time thing to finish what we'd started in the club. We were to prioritise the friendship and keep it simple. Could I do that? I'd just had the best, most earth-shattering sex of my life with someone I really liked.

A long silence stretched out between us as our breathing returned to normal and I tried to get my thoughts in order. I just wanted to cuddle into her, and make this night last forever, but the cool vibes I was getting from her silence and lack of eye contact suggested otherwise from her.

I rolled onto my side and rested my head on my elbow, somewhat confrontationally but I couldn't help it. Why did I think I could have *just sex* with someone I was emotionally connected to? It was better than not getting to have sex, so it had to be a win for both of us.

Kelly lay flat on her back. Apart from a couple of faint lines around her eyes and one or two silver strands in amongst that gorgeous thick brown hair, she didn't look that much older than me. She clearly looked after herself and kept in shape. I wanted to explore every inch of her gorgeous and very vibrant body, but our earlier discussion stopped me in my tracks again.

"Thank you for that," I said, smiling, and rested my hand on her tummy in what seemed like a riskier move than asking her to sit on my face in the heat of the moment.

She bit down on her lower lip and turned her head towards me. "You're welcome. And thank *you*." She was holding back, not quite meeting my eyes.

Her bedside clock spoke of the wee hours of the morning. Instead of letting this get uncomfortable, I decided that now was a good time to leave. She did say there should be no sleeping over. "I'd better get going. It's late."

We locked eyes. I couldn't make out her expression, frustratingly. For a second, it looked like she didn't want me to go, but then she didn't say anything so I must have been wrong.

"Sure. I'll see you out." She put on her dressing gown so elegantly and I couldn't take my eyes off her doing this simple action. I found my clothes and stepped into my dress again, skipping the underwear part. I wanted her to beg me to stay, but she wasn't and that was a huge disappointment after the way she'd made me feel tonight. If I hadn't known this was just a one-off, I'd have thought the way she touched me showed that she had real feelings for me. Or maybe she was just that good at sex, being older, and this was how she made every woman in her bed feel like. I had agreed to this being a one-time thing and I had to respect that. Anything more would need a proper chat, and I was not in the right frame of mind to be having one of those right now. I'd begged her to sleep with me, but I'd made her come really hard, so it wasn't just me who had done well out of this experience.

At her front door, I found my shoes and avoided her eyes. This was what we'd agreed. Just sex, keeping it simple. I had to keep reminding myself of that.

"Are you okay to drive home?"

"Yeah."

"Myla," she reached for my hand and held it gently. "I had so much fun tonight. Before and during our time in the bedroom." She planted a slow kiss on my cheek. "I hope we can still be friends, like we said we would? I really don't want to jeopardise our friendship. It means a lot to me. You mean a lot to me."

The more I looked into her eyes, the better I felt. Yes, we'd had sex and it was incredible, but we weren't committing to anything more here. We were still friends and that was the most important thing right now. I liked that I was showing her I could respect her earlier boundary, even if I was hoping it would come down sooner rather than later one day.

"Yep, still friends."

Ten

Barley came sprinting past after chewing a stick she told him not to. Spending Saturday walking through gorgeous woods up a mountain filled with wildlife for him to smell, she couldn't blame him for being excited. Myla was in front taking pictures as Barley ran up to catch her.

It turned out that Myla loved nature. Kelly hadn't expected this, for a city girl. It was sweet to see that she was soaking up as much of it as she could. Kelly, who had grown up in the Highlands and who was a country girl at heart, enjoyed trying to answer Myla's questions about things. Myla's knowledge of the natural world was limited, but she said she was keen to learn. Her enthusiasm rubbed off on Kelly.

Kelly hung back for a minute. She'd missed Myla all week, having not seen her since last Saturday. They'd texted, initiated by Kelly, and resumed their usual banter as if nothing had happened. But Kelly had *really loved* the night they'd shared and hadn't fully recovered yet from the impact it had made on her. She'd be at work doing something and be pulled into memories of the way Myla's back arched as she licked her or the sounds she'd made when she came.

Kelly had been about to ask Myla to stay at the precise moment Myla announced she was leaving. Kelly knew she would be sending mixed messages so chose to honour their prior agreement and respect Myla for staying true to her word too.

But it had been more difficult than she'd anticipated to let her go. Myla had put her cards on the table so bravely and they'd agreed to a simple one-night-only thing to finish what they'd started. They were on the same page and both clear about the situation. Plus, Myla was hot and had been coming onto her since the day she gave her the tour, and Kelly was not that angelic. There was only so much temptation she could resist.

After Myla left last week, Kelly had gone straight back to bed and curled up in the sheets that still smelled of her, keen to savour the moment for as long as possible. What was it about Myla that made her feel that way?

Having had the whole week to mull it over, she already knew she wanted Myla again. And soon. In her experience, sex that good, that soon, was not to be ignored. Myla's body was so responsive to her touch, and they'd only scratched the surface of their sexual connection and what they could do together.

Kelly had considered exploring the option of being friends with benefits, like Myla suggested. But she kept coming back to the complications with the distillery and who Myla was now. Those hadn't changed. Myla was still going through something monumental, even if she didn't think she was, she was still ten years younger and she was still her new boss. None of it bore well for them having a successful romantic relationship. So, proceeding with caution seemed to be the best option.

She hoped they could still stay friends despite having caved into her desires, and that, in some way was what today was about. No flirting. No touching. No thinking about when they had sex.

And it was killing her.

"Here," Myla pointed at a huge Scots pine as Kelly came to a stop beside her. "See the light coming through the trees like this. It's so beautiful."

The early spring sun was shining through a few particularly ornate trees, producing a kaleidoscope in the clear blue sky.

"I see it."

Only their breaths could be heard in the silence of the woods. Even Barley had come to a stop, attuning his ears to their surroundings and the odd tweeting bird. Myla was still, as if absorbing everything she could from the relatively untouched nature. Low sunbeams shone through the woods at an angle, casting gentle rays all around. Kelly didn't normally notice things like this on walks, or in as much detail, but today, with Myla, she was. Her senses were heightened. It was so beautiful and so peaceful being together like this.

Myla took some pictures of the trees and the sun coming through them. Kelly watched as Myla found more angles, loving how passionate she was about the area. Her eyes squinted as she looked into the lens and the shutter clicked, as did something in Kelly's heart over this wonderful young woman who had come into her life. She was twenty-seven but seemed older. Kelly wondered if that was due to the amount of suffering and loss she'd experienced at such a young age. Her heart lurched at the always-there-in-the-background sense of sorrow coming from Myla.

After they'd resumed walking Myla glanced over at her. "Where else do you like to walk Barley?"

"Lots of places. I try to take him somewhere different every weekend if I can. We haven't been here in a while, for example."

"Barley is very lucky to have a mummy like you. When did you get him?"

"When he was about one. I adopted him from a family who weren't able to look after him. He was obese and very timid."

"That's so sad."

"He's okay now. Seems to have bounced back."

"Bounced back with added zoomies. You'd never know he was ever timid, the way he welcomes guests."

At the top of the mountain, they stopped for a while and took more pictures.

"Can I get one of both of us." Myla said.

"Sure."

They sidled in close. This was the first physical contact they'd had since last week. Kelly tried not to focus on the fact that their shoulders and arms were touching.

"Relax," Myla said, laughing. "You look tense."

Kelly shook her head. "Sorry. I do this in photos. Clam up."

"Just be yourself. You're gorgeous so you don't even have to try."

Kelly bit down on her lip, loving how complimentary Myla continually was with her. Myla made her feel good. Desirable. Admired. She had to ask herself why those things were so appealing. Perhaps she was having a midlife crisis. Finally, they got a good one with the view in the back and even a bit of Barley sniffing around.

"Perfect," Myla said, looking at the image. "You look really lovely in this Kelly. I'll send it to you."

Myla held onto the camera now hanging from her neck looking out at the rolling hills and rugged mountain tops. "I love going on walks like this. It's beautiful here." She paused, turning her attention to Kelly. "I'm having the best time."

"Me too. I like hanging out with you."

"I like hanging out with you too."

Their extra special hanging out time last week still hadn't been mentioned. It hung between them as if they were both thinking about it at that exact moment. Kelly was happy they were still able to be friends and was relieved nothing had gone wrong. As they neared the end of the walk, Kelly's left knee was niggling from the deep steps they were going down.

Myla spoke after a while. "Are you happy living up here in the Highlands."

"It's a wonderful place. I'm very lucky. It's where I grew up, so it's not that exciting. But my family are here, my community, it's what I know. My job at the distillery lets me travel a lot, which I like. I think I mentioned that before."

"I remember." Myla glanced over at her as they walked. "You didn't say whether you were still happy to be here though."

It was impressive Myla had picked up on that. Kelly hadn't told anyone. "You're right. I didn't. I haven't been crazy about living here for a while," Kelly paused, catching her eyes briefly as they walked. "But I've been feeling better lately."

Myla smiled.

She hadn't felt this good with someone in a long time. Kelly was scared to lose that. She was scared of Myla returning to Edinburgh and not keeping in touch, and scared of messing up any chance of friendship by acting on their attraction to each other again. Because she *really* wanted to.

After a few more minutes Myla broke the silence. "Where do you feel happiest? Most yourself?"

"Oh. Um." Kelly had to think about that. She wasn't sure she knew the answer. Then she did. She was happiest out walking with Barley, in nature, alone with her thoughts. It was a far cry from her partying days in London, but it *did* bring her the most peace and it was where she felt most herself. And sharing it with Myla, like they were doing now, wasn't far off. But she wasn't going to divulge any of that. It was a bit much for a friend to say. She couldn't start saying 'being here with you is where I am the happiest', not after making such a big deal about them not exploring their attraction to each other further.

Last week had been a necessity, sexually speaking, and anything more was just plain risky. But what did it mean if it were true that she couldn't remember being as happy as she was now? Kelly pushed that thought from her mind. They barely knew each other. It was ridiculous.

"It's okay if you don't want to answer."

Kelly stopped walking. "Sorry." Ah, fuck it. *Tell her.* "I'd say I'm happiest when I'm out walking Barley in these hills. A bit like this."

A slow smile spread across Myla's face. Kelly felt better for being honest, at least partially.

"CEO slash nature lover," Myla said. Her eyes sparkled. "Is that allowed in your high-flying high-powered circles?"

Kelly ignored the sparkling eyes and the flirty comment. "What about you?"

"Mine is when I'm playing my music. I've built a music room in the house. It's my happy place."

Kelly smiled. It made sense for Myla. They held each other's eyes as a new level of understanding solidified between them. "I'd love to see it one day."

"You're welcome to come around any time."

They finished the rest of the walk passing comments on the trails and talking to Barley when he came back for attention now and then. Myla turned to her, looking shy again. How could someone so intriguing and so layered be so shy sometimes? It really fascinated Kelly.

Myla put her hands in her trouser pockets as they approached the cars. "I'll always think of this as our walk. Our mountain."

Kelly swallowed hard. There was just something about Myla in moments like this. She couldn't let herself fall for this captivating young woman.

Kelly dried the mud off Barley's chest and legs as he dissociated from the experience the way he always did. Myla hovered beside her, looking cute in her mustard beanie with strands of blonde hair falling at the front. Kelly liked the way she looked so comfortable in her own skin. So grounded.

Barley jumped in the boot and got settled. "Pub?" Kelly asked, closing the boot after giving Barley a treat. Hopefully Myla was still up for it. Kelly had suggested on Wednesday that they meet up today and go for lunch after. Today was about them being friends, and friends had lunch.

Myla smiled. "Yeah. I'm starving."

***

Kelly's cheeks burned as the hot air inside the pub met her skin. It had been a particularly cold day for early April especially up high in the hills with no cloud cover. Kelly was glad the log fire was burning brightly. The pub was nearly empty except for a couple of familiar faces at the bar – her friend, and local farmer Rory and his nephew, who worked for him. The men tilted their pints of beer towards them as they found a seat next to the fire. Barley pulled her along. He settled in front of the fire beside them. This was Kelly's local pub, The Crofter's Lounge, and that was Barley's favourite spot.

Myla was looking at a set of posters and flyers on the wall. "They do live music here?"

"Yeah, every Friday night."

"And folk bands," she pointed at a poster advertising a local folk band. "That's so cool."

"That's 'The Light Spectrum'. They're very good, and very popular up here. They should be household names." Kelly loved the local bands and Myla just so happened to point out her favourite.

"I'd love to see them."

"We should go next time they're playing."

"I'd like that." Myla smiled.

"This pub has been here for hundreds of years. It's steeped in history. It used to be an inn. The food isn't bad, too."

"It does seem pretty old. I like it."

"So, what would you like to eat?" Kelly asked, brightly.

"Something warming. And wine?"

"I'm with you on that."

After they decided on lunch, Kelly ordered at the bar and shared a few words with Rory. She knew Rory from school and his parents were part of the community council with hers.

"Not seen you at the pub quiz in a while. Still stewing over that loss?"

"Ha. No. What loss?"

"Never seen you so mad at losing, Kel. It's okay you're staying away to lick your wounds."

"I'll be back soon to kick your arses. I wouldn't get too comfortable."

"Aye, aye."

"You're on the sauce quite early today," Kelly nodded at the beers.

"This is an after-work pint. We've been up since five. Anyway, who's that you're with?"

Kelly secretly loved this small-town lack of boundaries.

"That's Myla. Margaret McAllister's great-niece. The new owner of Glenbuinidh."

Rory's eyes widened. "Is that her? She's a total legend. Fit, too."

While Kelly bristled at his last comment, she was proud of Myla. By this point, everyone in Balbuinidh knew that the distillery was safe. Kelly was proud of Myla for doing right by Balbuinidh even when she had no reason to protect their community. She could be forgiven for holding a grudge against the place given that her mum had run away from the town all those years ago, presumably for a reason. Kelly didn't know the reason, and she suspected that neither did Myla based on their chats so far. She hoped it was nothing too awful.

"For you," Kelly placed the wine on their far-too-small circular table as Myla looked up from the fire she had been staring into. She often looked like she was lost in thought like that. The flames cast a lovely glow on their table, and highlighted Myla's youthful and undeniable beauty even more. It was such an intimate space they shared. Myla seemed so calm.

Sitting down, Kelly was acutely aware of Myla's gaze on her. Myla tasted her wine and let out a satisfied groan which reminded Kelly of the noises Myla made during sex and warmed her to her core.

"Nice wine. Great choice."

"It's their best one."

"I bet you're as knowledgeable about wine as you are about whisky."

"I'm not actually that well-versed in wine. I know a little, but not to the same depth as whisky. Whisky is my job."

"Ah, so you are a mere mortal after all."

"What can I say? Cut me and I bleed."

"Whisky, probably. No," she dropped her voice to a whisper, "*tea*."

Kelly laughed. "True. Cut me and I bleed peppermint tea."

"Minty fresh. Is that why you taste so good?"

Kelly hesitated, stunned.

Myla continued, ignoring her own question, blushing. "I don't drink alcohol that often. I can't handle the hangovers. They're the worst."

Kelly puffed out her cheeks, still mostly thinking about what Myla had just said. "Wait until you're thirty-seven. Hangovers do get worse as you get older, at least that's been my experience. Way worse. Enjoy your twenties while you've still got them, if for this reason alone."

Kelly's eyes settled on Myla's lips, against her better judgement. Myla was such a good kisser. A knot gripped her stomach at the thought of it getting out to the whole of Balbuinidh that she was sleeping with the new owner of the distillery.

Myla tilted her head and looked at her in that admiring way she did. She could get used to that adoring gaze. "You know you don't look thirty-seven."

Kelly was amused at Myla's comment. She was still getting used to being in her late thirties herself and couldn't believe how quickly it had happened. Was this what getting older was like? Time speeding up on you. Kelly took some wine, enjoying the smell of it and how it warmed her mouth. "What age do you think I look?" Terror etched onto Myla's face. Kelly half-enjoyed making her squirm.

"You look younger. Maybe, twenty-nine?" Myla's voice went up at the end.

Kelly didn't believe a word of it, and it must have shown on her face.

"Okay, not twenty-nine, but I did think you were younger."

Kelly shrugged. "Please. You don't have to say that. I'm perfectly okay about being thirty-seven."

"Sorry—"

"It's interesting that we focus so much on a chronological number in this society, as if our meaning and worth are inextricably linked to it, particularly as women. We're fixated on it. I'm trying not to attach that much meaning to it but at the same time, I believe people are like fine whiskies – they get better with age. I know I've never been happier, in some ways. I've become much more comfortable and happier in my body and in my sense of self in my thirties. It's very freeing. A few lines and some grey hairs are inconsequential in the matter."

"I didn't mean anything—"

"Sorry. I didn't mean to give you a lecture. It's just something I've been thinking a lot about recently."

"What I was trying to say was that you look incredible regardless of your age. A lot of that comes from who you are – your confidence and how open-minded you are. Your spirit." Myla held her gaze, causing a warm heat to spread through Kelly again. It was not an unwelcome feeling. "The way your eyes crinkle a bit when you smile." Myla reached out and grazed the back of her finger over the skin around Kelly's eyes. "You really are the most beautiful woman I've ever met."

Kelly sat back, rubbing her hand around her neck, and getting caught in her hair. Kelly wanted to pay a similar compliment right back but was afraid it would come across as trite given what Myla had just said. The sexual tension between them had only intensified since last weekend. Kelly had still struggled to think about much else, particularly in those quiet moments when she could indulge in the memory of that night. The feel of Myla's mouth against her clit as she rode her face after fucking Myla within an inch of her life was all too real. The same mouth, slightly parted now, recently wetted after a sip of wine. Kelly blew out a breath, trying to steady herself. "Thank you."

Myla looked back towards the fire, as if contemplating something deeply. Something in the way her brow furrowed and her eyes softened made Kelly wonder what she was thinking. She could almost feel Myla's mind work. They were supposed to be just friends, not openly admiring each other next to a romantic log fire.

Since they were discussing age, Kelly thought again about how Myla was a remarkably well-adjusted young woman who was a lot more emotionally mature than she'd first assumed her to be. From the moment they first met in the gig, Kelly had been attracted to her. There was just something about her that Kelly found captivating, despite the fact that she was a lot younger. Younger women hadn't appealed as potential partners to Kelly before, but Myla was different. Now that Kelly had got to know her, Myla seemed older. Like an old soul. "You know you seem like such a mature person, for your age."

Myla turned back from the fire and shrugged. "That's trauma, baby." She laughed, nervously. "My quietness sometimes gets confused with maturity. Or maybe it is maturity, I don't know. Also, I'm not that young. Although sometimes I feel like I'm not acting my age because I don't have any responsibilities. Being up here with the time and space and, let's be real, the money now to process stuff is helping."

Kelly smiled, feeling even closer to Myla now given how honest she'd been. That kind of authenticity was exactly what she liked in a person. "Okay," Kelly held her hands up. "I hear you. I guess I still don't know you that well. It's just a very calm and grounded vibe I get from you sometimes. I know I wasn't like that when I was twenty-seven. I had my head up my arse. I probably still do."

Myla laughed. "Maybe that evens our ages up a bit then?"

Kelly had walked right into that one. They held an enormous amount of eye contact then. The more Kelly thought about it, the less important the ten-year age-gap between them was. They had a connection; they were friends. She was the only one who had made an issue out of it. "Maybe it does."

"I do like an older woman though," Myla said, eyes twinkling. "It's the confidence and the experience that does it for me."

Kelly took a sip of wine trying to distract herself from Myla's comment and the memory of taking Myla so thoroughly last week in her bed. She hadn't been able to get enough of Myla that night. Their sex had been a surprise. Everything just seemed to click. Even when Myla had insisted that she sit on her face and frantically finished her off. She hadn't seen that one coming.

"Be careful what you wish for." Her voice had inadvertently taken on the same tone that she'd used when they were fucking.

Must not do that!

Myla took a sip of her wine, blushing. Their food arrived and they both jumped back from the table as if caught in the act of something.

"Thanks, Alana." Kelly smiled, then added, after the eighteen-year-old was out of earshot, "Her dad, Duncan, works at the distillery. Kelly was glad of a change of subject. Barley sat up, eagerly awaiting the events to unfold on the table, ready to hoover up anything that should come his way. Kelly patted him on the head. He was her best friend. She'd been less present around him lately. She put aside a chip to cool down for him.

"Good boy," she said.

"I hadn't pegged you as such a soft-touch," Myla said, shaking her head and smiling.

"I am. He has me wrapped around his little paw."

They ate in a comfortable silence for a bit. Barley looked between them, hopeful.

"You still haven't seen the new beds I bought, have you?"

"No, I haven't." Where was she going with this?

"You might be happy to know I no longer sleep on camping equipment. My bedroom looks like a five-star hotel."

"Nice."

"But you know that saying, that money can't buy happiness?"

"Yeah."

"Well, I've been rich for a few months now and I'm still not one hundred percent happy all the time. It can make you more comfortable and it takes the worry out of putting a roof over your head, but it doesn't solve everything."

"I know." Kelly was super impressed with Myla's philosophical take on her new inheritance.

"What's with that, right? Our culture tells us that money is everything but when you get it, it isn't."

"True."

"Other things are more important… like how you feel about yourself, your health, living a meaningful life, friendship."

"I totally agree." Kelly paused eating, thinking about what Myla was saying. In what ways was she unhappy? Taking a deep breath, she felt like Myla was trying to tell her something. This whole day had been so intense, with Myla continuing to openly flirt and Kelly feeling things she hadn't felt in a long time. Could she honestly say to herself that nothing would happen if they were alone together again, privately? No. She couldn't.

Would that be such a bad thing?

She resumed her meal, taking a moment in between bites, feeling like something had shifted within her today. This pull towards Myla; this need to be around her and this desire to really know her just wasn't going away. It was only getting stronger. Why did she have to lose out on enjoying Myla's company in the best of ways through fear, when Myla herself said she was up for a friends with benefits situation? Yes, there were reasons not to take things any further but hadn't she been so good in her life these past few years since taking this job up here? She'd become someone she no longer wanted to be, so uninspired and tedious. Didn't she deserve to live on the wild side for once?

Fuck it.

Myla chatted more throughout the meal as Kelly solidified in her decision to broach the subject of them sleeping together again. When the plates had been taken away by Alana, and Kelly was satisfied they couldn't be overheard, she took a deep breath and went for it. "I've been thinking about what you said, last week, before we…" Kelly lowered her voice again, aware of the slow and seductive tone she was using. "Is a friends who sometimes have sex situation still of interest to you? I would like to try it."

Myla's mouth fell open, briefly, and then she smirked. "Define sometimes?"

"Whenever we feel like it?"

"Uh, hell yeah."

Kelly grinned. "Okay then. That's great. So, like you said, we just keep talking and let the other know as soon as possible if anything changes? We'll need to be open and honest with each other, as friends, I think, if this is to work."

Myla nodded, vigorously. "Yep. I'm happy to keep it super casual and just keep talking."

"Great. Great." She was starting to feel a little awkward about discussing this in the cold light of day, and, equally annoying, she was getting turned on by Myla's enthusiasm.

Myla took a sip of wine, looking off to the side. When she placed her glass back on the table, she seemed bothered by something. "Can I just ask though, last week you came up with tons of reasons we shouldn't get… I mean, do anything again. What's changed for you?"

She smiled and lowered her voice, deciding to keep it simple. "Well, I really enjoyed our night together last Saturday and I would like to do it again. I'm glad you've come into my life."

"Are you sure *you're* going to be okay with us just being fuck buddies?" Myla teased. "You're not going to fall in love with me?"

"I won't. You're far too young for me."

"And you're too old for me."

"It would never work."

"I agree. I think I'm also your boss?"

"That you are."

"But maybe we can have some fun in the meantime?"

"I like the sound of that."

They smiled at each other, all dimples and sparkling eyes. Deep down, Kelly knew this wasn't such a great idea but could do nothing to stop herself from going down this road.

Myla paid for the meal at the bar, she insisted on it, and then they braved the cold again. The pub doors closed behind them and neither of them was looking at the other. It was like this wall between them had been lowered and they were both scrambling to adapt in real time.

"Would you like to come back to the house?" Myla blurted out. "And Barley, of course. Goes without saying but just want to make that clear. Not unless you have plans, then it's no worries." Myla was blushing, hard.

She was tempted to say yes, so tempted. Kelly grimaced, desperately hoping Myla wouldn't take this as a snub, especially so soon after they'd talked about opening up the sleeping together thing again. "I'd love to, but I have plans tonight. I'm going round to Anna's for dinner."

Myla shoved her hands in her pockets. "Sure, yeah, no problem."

Seeing her disappointment cut Kelly up. This was crazy. "But I could do next Friday night, if that works for you?"

Myla's smile grew and grew. "Next Friday works. I'll look forward to it."

"Me too." Kelly was smiling now too. "I can't wait to see your music room. Will you play me a song?"

Myla smiled. "Sure. If you're interested."

I'm interested in you.

Damn, that was not supposed to be in her head. This was to be friendship and sometimes sex. That was all.

"I like music. I'd love to hear you play."

"Which song?"

Kelly shrugged. "Any song. You choose."

The smile that overtook Myla's face touched Kelly right in the heart.

Eleven

Kelly waited in Myla's music room. Their conversation a week ago felt like yesterday. Kelly had thought about it often, despite having had a busy week at work and despite being far too old for such nonsense. Myla had said she was okay with just sex, and she was going to choose to believe her. This *could* work. If anything, it seemed like Myla was rather too fine with keeping it casual, and she was the more invested one already. Myla was taking it in her stride. Kelly wasn't sure she could handle just being Myla's fuck buddy, but she wanted to give it a chance.

Of course she was second guessing herself and of course she wasn't sure that it wasn't going to end in tears, but something inside of her, something stronger, was pulling her towards Myla – something she couldn't control. Feeling reckless like this was such a thrill. Part of her was loving it. The part of her that was wild once, that was now lying dormant as she went about her daily life, one day much the same as the next, was screaming to be heard. Yes. Kelly wanted to enjoy this – whatever this was with Myla – even if it went against her better judgement. Maddeningly, Myla's texts this week contained zero flirting and zero mention of their new agreement.

Super casual.

Rain lashed at the old windows to Myla's music room. Barley was with his grandparents for the weekend. They were staying in a cottage on Mull for a short holiday. Barley loved it there. The room was nicely lit with salt lamps and a few candles on the mantelpiece of the burning log fire. The sofa had an oversized throw on it that spoke of bohemian artist – certainly not something Margaret would have owned. There was a piano in one corner and a full drum set in another. A number of guitars stood on stands, and a few were mounted onto a wall. A tambourine lay on the floor beside the drums. There was a mixing desk with a couple of desktop speakers and a large Marshall amp. She'd stocked a square shelving unit full of records which gave it such a homely feel. The room looked like someone had lived in here forever. Myla must have been busy getting it like this. It was like seeing inside Myla's head for the first time. She wasn't a particularly easy person to quickly understand, but that was one of the things Kelly liked about her.

Myla entered carrying a tray. "Two peppermint teas. Rock on!"

"You've made a lovely space in here. It feels very creative."

"I basically never leave this room."

"Your happy place."

Myla smiled, warmly.

Leaning against the piano, she then went on to point out the various instruments saying where she'd found them and how much fun she'd had researching them and ultimately, being able to buy them. She talked with such enthusiasm and gratitude; it was so lovely just to listen to her. Both Kelly's parents were into music and had encouraged her and the twins to take piano lessons. They loved putting on old Bob Dylan records and talking about the old days. Kelly found it comforting to watch them enjoy things together. And she found herself equally as engrossed in Myla's enthusiasm, too.

"This is my favourite acoustic guitar," Myla picked up a guitar and took a seat by the piano. "I've had it since I was twelve."

The lack of stickers gave Kelly the impression that young Myla might have been a little serious, which made sense. "Kurt Cobain would have been proud."

"He died before I was born. I was more of a Laura Marling fan."

Before she was born? "Oh, right."

"I've been playing more lately. Getting this room kitted out has got me all inspired." Myla stroked the guitar affectionately with it sitting on her lap under her shoulder and then looked at her fingertips. "Except my fingers hurt like hell. When you play guitar you get calluses on your fingertips, but when you stop, they go and it hurts to play. That's why it's better to keep playing because the skin stays hard," she held out her hand and showed her fingertips to Kelly.

Kelly examined Myla's fingertips, softly taking the injured hand in hers, noting the jolt of electricity when they touched. Her fingertips looked red. Kelly ran her own fingertips along them, causing another jolt of electricity to shoot right through her. "They look so sore. You poor thing."

"They'll toughen up soon enough. Just got to keep playing."

"Resilient."

Myla strummed the strings as one, making the familiar open guitar sound, and made a silly face. "That's me."

Kelly laughed, sitting down on the sofa, and clasped her hands in her lap. "I'm dying to hear you play something but now I'm not so sure that's ethical since you are in actual pain."

Myla blushed and Kelly recalled making her come last week with her own hands and mouth. She just wanted to taste her again.

She hung up her guitar and sat down at the piano stool. "I tell you what, I'll play something on the piano first."

Myla blew out a breath and fixed her posture. She went into a zone, back dead straight. When she started playing, a sort of haze came over her eyes. Kelly instantly recognised the music, as the hairs on the back of her neck stood up.

"Ah, I know this one."

Myla looked up, briefly, still playing. "You do?"

"Yeah. My parents love it. It's Beethoven, right? Moonlight Sonata?"

Myla nodded. Kelly inhaled as Myla continued to play the piece perfectly to Kelly's untrained ear. The quiet intensity of Myla's piano playing sucked her in and made everything else fade into the background. She ended the piece beautifully.

Kelly was completely blown away.

Myla finally looked up at her, eyes all open and deep.

Kelly was lost for words for a few moments, she was that moved. "You play so well. Brilliant."

Myla smiled, all youth and beauty, and Kelly just sat there, completely enamoured.

"Right. Guitar." Myla picked another guitar off the wall. It looked newer. "But be warned, I'm well out of practice." She strummed a few chords and then turned the nuts a few times, tuning it in. Kelly hoped her hand was up to this. "I'll do a cover." She looked through her as if deciding on a specific song. "I've got one."

"Okay, great. Hit me with it."

Kelly recognised the riff from a famous nineties American rock band and a shiver went down her spine.

What followed was an excellent rendition, to Kelly's ear, expertly played and sung, conveying her knowledge not only of the lyrics but also their cadence. She held back on the singing a bit, but it was still good. When Myla finished the last part of the song Kelly could only sit there and hold her breath as the guitar was strummed increasingly forcefully, amping it up louder and louder the longer it went on. Kelly was stunned at how powerful and haunting it sounded, mixed in with a talent that must surely be natural given how effortless it looked.

Myla stopped, resting her palm over the chords covering the hole, effectively silencing it. The final chord echoed around the instruments in the room. Myla took a deep breath, not meeting Kelly's eyes.

"Myla you're so talented. I can't believe you've kept this so quiet."

"I'm not. It's a really easy song to play. Just the same few chords over and over again."

"You're far too humble."

"I play because I enjoy it. Loads of people can play the guitar."

"Not like that, surely."

Myla tilted her head towards Kelly and they locked eyes again. A few moments passed in silence. Kelly swallowed, lost in Myla's intensity. "You said you write songs, too. "Can you play me one of those?"

Myla hesitated. "Okay. But only if you promise not to laugh at my singing."

"I would never. You sing well."

Kelly frowned. Myla needed to own her shit better. She was clearly talented, so this humility nonsense was going to have to go. Myla proceeded to play one of the most achingly beautiful songs Kelly had ever heard. Myla looked towards the floor as she played, lost in another world as she properly sang this time, perfectly in sync with the guitar that looked like an extension of her. The sound that emanated from Myla was like the embodiment of her personality: soulful, deep, and very individual. It was a sad song, but also life-affirming. It had this bittersweet melancholy about it that tapped into something bigger. The lyrics, the sound – there was such depth in them. It truly touched something in Kelly as she sat there perfectly still, afraid to breathe in case she missed any of it. When Myla's song ended, the room fizzed in the aftermath. Kelly *loved* discovering this about Myla. Loved it.

I could easily fall in love with her.

"I don't know what to say, Myla. That was beautiful."

"I wrote it a few years ago."

"I love it."

Myla sat back, the guitar now resting on her lap. "You don't think it's a bit… sad?"

That Myla was able to convey pain and suffering and make her feel something in under three minutes was a skill. "It was touching. Art should make you feel something, and yours definitely does."

"Thank you. I'm glad you enjoyed my mini gig."

Myla put the guitar back and then sat on the sofa beside Kelly, her shoulder slightly touching hers and her hand resting close to Kelly's. Myla was wearing a low-cut black tank top and colourful loose-fitting trousers. She looked so relaxed, and extremely hot. Kelly wondered if the cleavage Myla was showing was intentional or not, because it had been hard not to look. Her body was responding to Myla all on its own. Kelly moved away slightly to create some distance. She cleared her throat. "Have you thought about sharing your music? I'm sure others would love to hear it."

"When I was younger, I dreamed of a career in music. I wanted to be an internationally acclaimed musician who sold out intimate and exclusive venues around the world," she chuckled. "I guess I have my wounds and a strong desire to express myself through music. But with everything that happened with my mother and then me falling off the rails, I stopped playing. Some people channel their problems into their creativity, but I left it behind me. I couldn't *feel* things after my mother died. I did write a few songs in the years after her death but in the end I gave it up. I wish I'd kept my music going. I'm not as good any more. Since I've been here though I've started playing again just for fun. I've just been enjoying how it makes me feel. It's good. My lyrics are pure cringeworthy and totally from the heart. I'm not ready to share that level of vulnerability yet with people."

Kelly covered Myla's hand with hers, instinctively. "Then thank you for sharing it with me tonight. It's an honour." She ran her thumb over Myla's hand. "Do you have more songs I could listen to?"

"I have a SoundCloud with some bits and pieces on it from over the years. I could send you the link if you want?"

"Yes do, thanks." Kelly rotated Myla's hand and stroked the incredibly detailed tattoo on the inside of Myla's wrist with her fingertips. "I meant to ask about this before. It's lovely. When did you get it?"

"I got it when I was sixteen. It's a treble clef."

"What does it mean to you?"

"My love for music."

A silence stretched out between them, growing noticeably more uncomfortable the longer it went on. Kelly was acutely aware of Myla's slow and deep breathing.

Kelly wanted to lean over and kiss those soft lips so tenderly. That pull, that *want*, was back, stronger than ever. Not only was Myla beautiful and so attractive, she made Kelly feel inspired again. It was as if life itself had gone up a notch just knowing that Myla was a person in the world. Mundane everyday things felt more real and more meaningful somehow.

"Kelly," Myla faced her on the sofa, stretching her arm along the back of it, pulling Kelly out of her thoughts. "What was your first impression of me when we first met at the gig?"

That you were hot and sounded interesting.

"Um, I thought you were good-looking, and I liked your voice. You sounded very posh, and you were ordering my—sorry, our whisky."

"I'm not posh."

"Your accent is."

Myla sighed, as if giving in. "That's boarding school for you."

"Why do you ask, anyway?"

She shook her head. "I was just wondering."

"What did you think of me?" They locked eyes, facing each other on the sofa now. Kelly felt like she was falling into her orbit, unable to resist where this conversation was heading.

"Very confident. Attractive."

"Did you see me in the crowd during the gig?"

Myla nodded. "I did. You were watching me, you stalker," she paused, laughing.

"I was. I was totally stalking you." She hadn't been able to take her eyes off Myla as soon as she'd found her in the crowd again. From very early on, Kelly knew there was something special about Myla. She now felt that even more. "You had your eyes closed a lot. You looked like you were in your own wee world. What were you thinking about?"

Myla looked off to the side as if remembering that night. "I was feeling the connectedness in the room. The energy that night was intense."

"True. It was *full* of sapphics." Kelly laughed.

Myla laughed softly. "No. I mean, the shared love of the band and the music. I love it when you're in the crowd at a gig and everyone is just there and loving the same thing as each other. There's this shared feeling. It makes me feel close to people. Sometimes, I really crave that."

Kelly hadn't thought about things like that before. But she agreed. "Gigs are great for that. Human connection is really important."

Myla rested her hand on Kelly's knee, sending tingles right to Kelly's centre. There really was no controlling her body around Myla.

"I like connecting with you."

Myla's words hung in the air between them. Kelly lowered her voice, trying to sound like she was joking but didn't achieve it. "Myla, are you flirting with me?"

"I might be?"

Kelly's breath caught. She wanted to feel those soft lips again. This *wanting* for Myla was so powerful.

Myla touched the side of Kelly's face. "Is this okay?"

Kelly felt the rough calluses on her fingertips and nodded. "Yes."

"What about this?" Myla leant in so that their mouths were barely apart.

Kelly's heart pounded. Myla's lips looked so inviting, and Kelly knew exactly how they tasted. She wanted them again. Now. Everywhere. And all at once. "That's okay too," Kelly whispered.

Their lips brushed. Myla's hand went to the side of her neck and Kelly rested her hand on Myla's chest. The kiss was so tender and loving that it threw Kelly's head into a spin. She'd been arrogant to assume Myla would be the one to want more first, when she felt like *she* was the one falling hard and fast for a woman ten years younger, who she really had no business getting involved with. But they connected on a level that simply made Kelly happy. Kelly deepened the kiss as a raw hunger took over her. When their tongues met a rush of electricity shot between Kelly's legs. Neither was in a hurry to break away and by the time Kelly came up for air she became aware of how wet she was. "I can't stop kissing you."

"So don't stop."

Myla straddled Kelly's lap and ran her fingers through Kelly's hair. Slowly, she wrapped her arms around Kelly's shoulders as Kelly's hands instinctively went to Myla's waist. Kelly slipped her hands underneath Myla's top, making contact with her bare skin. Her spine tingled. Kelly's eyes rested on Myla's chest, as she bit down hard on her lower lip.

"Something got your attention?" Myla teased.

Kelly furrowed her brow. "No. I mean – yes."

Myla ran her thumb over Kelly's lower lip. There was such a dark look on Myla's face and it caused such a *want* deep inside Kelly. Myla planted kisses all over her jaw and neck, slowly working her way over Kelly's body and driving her insane with this desire. When Myla lowered herself down to her knees and lifted up Kelly's top to plant kisses on her lower stomach, Kelly's breath became uneven. Myla drifted further still, and Kelly's heart thrummed in her ears. Myla ran her hands along Kelly's lower abdomen, causing Kelly's clit to throb in anticipation. She was *nervous*, which was so unfamiliar to her in this situation. Come to think of it, she'd never had a friend with benefits before.

Myla stood and led Kelly towards the rug by the fire and guided her onto her back. Kelly went with it. Myla resumed her position between Kelly's legs, kissing her lower tummy. The kisses sent tingles to Kelly's clit, and a fresh wetness to soak her panties. This was insane. Myla wasn't waiting for some big conversation, she was just going for it, taking what she wanted. It was driving Kelly mad with this need for more and also a strange insecurity that this might mean a lot more to her than it did to Myla.

Myla unbuttoned Kelly's jeans and pulled them down and off, socks and all, taking her time, before hooking her fingers into Kelly's panties and sliding them off. They locked eyes, briefly, before Myla lowered her mouth and made contact with her centre. Kelly arched her back, moaning, as Myla's mouth explored and gave her everything. Myla's breathing became more ragged against her, and the sensation was overpowering. Myla made her feel so wanted. Kelly's body began to shake uncontrollably and despite trying to fight it she came, moaning and thrashing under Myla's mouth quite unhinged. Kelly's heart raced in the moments after, embarrassed at coming so quickly.

Myla knelt back and rested her hands on Kelly's knees. Kelly shut her legs and pulled Myla down beside her. Her being half-naked and Myla fully clothed was so symbolic of how Kelly felt right now, and she couldn't have that. Kelly switched places and intentionally took off all of Myla's clothes, as the fire crackled beside them. Seductively, Myla let a leg fall open giving Kelly full glorious view. Her body held all the delights of youth: firm, supple and glowing. She was slim with curves in all the right places. Her nipples were small but hard. There was something so sexy about her. Kelly just couldn't get enough. "Touch yourself for me."

"What?"

"I want to see you touch yourself."

Myla swallowed. "Now?"

"Yeah."

"I'm too shy."

"I think we're way past that now."

Slowly, Myla started touching her clit. "I can't believe I'm doing this."

"Tell me how wet you are."

Myla clenched her jaw. "I'm so wet."

Kelly leaned over Myla, desperate to put her fingers inside her. She whispered in her ear. "Did you fuck yourself and think about me like I've been thinking about you?"

Myla's hand moved faster, her fingers working hard. "I did." Myla whimpered, stoking the fire within Kelly.

"Do you want me to keep watching?"

"Keep watching," she breathed. "Please."

Kelly bent her head down to Myla's mouth for a deep and passionate kiss, feeling Myla's pleasure every time she moaned. Pulling back, she propped herself up on her elbow and lay beside Myla and just… watched. That Myla was getting into it and taking her time pleasuring herself was like witnessing Myla's most vulnerable and intimate self. Myla's breathing became uneven, coming out in short sharp rasps. A full red rash spread across Myla's chest and neck. The sight of her fucking herself was just so unbelievably hot. They locked eyes as Myla came, hard, right beside her. It was the hottest thing Kelly had ever seen.

Myla closed her legs and rolled towards her. "I thought having a friend with benefits meant I didn't have to do that any more?"

Kelly remembered Myla's hand was sore. "Fuck, I'm so sorry." She brought Myla's hand up to her mouth and kissed her fingertips so gently, tasting Myla's juices on her fingers. Her smell drove Kelly wild and she wanted to suck each finger dry but held back. Myla's skin was soft, except her fingertips, which were rough. "You poor thing. You should've let me know you weren't up to that."

"The pain was kind of part of the pleasure."

"I can't believe I forgot. I got carried away there."

"I like it when you get carried away. It's hot. I can't believe you asked me to masturbate in front of you and I did."

"It's important for me to see how you like to touch yourself so I can learn what you like."

"Thorough."

"I don't like causing you pain," Kelly kissed her neck. "That doesn't do anything for me. Not unless it's something we've agreed on first."

"Got it. You're such a top."

Kelly scoffed, simultaneously brushing a strand of Myla's hair behind her ears. "I prefer to call it dominant energy."

"Of course you do," Myla said, hooking a leg around Kelly's beckoning her towards her.

About an hour later they rolled away from each other. Kelly rested her hand on her chest, trying to wrap her head around this crazy connection they shared, as her breathing came back to normal. They'd both had about three orgasms each, or maybe more, she'd lost count. For friends with benefits, it didn't *feel* like just fucking. What was this?

She turned onto her side and wrapped her arm around Myla's waist. Myla's light hair was wild, and her cheeks were rosy. Kelly caressed her shoulder and then the side of her face, and then planted a slow kiss on her cheek.

Myla watched her closely, with a soft smile playing at her lips. "So affectionate."

Kelly registered the meaning of her actions and pulled away, trying not to make it obvious. "Just being friendly."

"I like it when you get friendly."

Reluctantly, Kelly realised it was time to go. Staying late and sleeping over wasn't a good idea, especially if she didn't want to let it slip that she was crushing on her supposed fuck buddy. "I should get going."

"It's early. Can't you stay a little longer?"

"I'd better not."

A flicker of disappointment flashed across Myla's face but then quickly disappeared. "Yeah, sure. Of course."

Kelly picked up her clothes from the floor and got dressed. Myla did the same, throwing on her tank top first, and then her panties and then her socks and trousers. Just watching Myla get dressed fascinated Kelly.

"Here," Myla found her socks. "Yours."

"Thanks."

"Kelly."

"Yes?"

"Before you go. Can I get a hug? Or is that not part of the whole friends with benefits situation either?"

Kelly's heart skipped a beat. "It's part," she stepped in close to Myla, who looked lost and vulnerable, and wrapped her arms around her. She inhaled into Myla's hair smelling both sweat and sweetness. She ran her hands up and down Myla's slender back, feeling so connected to her in this moment.

Keeping things casual had to be the safest option here, at least for now. Kelly would hope for the best but expect nothing in return. There was no guarantee Myla was interested in pursuing an actual relationship with her anyway. Is that what Kelly wanted? The things worrying her about them being together still danced around in the back of her head.

"You're a great cuddler," Myla said, squeezing her tightly. Myla tilted her head towards Kelly, brushing her nose against her cheek. When their lips met, Kelly was back there again, completely lost in their connection and in Myla's softness. For a goodbye kiss it quickly escalated into open mouths and hands gripping clothes before Kelly pulled back, trying to regain the control that was fast disappearing from her.

Myla spoke first. "When can I see you again? I mean, when are you free to hang out?"

Kelly sighed, inwardly at her packed schedule coming up. "I'm not sure. I have a lot on next week." The disappointment that appeared on Myla's face wasn't what Kelly wanted to see, especially not right before she had to leave; she was just being matter of fact but clearly it had caused a reaction. A reaction that suggested this meant more than just casual sex for her too? "I could do lunch a week on Tuesday though? You could come by the distillery? Catch me in my natural habitat?"

Myla smiled, the lightness returning to her eyes. "Perfect."

Louder Than Words

As Kelly drove away from the house with Myla waving from the doorstep, all she wanted to do was turn the car around and go straight back into her arms and never leave. Kelly was falling, and she was falling hard.

Twelve

I opened the door to Kelly's office feeling like a bit of an intruder. Kelly looked up from her laptop and smiled warmly. God, she was so beautiful.

"Hey."

"Hi. Lucy let me in. There were lots of visitors in reception, so I don't think she had time to call you."

"That's fine."

Kelly stood up from behind her desk and crossed her office towards me. She was wearing the sexiest black pencil skirt and high heels, with a long-sleeved blouse buttoned up to the top. Her hair was down and wavy and her soft-brown smoky eye make-up highlighted her eyes. That Kelly might have dressed up for me was thrilling, if likely inaccurate.

I cleared my throat. "You look great. Very smart."

"Not *quite* what I was going for, but thanks."

"You look really fucking hot as well, but I'm not sure I'm allowed to say that."

"You're allowed. Thanks."

Kelly was blushing. How that was possible was beyond me. She was a successful woman in her late thirties with her shit together yet here she was looking all angsty and adorable with me. The friends with benefits situation was exciting, if a little hard to get my head around. It was clear that Kelly didn't want any more than what we'd agreed, even if she was affectionate or sweet sometimes. When she left on Friday night, I was very in my feelings and really wanted her to stay, but I knew that she wasn't going forever, we were friends now first and foremost. I liked her as a person and while I *really* liked it when we had sex, I vowed not to let my emotions get the better of me and just enjoy what this was, free of any expectations from her and not putting myself under any pressure either. Strangely, it made sense for me right now.

"How's your morning been then? Any whisky drama to speak of?"

"Oh, there's always drama." Kelly closed the door and we hovered by it. "How's yours been? Have you been up to much?"

I took a deep breath, looking into her warm brown eyes, already feeling fuzzy inside. "I have actually. I've been exploring the town a little more, exploring my roots. I went back to the library. I love looking at the exhibition downstairs. It tells such a story. I visited the school my mother went to. I sat on a bench watching the kids play at break time, imagining it was my mother running about… I know, I'm a bit weird."

Kelly laughed, good naturedly, and I swear it permeated my soul.

"And I love the park. It's so beautiful. I like to walk through it on my way into town."

"We're very lucky to have that park. It has Green Flag status, the UK park Oscars, basically. Funding is always at risk, but the local community keeps pressuring the council to prioritise it. It makes me proud."

"Good for them. Maybe I could help one day? I'm not sure if I mean personally or financially or both. The park has grown important to me since being here."

"Wow. Yes. I'm sure that would be much appreciated. I can put you in touch with the right people."

I held up the paper bag and drinks tray I was holding. "I've got lunch." I'd stopped by the café en route and picked up some paninis and English breakfast tea. We'd texted about it earlier. We'd been texting a lot since that glorious Friday night in my music room, yet I still felt a bit nervous about seeing Kelly today. We hadn't hung out since that night, and it was yet to be seen how we were going to make the friends with benefits work in reality.

"You're a star, thanks."

We sat in the same seating area as when I first visited with Graeme. That felt like an eternity ago. The difference in Kelly was monumental. That day, she'd been cold and distant, and understandably shocked. Today, she was warm and open, and had let me call her hot. We sat across from each other and started on lunch.

"What else have you been up to?" Kelly said, unwrapping her panini and leaning towards me slightly. "If feels like ages since I've seen you."

I got the distinct feeling that Kelly had missed me. There was just something about her tone and the way she was looking at me. Were we becoming more than friends to her? "I had tea with Hilary again. I popped in on her and we had a nice chat. I want to claim her as my own grandmother."

"I think she'd love that. She has such a big heart. I'm very fond of her too."

I didn't mention that I was struggling to find the courage to ask Hilary to tell me everything she knew about my mother and my grandparents. I wasn't strong enough yet to know the truth, as I knew that it wasn't going to be a very happy story. I wasn't ready to face it yet. So instead, I'd kept it light with Hilary and we talked about life in present day, rather than the past. "I've also been writing some lyrics. They're not awful."

"I'm sure they're not."

"Um, you might want to see them first before saying that."

I finished my lunch and scrunched up the wrapper. Kelly was still going. I loved watching her mouth as she ate. I could hardly take my eyes away. I loved just hanging out like this. She was so genuine and down to earth, and good. She was so safe. Another few moments passed with us just sitting with each other. I loved just sitting with her. "So, what's the drama?"

"Sorry?"

"You said there was drama this morning. Anything interesting? Concerning?"

Kelly's eyes widened in alarm. I hadn't meant for that. "Oh. Yes. Did you want like an update or just…?"

I shook my head numerous times. "No, *no*. I was just making conversation."

"It's your company, Myla. If you want to know anything, just ask."

It's not that I wasn't interested in the distillery, I was, but today I just I wanted a nice lunch with her not a business meeting. I guess we hadn't discussed my involvement in the distillery yet. Was that why she invited me here today? To talk to me as the new owner? My mood soured at the thought of that.

"Are you okay?" Kelly's eyes were kind.

"Yes. Sorry."

"There's no need to apologise. Where did you go?" Kelly took a sip of tea.

"Nowhere." Why was I second guessing her? She couldn't be any more trustworthy, and it was me who asked about the drama.

"Okay. Well, we received a shipment of new casks from Spain but they are faulty. The supplier is refusing to replace them but I will have my way, in the end."

"I'm sure you will."

Kelly gave me her CEO smile and a little part of me wanted to giggle like the child I was in such a grown-up's domain. I did my best to gather myself. "Anything else exciting?"

Kelly smiled. "Exciting? Well, I'm launching a new initiative called Women in Whisky. It's aimed at increasing the number of women working in the whisky industry in Scotland and debunking some myths. There already are many women working in this industry and doing great things. I want to ensure more girls and young women feel like it's an industry that welcomes them."

"That is such a good point. It does come across as a very male-dominated thing."

"I'm keen we lead by example. Women account for over half of the sector yet men still disproportionally lead it and get paid more. There's a huge visitor attraction element to the whisky industry and that is mainly staffed by women but is often the least well paid. Not at Glenbuinidh, though."

This information made me swoon. Not only was Kelly the way she was – kind, intelligent and beautiful – she was also an advocate working tirelessly to improve things for others. Could she *get* any more attractive? This was doing nothing for my growing feelings towards this ridiculously attractive older woman. My friend with the most mind-blowing benefits. "It's commendable of you."

"I'm strict about equal pay. I implemented it a few years ago at Glenbuinidh. I was shocked when I took over and found out it was an issue here too."

"What's your game plan with the initiative?"

"At the moment it's mostly a network of other women. We're building a website showcasing the array of talented women already working. Then we plan on doing outreach events and picking up some sponsorship."

"You're pioneers."

Kelly frowned. "Thanks. I haven't had everyone's full support on this. Some people think it's too big, too difficult, and might endanger the brand. We're known as a traditional brand and many are scared to change that. My senior team, my parents, and Margaret before she passed. She thought it was a silly distraction from the real business of making good whisky. People can get very set in their ways. When it comes to the crown jewel of the area, people are nervous to mess with it."

"I get that your team and Margaret had views but why do your parents come into it?"

"It's just my dad, really. He thinks because he gave me the job I'm indebted to his superior experience or something."

I scratched my ear, thinking. "That doesn't sound like fun. It's your distillery now. Not his."

Kelly's eyes lit up as if she was finally being seen. Sometimes she seemed much younger than her thirty-seven years. I continued. "You've got to move with the times. I sometimes think life is like a raging river, all flexible and subject to change over time. Nature never stands still, so why should we?"

"Exactly." Kelly's eyes were still bright, and she was smiling broadly. "I think like that too."

"This initiative sounds really important to you."

"It is."

I nodded. "And along with your new folklore malt, it probably threatens people."

Kelly took a sip of tea. "Queen of Spirits. Yep, Margaret wasn't up for any of that. She was the truest to the old ways, as you might expect." Kelly paused. "Since she passed, I've been doing more on the Women in Whisky initiative. I hope that's okay?"

It took me a few moments to realise she was asking me for an opinion. "Are you asking me?"

"Yes. It's only fair."

"I think it's a brilliant idea. I fully support it."

Kelly just stared at me as a slow smile crept onto her face. "You've no idea how happy that makes me."

"I still don't feel like it's my place to have an opinion around here, but I do like the sound of what you're saying, much like Queen of Spirits. I'm all for dismantling the patriarchy one bit at a time."

Kelly laughed. "You might not feel it yet, but your opinion does matter. I want you to feel involved and I'll do my best to make that happen, starting with meeting the people that work here, if you like?"

"What do you mean?"

"Everyone is dying to meet you. I could give you the real tour, if you're interested?"

I didn't know what to do with that, but I agreed in principle about meeting the people. "Just tell me when and I'm there."

"How about now?"

I sipped some tea not immediately taking to the idea and utterly failing at being spontaneous. "Now?"

"Why not? You're here. I can walk around with you and introduce you to people and move us on when you start getting life stories, which you will. Only if you want to, of course."

My thoughts scrambled. Spontaneous socialising was not my strong point. Usually, I needed time to prepare for things like this; although, come to think of it, I couldn't recall ever having been in a similar situation. With Kelly next to me, however, it might be okay. "Sure. I can do now."

***

Over an hour later we were back in Kelly's office so I could pick up my backpack. She'd introduced me to pretty much everyone who was working today, and we had a little chat with most people. Everyone was so friendly and interesting, but I'd already forgot most of their names. I was terrible at remembering names. I remembered what they said, though. Like the man in overalls walking around the casks saying that a small percentage of the whisky evaporates while maturing and is known as the angel's share, or the middle-aged mother of three in the office who doesn't even like whisky. The manager, Georgia, was nice and welcoming. I loved her accent, too. She did not mince her words either as in the five minutes we spent together she summarised the last fifteen years at Glenbuinidh from her perspective.

Back in Kelly's office, I was glad to be alone with her again. I wanted another chance to chat after such a stimulating afternoon. Being around her was fast becoming my favourite thing. She'd introduced me as simply 'Myla Murray, the new owner of Glenbuinidh'. I was still getting used to that title.

"Thanks for doing that," Kelly said. "It's really made everyone's day, I can tell."

While I doubted that were true, it was a nice thought and an even nicer thing of her to say. "It was lovely to meet everyone. The real tour was even better that the first. Me getting pissed in the bar after aside."

Kelly laughed, gently. "I'm glad you enjoyed it. It means a lot."

I swallowed hard, still not sure what my role was going to be here. I also didn't really want to leave, but it was time.

Kelly smoothed out her blouse that was tucked into her skirt. "This year's Scottish tourism summit is in a fortnight. It's a conference for the main visitor attractions and industry bodies in the country. There'll be presentations and talks, and networking. We'll be displaying a stall in the main foyer, which Anna and Georgia are going to staff. The lunch usually isn't bad. Would you like to come? It could be a good way to get your head around what Glenbuinidh is all about out there in the real world."

"Yes I would. Thanks for inviting me. I've never done anything like it."

"Brilliant."

"Is it a day trip or stay over in a hotel situation?"

Kelly raised an eyebrow as a small smirk appeared on her lips. "Which would you prefer?"

"Stop teasing. Which is it?"

Kelly became serious again. "It's a day trip. About an hour's drive south. We could travel together, if you like?"

"That would be great, thanks."

"I wouldn't get too excited. Some of the presentations can be a hard watch."

"As long as you'll be there with me it'll be perfect."

Kelly bowed her head, thinking something but I couldn't work out what.

"I'd better go. I've already taken over your whole afternoon as it is. Sorry."

"Myla," she reached out and held my hand and then gently stroked her thumb over it. Her touch made me all gooey inside. "Please don't apologise. It was my pleasure. I can catch up with my work later. I've loved having you to visit Glenbuinidh again. You're welcome here anytime. I mean that."

The sincerity in her words nearly made me crumble. What was it about this woman and making me feel better with just a few words? "Cool," I murmured. "Thanks."

"Actually, I was hoping we could have a quick chat about something before you leave?"

Oh fuck that didn't sound good. My stomach dropped in dread. Was she ending our sexy times agreement? "Sure. What about?"

"I was wondering if you'd had a chance to think about what level of involvement you want in the distillery. I want you to be happy about how much control you have, or at the very least, for us to be clear about what the terms of engagement are."

'Terms of engagement' didn't sound like much fun at all. Then again, from the people I'd met this afternoon, the cool new folklore bottle coming out, and Kelly's insight into the Women in Whisky thing, I was getting more intrigued. I didn't want any responsibility though. I wasn't ready for that. I probably would never be. It wasn't in my nature to grab the power. Others would probably have jumped at the chance, but it didn't appeal to me in the slightest. And most importantly, being Kelly's boss didn't sit great with me either. I didn't want it to get in the way of our *friendship*.

Kelly sat, hands clasped on her lap, legs crossed. She looked so sexy it was hard to think clearly. She was obviously waiting for me to say something. In fairness, she had waited long enough already.

"I guess I want you guys to continue doing what you're doing, keep making it a success. I'd be happy to get involved in the fun stuff, like drinking the said whisky?" Kelly just nodded, as if this still wasn't nearly the level of detail she was looking for. I sighed, feeling bad about not having an answer for her and shit about myself for not being good enough for her. "I can see there's a lot more to this than I realise. Trouble is, I don't know what I don't know. That's all I've got for you, I'm afraid."

Kelly's eyes crinkled kindly as she smiled with her lips firmly closed. "That's okay. I tell you what. I'll set up a meeting with Georgia and she can talk you through each of our departments. Then, once you know a bit more you can let me know if anything interests you. Apart from propping up the bar, which you're more than welcome to do by the way, it might be that you want to know more about a specific area such as marketing or part of the whisky making process itself or even the bottling. Whatever it is, I want you to feel like you are involved and that you're part of the Glenbuinidh family. Because you are."

A lump formed in my throat and I gulped. I wanted to ponder this more but she was staring at me so I couldn't dwell on her words any longer. I sat up straight again and faced Kelly directly. "You know I really did like the bar. I'd love another visit and to meet Anna again, she seemed cool."

Kelly laughed. "Okay. Speak your truth. I love it. I just want you to get something out of this, too."

I smiled. I was already getting so much out of this experience and was intrigued to see what it was that I could offer Glenbuinidh, if anything. My life had completely changed, and I was loving every second of it. Not even my predisposition for melancholy could compete these days.

"You just need to tell me what you want, and I'll make it happen." Her voice was smooth and sexy and had gone done a notch.

Kelly was still trying to be so polite and professional, but my head was now in the gutter. She was so warm and kind, and just so fucking... *hot*. I still had a hard time concentrating on much of what she was saying. My eyes raked over her toned and slender body, wishing I could run my hands through her hair again and explore her body at will.

"There is something else I want."

"Yeah, sure. Anything. What is it?"

I paused. "To kiss you."

Kelly blinked in disbelief, it seemed. Our eyes locked. Even I could hardly believe those words had slipped out of my mouth. Kelly *did* approve of me speaking my truth, and we *were* fucking. I would never have been so forward during the day like this normally but from the passion Kelly had shown the two times we'd slept together, and in that gloriously epic first kiss in the club, it was hard not to keep growing in confidence. I think she liked it when I was bold like this. I did too.

She walked to the door and gently locked it. She crossed the room, closed the blinds, and then leaned against the wall. My heart started pounding. She tucked her hands behind her back and rested on them. "Come over here," she said, eyes fixed on me and dark.

The kiss started slow, barely registering on each other's lips as our noses danced for a moment. With her hands still tucked behind her back, I was free to touch her, and I think she wanted this. She was inviting this. I traced my fingertips across her cheek and then into her hair, feeling like that was such an intimate move, but what the hell, we were doing this. I deepened the kiss, confidently taking it in the direction I wanted. I leant down and kissed her softly on the neck. Tracing kisses on each side until I ran into blouse.

Kelly's throat tightened. "Is there anything else that you want?"

My heart still pounded. She was letting me live out some sort of fantasy here. "This." I started unbuttoning her blouse, unable to hold her gaze for long. With trembling fingers I carefully dealt with the buttons, determined not to give into the nerves or ruin her nice top. When no objection came, I tugged the fabric up and out of her skirt. Her eyes were trained on me the entire time, encouraging me to go on. I put my hands inside her blouse and touched her sides, then travelled upwards towards her shoulders before she brought her hands from behind her back and let me slip her blouse off. Standing there in her lacey white bra Kelly looked like a dream. I couldn't believe she was letting this happen, and in her office.

She tucked her hands behind her back again, leaning onto the wall. Her nonchalance was so hot.

"Is that all?"

I swallowed, kicking into gear as desire mixed with something fuller took root in me. I stepped right into her

Louder Than Words

space, so that our bodies were touching, and her breasts pressed into mine.

"No. Not by far."

From the look in her now-hooded-eyes, I knew exactly what she wanted and I wanted nothing more than to give it. Her head fell against the wall as I planted kisses all over her neck and jaw, pressing my thigh in between her legs. I got goosebumps when she moaned softly. When I pressed my hand to her centre, her legs buckled momentarily, and she gasped. I tugged her pencil skirt up high as I kissed the fleshy skin just above the cups of her bra. I hooked my fingers underneath her panties and rolled them down to her knees. Leaning into her, I found the wetness between her legs and drew small circles with two fingers across her swollen clit as I pressed the side of my face against her soft cheek.

She freed her hands from behind her back and put her arms around my shoulders. It was a small move but there was such surrender in it. I searched and explored her wetness, teasing and rubbing. She felt incredible. Her moans were low and *deeply* sexy. I kissed her shoulder while putting two fingers deep inside her and pressed my palm against her clit. Her body rose upwards, onto her toes, and since she was already in heels I had to rise with her. Her breathing became ragged, as had mine, which only strengthened my resolve to keep her on the edge for as long as possible. Kelly's moans intensified, though she was trying to muffle them, and her body trembled. I wanted nothing more than to hear her cry out in pleasure, giving herself to me completely, but she was near silent as she came in my arms.

I rested my forehead against her shoulder for a few seconds, savouring the moment and wondering if I was lying to myself that I hadn't already gotten completely attached to this woman. We looked at each other, with my fingers still inside her. Her face was bright red and her eyes were hazy. My panties were soaked.

With a small smile playing at her lips and a sexy look in her eyes, Kelly ran her hands down my back, coming to a stop where my lower back ran into my bottom. I curled my fingers towards me. She juddered, then tilted her head to the side, allowing me to kiss her mouth and find her tongue.

"Dare I say it, but are there any more... *demands?*"

The need between my legs drew my attention. Carefully, I removed my fingers, and licked them. The look on Kelly's face was of pure desire and mild shock. I moved backwards a few paces to rest against the edge of her desk, putting my hands on the edge and leaning back. I opened my legs. "Just one."

Kelly opened her mouth to speak but no words came out. I loved surprising her like this. She removed her skirt and bra, to stand completely naked in front of me except for heels and stockings. She stepped towards me and lowered herself to her knees, and I nearly died.

Thirteen

Kelly ran behind Barley on the trail, her breathing steady and strong. Mud splashed up the back of her calves. She loved a good morning run. Since that day Myla came into the office, they'd seen each other every other day, as often as Kelly's schedule would allow. Last night, Myla had turned her over and fucked her so hard she actually shouted when she orgasmed. Kelly had *never* been this compatible with a lover. Myla's youthful energy seemed to match her own so well. They just got each other. They clicked. Myla knew her body well by this point, what she liked, what she was less keen on. Their openness to discuss their sexual preferences was refreshing.

The underlying friendship was still there, but it was becoming increasingly difficult to separate the two, as when they would message each other during the day, it quickly turned flirty. Myla sometimes mentioned snippets about what she was writing and things she was finding out about her family. It just always ended up coming back to them meeting up and tearing each other's clothes off. Barley even had a favourite spot on Myla's sofa that suited him fine as they… attended to other things upstairs.

Georgia had said she hardly recognised Kelly any more, given how much happier she seemed. Georgia had no idea it had anything to do with having the owner of the distillery as a fuck buddy.

Kelly's muscles were sore from all their activities in the bedroom, but she needed this run to work out some energy and work through her feelings. She needed to clear her head and a leisurely walk wouldn't cut it. They still hadn't spent the full night in each other's beds and generally didn't talk about how either of them felt about the situation, which was fast becoming silly. Kelly's feelings landed mostly on worry, frustration and hope: worry that this would all end in tears, frustration that this wasn't simple, and hope that soon Myla would ask for more than their current situation. Kelly didn't want to pressurise Myla into getting into a relationship before either of them was ready. Falling for your friend with benefits who was also your boss and ten years younger wasn't a straightforward idea in anyone's playbook. Kelly had to figure out a way to come through this situation in a way that was healthy for both of them and keep them in each other's lives.

Her head was in a spin but she knew one thing for sure: she was in love with Myla Murray, the new owner of Glenbuinidh. God, she was such a typical lesbian falling for someone so quickly.

She was due a visit to her parents. After her run she showered and went over for elevenses. Her mum was on the phone when she got there and mouthed 'I'm sorry won't be long' while holding the phone away from her ear and covering it with her hand. That her mum still didn't know how to use the mute button made her smile. She went through to the conservatory where her dad was reading a book.

"Ah, there you are," he said, mostly to Barley. Barley sat by her dad's feet wagging his tail, quietly accepting his pats on the head. "Your mum answered the phone just before you arrived and now she's on a roll. Same as usual."

"I don't mind waiting." She took a seat across from him, relieved to be sitting down for a second.

"How are things going at Glenbuinidh?" An update on the distillery was one of the first things Kelly's dad usually asked her about and today was no different. He was still focused on the distillery and his various committees and boards that he sat on. Kelly was okay to talk shop normally but today it triggered her a bit. Why didn't he want to ask her about *her* first?

"Yep, fine."

"Good. And how is Myla? Has she said what she wants from Glenbuinidh yet? Does she know?"

The mention of Myla from her dad jarred, and the fact that he only wanted to know how she was in relation to the distillery too. Did everything come down to that for him? "She's well. She's going to join me at the annual tourism summit."

"Hurrah," he sang. "Good for her for getting involved. I'm sure everyone will be interested to know who she is after all this time."

"I'm not sure they'll care that much, Dad." This she knew was inaccurate. She knew people would be interested, just not as much as *she* cared about Myla for more reasons than she had any business in having. For one, she was presenting at the conference. It had been a spur of the moment thing to invite Myla along. While it would be good for Myla to get acquainted with the world that Glenbuinidh inhabited, Kelly hadn't thought through the implications of bringing along the new and very young and inexperienced owner of their internationally acclaimed whisky brand.

Would she send Glenbuinidh off the rails? How was the relationship between the CEO and new owner? Do they get along? Would there be changes? Drama? These were the questions she knew the people would be asking among themselves while looking over their shoulder at the young and very beautiful new owner with a rather unclear link to Margaret's family other than blood line. It was quite possibly the worst thing she could have done for Glenbuinidh, herself, and Myla at this point in time, hence the overall sense of dread about the event. Yet, part of Kelly wanted Myla to jump in at the deep end. To finally see for herself what it was all about, other than a sleepy distillery in the middle of the Highlands. Sometimes, seeing something for yourself was the best way to understand it.

"I'd keep an eye out for any dodgy players at the event. I'd rather they don't have much access to Myla, for her sake as much as anything."

Ah yes, those guys. She hadn't heard anything about their enquiries since Myla had shown up. Their disappearance was ominous. Hopefully that was the last they would be hearing of them. Myla wouldn't sway, not now. She also appreciated the concern for Myla's wellbeing, finally, from her dad. "If anyone makes a move, I'll tell them where to go. Don't worry."

"Tell who where to go where?" Her mum came in, phone still in her hand.

"Anyone who wants to stick their nose into the distillery's business," Kelly's dad said.

"Quite right." Mum sat down. "That was Nicole by the way. She was out last night and has a hangover but all's well. She sends her love." Her mum regarded her carefully. "You look a bit tired, my love. You're not doing too much again, are you?"

"It's just been a busy week. I'm going to relax today."

"Good. And how is Myla?"

Her mum asked this innocently enough, and Kelly was strangely grateful that she'd thought to think about Myla's wellbeing, but Kelly prickled at the question nonetheless. "She's fine. I think she's getting on okay. Why do you ask?"

"Oh, you know, every time you're here you talk about her. Are you seeing a lot of her these days?"

"Sometimes."

"That's good. She's a lovely girl. I'm glad you've found a new friend in her."

Kelly tensed up. Did her mum know something she wasn't letting on? Kelly didn't want to talk to her parents about Myla. She didn't think they would approve of what was going on between them if they knew. "Yeah, she's great."

"Great. Now, who's for elevenses?"

"Thought you'd never ask," Kelly said, glad she was in the clear from any further talk about Myla with her parents.

***

Kelly arrived at the bar at the tail end of Anna's photoshoot and interview for the Women in Whisky initiative. Susan, one of the members of the initiative who worked in PR and Marketing for another large distillery, had volunteered to organise and do all of the interviews herself. Kelly had done her interview months ago, as one of the first. She waited behind the camera while Anna chatted away. Anna could tell you everything about Scotch whisky, its many different smells, tastes, ingredients and more. Her nose was a pro, and she held her own with the self-proclaimed, mostly male, 'master whisky tasters'. She was excellent at her job and this place wouldn't be the same without her. This type of insight into Anna's world was exactly what was needed. Kelly was bored of the stuffy-old-man image that sometimes came with the drink. Or of the high-powered executives and their glamorised low-key alcoholism. It was time for a new image.

"It was a pleasure talking to you, Anna. All the best."

"Thanks for coming all the way up to speak to me."

Kelly took her cue and joined them as Susan's assistant dismantled the camera equipment and lighting. She had a quick chat with Susan and Anna about how the interview went and when it would be ready for sharing. Two weeks, apparently.

"Could we do a feature on the new owner, Myla Murray?" Susan said.

The question threw Kelly off her stride. She hadn't thought of Myla in that way yet, but the link that Susan was making now made complete sense. Was Myla ready to tell her story yet? Did she have enough of a role in the distillery to say much? Despite knowing it would come off sounding dismissive, she had to tell the truth to Susan. "I don't think now's a good time. She's still getting her head around it all. But maybe in future?"

"Sure. That's fine. Do see if she's interested though. She'd be great for the initiative. It's a fascinating story. I'd love to meet her."

Kelly felt uneasy about Susan's request, but she knew it was a good idea and would ask Myla about it soon, perhaps after the summit. It might not be wise to overwhelm Myla with everything at once.

Susan didn't hang around for long after that. She had a demanding job in a big distillery in the lowlands and the initiative was on her own time. Before long, the bar was quiet again and it was just Kelly and Anna.

"How'd it go?" Kelly took a seat at the bar.

"Really good. It's fun to be asked to talk about what you love doing. I enjoyed it."

Kelly smiled. "Glad to hear it."

Anna looked up at the clock. "Next tour will be here in twenty minutes."

"I'd better leave you to it then."

"No, it's cool. I'm prepared. Just thought you should know."

"Okay." Kelly was dying for a chat with Anna, what with everything going on with her and Myla, and they hadn't caught up in ages, it felt. "So what's new?"

Anna slid onto the bar stool next to her. She blew out a deep breath. "I heard from Hayley."

"What did she say?"

"She sent me another long email. She's serious about it. She's going to quit her job and come back to Scotland."

Kelly's eyes widened. "Really?"

"I'm trying not to get my hopes up."

Anna had met Hayley at university while Hayley was doing an exchange year from the US. They were friends. Anna had fallen madly in love but had never said anything. They slept together once, on Hayley's last night before she left to go back to the States, but it didn't go anywhere. They lost touch but started talking again last year.

"Why is she coming here?"

"She hates her job. She wants to start over in the place she loves, which is Scotland. She wants to buy a campervan and travel and be free. And then go all over Europe. Find herself and all that. She'd just be coming here for a long holiday. It's not for me."

"From what you've told me about her she seems quite corporate."

"That's what she says she hates. She never used to be like that. She's a free spirit who's followed the path but now wants out. She wants to prioritise joy and pleasure. I'm even more in love with her for that."

"Brave girl. Not many people have the courage or the means to walk away."

"I know. She says her family are going to be so pissed, but she has to do it. They paid for her education, and she's worried they're going to think she's not grateful, but she can't go on working for some big company being absolutely miserable for the rest of her life."

"Didn't she go to Princeton or something?"

"Yeah. Exactly. So it is a lot bigger than her coming back here for me, as in, it's got nothing to do with me, really." Anna shook her head. "We haven't seen each other in person in years. She doesn't know how I feel about her."

Kelly highly doubted that. "Yeah. Right."

Anna scratched her chin and looked away towards the window and the rugged mountains. Dark clouds bunched above them, threatening an afternoon of rain. Kelly knew how much this had cut Anna up and hated to see her like this. Anna had thought her feelings would go away over time, but they hadn't. And when they'd started talking again, Anna had been a different person – much happier, but also, it had re-ignited a painful unrequited love which came with its own downsides. And Kelly had been trying to support her through it.

Anna turned towards Kelly again, seemingly having shrugged off whatever thoughts she was having about Hayley for the moment. "Anyway, how are you? Not seen you as much lately."

Kelly bit her bottom lip, aware how shocking this was going to sound. "I'm sleeping with Myla."

Anna's eyes widened. "Really?"

Kelly nodded. The words sounded so outlandish saying them out loud. "Yes."

"Fuck me. Right. Tell me everything." Anna glanced up at the clock. "Fuck. Tour. Right. Will you come by afterwards?"

Kelly grimaced. "I have plans. With Myla."

Anna shook her head. "Of course you do. Right. Okay. Is everything okay?"

Kelly found herself smiling from what felt like ear to ear. "I'm really happy. That's about all I can give you right now."

***

The packed conference loomed over Kelly. She was on stage behind a lectern underneath a huge screen showing her slides. In truth, it wasn't the venue or the large audience making her feel self-conscious, but one blue-eyed young woman looking directly at her. Myla's gaze penetrated something in Kelly. She'd never felt so *seen*. So utterly raw and exposed – physically, mentally, emotionally, and well – sexually. Kelly was starting to feel like her old self again. Even being here at this event felt fun again, and that was truly a feat given she had grown so bored of attending this every year. Kelly was in love. She knew this feeling, she'd felt it once before, but not nearly as strongly.

Myla was wearing a smart fitted suit and heels for the summit. The professional outfit accentuated something about Myla's calm and considered nature. Kelly could visualise Myla in ten years, the epitome of elegance and poise. More grounded and sure of herself. But today, Myla was young, all fire and quiet passion. She was blossoming. It was truly hard to look away from her. She was a beautiful, kind, and creative young woman with her whole life ahead of her. In many ways, they were in two very different places in their lives, weren't they? Kelly's was slowing down while Myla's was speeding up. She didn't want to hold Myla back. She already cared about her too much to do that.

Could it really work out between them?

Taking a deep breath, she continued her talk, thankfully nearing the end, and thankfully able to talk on autopilot given that her attention was elsewhere. Glenbuinidh's continued success was of interest to other businesses who received knock-on trade and was why Kelly had been invited to speak today.

"Before I end, I want to make a quick announcement, if I may." In a split-second decision, she decided to introduce Myla to the world, hoping that Myla would be okay with not having been warned in advance. "In light of the recent passing of our former owner, the beloved Margaret McCallister, we have a new owner of Glenbuinidh Distillery. Her great-niece, Myla Murray, has taken over the business. We are delighted to be working with Ms Murray and look forward to a successful partnership. I'll be happy to take any questions throughout the day or later by email on the matter. Thank you."

And with that, she picked up her notebook and took her seat to the polite applause that followed. She leant over and whispered into Myla's ear. "I hope that was okay to introduce you like that? I just thought of it."

Myla shrugged, not looking bothered in the slightest. The confidence of youth was a beautiful thing. "Sure thing. If it helps you out."

Lunch followed the speaker after Kelly. About two hundred people in business attire headed straight for the buffet, forming a very British queue that snaked right back into the auditorium.

"These people are *really* wanting their lunch," Myla said, queuing beside Kelly with an amused grin.

Kelly shrugged. "It's a free lunch at a work thing. It's probably why most came."

Myla laughed, good-naturedly. "I like their priorities. The beautiful remote location on the banks of that loch can't be hurting either."

"True," Kelly looked towards the windows lining one side of the sprawling country hotel with stunning loch views. Living among this natural beauty was such a privilege. "It doesn't hurt."

"Kelly?" Wincing, she turned around to see her ex-girlfriend. She hadn't seen her since this event two years ago.

"Gemma. Hi."

"It's good to see you." She leaned in to peck her on the cheek and she obliged, out of habit and politeness more than anything.

"And you."

"I saw your presentation. That was some bombshell you dropped in at the end there. But then, you always did know how to work an audience."

Ah, Gemma. The perpetual flirt. "This is Myla," she paused, unsure how to introduce Myla to Gemma. "The new owner of Glenbuinidh." Was it cold to introduce her like that to Gemma? What else could she say? Her much younger friend who she was currently fucking?

"The very person. Good to meet you, Myla." Gemma held out her hand and regarded Myla closely, pissing Kelly off.

"Pleasure," Myla said, coolly.

"Myla is staying up in Balbuinidh these days." What the hell was she saying? Why give Gemma more ammunition?

"Oh really," Gemma replied, eyebrows raised. "And how do you find it up there in the middle of nowhere?"

Myla took her time in replying, which Kelly loved. Gemma waited for her response. "It's like heaven on earth. I love it."

"To each their own." Gemma's accent had come back a bit stronger after having moved back to Glasgow, Kelly noted. "I prefer a bit more life about me, but hey, whatever floats your boat."

She'd split with Gemma five years ago. They'd met in London towards the end of Kelly's time down there. Back then, they both enjoyed the same things – going out all the time and partying hard. Gemma tried living in Scotland again for a while after Kelly took over as CEO, more like two weeks, but Gemma couldn't settle in Balbuinidh. It was too small and unstimulating for her. Their split was amicable enough. Kelly hadn't dated anyone seriously since.

For a few more minutes she and Gemma caught up on some pleasantries and she was reminded just how much she liked her, despite her somewhat annoying introduction to Myla. She was clever and kind, deep down, but the relationship was never going to fulfil her. It never had. Gemma wasn't a very emotional person and Kelly had found herself pretending to be a similar way sometimes, which she despised. Plus, the sex just wasn't good enough considering they didn't have the complete package. The longer they stood chatting Kelly wondered why she had stayed with her for so long.

They agreed to keep in touch more as the conversation came to a close. Kelly turned back to face Myla, after somewhat neglecting her to talk to Gemma, and having barely made any progress in the queue.

"Who was that?" Myla's voice was flat and her expression faintly hostile. Myla had her arms crossed and a tightly set jaw. Kelly hadn't seen her like this before. It could only be described as jealousy. That had to be a good sign she was into her too, right? Feeling guilty for coming to that conclusion despite Myla's obvious discomfort, Kelly treaded softly, keeping her voice low. "My ex-girlfriend." She watched as Myla turned away from her, facing the back of the person in front of her and stared ahead. She seemed upset. Kelly's stomach knotted. "Are you okay about that?"

"Yes. Fine," she turned towards her again, searching her eyes sincerely, it made Kelly's breath catch. "Sorry." She shook her head in that way she did, almost more for herself than anything else. "She seemed nice."

"She is. We split up five years ago."

"Oh."

As they neared the buffet the smells were making Kelly hungry. She was starving, having only had a banana for breakfast in the rush to get here this morning. Once they got their food, Kelly led them to a free table, wanting a bit of a breather before all the networking this afternoon. Almost as soon as they sat down, two men in suits asked if they could join them. Kelly didn't recognise them.

"Congratulations on taking over Glenbuinidh," the older man said to Myla. "You must be very pleased."

Myla didn't bat an eyelid. "Thank you."

Kelly listened as the men chatted to Myla and only Myla about 'the whisky business' through their meal. She wasn't bothered about not being brought into the conversation. What bothered her was that the men were trying to manipulate Myla, and so blatantly right in front of her.

"We'd be interested to discuss some ideas with you." A business card was slid over the table. Kelly didn't recognise the name, which was a red flag on top of the already outrageous approach. Who were these two jokers?

"Is there a number we can reach you on?"

"Oh, I don't have a business card," Myla said. She picked up an unused napkin and a pen. "Here, let me write it on the back of this."

"What was it, exactly, that you wished to discuss?"

Begrudgingly, the two men acknowledged Kelly.

The main guy frowned.

Myla stopped writing.

"You can direct any enquiries you have to me."

"Certainly."

Kelly tossed them both one of her business cards each, hoping to demonstrate her utter disdain for this performance and her wish for them to fuck off immediately. "Here you go."

After some further painful small talk, the two men left the table, leaving their dirty plates and empty glasses. Assholes.

"Sorry," Myla said. "I thought I was being helpful."

Kelly's heart melted. "Please don't say sorry. But if you get any more pushy enquiries like that would you mind referring them to me or the distillery management team? Equally, you could just say you're not interested at this time."

"Sure thing. I don't even know why they were so interested in me."

"You're in a powerful position. Some of these people will want to get in with you for their own gain. I don't mean to sound patronising, but you should be aware of it, if you aren't already."

"No problem. Be the aloof top-dog. Got it."

Back in the auditorium after lunch there were three more speakers. Myla seemed greatly interested in them, leaning forward and hanging off their every word. Who knew that national parks, visitor numbers and sustainable tourism practices would be so riveting?

When they moved onto the breakout rooms and networking, Myla seemed full of energy. "This is so much more interesting than I thought it was going to be. I had no idea so much went into these things. So many organisations doing so much."

Her comment was cute, and it lifted Kelly. She'd attended countless summits like this before but seeing it from Myla's perspective made it seem that bit fresher and more stimulating. This was just another example of the ways in which Myla made her life… *better*. She just seemed to infuse things with a new energy that Kelly had been lacking in recent years. "Scottish tourism is diverse. I like your enthusiasm. It's infectious."

"I'm glad I can be useful for something."

"Which talk did you like the most?"

"The one about visitors. It got me wondering about how we cater to visitors at Glenbuinidh."

"Then you should talk to Linda, the Visitor Experience Manager. I'm sure she'd be happy to go into it with you."

The Glenbuinidh stall was big and bold, and exuded quality and luxury. Georgia was talking to someone, but

Anna was free. Kelly was proud of their brand, and even prouder of her team on days like this. "Great job, Anna. Stand looks wonderful."

Anna smiled. "Cheers boss. Nice to see you again, Myla. How are you enjoying the summit?"

Myla fiddled with her lanyard. "I'm totally out of my depth but I'm loving it."

"And you got outed this morning, I hear?"

Myla glanced at Kelly.

"Yes I did that on the spur of the moment."

"I don't mind."

Kelly shared some words about the event with Anna as Myla looked around the stall. Myla was studying the timeline of the history of the distillery displayed across the whole back wall. She was having such a great day because Myla was here. This feeling was deeper than just a better than average workday. She loved it when Myla was around. It was that simple.

Later at the networking part of the conference, Kelly looked up from her spot beside a pillar in the main foyer surrounded by people, to see Myla making her way through the crowd. Just like when they first met, Kelly was mesmerised by her. They locked eyes and Kelly's tummy fluttered. She had this ethereal quality that Kelly was so enamoured by.

"Your coffee, *mademoiselle*."

"*Merci beaucoup*."

Kelly took the cup from Myla and not so subtly raked her eyes over Myla's mouth, putting Kelly in mind of all the things they could be doing right now instead of networking at an industry event.

Frustratingly, that was the last of their private interaction. The afternoon ran away with itself, and they got firmly caught up in the whirlwind. Kelly networked and Myla stayed by her side like a lost puppy. Myla became increasingly subdued as the afternoon went on. She seemed to just sink into herself and became very quiet. It was a worry. Kelly didn't get a chance to ask her if she was okay due to being locked in conversation with so many people for so long, but it was on her mind the entire time. Myla's face went from vaguely bored to completely checked out towards the end. It wasn't until six that they finally made it through the gauntlet and back to the car. Myla hadn't said a word since they got in and they'd been driving for a while. It had been a long day, maybe Myla was just tired?

"Hey," Kelly said, gently. "Are you asleep over there?"

A beat passed before Myla spoke. "No. Just watching the road."

"Is everything okay?"

"Yes."

"How did you find the summit?"

"Interesting. I understand the world a bit more."

"That's good. I'm glad."

"You were brilliant today." Myla was still quiet. Her words conflicted with her general vibe.

Kelly was confused. "Thanks."

The rest of the drive home passed in silence. They were nearing home. Kelly had to make the decision about which route to take if they were going to be seeing each other tonight. "Do you want to come back to mine tonight?" Kelly glanced over at Myla.

"Thank you but I think I just want to go home tonight. Be by myself."

The tired tone of Myla's voice suggested a weariness that not even a friendly chat and certainly not a serious conversation about their *friendship* would help.

"No problem."

When Kelly parked in front of Myla's house, part of her screamed inside to just tell Myla how she felt – to finally reveal the depth of her feelings, and to just cut through this lack of honest communication. They needed to talk. But sitting in the car across from each other in the dark didn't feel like the right time to discuss anything important. It didn't feel safe. Kelly's wiser side *insisted* that she hold back, at least for now. Myla had withdrawn and Kelly knew better than to chase someone when they were like that. It would only make matters worse. She could tell there was a lot going on inside Myla's head and she wasn't prepared enough for the answer that might come. Kelly couldn't think of anything to say that would make it better right now without sparking a whole conversation about things that neither of them seemed to be in the right place to discuss.

Instead, it was Myla who spoke first. She cleared her throat. "Thank you for today and thank you for the lift. I appreciate it."

"You're welcome." They held each other's eyes. So much unspoken hung between them. "I'm really happy you made it."

Myla averted her eyes and stayed quiet, giving her no response. It was like she'd completely shut down. Kelly was going to the US for work soon so they might not have time to sort this out before she left. The trip was to meet with major importers of Scottish whisky in the US and hopefully sign an exciting distribution deal. She couldn't skip it. She didn't want to skip it. She'd been looking forward to it for months. "I'm going to New York in a couple of days."

Myla still didn't say anything.

A few moments passed. "So, I'll see you a couple of weeks?"

"Yeah," Myla said, hooking her fingers around the door handle. "Thanks for today. I hope it goes well. Have a good trip. I'll see you when you get back."

And with that, she opened the door, got out, and shut it behind her with another sad and small smile that did nothing to make Kelly feel any better. Myla's mood was like a punch in the stomach. Kelly had no idea what was wrong. Today had been a bad idea. A stupid idea that had messed everything up. Something had got to Myla today. Kelly took a deep breath, looking out of her window as Myla went into the house and closed the door. Pushing herself back into her seat with all her strength she gripped the steering wheel tightly until her fingers began to hurt.

As much as she hated to admit it, because she was rarely as happy as when she was in Myla's company, maybe some breathing space between them was what they both needed right now. With that, she let go of her grip on the wheel, turned on the car and drove the short distance home.

Fourteen

The house was cold when I got in. All I wanted was to sit in front of the fire and cry into a hot water bottle. I felt like shit. I needed to get out of these clothes. They were restrictive and uncomfortable. I hadn't worn anything as smart since a failed job interview years ago. They just weren't me. I trekked up to my room, took a quick shower and got into my pyjamas, thinking about Kelly the whole time. She was magnificent, beautiful, radiant. Words couldn't describe how much I admired her. She was a respected professional with the skills to command an entire audience and endless people wanting to talk to her all day.

What she saw in me, I did not know.

As the summit wore on, I saw our situation for what it was, and the dawning realisation made me so depressed. Yes, we were friends, and I was happy about that, to an extent. But my feelings for Kelly were only growing stronger. Clearly, the only thing that was going to happen here was me getting hurt. Big time. Kelly didn't want a real relationship, that much was clear. She just wanted a casual fuck buddy whenever it suited her, away from the eyes of anyone that really mattered in her life. I thought I could do casual sex with a new friend, but I was fast learning that I could not. Not when that new friend was the best person I'd ever met and makes me feel like the sun is rising inside my heart every time I'm with her.

Logs were thrown into the fire and set alight, and a hot water bottle was made. I threw a blanket around my shoulders and pulled the wing-back chair closer to the fire. I was so cold. Staring into the flames that were now licking at the top of the stove, I started to warm up a bit. The summit had been a lot to take in. The whole day had got under my skin in so many ways. Having people come up to me and wanting things was such a head-fuck. At first, I was kind of flattered. But soon it became obvious and kind of absurd. The men at lunch were probably the worst. I handled them so badly, and Kelly had had to step in. She was kind about it, but I just felt like an idiot. I realised afterwards that the two men must have thought I could be easily manipulated, and I *hated* being underestimated.

Kelly's ex showed me just how out of my league Kelly truly was. The woman was attractive and classy. The way she'd looked at Kelly, with that knowing look that only past lovers shared, made my insides boil.

Yes, I was jealous.

I wasn't good enough for Kelly, and that was why, ultimately, she was never going to choose me in a meaningful way. All this talk about me being her boss, me being too young for her, or even, and this was the biggest stretch – that I was 'going through a lot', all screamed of one thing: Kelly just wasn't into me as much as I was into her. Sure, Kelly seemed to be enjoying fucking a younger woman and we did have a connection, but that 'thing' that I felt in my entire body, that light that was now firmly lit for her, just wasn't being reflected back to me. I gulped, pushing down the emotions that were threatening to boil over into tears.

I shouldn't have let this happen. I shouldn't have opened myself up to Kelly and made myself so vulnerable. What was I thinking! I'd had to practically beg to sleep with me that first time. She never stayed with me after sex, and she wasn't a cuddler. Not even after some of the most life changing orgasms I'd ever had.

That in itself spoke volumes.

It was never going to happen. I couldn't go on like this. It killed me to admit it, but it was true. I might as well realise it now and begin the process of protecting my wounded little heart. I sat back in my chair and a rogue tear slipped out from my eye. This feeling of being hurt had been building since the first night we slept together, and Kelly hadn't even asked me to stay over. I couldn't take this. I wasn't as strong as I thought I was. I didn't have it in me to wait and pine and hope. As I dried my cheek with the back of my sleeve, the only thing that made sense was to stop having sex with Kelly and hope that in time we could still be friends.

Over the next few days, I got serious about the house by getting in touch with Jenny's husband and an electrician. I bought some new paint and made a start in the bedrooms. Doing this gave me a purpose and it made me feel like I was doing right by Margaret and the house. It also took my mind off Kelly... until it didn't.

I picked up my guitar, randomly, and started feeling out some new songs. I wrote a bit, but it was all terrible. Well, most of it. I did make one song about Kelly that got all my feelings out in a cathartic sort of way. But there was nowhere for my feelings to go now but away. It was never going to happen. All I needed now was to restore this house, sort out my life and go back to Edinburgh and figure out what I was going to do next.

***

"You're moving out?" I felt sick. Rebecca and I were sitting in our old seats. It seemed so normal, but it wasn't any more. I'd come down to Edinburgh for a bit of normality and a break from Balbuinidh. I also had to deal with some letters and speak to Michelle. I'd neglected my life down here and now Rebecca was leaving. It was all getting very real.

"Josh and I are moving in together. You've been so generous covering the rent here, but the lease is up soon so I thought you wouldn't mind seeing as you're living up north now. I'm sorry. I hope that's okay?"

I felt shaken. Rebecca had been my safety blanket since I'd moved to Edinburgh, but she was absolutely right to do what was best for her and had nothing to apologise for. I had to get a grip of myself here. "No, please, don't apologise. I'm being ridiculous. This is wonderful news."

"You don't look like it's wonderful news."

"I'm sorry. It's just that everything is changing so fast. But you're doing the right thing. I'll be okay. We're all good."

"I know it's huge, Myla. I'm glad we got to talk in person though. It's great to see you. I've missed you."

I smiled. "I've missed you too. Where is the new place?"

"It's beside the university. Easier for both of us."

I took a deep breath, thinking about when Rebecca and Josh had first got together and how ecstatic Rebecca had been. How in love. I was happy for my friend and knew deep down that we wouldn't have stayed sharing a flat forever.

"How are things at the mansion?"

"Yeah, great. I'm getting it fixed up. I want to return it to its former glory."

"Check you out, you proper grown up. You've got it so made. Millions of pounds in the bank and a hot fuck buddy situation with a powerful and beautiful older woman. If I was a lesbian, I'd be jealous."

Rebecca was right. From the outside, I had a lot. And I was immensely grateful for my good fortune. For the inheritance. For meeting Kelly. But was being with Kelly but not really being with her good for me? "I'm thinking of ending being friends with benefits."

"Oh no. How come?" Rebecca was interested without judgement which was such a gift in a friend. It wasn't easy for me to open up like this, but I needed to talk about it.

"Because I think I'm going to get hurt. I think I already am."

"What happened?"

"She's not interested in a real relationship with me and it just... hurts. I shouldn't even be feeling this way because she's always been clear that it wasn't going anywhere."

"Do you know that for sure?"

"It was to be a one-time thing at first, because I basically begged her for sex. I know, so embarrassing. And then she wanted to be friends with benefits. We do get on well and I do value her as a person in my life, but overall, her stance is still the same. It's just a casual thing for her. She doesn't even stay after we... you know."

Rebecca had her thinking face on, absorbing the information. "Hmm."

"And that's not even mentioning the reasons she's overtly given for why it wouldn't be a good idea. There's a ton, apparently: I'm her boss, I'm ten years younger, and she even says I'm dealing with *a lot* because of the inheritance and stuff. It's like she's clutching at reasons for us not to explore whatever nice spark we had between us."

"Had?"

I shook my head. "It's still there, which makes this all the more complicated."

Rebecca tapped her fingers together. "If she's your friend then I don't think she's intent on hurting you, and if she's having sex with you then she obviously likes you more than a friend. I've never understood the whole friends with benefits thing, but maybe that's just me. Maybe she does want more and is just scared? It sounds like she has more to lose than you do."

What Rebecca said got me thinking. Hoping, even. But hope can be a dangerous thing. It can hurt you more than anything else in this world.

"She's too good for me."

Rebecca scoffed. "She runs a distillery, so what? Didn't her dad give her the job? I mean, come on… And you're definitely in her league looks wise. That picture you sent of the two of you on the hill was so sweet. You look great together. The same level of hot."

"It's not about looks, though, is it? I'm broken inside and she's… well, she's just perfect."

Rebecca held her arms out. "Hug. Now." I leant into my best friend's arms, savouring her warmth and kindness. "You're a wonderful person. Hard as fuck to get to know but once you do, you're a gem. Kelly would be lucky to have you. Don't forget it."

I laughed. "Thanks, Bec. Keeping it real, as always. I'm glad we got to live together for such a long time."

"The glory days."

We lightened up after that and started talking about the good times we'd had in the flat over the years, like Rebecca's twenty-fifth birthday party where half of her class at university ended up squashed into our tiny flat. Rebecca said she wasn't drinking tonight, and I couldn't face drinking alone, so we made a big pot of tea and shared that.

Closing the door after a long hug goodbye and then watching from the window as she got in the cab with the last of her plants, the world felt *changed*. My world was changing. It had already changed. Sitting down on our sofa stripped of Rebecca's comforting cushions and her nice throw, I didn't know what to do with myself.

It was just so empty.

It didn't feel like home any more. I could renew the lease, and try to revive it, but that was unlikely. It was tiny and cramped. No. I had a new home now. Up in the Highlands. My great-aunt's home. My grandmother's childhood home. Somewhere my mother would have known and visited. That was where I needed to be right now. It was pulling me back. I could always buy a city centre penthouse apartment at some point and watch the sunset from my floor to ceiling windows sipping champagne from the bottle on the balcony if I wanted. But I was in no rush to live that dream lifestyle. Would it make me feel any better, anyway? The money hadn't magically made me happy all the time so far. And I already had one house to focus on.

If someone had told me six months ago I'd inherit a family fortune and be living in a mansion in the Highlands, I would have laughed in their face. But it was true. The estate was mine now. I was making connections up there. I liked Balbuinidh. I liked the people. It made sense to me.

I thought of Kelly as I got into bed. My old bed was so warm and cosy, even if it didn't cost a fortune. Maybe Rebecca was onto something. What if she did like me more than she was letting on and was holding back for some reason? That would be *everything*.

I wanted Kelly in my life, ideally as my girlfriend, but if not, once I got over her, maybe I could accept just knowing her as a friend, in the long run. All I knew was that I couldn't go on being friends with benefits any more. And I had to talk to her about it. We always said we'd be friends first and tell each other how we felt, and well, I had to actually do that now. For my sanity, as much as anything else.

With my eyes closed, drifting towards sleep, thinking of her brought me comfort even while contemplating never being close to her again. Warm brown eyes and thick dark hair enveloped me like a blanket. Seeing her face, seeing her smile, cast a warm haze over me as I slipped off into sleep dreaming of the only person who had ever made me feel happy.

***

The next day I pulled myself together and walked to the café to see Michelle first thing in the morning. It was strange, taking my old route to work. So much had changed since that cold and dark morning in the height of winter before I got the call from Graeme.

"There you are!" Michelle came in for a hug, her order pad and pen pressing into my back. "It's great to see you."

The café was full, which was always good to see. Michelle had two new people working.

"Let's go in the back. Too busy out here."

Michelle passed her orders to the young girl over the counter. Her youth reminded me of who I used to be. Fresh-faced and eager to please.

We took seats in the cramped office-come-store cupboard and caught up, finding a surprising amount had happened for both of us. Michelle was in the process of listing the café as an LGBTQIA+ friendly café in local food and drink networks and on the website. She was going to put a pride flag in the window. I would have loved to have been around for it.

The familiar noises of customers chatting, chairs moving on the wooden floor and the coffee grinder soothed me. Yet, this no longer felt like the only place I could go to for comfort. I'd decided to quit the café and needed to tell Michelle face to face. It was only right.

"I've decided not to come back. I'm sorry I messed you around these past few months."

"You haven't. I didn't think you would be back, to be honest. I hired some students. Everything is fine here."

"As long as you're not in the lurch." I'd been easily replaced, but I understood.

Michelle's eyes were kind. "I will miss working with you, Myla. You've been my friend here all these years. You've helped me make this place what it is. I'll always be grateful to you for that."

"Aw, shucks, Michelle. If I'd known you were going to say something as sweet as that I might not have quit."

Michelle laughed. "Go, be free and do whatever your heart desires. It's what most people can only dream about. We'll stay friends, regardless of if you work in the café or not. I hope you know that, right?"

"I know."

"So, what are you up to? What are your plans?"

I ran my hands through my hair, unsure of where to start. "Loads. I'm renovating the house. You'll have to come up and visit once it's been done up."

"I'd love to."

"I'm playing music again. I want to find some people to collaborate with. Or join a band. There's a big folk scene up there that I want to get into. Then," I was aware that I was rambling now and how much had changed since just a few months ago when most of my days consisted of serving coffee to Michelle's customers and not much else. "I want to build an animal sanctuary on the land. Dogs, cats, horses, hedgehogs. Everything."

"I always knew you were a good 'un."

"It's the best thing I can think of. That and giving to various charities which I'm already doing. Give it away, that's my motto."

"So decent of you. And how's the distillery?"

"I'm getting a bit involved, but it's very light touch. It's interesting though. I literally have no idea what I'm doing but I'm keen to learn."

"I don't know what to say. It's all so amazing."

Michelle's reaction reminded me just how awesome things were now. How incredibly lucky I was. And I hadn't even told her about Kelly – well, the good things about Kelly. I shrugged, feeling reflective. "As cheesy as it sounds, you never know what life is going to throw at you."

"I'm happy for you, Myla." Michelle smiled, coffee machine grinding in the background.

I reached into my bag. "This is for you." I handed her a bottle of whisky in its case. "One of our finest bottles."

Michelle's face lit up. "Seriously?" She studied the bottle, turning it in her hands. "This is such a treat, thank you so much."

"There's more." I handed her an envelope.

"What's this?"

"Open it."

Michelle slid open the envelope and took out the letter I'd wrote to her expressing my gratitude for the past few years and a cheque for her to buy the café premises and potentially another one too. Her mouth fell open and she looked up at me in complete shock. "Myla this is too much! I can't accept this!"

"It isn't and you will. It's the least I can do. I've seen you struggle for years to keep this place afloat and create the life you want. You've made a space here that people love. Take it and enjoy it. Please."

Michelle continued to look at me for a few moments, clearly trying to process what had just happened and instantly looking less stressed. It made me so happy to see her like this. "Lovely Myla. You really do have a heart of gold."

I walked back to the flat, which was soon to be a thing of my past, on a high looking forward to fully embracing all that was unfolding, without having one foot in the past. I was going to jump in with both feet and see if I could create the sort life I'd always dreamed about, too. There was so much that I wanted to do.

Back in the flat, I made good time at gutting it and tidying up. A few hours later, my bags were packed, and a stack of full black bags sat at the front door. I'd finally thrown out all the clothes I used to wear in my partying days. A trip to the recycling centre and charity shop took up most of the afternoon. It was surprising how quickly I'd been able to pack up my life here.

I ordered pizza later that night and hung around the empty flat, thinking about my life. Kelly was the missing piece in my new life in the Highlands. Would we move forward just as friends? Or were there ingredients for an actual relationship between us? After everything that had gone through my head since the tourism summit, in the end, I knew I just needed to tell her how I felt and that was what I was going to do. I wanted more. Hopefully she did too.

The next morning I took a selfie before I locked the door for good and sent it to Rebecca and then Kelly saying I was moving to Balbuinidh. I only realised it was probably the middle of the night for Kelly in New York once I'd sent it. Hopefully I hadn't woken her. I wanted to show her that I was committing to Balbuinidh.

Rebecca replied immediately with a series of crying face emojis and broken hearts. I replied with a series of happy faces wrapped in hearts which were quickly reciprocated. I slipped my phone into my bag and left the flat for good, feeling surprisingly upbeat after all was said and done.

Fifteen

Kelly sat back in the comfortable leather chair and held her nerve. Victory was in sight. Her mission here was about to be realised. She had a new and highly desirable product. Buyers had been lining up, giving her the bargaining tools she needed to play them off each other. Being in the position of power made her job easier, of course, but she'd honed her negotiation skills over the years and now she was putting them to the ultimate test. She'd kept production costs low and was now about to sell high. *Very* high. It didn't get any better than this for their business. She was nearly there. She could practically taste it. "So do we have a deal?"

Ryan McCafferty, head of one of the largest distributors in the US, sat across from her. They'd been out to dinner twice this week and chatted after the New York Scotch Whisky Society's annual meeting, in an exclusive venue in the Upper East Side. The old leather chairs and paintings put Kelly in mind of the old boys' clubs that her dad would have fitted in so well at, in years gone by, and before that, Margaret's husband, who was known to have handled these types of things back in the day.

But now, she was the face of Glenbuinidh, and she had created a new and more feminine malt for the world to enjoy – Glenbuinidh: Queen of Spirits. The established brand was doing fine, but Kelly firmly believed they needed something different to offer as well.

Ryan held her eye for another beat and then she saw it, the moment of acquiescence in his eyes. "Yes. I think we do." He stood up and thrust his hand out. "Thank you for choosing us, Ms MacGregor. We'll push it far and wide."

Kelly was amazed that *he* was thanking *her*. They were agreeing to buy a shitload of their new whisky in addition to their signature twelve-year-old single malt in what must surely be one of the biggest distribution deals in recent years. Kelly had brought three bottles of Queen of Spirits with her to New York so she could let potential buyers taste the new malt. It had all been handled by their contact at the New York Scotch Whisky Society. From something that had come out of her suitcase, the fanfare that they'd made in the clubhouse bordered on the ridiculous. But she was immensely proud. "No, thank you. I'm glad we could come to an agreement."

Ryan stood with his hands on his hips in a state of glee. "I can't wait to get my hands on the new bottle. Queen of Spirits by Glenbuinidh is going to take the world by storm. It's got such a classic taste and invokes a Scotland that we want to know more about. Feminising whisky is long overdue. There's a huge market there. I think it's going to be a real game-changer."

"I'm delighted you think so. We're really looking forward to sharing it. I'd be more than happy to send you an advanced batch, if you like?"

The smile that grew on Ryan's face reminded Kelly of an excited five-year-old. He must have been over sixty, so it was kind of sweet. Kelly smiled back, loving this moment.

"That's very kind of you. Thank you very much."

After her meeting, Kelly headed across the city to meet Adam for dinner. The streets were packed full of people and traffic coming from all directions. Yellow cabs sped past as tall buildings flanked her on every side. She walked through the streets of New York on a high, feeling like a character from a TV show or film. She was *thrilled* with the deal. She stopped at the lights, brushing shoulders with fellow pedestrians, and buzzed with excitement. When the loud beeping sang out for them to cross, Kelly joined the crowd and thought back on her successful week here.

She'd presented the brand and marketing for the new bottle five different times in various boardrooms across the city, and everyone who'd seen it had seemed excited about it. The campaign centred around the Scottish folklore of Neachneohain, an ancient Gaelic Goddess. Something about the short film her team had made really seemed to capture the hearts and minds of people. There were too few Scottish female legends, and it was Kelly's mission to bring this particular Goddess to light.

It had been fun. She'd spent time in the New York Scotch Whisky Society, high-end bars, and quality restaurants not matched anywhere in the UK, in Kelly's opinion. She'd made a new connection with the Director of the New York Tartan Week and attended the Tartan Day Parade; the scale and passion of the celebration had made her feel proud. She'd enjoyed meeting people from around the world and was happy to have visited at a time when all things Scottish were being celebrated, although this was entirely intentional on Georgia's part.

A few clever and well-informed people asked about the new owner of Glenbuinidh; they wanted the low-down on the big news. Kelly steered those conversations towards something else.

And she'd received a once in a lifetime potential job offer. It started with an unexpected chat with the CEO of a global drinks corporation, Jeff Barry, at the Tartan Day Parade drinks at the whisky society. She'd seen him watching her at the event for a while before he came over when a gap allowed. The first thing Kelly noticed about him was his expensive suit and bright, sharp eyes. They'd made the usual pleasantries and he'd been super easy to talk to – charming, and with an intensity about him that Kelly liked.

"We've been watching your progress at Glenbuinidh for a while now. We think you'd be great for our company, and I'd love to discuss it further with you and introduce you to my colleagues." He'd said, with a captivating smile but a serious look in his eyes. "Is a new opportunity over here something you'd be interested in?"

Kelly just looked at the guy for a few seconds, unsure if she'd heard him right. She'd received one or two job offers when she networked or travelled to different countries in the past and had never considered them. But something about this man and the scale of his company gave Kelly pause. His world seemed bigger, and more exciting – all things that massively appealed to her. It was the best opportunity she'd been offered in years, since her embarrassingly nepotistic appointment as Glenbuinidh's CEO.

He had given Kelly his business card and she had taken it. "It might help to see it for yourself. If nothing else, it'd be great to have a coffee and more time to talk before you head back to the UK. A move of this nature would need to be discussed fully. I understand how serious a decision it would be."

Throughout her time in New York, she got increasingly interested in what he had to say. Living here, working here, the many things she could do in her spare time. Her life back in Glenbuinidh seemed so... *small* in comparison.

And with no word from Myla, Kelly was struggling to see what would keep her and Barley there any more.

So, she'd met with Jeff Barry and his team. They courted her rather than the other way around, which was so weird. Their office was at the top of some skyrise, and she'd felt so outside of herself the whole time. Like she was watching herself from above go in and meet with the high-powered executives and get shown around as if she belonged there. It seemed like a good fit. It was all very casual and slick. There were more people to meet before Jeff could make an official offer. He had to float it up the chain first, and his Board would want to meet her, but Jeff was fairly certain those video call meetings would be a formality. It was all just talk at this point, though.

While she'd been looking for change in her life, she wasn't sure if she wanted *this* change. Where would she walk Barley and would he be happy living in such a big city? Could she leave Balbuinidh and everything she'd built at Glenbuinidh? Her family? Her friendship with Anna? Could she really leave Myla and move to the US given that Kelly was in love with her?

She didn't know the answers to these questions, yet she couldn't deny she was tempted by the offer. This week, this walk down Fifth Avenue, everything here was heightened and exhilarating. She'd have her own corner office, assistant, and would work with clients from around the world. It was an exciting opportunity and would allow her to stretch herself.

"We'll double whatever compensation you're currently receiving, and you can have whatever car you want from our fleet," Jeff had said. "We're a family. We have people from over fifty countries and plenty of social activities. We look after our own."

Louder Than Words

Kelly had had an excellent week.

Yet internally it wasn't the same story. She'd missed Myla the entire time, carrying around a dull ache that never really went away. It didn't help that she spent every night listening to Myla's music on SoundCloud, in total awe at her creativity and fascinated to get such an intimate insight into Myla's past, her thoughts and her feelings. She'd published a lot between eight and ten years ago, so it really was raw talent she was hearing. Other songs appeared in randomly over the last decade, getting more sophisticated and distinctly sadder as time went on. It really didn't help with trying not to think about her all the time. They hadn't spoken or texted since the summit, nine days ago. Checking her phone to see if Myla had reached out was becoming a bad habit and one that was starting to drive her crazy, so she had forced herself to turn the phone off when it wasn't needed. Kelly was determined to give Myla some space, but it still stung.

She neared the Italian restaurant she was meeting Adam at. Her feet were starting to get sore walking in these four-inch heels.

She was also bothered by the fact that her dad wouldn't be fully on board with her success this week. He would describe it as a huge risk, but her instincts told her it would be worth it. Without Myla's encouragement or her blessing, she might not have pursued this deal with as much passion, either. There were no guarantees that the new bottle would sell as well as expected, but she was optimistic and it had been testing well. Even Georgia had come around to Queen of Spirits, lately. Something about it just *felt* right. Like this was the right time to take the old-fashioned whisky industry out of the past, finally, and modernise.

Adam was waiting outside on his phone, looking all busy and important. She hadn't seen him in nearly a year. He had on a nice shirt and jeans and had some dark stubble on his square jaw. He seemed so grown up and sophisticated, which made her feel ancient for a split second.

"Hey," Kelly said, smiling broadly. "If it isn't my wee brother standing in the middle of New York like a local."

He looked up and grinned, wrapping his arms around her in a big hug. Had he got stronger too? "Kelly. How are you?"

"Good. You're looking well. This place must agree with you. It's great to see you in the flesh."

He shrugged. "There was no way I was going to let you fly to the States and us not meet up."

"Aww. You miss me."

"Shut up. No I don't."

"So cute."

"Anyway. I thought we could do a bit of a bar crawl after dinner? There are a couple I'm dying to try out."

Kelly nodded. "Sounds great."

"There's the Kelly I used to know!"

"When did you ever know me like that? You were a child when I used to be fun."

"What can I say, you were my role model."

"Have you been doing *any* studying? Mum seems to think you're on track for a Nobel prize."

Adam laughed. "All the time. That's why I need to let off some steam tonight. I have an exam in three days!"

"And what better way to prepare than a night out drinking with your sister."

"Exactly." Adam laughed.

They went into the restaurant and were shown to their table. Kelly asked Adam about his year at MIT and how he was getting on. He'd met a girl and made lots of friends. Adam ate solidly for over an hour and Kelly told him about her new deal that she'd agreed this week and about the potential job offer. He stopped eating for that.

"Seriously?"

Kelly nodded.

"You might be coming here?"

"I don't know."

"That's so cool!"

Kelly looked down, touched by his enthusiasm but torn over what to say next, because she hadn't decided how she felt about it yet, and she didn't want him to get his hopes up. She sighed. "Adam. I'm not sure. My life is in Balbuinidh. I'm probably not going to take it. Please keep this to yourself for the time being."

"Kelly." He mirrored her tone, jokingly. "We both know this is a million times better than living the rest of your life in Balbuinidh where nothing ever happens. You'd be mad not to say yes. You're still young… sort of."

"Steady," she warned, teasingly.

"…what I'm saying is there's nothing holding you back. I'll be here too."

"I need to think about it." She paused. "So, are you staying on here then, after you graduate?"

"Yep."

"Good for you."

She picked up the tab and left a generous tip. Tipping was on a whole different level in the States, and she always tried to make sure she got it right. Outside the restaurant on the bright and bustling street, Adam practically bounced with excitement as he led them to the next place.

She had paid for him to stay in the same hotel as her, so he could enjoy a proper trip to the city, and they could catch up.

New York in the evening had to be one of the world's most exciting sights but could she really live here? Did she want to? Maybe she was happier in her sleepy close-knit Highland town than she realised. Or maybe she was feeling this way because of a certain person that had come into her life. There she went, thinking about her again. How did it always come back to her? That ache came back. She missed Myla. Pining for someone had never been her style yet here she was, thinking about Myla constantly and wishing there was a future between them, free of complication. But what future? It was yet to be seen if Myla would ever make Balbuinidh her home, or if she would go back to Edinburgh or even somewhere else. She could go anywhere in the world if she wanted. It bothered Kelly that she didn't know. Someone slammed into her shoulder as she walked down the street next to Adam, momentarily knocking her off balance. "Sorry," she said, involuntarily, even though it wasn't her fault.

Adam laughed. "A Brit abroad."

Once settled on her stool at the cool East Village bar, she probed into his thinking about staying on if he could get a work visa. He seemed serious about it. She would support him, but she knew their parents would be devastated initially that he wasn't going to come home any time soon. They'd had a hard enough time getting used to the fact Adam was going to study here – which was assumed to be a temporary situation. They'd come around, though, they knew he had to properly fly the nest someday. Kelly wondered how they would react if she moved here, too.

"Nicole says you're spending a lot of time with the new owner of Glenbuinidh?"

Kelly looked down at her drink.

"You're totally blushing!" Adam laughed.

Kelly snapped her head up, a smile threatening at her lips. "I am not."

"Are so."

Kelly glared at him. "Look. You saw nothing."

He raised his eyebrows and held up his hands in defeat. "Okay." Adam's phone rang. He looked at it longingly.

"Do you need to get that?"

He grimaced. "Would that be okay?"

"Sure."

He sped off to take the call outside.

Kelly returned to her Manhattan cocktail, thankful for the interruption to that conversation. After a couple of minutes, a woman approached her.

"So, are you into younger guys then?"

Kelly's eyes bulged and she nearly choked on her drink. "Excuse me?"

"Your date. He's a lot younger than you, right?"

"He's my brother."

The woman smiled. Perhaps too much? She had perfect white teeth and a slightly lingering gaze. "Ah. That makes sense. Come to think of it, you do look a bit alike."

Kelly desperately needed a change of subject or for her to leave her alone.

"I love your accent, by the way, it's so cute."

Kelly was used to this. It was always like this when she travelled. It was flattering, in a way.

She asked Kelly what she did in New York, and she said she was just in town for business and that this was her last night. On another day, Kelly would have been interested.

But she wasn't in the mood to flirt with strangers tonight, not even hot ones. She was here with her brother, it was her last night, and she was missing Myla. Badly.

The American took a sip of wine. "That's too bad. I would have asked you out had you been staying longer."

And there it was. They caught eyes. She was very attractive. Kelly smiled, politely. "It is too bad."

"Are you seeing anyone back home?"

Myla popped into her head and that familiar ache came across her body, again. Part of her felt like she was grieving something that hadn't technically started. Theoretically she was single, but she didn't feel single. She'd lost the urge to sleep with anyone else as soon as she and Myla started having sex. That had to be a sign, right?

"Yes." Wow, that felt good to say. But it wasn't true. Her shoulders sank as she sighed. "Sort of."

"How does that work in Scotland?"

"Same as anywhere, I guess."

"You're not on the same page?"

For a stranger, she was surprisingly perceptive. Kelly's defences lowered. "I have a friends with benefits situation that's currently imploding. I want more but don't want to scare her away and ultimately ruin the friendship. I also don't want to get my heart broken by not addressing it. Plus, she's my boss and ten years younger. It's just really complicated."

"Okaaay, good luck with that." She tilted her head and pretended to leave. "No, seriously. That sounds super tough. Have you tried just talking to her about how you feel?"

Kelly blew out a breath. She hadn't. Not yet. Kelly had no business feeling this way about Myla given that it was *she* who'd stopped their relationship from evolving naturally in the first place. If Myla backed away now she had every right to. Kelly couldn't blame her. The whole situation was too intense and couldn't go on indefinitely, it turned out. "No."

The sexy American shrugged as if her point was made. Bowing her head towards Kelly, she lowered her voice. "Talk to her. Clearly, she must be madly in love with you. I mean – look at you. From the second you walked in here I haven't been able to take my eyes off you. That bitch must be crazy not to want you."

Kelly laughed. "I'll keep that in mind."

She picked up her drink and moved away slightly, one hand still on the bar. "You have a good night, gorgeous, and a safe journey back to Scotland." And with that, she was gone, back into the crowded bar.

Adam returned just as she was leaving, with a spring in his step. He looked between the departing woman and Kelly, a questioning look growing on his face. He raised an eyebrow as he sat down. "Making friends?"

"*Aye,*" she exaggerated. "Everywhere I go."

He laughed. "Right. Next bar?"

"You got it."

They went to two more bars in the area. It was fascinating to see the people in another country go about their day. The bars were also distinctly American or, well, like those in New York. She loved spending time here and wanted to take a trip across America one day. Before she knew it, she was picturing her and Myla taking a road trip and ending up on route sixty-six in some open-aired convertible, holding hands and driving off into the sunset together. The idea of seeing the world with Myla set her heart alight. Why was she getting her hopes up like that though? Sighing into her latest and, for definite, last of the night, that ache came back. Fuck's sake, why didn't alcohol take such feelings away any more?

"You okay, sis?"

Adam was twiddling his thumbs and people-watching by this point and Kelly was starting to feel sorry for him.

"I'm okay. Just got a lot on my mind."

He nodded. His expression was thoughtful and kind, a bit like their mum's. "I kind of got that feeling."

"Maybe it's time to call it a night. I'm no fun any more."

Adam agreed on both accounts which lifted the mood again, and then he called an Uber. Kelly looked out the window on the drive back to the hotel, in awe of the city. They got back to the hotel around twelve-thirty. Her flight was at ten-thirty so hopefully she would still be able to get a half-decent sleep.

Adam's room was on the second floor while hers was on the fifth. He stopped in the foyer. "I'm going to take the stairs."

"Okay," she tilted her head. "Time to say goodbye." She held out her arms to hug her baby brother, and he held on for a moment or two longer than normal.

"It's been great seeing you, sis."

"You too, wee man." This was her pet name for Adam growing up, and it used to really annoy him, until he outgrew her and then it became an ironic thing for Kelly to tease him with.

He laughed. "Still using that."

"Always."

"See you for your graduation party soon, yeah? Mum and Dad have a whole thing planned."

"Yep," Adam stepped back. "See you then."

"Get some sleep. Enjoy the hotel. And get studying soon, right?"

He smiled. "Will do. And hey, Kelly, thanks for tonight. Believe it or not I have been missing home."

"Let's call more often, okay? You tell me when works for you and I'll be online."

With a final wave, which was more like a salute, he was gone. She was proud of him for getting out there and living his life to the fullest like this, but she did still miss him.

Back in her room, the door clicked shut behind her and all she wanted to do was get into bed. Her head was already sore. She drank a bottle of water and took a hot shower to wash away the evening. Crawling into bed, she fell asleep almost instantly.

Blinking to assess the severity of her hangover when her alarm went off at six-thirty, she sighed realising that her head hurt a lot. It was going to be a rough trip home. Reaching for her phone to turn the alarm off, she noticed a message on it.

A message from Myla.

Adrenaline rushed through her as she tapped off the alarm and opened Myla's message. It was a cute photo of her in an empty flat, presumably her flat in Edinburgh. She was moving to Balbuinidh. Wonderful news. Kelly stared at the photo for longer than she had time for. She had to get up and get to the airport so there was no time to reply; she wanted to think carefully about what to write first.

She got to the airport for eight-thirty and made her way through to departures. She was cutting it fine. Her plan was to get a coffee and bagel and then reply to Myla when she was settled and where she needed to be. Normally she loved to people-watch in the airports of other countries, but this morning she almost felt like a commuter. She was certainly grumpy. There was so much noise. She went into Hudson News and bought some painkillers and water. Her head was fragile, and she needed to eat something so she could take a double whammy of ibuprofen and paracetamol – or Advil and Tylenol as she found they were called in the US.

Something about the expansiveness of the US or the sheer scale of this airport got Kelly thinking about climate change and the state of the world. She'd been wanting to do more on making the distillery greener for a long time. Switching to renewable energies throughout the business had to be done. If everything went well with the Queen of Spirits launch, she could start making further changes along those lines. People loved knowing their product was carbon neutral and could be enjoyed guilt free. She would ask Myla what she thought.

Sighing in relief, she finally sat down with her coffee and bagels, ravenous. She relaxed with the first sip of coffee, took her phone out and stared at Myla's message. She took ages to compose her short reply.

Kelly: *I'm glad you're moving up. A new beginning* :)

Myla replied quickly. It must be mid-afternoon back home.

Myla: *Yes! Onward! I'm here now. Just been unpacking the car. How's your trip going? When are you getting home?*

It was as if they hadn't stopped talking for over a week. Kelly wasn't overly keen on Myla just withdrawing from her like that and coming back as if nothing had happened. But she would try to go with the flow. They weren't in a relationship. They were just friends. She had no right to expect Myla to stay in touch every day. And it wasn't as if Myla had said anything bad after the summit. She'd just gone quiet.

The bagel was divine, and Kelly's spirits rose with every bite. Myla's use of *home* was promising. She'd picked Balbuinidh, at least for a while, and they now lived in the same place. It was exciting.

> **Kelly:** *Trip was a success. I signed a major new deal for Queen of Spirits (will tell you all about it). In the airport just now. Home later tonight.*

She held back telling Myla about the potential job offer. It was still just talk at the moment so there was no point in bringing it up yet.

> **Myla:** *Awesome! I can't wait to hear about it. Would you like to come over soon? This should be celebrated! I also want to apologise for my behaviour after the summit. I wanted to have a chat about things, too.*

> **Myla:** *I also just can't wait to see you.*

She wanted to talk? She wanted to apologise? What did that mean? Kelly's pulse started racing.

> **Kelly:** *I'd love to come around. Tomorrow?*

Kelly wanted to say that she missed her but stopped. That wasn't something a friend would say and would be better said in person.

> **Myla:** *We always seem to message each other when you're in an airport ;)*

> **Kelly:** *We do! You have a great memory. That was ages ago!*

> ***Myla:*** *Have a good flight. See you tomorrow xx*

There was an openness to Myla in her texts. It was decent she acknowledged her behaviour at the summit and sweet that she wanted to celebrate Kelly's success. Kelly looked up at the departure board next to the gate. They should be boarding soon. She couldn't get home fast enough now. She wanted to see Myla right away. So, failing that, she put her earbuds in and listened to Myla's songs again. Before long, she was on the plane and feeling better about things, floating above the clouds with the sound of Myla's voice soothing her brain from the inside out.

Sixteen

Kelly was coming over for lunch in an hour. I'd spent the morning cleaning the house, preparing an elaborate celebratory meal and getting ready *to talk*. We either needed to become a couple or move towards being just friends. It was either or. I wanted more, and I couldn't go on sleeping with her unless it was going somewhere. I was also going to apologise for shutting down on her after the summit. It was immature and not a good way to communicate. I wanted to be better than that. I needed to behave better than that if I was going to get with someone as out of my league as Kelly.

Needless to say, I was nervous.

When the doorbell rang a while later, I was in no better a place, mentally or emotionally than before, but the cooker was now gleaming. My heart pounded so hard as I opened the front door.

Barley dashed into the house, wagging frantically. He circled my legs but before I could pat his head he was off again. Kelly and I stood at the front door just looking at each other. It felt like I hadn't seen her in ages, yet it had only been ten days. It was awkward, and by the looks of her rigid stance, she felt awkward too. She was wearing a comfortable jumper and jeans and trainers. Her hair was tied up in a messy bun. She seemed more approachable and… gay. "Hey."

"Hey," she said, hesitantly.

"Come in."

Kelly's lips were set hard, and she had worry lines between her eyebrows. She also looked a bit tired, probably from the jet lag.

"How was your trip?" I'd already asked this via text, but I felt like I needed to ask again in person.

"I got the deal."

"I know, congratulations! I've got some champagne and I made lunch."

Kelly looked at me funny. "Thank you."

"Not bad getting to go to places like New York."

At this, Kelly's face relaxed, but only a bit. "I know, I'm very lucky."

"Great," I said, still too keenly. I forced myself to take a breath and calm down.

"You've moved out of your old flat?" Kelly said this casually but the look in her eyes was anything but casual. There was an intensity in them about the question that I hadn't seen before.

"It's official. I live here now. Even the Royal Mail knows."

Kelly's eyes softened, making me feel warm and fuzzy despite the awkwardness of our conversation.

"I hope you'll be very happy here."

"I've got big plans. Like brightening up this whole ground floor and sorting out the study."

"I'm sure you'll look after this place very well. Margaret would have wanted you to enjoy it."

I swallowed, enjoying the moment and that familiar feeling of comfort that I got from just being around her, but aware that I still had to follow through and address the pressing issue or I never would. "I'm sorry I gave you the silent treatment on the way back from the summit. I was just in a weird head space that day. I'm fine now." I forced myself to smile but couldn't bring myself to commit to it. My stomach was too full of butterflies still.

"It's okay," Kelly shifted on her feet, but her eyes were still soft. "I figured there was something going on with you. I didn't want to pry."

Of course she had a healthy way of looking at it. At times like this, I could see why being with someone who had their shit together was a good thing, especially if they were as emotionally healthy as someone like Kelly. I craved her stability and her warmth. I wanted to reach out, wrap my arms around her and pull her in close but I hesitated. She played with her hands and looked anywhere but at me. After a few seconds of this, I realised how silly this was. I stepped into her space, inhaling her perfume, and gave her a gentle hug. It felt so good to be in her arms again, to inhale that spicy citrus. She smelled so fresh and clean. I'd missed her.

Kelly then put her arms around me, resting her hands on the small of my back, making me feel so… loved. Was that what someone who just wanted a friend who they slept with occasionally would do? Our bodies pressed against each other. How had that happened so quickly? So easily?

Resting my head on her shoulder, my heart thumped and my palms began to sweat. We needed to have the talk. I needed to say the words that I'd been holding back and address the situation between us. But I couldn't. The anxiety of potentially pushing her away was crushing. Instead, I remained quiet and let myself fall into her. She didn't step back. She squeezed me tighter. It was as if we were melting into one another. I was safe in her arms.

About a minute later Kelly turned her head towards me and spoke into the side of my face. My heart was still pounding, and I swear hers was too.

"I've missed you," Kelly whispered.

My tummy flipped. She did? As a friend? As a lover? Did it matter after this hug? "I've missed you, too."

Kelly pulled back and gently held my face in her hands. We locked eyes. Kelly was here and she was different today. More open. Softer. When she leaned forward, tilting her head slightly, my lips parted in anticipation. Kelly kissed me so softly and tenderly. She didn't push or take, she just gently let me know she was there. I held onto her waist that bit tighter, feeling almost dizzy, as the slow and emotional kiss went on. When a small moan escaped the back of her throat, tingles spread to my centre and a warmth engulfed my entire body. We weren't supposed to be kissing, we were supposed to be talking about the burning issue between us, but I couldn't bring myself to stop this. I couldn't bring myself to break this spell. It was so real and true. Surely she felt it too. Surely this wasn't as one sided as I thought.

Kelly pulled back, breathing hard like me. Her eyes spoke of a million things unsaid. Kissing me like that after a spell apart was not part of the fuck buddy package, right?

Barley nudged at our legs, causing us both to lean away slightly. He was sitting at our feet looking up at us, expectantly. His little face was so cute.

"Sorry, buddy. I've commandeered your mummy."

"He's just happy to see you. Like I am."

I bit my bottom lip trying not to smile too much at that. "I've missed my two walking buddies, too. Um, I've got him a present. Can I give him it?"

"Of course. What a lucky dog."

I led them both into the main sitting room where the fluffy penguin, which I'd wrapped, and bag of treats were. My resolve to have a conversation disintegrated with each step. What if it burst the bubble?

"Barley, sit," Kelly said in her stern Barley voice. Barley's nose was already on his presents, knowing they were for him.

He obeyed, tail sweeping frantically over the floor behind him. He made quick work of the wrapping paper and claimed his rightful toy. It was pawed at and squeaked and paraded around. We laughed as he lapped up the attention then settled himself in the sitting room floor where he set about tearing it up on the hearth rug.

Kelly took off her jacket, still looking flustered. I hadn't recovered from our kiss yet, either. "How's the jet lag? Did you get some sleep last night?"

Kelly ran her hands through her hair. I ached to be the one doing that, still tingling on my lips from her kisses. She smiled, but still a little unsure. What was that about? "I did. I'm still a bit out of sync, but I'm getting there." Kelly paused, not looking finished. "Actually, I hardly slept at all. I've a lot on my mind."

I shifted on my feet. "Oh."

Kelly cleared her throat and smiled again, this time a bit fuller. "I brought you back something."

"Really?" I heard the surprise in my voice. I inhaled, excited about the gift and the potential meaning of it, before quickly doubting myself. Friends bought each other gifts. It was no big deal.

Kelly picked up her bag and brought out a small present wrapped in silver paper shaped like a book and handed it to me. It was carefully tied together with a purple bow.

"You shouldn't have." I cautiously moved the bow off to the side and took the paper off. Inside was a slim book: *Here is New York* by E.B. White. I read the back cover and inside pages. It was first published in nineteen forty-eight. "About the same time *The Price of Salt* was written! I love it."

"I did a lot of walking around the city when I was there. I stumbled across a bookshop and this book. It reminded me of you."

We locked eyes. I was touched that she had thought of me. Kelly paused, as a red blush crept up her neck and onto her face.

"I wished you were there with me. I think we would have had a lot of fun exploring the city together. I knew you would see it in a unique way. I thought maybe you would enjoy this take on the city," she nodded at the book in my hand, "because I can't do things like that justice. I'm not creative like you. I'm not poetic."

I looked down at the book. A review said it was the best love letter to the city. That word: *love*. I found her gaze again and held it. "Thank you."

Barley squeaked the penguin a few times causing us both to flinch. I smiled, uneasily.

I had to do this. "Um, I wanted to talk to you about something."

"What about?" Kelly sat down on the sofa looking curious. Barley lay on the floor by her feet looking at me with his head tilted and ears high.

"Sorry, I'm..." I scratched my head.

Kelly leaned forward. "It's okay. You can tell me."

I sat down next to her. "About us. I feel it's time we start talking more honestly with each other."

Kelly's brow furrowed. "I agree."

My stomach flipped. I held my breath. She was going to back away from me, from our friendship, from our benefits.

And then she smiled at me and ran her thumb over my hand. It was such a loving smile. She'd never smiled at me quite like that before.

I blew out a breath, feeling slightly less anxious, and tucked some hair behind my ears.

"We said we'd be friends who sometimes sleep together and nothing more because of various complications, and that we would be honest with each other if anything changed, right?"

"Yes." Kelly nodded.

My heart raced. "Things have changed for me. You've become so much more to me in these past few months. I can't keep doing this as we are. I want more. Or it has to stop."

She touched my face, her eyes were soft. "I was thinking about the exact same thing."

"You were? Which part?"

"I'm done pretending I don't have feelings for you. I want to fall asleep holding you and wake up with you in the morning. I want to know everything about you. I want this. I want you."

Before I could react, Kelly leaned forward and brushed her lips against mine, cupping my face in her hands. She kissed me with such tenderness that all I could do was lean in and let her do it.

I pulled back, unable to string my thoughts together except one that solidified. Kelly wanted more too. *She wanted me.* Kelly, the hot CEO, the gorgeous and successful older woman who had made my pulse race in the club all those months ago. I was shocked, elated, happy, excited, and well, horny.

"I want you, too." Kelly was looking at me with such affection, that it was hard to believe she would ever hurt me. "I was worried I'd messed things up, after the summit, even our friendship."

Kelly tilted her head, brow furrowed, almost affronted. "You didn't. I said we would be friends no matter what. I always said that, right at the start."

"I was worried, given how many reasons you gave for us not being together. The distillery—"

Kelly bit down on her bottom lip. "I know."

"I thought you didn't want a relationship with me."

She took a deep breath and looked at me squarely. "There are some things that scare me but that doesn't mean we can't work things out and shouldn't try to see where this goes."

"I can't do anything about being younger."

"I don't care about that any more."

"Oh." I cleared my throat, trying to sound normal about this. "So does this mean you want us to be a couple now?"

She smiled so warmly and pulled me towards her, onto her, wrapping her arms around me. "Yes. Myla Murray, will you be my girlfriend?"

My heart swelled hearing those words. "Yes! You had me convinced you weren't wanting to go down this road though," I said through my grin, still half-confused.

"I want to go down it."

"But I'm a mess. I'm broken. My past—"

"What do you mean?"

I sat back up, pulling away from her, and shook my head, utterly enraged at the callous way I was endangering my own potential happiness. Barley lay sprawled out on his side now, fast asleep, his soft snores permeating the room. "Would it be possible to forget I said that, please?"

"I'm sorry you feel that way. I didn't know. Do you want to talk about it?"

"No. Thanks."

Kelly nodded, taking this very seriously. "From what I see from the outside, you are strong, you are resilient, and you so deserve the time and space that you've got right now to just... be. I want you to be happy. And if you're not, then I'd love to support you in that journey. No one's perfect. That's not what I'm looking for in a partner. That doesn't interest me. I want you for you, not someone you think I want you to be."

I tilted my head towards her. "Well, if you're going to put it like that..."

"You're also very talented. Your SoundCloud is outstanding."

"You've heard my songs?"

"I might have binge-listened to them all on my trip."

I didn't know what to do with that. I was flattered, proud, and a little bit excited by it. Kelly taking the time to listen to my awful music was just *everything*.

"Come here." She pulled me back onto her and I let myself fall into the glorious feeling of being held and accepted. We were quiet for a while just cuddling into each other. We'd never done this before. Heat emanated from her body and the slow rhythm of her breathing was hypnotic. Even if this didn't last, I would remember this feeling forever.

She planted slow kisses on my cheek and ran her fingertips up and down my arm. A rush of arousal spread through my entire body, mixed with something more certain now. She wanted to be in this with me, whatever this was. I let myself feel how much I wanted her. How much I needed her. It took my breath away. It wasn't until now that I realised how much I'd been holding back.

"Our first kiss as a couple." She held my face and leaned in again. Her lips felt like home. I knew kissing Kelly by this point. The way she usually held the side of my face and the way her lips moved against mine. Kelly was so at ease with herself, and I loved being around that level of harmony. She was so trustworthy and kind, while also powerful and exciting. Strong. She was everything I wanted in a woman and then some. A hunger took over me the longer we kissed. I ran my hands up her thigh, causing Kelly to moan quietly into my mouth, and me to soak my panties.

"Hey," I said, moving some hair out of her eyes. "I can think of another first time we can have."

Kelly swallowed, hard. "Yeah?"

Holding hands, we went up to my bedroom. My room was bright with sunshine streaming through the large bay window, casting light across the whole room. The bed was bathed in it, like benevolent energy pouring into this moment encouraging us to be together and be happy. Kelly lifted my top up and over my head. The action left my hair in a mess and she fixed it, affectionately, with an easy smile. We stood by the bed slowly undoing buttons and gently guiding each other's clothes off. There was no rush. Her skin was so soft and her eyes never left me. With our feelings out in the open now, we were connecting on a whole different level. This was way more intimate and exposed than anything we'd done together before.

Lying in bed, wrapped up in each other's arms and legs, bodies pressed against each other, neither of us made a move to get things started. We just gazed into each other's eyes. She ran her hand through my hair. I'd never been as connected to someone. I was simultaneously hot for her and content to take it slowly. We were like two guitars calibrating to each other's frequency again after a small time apart. I traced her jawline with my rough fingertips.

Kelly brushed her nose against mine. "You're like a little radiator."

I squeezed her arm, with my leg wrapped around her waist. "I've got more heat if you need it."

Kelly buried her face into my neck, inhaling, and murmured. "I need it."

I melted at that, with nothing left to say or do but kiss her. All my feelings came through the kiss. Affection, lust, relief, possibility, hope. Kelly was here and she was mine now. It just blew my mind. I rolled on top of her, less gracefully than I would have liked, but I didn't have to be perfect or worry that one false move would put a stop to our situation any more. She wanted me, and just thinking about it made me smile.

"You have such a goofy grin on your face," Kelly said, reaching up and touching the side of my mouth. "I've never seen you smile like this before." She touched the end of my nose. "It's so cute."

Immediately, I fixed the smile into something sexier, furrowing my brow, and no doubt failing.

"Oooh. Sexy eyes now," Kelly smiled, then flipped me around so that I was lying on my back. She shrugged off the covers. "Too hot," she grinned, naked, sitting on my hips above me with the covers falling down her back. And then she just... *looked* at me. Her eyes drank me in. She was so still. Her probing gaze was in no hurry at all. I lay still too, aware of the warmth spreading through my body and my racing heart, relishing that she was looking at me as if she'd never seen me before. I shivered when she touched the bare skin by my navel. With a small smile she leant down and kissed me. This kiss was slower, deeper and so full of emotion. She kissed my neck, and stroked one of my breasts, before finding my nipple with her teeth and squeezing lightly. When she flicked her tongue over my nipple a hot rush of arousal coursed through my body. If this continued much longer I would surely combust from this fire between us.

She rested herself fully on my thigh, pleasuring herself against it as we kissed. Her unselfconscious taking of what she wanted was almost too much. Kelly's heat and wetness rubbed against my leg, sending waves of electricity straight to my clit. She stopped kissing me and manoeuvred herself onto me so that we were pressed together in just the right spot. In *exactly* the right spots. It was the best feeling in the world being that close to her. There was nothing more intimate. Nothing could compare to this connection we shared.

"Can you feel that?" she murmured.

"Yes," I breathed. My voice came out low.

Kelly lay on top of me, grinding herself against my centre. The way she moved her hips was so good, and so fucking sexy. My leg muscles were completely tensed up, only adding to the friction between us.

I might die from this.

As our hips rocked together, the tension kept building. Kelly had this way of finding the most decadent rhythm and making me want so much more. I was completely at her mercy. Kelly moaned, breathing harder. I was going to come, already. I prayed that she would just keep doing what she was doing as I had never come from someone on top of me like this before, and with Kelly being the one to do it, it was just even more special. *She* was so special.

"Oh my god that feels so good," I cried out, digging my fingers into her back. The heat between our bodies intensified. I ran my hands over Kelly's body, feeling her every curve, tracing the muscles that were working hard against me.

"Myla…" Kelly trailed off, squeezing her eyes shut and then opening them again to look right into mine. The eye contact sent me over the edge, wave after wave of intense pleasure built within me. Kelly rested her head on the pillow over my shoulder, pressing her whole body onto me now, and fucked me faster in a much less controlled way than before. I'd never seen Kelly be so free. She was so fucking sexy and caused me to cry out as I exploded underneath her.

She held me in her arms as I came. The way she stroked my arm and patiently waited as I recovered was so loving. This connection with Kelly felt primal. Hot emotion bubbled up to the surface, threatening to pour out of my eyes, as I desperately tried to prevent it and hide my over-emotion from the woman of my dreams.

I failed.

Kelly whispered. "Are you crying?"

"Nope." I turned away, discreetly trying to wipe away the tears that were now falling from my eyes. It was *embarrassing*. I was embarrassed. I'd put my heart on the line this afternoon. I wasn't used to doing that. I was raw, even though they were positive emotions. My heart was both on fire and about to burst, it was so full.

I think I'm in love.

Kelly's voice was soft. "It's okay."

Oh my god.

I rolled away further, trying to hide, but she followed me, spooning me closely and tucking her head into my neck. "Why are you crying?" She whispered and kissed my shoulder.

"They're happy tears."

She gently pulled me back towards her, so that I was lying on my back, as she propped her head up on her hand. "It's okay if they aren't. You can tell me anything."

I was lost for words, having just realised I was in love with her. That I loved her so much it made me feel so completely overwhelmed.

"They are. I'm just a very emotional lesbian, don't mind me."

Kelly squeezed my waist. "As long as you're okay. I can't have my woman crying after we have sex."

My woman? I *loved* the sound of that coming from her. It sounded possessive. I never thought Kelly would be like that with me. "I promise you they are."

Kelly rested her head on my pillow and bit her bottom lip. She stroked my cheek. "You said something about a celebratory lunch?"

"But you haven't—"

"I'm a big girl, I can handle it."

***

Later that night, Kelly's slow and steady breathing was all I could hear. My room was pitch black. She was cuddling into my back, spooning me. I was so excited to be taking this step with her. I let out a contented sigh, feeling so safe and protected in her arms. Her breathing had gone into that deep sleep state. I, however, could not sleep at all. I was still buzzing and wanted to remember every second of this – even down to the way she sounded when she slept.

Earlier at lunch, we chatted about her trip to New York over champagne and my best smoked salmon risotto followed by Italian cannoli. I loved hearing about everything she got up to. We wrapped our feet together underneath the table. I ran my toe up the inside of her leg from time to time. She was a rockstar, getting that deal for Glenbuinidh. I liked the sound of Adam. She spoke so affectionately about him. I wondered what it would be like to have two siblings, it sounded wonderful. And then, that empty feeling came back in, but I pushed it away, as I was having the best time ever with Kelly. Kelly asked about the café, my old flat, and Rebecca and Michelle. She was supportive about my decision to move up to Balbuinidh.

Kelly was so light and full of energy; I really enjoyed this side of her. I enjoyed having a laugh with her. We kept hugging or holding hands. I stood behind her and squeezed her tight as we did the dishes. At one point, she had to ask to be released so she could move. We'd never been this openly affectionate before. I hoped she didn't find me too clingy.

I'd bought some dog food for Barley before, I couldn't remember when, in case they ever did stay over, and when I told Kelly I had some in the cupboard she was really surprised by it, and happy.

We walked around the estate for a bit, letting Barley explore the grounds and play in the river. It was so romantic to stroll around hand in hand like that. Having her in my space, spending the day with her, it was everything I thought it might be and more. It wasn't long after we made it home that we found ourselves back upstairs in my bedroom, well, I did practically pull her back up here as soon as we got in the door. I'd put my hand inside her pants the moment we fell onto the bed together and she'd come within minutes. I loved every second of it.

And now, countless hours and orgasms later I replayed the day over and over again in my head as she slept all nuzzled into me and warm because it might just have been the best day of my *entire* life. It was very near perfect except for one annoying niggling thought at the back of my mind.

Was this too good to be true?

Seventeen

Myla's hand fit perfectly in hers. They were strolling along the lochside after a romantic meal overlooking the loch. Kelly didn't care who might have seen them and wondered if they were together. She was in love. That was all that mattered. It was so light out, despite being well after nine in the evening. The water lapped gently at the shore in the slight breeze. The restaurants were still busy, with some people braving the cooling air and still sitting outside. Kelly had been here a million times, had grown up here, yet she had never been this happy walking down the promenade as she was right now.

"If you could tell your younger self one thing, what would it be?" Myla said.

Kelly didn't think about it long. "To have more fun, take more risks and just live more. Say yes to more things and be free while you still can because you're going to grow up and have to do adulting one day and it's going to be a real shock to your system."

Myla smiled warmly, then took her arm. "That was about ten things, but I'll forgive you."

"What about you? What would you tell your younger self?"

Myla thought about it for a moment. "I'd tell her that it's okay you're overwhelmed and falling apart and broken. It doesn't define you. One day you're going to get so lucky. I'd tell her that she's not alone. That she's loved. That I love her, and I'll always be here for her."

Kelly stopped walking and hugged Myla tightly, feeling Myla's breath on her neck. "I'm sorry you've felt that way. You're not alone any more."

Myla stiffened, and Kelly felt a lone tear on her neck fall from Myla's face.

"Come on," Kelly said. "Let's go home."

***

Kelly huddled around her parents' laptop at their kitchen table next to her mum. They were on a family video call with the twins. They spoke together at least once a month, usually on a Saturday after her mum finished surgery. Her dad was moving about in the kitchen behind them making a snack and noise.

"You've invited half of Balbuinidh," Nicole said, shaking her head.

Kelly knew how much their children's education meant to them. Her own university graduation felt like a long time ago. Fifteen years ago, to be precise. How had that happened?

"Would it be possible to put a blanket ban on people asking us what we're going to do next?" Nicole said, touching her forehead, looking stressed.

"Honey," Kelly's mum said. "People will ask that."

"You've got the rest of your life to figure it out," Kelly said, aware that her parents had been worrying about Nicole's next steps an inordinate amount. Nicole was on track to graduate well from Cambridge but was struggling to know what she wanted to do next. She hadn't applied for any jobs and seemed strangely out of ideas for further academic or career opportunities. It wasn't like her to be so indecisive, and she apparently didn't want to do anything related to her actual degree in physics. "Why not just focus on your final exams for now?"

"What about a master's and then a PhD?" Kelly's mum said. "You enjoy academia."

Nicole nodded, lips firmly pressed together. "I think I just need a break from studying for a while. It's literally all I've been doing, and I can hardly think straight, let alone plan my whole future." She sat up straight, head half disappearing off the screen. "I think I want to do a gap year."

"Then you should do that," Kelly said. Her mum gave her a sideways stink-eye and her dad momentarily stopped clanging around behind them. Adam was resting his head on his hand, doing well to stay out of this. "It does sound like you need a break."

"Finally, someone who understands me."

"Let's not make any major decisions right now, shall we?" Kelly's mum said. "Kelly's right. You should just focus on your final exams for now and then you can figure out what to do next once that's done. We'll be right behind you, whatever you decide, even if it is a bloomin' gap year."

Nicole's eyes softened. "Thanks, Mum."

"So!" Kelly's mum changed the subject. "Not long until we're all back together."

A chorus of nods and general agreement went around the screen and the kitchen, relief evident at the change of subject. Adam cleared his throat. "Um, I hope it's okay, that I, um, have invited Christen."

Kelly's dad called out from looking inside the fridge. "Nope. No visitors here. Standing room only."

Adam frowned.

"Malcolm!"

"I'm joking! Of course you can bring your girlfriend home, boy." Kelly's dad hovered behind them. "We can't wait to meet her."

They chatted for a while longer and one by one Adam and Nicole left the call. Kelly's dad left to go fishing with his friends, leaving her and her mum alone in the now quiet kitchen.

"You know I'm so proud of you," Kelly's mum kissed the side of her head. "That American deal was just so impressive."

Kelly's dad hadn't seemed that impressed. When Kelly told him a couple of days after she'd got back from New York, he'd simply raised his eyebrows and said 'very good'.

"Dad wasn't too bothered, though." Kelly was annoyed at how much his lack of enthusiasm had got to her.

"He's probably just jealous because he never achieved anything like that while he was in charge," Kelly's mum said, squeezing her arm.

Kelly looked down at the kitchen table, registering the accuracy of her mum's point. "How petty is that?"

"He's only human. He is very proud of you, you know. Never doubt that."

It was exhausting, this competition with her dad, and she was very nearly done with it. So done. She just wanted him to be her dad and not some pseudo boss or rival. *She* was the boss now for fuck's sake.

She'd spoken to Jeff and his board of directors on a video call, out of curiosity, nothing more, and then Jeff officially offered her the role. She hadn't expected it. Jeff reiterated how much they wanted Kelly to join them and talked in detail about how they wanted her to help them grow their international division. Kelly was excited about it, and the guilt was killing her. She hated carrying this secret, but the truth was she couldn't say no yet. The fast pace, the hustle and bustle and the thrill of it all just appealed.

She hadn't told her parents that she'd pushed ahead with Queen of Spirits and the Women in Whisky initiative despite their reservations. They thought the deal in America was around the signature bottle. With increasing numbers of women signing up for the initiative and early interest building for Queen of Spirits, she was at the peak of her game. She wasn't ready to tell them about what she was doing at the distillery yet, but it was time to tell them about this job offer. There was no telling one without the other, and it was easier to talk to her mum. She wanted her mum's opinion. They'd always been close. And showing her dad she was in demand couldn't hurt, either.

"Can I tell you something?" Kelly took a deep breath.

"Of course."

"I've been offered a job. In New York." Kelly paused. "A good one."

Kelly's mum blinked rapidly. "You have? What sort of job? By whom? Did you apply for a job over there? Are you thinking of leaving us?"

"Mum, wait. Calm down." This was the reason she hadn't told anyone yet. "It was just an offer. It came to me. I didn't go looking. It's with—"

"You got headhunted?"

Kelly paused, mouth open. "Yeah. The CEO approached me."

Kelly's mum had her thinking face on. "You must be making some waves."

"Maybe."

"Being completely honest, I don't want you to go, love. I've loved having you back home with us. But," she tilted her head and half-smiled, "you have to do what's right for you. It's your life, and life is short. You've got to grab it with both hands and hold on tight. I want you to be happy and I'd understand if you want to take this job and start a new life in the US. I know you've been unhappy here for a while."

Kelly filled her mum in on everything she knew about the company and the main pros and cons, except the biggest reason not to go, which was her and Myla.

"It's a tough one. But it's your decision."

She hadn't told her parents about her relationship with Myla yet, nor had she told Myla anything about the job offer in New York either. Neither was good, and she was going to – had to – address them both very soon. The more time went on, though, the harder it got on all fronts. The guilt was eating her up inside.

"Could you tell dad and tell him not to tell anyone else yet? I'm still making up my mind and I don't want to worry people for no reason."

"Of course. Whatever you decide, we'll support you."

It was good Jeff was being so patient for her answer – 'take as long as you want' he had said, although the subtext was also 'but not too long'.

As Kelly drove home with Barley, she was conflicted. After living away from home for so many years, she'd come to value the time spent with her parents living in Balbuinidh as an adult. They wouldn't always be around. Her mum was correct though, she had to do what was right for her. She was grateful for her mum's blessing to go, but there was something else keeping her in Balbuinidh now.

There was something *special* going on between her and Myla. Neither had mentioned the word 'love' yet but it was there. It was present in Myla's eyes and in her actions. It was wedged deeply in Kelly's heart. She couldn't quite pinpoint the exact moment she knew, but it was early on, perhaps as soon as they first slept together. The more she learned about Myla the more she wanted to learn. She cared about her. Kelly was in love. She didn't dare jinx it. She didn't want to.

She was so torn.

Kelly knew Balbuinidh would always be there. It was home. She'd pictured herself growing old in this place. Watching the years go by and the changing seasons, seeing the children grow up and new children being born. Strolling around the park with a head full of grey hair remembering when she used to play in it as a child or run around it with Barley. This place had given her the stable platform from which to go through life so confidently and so adventurously. She'd been lucky to have had such a good childhood and community. It wasn't always perfect, but it was good. She was grateful. But did she still want to be in Balbuinidh at this point in her life?

With Myla's arrival, everything had changed. Kelly was loving exploring this new and soul-satisfying *thing* that was blossoming between them. And having this experience with Myla in Balbuinidh itself was unexpected but also so perfect. Like last week, when they'd went for a day trip to see some standing stones, and it was just about to rain yet the sun was shining through the dark thick clouds lighting everything up and there was this stillness in the air and this feeling of *aliveness* as Myla described the scene and drew Kelly's attention to it.

"You feel how quiet it is?" Myla had said, before taking a deep breath. "There's so much potential in moments like these. Makes you feel like anything is possible."

Or two nights ago, when Myla had finally opened up more about her past while they were strolling along the waterfront. Kelly didn't think she could care about another person as much as she cared about Myla now. It was overpowering.

But then there were moments when she didn't feel like she really knew Myla at all. There was this hidden inner layer. Sometimes, Myla would withdraw from her or look so sad that not even their newfound and growing connection could pierce it, and that made Kelly feel sad too. Nothing that bad or traumatic had ever happened to Kelly. She felt pretty stable, emotionally.

Would Myla ever fully open up to her?

Lately, however, they spent most of their time in the bedroom, so that was where the focus was going. In the weeks since she'd got back from New York, they'd spent every night together, except for one night when Kelly had an overnight stay in London for work, which had resulted in rather explicit phone sex and an orgasm each.

The sex was intense and deeply satisfying. Kelly was exhausted most days from staying up until the wee hours, but she was loving every second of it. It was like they were trying to create the basis of a healthy relationship through all this lovemaking, through physical touch and exploring each other's bodies, what they liked, disliked, how they felt about certain sex positions and various sex toys. What their limits were. The sheer ambition of their lovemaking had lodged such a warmth in Kelly's chest, a warmth that had transformed this crush into something real and potentially permanent.

And they played. Such dualities kept Kelly on her toes and constantly coming back for more.

"You have a lot of energy for your age." Myla had said one night at one in the morning after they'd been fucking for hours. This only served to cause Kelly to don her favourite strap-on and take Myla from behind for such insolence, which Myla seemed to love based on the orgasm it gave her. Kelly thought she'd said it on purpose to elicit such a response, which turned Kelly on even more.

As Kelly arrived home and fed Barley and got changed to go around to Myla's, she realised that it was still relatively early days in their relationship and that this phase was to be savoured and enjoyed, and not rushed. Falling in love with someone and getting to know all of them is a process that unfolds in its own unique way depending on the two people involved and what initial barriers there may be to overcome. And Kelly and Myla were dealing with a few.

In her quieter moments, those early doubts about their age difference and Myla's connection to the distillery kept coming back. Was it worth saying no to a life-altering career opportunity for a relationship that might not last long term? With everything still so fragile and new between them, dropping the job offer in another country into the mix was a risk she couldn't yet bring herself to take.

Eighteen

The pub was packed. Kelly and I sat closely together across from Anna and Rory at a small table. The Light Spectrum were playing in one corner of the cosy pub, but they could have been headlining a festival, they were that good. They were a full-on Highland folk band, with a modern twist. The singer was a dark-haired woman with thick eye make-up and a gravelly voice that oozed so much soul. The drummer was a skinny guy with tattoos and long, sandy blonde hair. The guitarist was a big guy with a long beard, and there was an even bigger guy playing the smallpipes. The violin player had her back to me. They could all play. The whole pub was pulsating with the live music and energy from the band. Everyone seemed to know each other. I'd never seen anything like it. I loved it. Kelly squeezed my leg, smiling at me.

"You seem happy."

Kelly looked so hot tonight in her short-sleeved black shirt and little denim shorts. I couldn't wait to rip them off her later. "I'm loving this band and this pub. I'm glad we came out."

"You should go and talk to them after their set. They're all really nice."

I inhaled, sharply. I wanted to. And I probably would. But that didn't mean I wouldn't be nervous about the prospect all evening. I nodded back at Kelly. "I might."

"Best kept secret in the Highlands." Anna said, turning to us both.

"I should get a record deal," Rory said in his thick accent that I found hard to understand sometimes. "Grant's a mate of mine. They deserve it, the amount of work they've put in."

I picked up my pint of beer, nodding along to the raw Celtic drumming, half wanting to get home and play some of my own music.

By the time the band was playing their last song, the whole pub seemed like part of the band. Everyone was tapping their feet to the beat and clapping their hands on the offbeat. The occasional 'whoop' could be heard. The experience was visceral. I could feel the music in my bones, in my genes.

When the band finished a wave of butterflies ran through my stomach. We chatted at our table for a while, and I kept one eye on the band packing up when I got a glimpse of them through the crowd of people.

"Hey Grant," Rory said, calling the guitarist over. "Nice one tonight, mate."

"Aye, it was fun."

Grant found a stool and pitched up at our table, at the same time as the lead singer put a pint down on the table in front of him. "Cheers, Susie."

Susie smiled briefly and returned to the person she was chatting to. I listened as Rory, Anna and Kelly chatted with this guy as if they were old friends. I guess they were. I loved this place.

"Have you met Myla?" Kelly said. "She's a solo artist. Very talented."

"Oh really?" Grant said. He took a big gulp of beer. "What do you play?"

I cleared my throat. "A bit of everything."

"Can you play the fiddle? Heather is leaving the group. She's expecting a baby and wants to focus on being a mum for a while."

"Yep. I play."

"Concert level." Kelly said. "She's incredible."

"Then drop by sometime. We rehearse just up the road. Let me give you my number and you can drop me a line if you want to jam with us for a bit."

***

Cup of coffee in hand, I stepped into the old study at the far side of the house. Sunlight was streaming in, making some dust particles visible in the mostly untouched room. I hadn't been in here much since arriving. The room was ancient. Some of the books were bleached from being in direct sunlight, and all of them needed to be dusted. The desk was covered in papers and the drawers were ajar, bursting at the seams with junk. It looked like it had been abandoned after a long week's work fifty years ago. I was going to declutter the whole room and redesign it into a gorgeous work and reading space.

Barley did laps of the room, sniffing out the perimeter. Kelly had gone into work this morning, despite it being a Saturday. I'd been looking after him more when Kelly was at work. Hanging out with him, taking him for walks. Kelly had been staying over a lot, or I would stay at hers. I was getting used to waking up next to her, her clothes in my room, making coffee for her in the morning, her arms wrapping around me. Her smell. The ease with which we'd slotted into each other's lives and personal spaces was astonishing. It was astounding how more fully myself I was able to be in her company. No one else had ever made me feel like that. She'd shown me the archives at the distillery, and it turned out my family line had been pretty decent employers over the years, which was a relief. Kelly seemed as interested as I was in finding out about my history. She was amazing.

I sat down in the old chair, letting my head flop back, contentment washing over me. I'd never been this happy. The past few weeks had been a blur of sex and unprecedented joy. Kelly was way more tactile and affectionate now. It was all so fucking good. I'd never fully understood the term 'loved up' until now. Barley lay down beside me, seemingly satisfied that the room had been checked.

I took a sip of steaming hot coffee. We were going to a party today. Kelly's brother and sister had both finished university and her family were throwing them a graduation party in their garden. Their graduation ceremonies weren't for a wee while and were in separate countries, so they'd wanted to do something sooner and with the whole family together. It was sweet. I'd never seen anything like it up close. I was a bit apprehensive about going and for some reason chose today to start sorting out the study. Having a task would give me something else to focus on besides my low-level social anxiety, which was rearing its ugly head. The fact that we hadn't come out as a couple yet was not helping. I guess I was hoping Kelly would tell people today, but then again, maybe she didn't want to upstage the twins' party? So it probably wouldn't be today.

Sighing, I got to work on one wall of bookshelves and tried not to think about these things that were worrying me. I placed the stepladder where I needed it and began emptying the bookcases. Barley sniffed around where I was working. I handled each book as if it were an endangered species. It was slow going because I had a little read of each one. I put them into two sections: one to keep, and the other to be given to the town library. It was hard to throw them out even though they weren't mine.

An hour or so later I sat back in the chair again, tired from going up and down the ladder and shifting the books around. Barley was curled up on an armchair now. My eyes rested on the messy desk again and I started tidying it up, because I was on such a roll, and cleared some space to uncover a rich mahogany desktop underneath. I looked through the drawers for anything interesting, pulling papers out and stacking them on the floor for now. There were some papers relating to the distillery or random invoices dated twenty years ago. I slid open the top drawer and closed it again a few times. The smoothness was so satisfying. I loved old chunky furniture like this. It was so well made. So reassuring. The bottom drawer was packed full. It looked like piles of old letters under paperweights mixed beside random items. An old stopwatch. A long stapler. Some paperclips. Something about the letters caught my eye. It was like they'd been hidden.

Digging deep into the drawer and scooping them out, I laid them on the desk. Picking one up, it was addressed to Margaret and the stamp was dated nineteen ninety-six. The handwriting was elegant, old-fashioned, and quite beautiful. I would have been about a year old when this was written. I took the letter out of its envelope to find a short one-page letter addressed to Margaret from Hazel, my *grandmother*. I gulped, averting my eyes from the piece of paper for a moment.

Margaret,

I hope this letter finds you well and that you and James got back from France safely. I've been in London with Sarah for over two weeks now.

What? My heart pounded. Was I ready for this? I had a feeling something would turn up one day inside this house that would reveal my mother's past to me. Now that it was here it felt... inevitable. With a racing heart and a feeling of being cursed, I read on.

I am relieved to say that Sarah is coping a bit better now and that the baby is healthy. I wanted to put your mind at rest as quickly as possible.

Sarah has not changed her mind about coming home. She is quite determined to stay in London by herself and I can't do anything to convince her to come back to Balbuinidh, at least not until Myla is due to start nursery. She has no one, Margaret. I can't fathom how she is going to bring this baby up alone, especially given her poor mental health.

I've been looking after Myla around the clock since I arrived. Sarah has calmed down for now. She has been sleeping a lot. She seems to be doing better now that I've given her a break. The underlying problem is still there though. I just don't know what to do about it. She won't go to the doctor. She is in complete denial. I worry for Myla. She is such a sweet baby – so gentle and so quiet. An easy child, quite the opposite of what Sarah was like!

I'm not sure Sarah can cope on her own. It would make sense for me and William to look after Myla for a spell but Sarah refuses to hear of it. Do you think I should be getting help from social services about this? You know I would hate to do that to Sarah but I'm not sure I have any other choice.

I plan to stay here for another two weeks, if Sarah will allow it. I will keep you posted.

Love,
Hazel

Carefully, I placed the letter on the desk, staring at it like an unexploded bomb. But it wasn't, it had already detonated. Its truths hit me like shrapnel. I never knew my grandmother had stayed with us in London when I was a baby. This was yet another thing my mother hadn't told me. I gritted my teeth. Rage towards a dead person you loved is hard to reconcile. If she were here now I'd tell her how fucking pissed off I was. I could have *known* my grandmother. I could have had a constant loving presence in my life. Why the fuck had she kept that from me? Clearly, Hazel had wanted to be part of my life. She wanted to have a more active role. She said so to her sister in this letter.

I picked up the other letter, this one dated nineteen ninety-five. A few weeks after my birthday. I read the letter quickly, slowing as it progressed and the words became something lodged in my life never to be unseen.

Margaret,

I'm scared. Sarah is not well. The birth was very hard on her. Physically, she has recovered but mentally, she is not doing well. She has taken to her bed and is shunning the baby. I can't bear to see it. Myla is so tiny. She cried so much at first but now she is becoming quieter, but she wants her mother! Margaret, I don't know what to do. Sarah is reluctantly accepting my help. But she won't let William inside the flat. She says she hates him. She is convinced he's a threat, that he wants to take Myla away from her. He doesn't. Neither of us want that. She keeps saying that he wants to kill the baby. It's scary. At least she has allowed me in to help. The flat is not fit for bringing up a child. It's tiny and damp. She had hardly any things bought for the baby. I had to send William out to the shops for baby clothes, nappies and formula. We are staying in a hotel nearby. They're sleeping just now. I will keep you posted.

Love,
Hazel,

I threw the letter down and moved back from it, as if it were something toxic. Numb. I was numb. My mother had struggled after I was born. They thought she had mental health problems. My grandmother wanted to be there for us. She had concerns about my mother's ability to look after me. My mother pushed them away.

I searched for another letter, but the desk had no more for me.

***

I drove over to Hilary's house across town with Barley in the back, hoping she wouldn't mind the intrusion and that Barley would be okay in the car for ten minutes. I had a sense of dread but also certainty. I had to know what happened. And I needed to know now. I parked in the shade and opened the windows as low as they'd go without Barley being able to fit through them.

"Oh hello," said Hilary, opening the door. Hilary squinted into the sun behind me, holding her hand above her eyes, smiling. "Myla."

"Hi Hilary. I was wondering if we could have a quick chat for a minute?"

"Yes, of course."

"About my family."

Hilary paused and then lowered her hand from her eyes. "Oh. Very well. Come in."

Her living room was cosy despite being so large, bright and floral. Before visiting Hilary, I'd never been in such a room before. Never known a grandparent. What *else* had I missed out on?

I was close to tears already. Tea was offered and refused. Hilary already had one on the go. She was as close as I was going to get to the truth. Hilary adjusted her cup on its saucer. She had liver spotted hands. I'd never really looked at an old woman's hands before. I'd never even considered to. There were so many things I'd missed out on. This being one of many little things that, when added together, made me feel like I'd only lived half a life. This pain just kept twisting inside me.

She was so warm and nurturing, I wanted to adopt her as my grandmother if she would have me, which of course she wouldn't because that wasn't how things worked. She had a family of her own, like most people.

"What did you want to talk about, pet?"

"I found some letters in Margaret's study. They were from my grandmother." I paused to gather myself. "One was written just after I was born, the other a year later. Hazel was in London. My mother wasn't well; she said my grandfather wanted to hurt me." My voice broke. My mother's fierce independence, her protective love for me but also her mental health struggles and her failures as a parent clicked into place the second I'd read those letters. So much of who my mother was and what my relationship with her was like now made sense. But I needed to know more. I needed the whole story. I was done waiting and living in the dark. When I first met Hilary she invited me to ask her anything I wanted, but I was too scared. Those letters had ripped away my ability to bury my head in the sand any longer. "If it's not too much trouble, and please tell me if it is, I am ready to know more about what happened to my mother. Could you tell me everything that you know about why my mother left and why she cut off my grandparents?"

Hilary nodded, sadly. The expression she gave was one that suggested she'd been expecting this moment ever since she met me. "All right. If that's what you want. I will tell you what I know."

I was both relieved and terrified at the same time.

Hilary began, gently. "Your grandparents were so happy when they had your mum. They tried and tried to conceive a child so when she came along they were besotted. Hazel was forty by the time and William was a few years older, so there was quite a big generation gap already. Your grandparents grew up during World War Two. Your great-grandfather fought in the war. Did you know that?"

"I've seen photographs in the house, and some bits and pieces of war memorabilia but I don't know any details. So they were from a very different generation then?"

"Yes. As you know, your mum was very headstrong and clever. She was always that way. When she was five she was able to hold her own in a conversation. Your grandparents were quite traditional people, and your mum, she was not. She rebelled against them as a teenager and by the time she went away to university, they knew she was getting up to no good, going out to parties and drinking and what not. It was the nineteen nineties and more and more young women were behaving like young men. That's just my opinion, please forgive me. I'm old. I understand that they have every right to, I'm just saying that was when we started to see it."

"She told me she spent less than a year at the University of Glasgow, then dropped out."

"Yes. She came home pregnant at eighteen." Hilary paused. "William was adamant that she either marry the boy or have an abortion. He felt that it was wrong to have a baby out of wedlock and at such a young age. He was worried what people would think. He thought it brought shame on the family. He was quite obstinate, you know, stubborn. Your grandmother didn't share his feelings, but initially, she stood by him. He could be very controlling sometimes. Sarah felt betrayed by her parents and left. It tore the family apart."

I heard the words but they weren't sinking in. It was like I had a thick wall up against this new information. "She never told me any of this."

"She must have wanted to protect you, pet. That will have been the reason. That was why she left. To protect you. To bring you up herself because she already loved you."

"Hazel said in a letter they were thinking of calling social services. Did they?"

Hilary grimaced. She took a deep breath. Hopefully this wasn't too much for her. I waited for her to continue.

"They wanted to bring you back to Scotland and look after you for a while, until your mum got better. They were very worried, Myla. Your mum wasn't accepting the help she needed. Looking after a baby is hard for anyone, and your mum wasn't... she wasn't well. They were worried about you. One night, when your mum had an... *episode*, Hazel suggested it but Sarah wasn't happy about it. She asked your grandmother to leave. When Hazel went back the following day, Sarah had gone and taken you away."

The grandfather clock in the room ticked away loudly. It was annoying and making it difficult to concentrate on what Hilary was saying. Or maybe I just didn't want to hear this.

It felt true, though.

Hilary continued. "Your mum's mental health wasn't great. I know that she often got very agitated and would then take to her bed. She could be very paranoid. Hazel thought the birth might have exacerbated it, especially since she had no support. What do they call it now... postpartum psychosis? Hazel would talk to Margaret and me about it, mostly Margaret, of course. It broke her heart to see her daughter like that. Hazel found it very stressful. And then she got sick." Hilary frowned. "It broke my heart, too, everything that happened." She paused. "Are you okay, pet? Is this too much to hear?" Hilary's gaze was steady, as if she understood the gravity of what she was telling me.

"No. I need to hear this." I took a deep breath and then exhaled slowly. "How did my grandmother die?"

"Cancer."

"Same as Margaret."

"Yes."

"I'm sorry to hear that." I went quiet for a few moments, absorbing all this. "Going back to my mother... and her mental health. I just figured that was who she was.

I never realised until I got older that that sort of behaviour wasn't normal."

Hilary smiled sadly. "I'm so sorry to hear that. Did she ever get help?"

"No. She said she didn't need any help."

Hilary nodded. "Your grandmother thought that Sarah would come around, come home and they would put it behind them. But she never came home. When your grandmother passed away, far before her time, there was no way to reach your mum to tell her. It destroyed your grandfather, I'm sorry to say."

I nodded, not yet fully absorbing any of this. "Did my mother ever know that her mother had passed away?"

"She called home about a year later. William told her. He tried… She hung up. That was it."

"William tried what?"

"He wanted your mum to come home so you could grow up here. Your mum hadn't forgiven him, and she was happy in London."

A long silence passed. I had reached my limit of tragedy for today. The chair dwarfed Hilary. She seemed tired. "Thank you for telling me this. It can't be easy to dig this up."

"Not at all, pet. I've been preparing for this since I heard you had come home. I'm just glad I'm still alive to tell you what I knew of the situation, seeing as Sarah left some gaps."

"I'm glad too." I half-smiled.

"But you seem to have turned out well, hen. You're a sweet girl. You have a kind heart. I know your grandparents would be proud."

I bit my lower lip, feeling my chin wobble and my eyes water.

"Your mum clearly did a good job with you. They knew she cashed in her trust fund and lived off that. We assumed she made a life for herself down in London and enjoyed it enough not to come back. That's what we hoped for anyway."

"I didn't know she had a trust fund. I knew she had money because she was able to send me to boarding school but I never questioned where it came from." God, I was so naïve never to have questioned that.

"You had everything you needed then?"

"Yeah. I guess. We rented a nice home in north London. I never went without."

"That's good."

I couldn't get comfortable in the chair. My clothes felt like they were sticking to me. "Yes, she bought food and clothes for me and kept a roof over my head, but she was a terrible mother. Sometimes she would fly into rages and take out her anger on me. One minute she'd be fine, and the next, she was a different person. She could be so scary when she was like that. Right up in my face screaming at me. She'd grit her teeth and make this face of pure hatred. I've tried to forget that face, but I can't. She could be an angry drunk and could cut you with her words more painfully than any knife." I was inflamed, as if I was shedding my skin. I needed to get this out. "I remember her telling me that I had been a mistake. That I had ruined her life. That she wished I hadn't been born." I scoffed, feeling disgusted at the memory of her. "She went through relationship after relationship, always repelling them when they got to know the real her, if they ever got that far. There was one boyfriend who stayed for a while, he was okay. But then he left. She took that one quite hard. The only thing that kept her going was her job. She loved that job. It kept her anchored to reality. It gave her a purpose. I used to worry that she would completely fall apart if she ever lost it."

Hilary listened, patiently. If she was shocked, she was doing well to hide it. My head was starting to hurt. Reliving the past was compressing my whole life into one solid headfuck that I was struggling to understand. I was having trouble remembering the details. There were huge gaps in my memory. What was that about? I sighed. "But then sometimes we would have these great talks and she would show an interest in me. We'd go for walks and feed the ducks. She'd ask me about school, and we'd talk about my music. Then her work would get busy or there would be some big drama with the guy she was dating, or she'd get some crazy idea into her head like she was famous and people were watching her in the street. She would monologue about it for hours and hours, talking at me, past me, and there was no way I could question it. It was terrifying. I never knew where I stood. She was so inconsistent. Chaotic. She was a slob around the house, too. I used to do all of the cooking and cleaning. I couldn't rely on her." I took a breath. "But she was all I knew. After she died, I found it hard to know where I belonged. I still don't know, to be honest."

"Oh sweetheart. Can I give you hug?"

If this sweet little old lady showed me an ounce of physical affection I was going to have a breakdown and it would get ugly. I was hanging on by a thread here as it was. "Um, well, I don't think that's necess—"

Hilary had hobbled over to me and gave me a hug. I let it happen, willing myself to hold it together. I made a valiant effort but crumbled when Hilary and her watery brown eyes started speaking. "Your mum wanted you very much. That was clear for all to see. She wanted to protect you, so she must have loved you very much even if she had issues. All mothers do."

Painful emotions bubbled up and poured out of me and I could do nothing to stop the tears that fell. My face hurt from crying so much. The pressure in my head became intense, my nose blocked, and my eyes stung.

"There, there," said Hilary, triggering another round of tears.

"I'm sorry. I don't know where this is coming from." Finding out what had happened to my mother all those years ago had shaken me to my core.

"You have nothing to apologise for, sweetheart. It's a lot to take in." Hilary pulled back from the hug and held my hand in between hers.

I knew the moment I met Hilary that she would hold the truth to my past. I shouldn't have left it this long. I didn't have the strength in me to ask her before. I wasn't sure I had the strength now. Yes, my mum wanted to keep me, but even from before I was born there were problems. My grandfather didn't want me. My father was never told about me, or maybe my mother lied about that too. My mother probably only kept me to spite her father, and my grandmother didn't have the guts to stand up to her husband and make it right. I was from a family needlessly ripped apart and my mother had lied to me my whole life. Had I ever really known her? I grew dark with these thoughts.

We sat there in silence for a few minutes as I gathered myself. Bless Hilary's heart for waiting patiently for me to come to her for answers. This wasn't a story you forced onto someone. My mother's life made more sense now. It was like I was seeing her for the first time. So tragic to think that she died never having been able to be fully open with her own daughter. It was like I had a spiky concrete chain around my heart preventing me from living the life that I wanted. I was emotionally raw. As if my whole heart had been dissected in this sweet little old lady's living room.

Hilary gave my hand a squeeze. "Take some time to come to terms with the past, pet, but you mustn't ruminate on this forever. You have your whole life ahead of you. You don't want to spoil it by spending your time looking backwards at things that were beyond your control. Things that are over now."

I nodded, knowing that I could easily end up doing that if I wasn't careful. I didn't want my past to dictate my future. "I'll try not to." Kelly popped into my head. Was she my future? But then, this pain and unhappiness surged within me again. Why would she want to be with someone like me? Someone so broken?

"Good. Now, I hope you are going to look after yourself today."

"I have to go to a party." A party was the last thing I wanted to go to right now. I knew my eyes would be puffy and my face would be a mess. Why did my depressing life have to get in the way all the time? I was triggered and I was sad. I wanted to cancel, but how would that look? I'd be letting Kelly down. Although it wasn't as if I was going there as her girlfriend.

"It doesn't sound like you want to go. Is it the MacGregor twins' graduation party?"

"It is, yes. I did want to go, before I found those letters."

"Pet, maybe you should skip the party today and focus on yourself. Take some time. I'm sure they will understand. Sometimes you have to put yourself first."

"I don't want to cancel."

"I was going to go to that too, but my arthritis has been flaring up recently so I cancelled."

Oh god, hopefully I hadn't tired her out with my questions about the past.

"You're more than welcome to stay here with me, Myla. If you don't feel like going."

That sounded very appealing. But there was no way I was not going today. I'd plaster on a smile and be there for Kelly. I wanted to meet her siblings and the rest of their friends and family. I'd heard some people from the distillery would be there too. "Thank you for the kind offer but I'll be fine. It might cheer me up."

"Okay then. If that's what you want."

After I left Hilary's house I started to wonder: did everyone know about my sad past? Did Kelly's parents know? *Did Kelly?* I should have asked Hilary. My whole existence had been based on a lie. I was so *angry* at my mother for putting me through this. For not being there for me when I needed her. For being such a selfish chaotic mess who made me the parent. For being so shit and leaving me to find out all this on my own.

Nineteen

I was parking at Kelly's parents' house before I knew it. I texted Kelly from the car to let her know I was outside. I didn't have it in me to dress up. I was in the same jeans and t-shirt I'd cleared the study out in and worn to Hilary's. The party was mostly in the back garden by the looks of it. It was a hot June day, and I hadn't put on any sunscreen. At their door with Barley beside me, I was reminded of the time I came around for dinner. I was so innocent then, unaware of my true place in this town's history – the shameful unwanted child of a castaway teenager who wasn't mentally well.

"Hey there, beautiful," Kelly said, all radiant and smelling amazing as she came in for a peck on the cheek as she met me at the door. Her affection felt bittersweet. I couldn't take it in. I was so spaced out. "How are you? Had a good day with Barley? How's my amber malted Barley boy?" She bent down to talk to Barley.

I didn't want to spoil anything, so I pretended to be okay. That was what people did, right? "Barley's good. You look," Kelly was looking particularly beautiful today, her eyes and hair were sparkling, and a lovely smile played on her lips. "Glowing."

She leaned in close to my ear. "Even though sleep deprivation isn't good for the skin, at least something else is."

I half-smiled, looking at Barley who was wagging at Kelly, having not seen her for half the day. I couldn't connect with her as normal, and I couldn't tell her what was going on with me.

Kelly scratched his head. "Missed you." She leant down and kissed his ear, which he wagged extra at. When Kelly stood back up, she tilted her head at me and furrowed her brow. "Is everything okay? You don't seem quite yourself?"

I shrugged, clenching my jaw, irrationally annoyed with the question. "I'm fine, thanks."

Kelly looked at me carefully, but I wasn't budging. After a moment she nodded. "Okay," she entwined my hand in hers, bringing the back of my hand up to her mouth and kissed it. "You can meet Adam and Nicole. Come on," she gestured with her head, smiling, then let go of my hand.

There was no use in being here unless I could act normal, so I forced a smile out and followed her. There were loads of people in the house. It was a blur. Barley said hello to everyone, loving the attention. It was very bright and airy leading out to the back garden, where there were even more people, including Kelly's parents. I was introduced to Kelly's brother and sister as her friend. Adam was a muscular guy with Kelly's eyes. Nicole was petite and wore glasses. They both looked young and very comfortable in themselves.

"Nice to meet you." Adam held out a large hand. He had a confident, wide stance, and a kind manner.

"Likewise."

"This is Christen, my girlfriend."

"So nice to meet you," she said.

I shook hands with a stunningly attractive girl who had long curly brown hair, bright blue eyes and an American accent.

"Great to finally meet you. Congratulations on taking over the distillery. I wish it was in better circumstances," Nicole said.

"Thank you. And you. I've heard so much about you all. And congratulations on getting your degrees."

We chatted politely for a bit longer and then the conversation fizzled out. Unsurprisingly, I wasn't in a chatty mood. I couldn't think of anything to say, despite being interested to know more about them all. I hated being so in my own head sometimes. It was so frustrating. Kelly wasn't saying much, either.

Eilidh came over holding a tray of drinks. We each took a cup of wine. "Where's my little Barley? There you are my little sunshine angel baby boy!" Barley nearly knocked her over. It was obvious how much she loved her Barley and her children, too. An irrational stab of loss hit me.

"Geez, Mum, anyone would think Barley was your dog, not mine."

"I'm his grandmother. It's allowed." Eilidh looked at me. "Myla, thank you so much for looking after Barley today. Today was a bit manic getting ready for the party. It was a big help."

Kelly glanced at me, smiling, but didn't linger or say anything further. I wasn't expecting her to out us as a couple today, but it still jarred.

"No problem."

Malcolm turned up, and put his arms around Nicole and Adam, affectionately. Kelly's family started talking about their previous dog, who'd passed away a couple of years ago. Honey, the yellow Labrador, loved parties and being the centre of attention. Bore seven puppies. Had her own double bed when Nicole moved out. Stole any unattended food.

"Bloody dog," Malcolm mumbled. "Could eat for Scotland."

I just listened in as they had fun chatting as a family. I was distracted by my own thoughts and didn't feel part of the conversation. Sometimes it was hard to follow what was being said, as I didn't get the references. I was in no mood to talk anyway. There was such an ease about them with each other. Such unity. I'd never known anything like this. I'd known inconsistency, chaos, and feeling like a burden. Sometimes I felt loved, but that only made it more painful when my mother withdrew it. I'd missed out on the basic human need of secure parental love and was now doomed to sail through life unanchored and alone because I was so fucked up. No one understood.

Kelly chatted more now, central to the conversation and fully engaged with her family. The lack of her direct attention was like an abandonment. I gulped, feeling emotional, wishing that she would just talk to *me* instead. Go home with *me*. It was so irrational, but I couldn't help it. As time went on, the feeling got worse.

Kelly was ignoring me. I hated it. Everyone was laughing and having a good time. She didn't really want me. I didn't fit in here. I'd never fit in here. Or anywhere for that matter. My mother and her parents had been torn apart – and for what? Because my grandfather wanted my mother to have an abortion because he was ashamed? Because my mother was mentally ill and never got help? I hardly spoke as people chatted around me. Kelly didn't even check in.

What the fuck *was* that?

"I first knew you were really clever, Nicole, when you were five and you had the whole periodic table memorised. You used to sit staring at that huge poster on your wall for hours. I'd never seen anything like it!" Eilidh said, bursting with pride. "And now to get a first from Cambridge," she paused, swallowing an obvious lump in her throat. "You deserve it sweetheart."

Nicole gave her a hug. "Aw, thanks mum. Does that mean you don't mind me taking a year off?"

Eilidh frowned then gave her a scalding look. "Anyway," she turned to Adam. "What an achievement, son. I've said it before and I'll say it again, going abroad and doing what you've done, it's a triumph. We're so proud."

Adam blushed a bit and glanced at Christen. "Thanks, Mum."

"Again, well done the both of you," Malcolm said, before moving away.

Kelly was smiling broadly. God, she was so beautiful and perfect. "The rug rats are all grown up."

This was what a family should be. Together, warm and loving. Parents who behaved like adults. No lying. They were the epitome of the perfect family.

There was something about the way Kelly interacted with her siblings that made me feel like an outsider. I couldn't put my finger on it, but I knew that it bothered me in some way. I was way out of line here, but I couldn't help it, yet another sign I was damaged goods. Being here at this party combined with the news I'd had today was just too much. I should never have come when I was feeling so triggered. Hilary was right. What was I thinking?

I wanted to be there for Kelly. To be the nice and normal girlfriend she wanted me to be, but I wasn't. I was broken. She would never understand. How could she? Kelly hadn't even introduced me as her girlfriend. Why was she with me, anyway? She could do so much better.

Was she ashamed to be with me? With the girl whose family fell apart? The loner?

Probably.

I needed to get away from this party, and fast, before I let my emotions become visible to anyone who cared to look closely for a second. Twenty more minutes would do it, so I didn't appear rude. They were good people. I was just hurting. I walked around the garden, pretending to be interested in the pretty flowers but couldn't enjoy them. I could so identify with the rose bushes and the thorns they were stuck with. I wandered around the house with my plastic glass of wine, looking at their choice of furniture. They had good taste. It was all so homely. Classy. Nice. Just like them. The art on the wall was initialled E.M. and was of gallery quality. There was a family photo of them taken some time ago. Younger Kelly was so cute and fresh faced. Their family portrait was perfect. Happy. Together. Whole.

The house was quieter than the garden now, but some men were talking in the conservatory. Their conspiring tone gave me pause. When I heard 'the distillery' I stopped and listened.

Malcolm was speaking. "For a while there we were terrified. She could quite easily have sold up to the highest, or lowest, bidder. We knew that buyers were circling but they disappeared after Kelly sorted it out. Massive relief, I tell you. Kelly did well to keep the girl close. I advised her on that. It seems to have worked out well."

My breath caught. I froze. *What the fuck?*

"And now Kelly has been offered a job in New York with Matteo, heading up their international division. She's in talks with them right now. I never thought I'd want her to join the dark side, but I must admit I've never been prouder of her."

Another man spoke. "Matteo? New York? That's impressive, Malcolm."

Kelly is moving to New York?

And another man. "It's good the girl kept it in the community. God only knows what would have happened to the town if a huge chain got its stranglehold into the distillery before Kelly went onto bigger and brighter things."

The girl? Don't I have a fucking name?

"And thanks to me you'll never find out."

A snap of heads turned to face me at once.

"Myla. We, we were…" Malcolm stammered.

"Just talking about me?"

Malcolm's face went bright red. The other men weren't nearly as embarrassed as I would have liked them to be.

"Um, yes. About how pleased we are that you kept the distillery."

He was bragging to his friends that he'd orchestrated me keeping the distillery, which couldn't have been further from the truth. Kelly hadn't even been involved in my decision except to help me understand what the distillery was all about and what it meant to the people around here. It was in the interests of the town and the last dying wish of my great-aunt that had made it a no-brainer. What sort of person did he think I was? How pathetic was it that he was trying to take credit like this through his own daughter?

"That *I decided* to keep it, you mean."

"Well, yes but…"

I walked away without another word. I threw open my car door and slammed it shut. Had Kelly and her family only bothered with me because they were worried I was going to sell up and ruin their livelihood? Is that why I was feeling like such an outsider today? What the fuck was this about Kelly moving to New York? Why hadn't she told me about it? Was what we had even real? Did she even care about me at all?

I turned on the engine and tugged my seat belt over me. I missed the hole a few times. Deep down I knew that what Kelly and I had was real and there must be a simple explanation somewhere but with everything else that I'd found out today I just couldn't deal with this right now. I was already triggered before coming to this party. It was like I'd been hit by a double-decker bus today. It was overwhelming. I left the house immediately and drove straight home.

Twenty

Kelly hadn't seen Myla in a while. Maybe ten or fifteen minutes? She'd seemed down – depressed even – when she'd arrived. Kelly was sorry to see her that way. She thought the party might cheer her up, but Myla had been quiet again while they were hanging out, and then she'd disappeared. Something didn't feel right the more time went on and Myla hadn't come back.

Kelly excused herself and went to find her. But she couldn't see her. Anywhere. Weird. Where could she be? Kelly started to worry when she'd searched the whole house and garden to no avail.

"There you are," Kelly's dad said, flustered.

"What's wrong?"

"It's Myla."

"What? What's wrong with Myla."

"Hear me out." Her dad held his hands up in a sort of surrender then gestured for Kelly to join him in the sitting room. When the door was closed, Kelly crossed her arms over her chest. "Myla overheard me talking to Jim and Andy."

"So?"

"I was telling them about how you kept an eye on her and that it helped Myla not to sell up."

Kelly froze, simultaneously feeling her blood boil. "What?"

He lowered his head.

"What exactly did you say?"

He paused. "I said that it was my advice that you keep her close. And I think I mentioned that you were going to work in New York."

Kelly gritted her teeth and glared at him.

"I'm sorry. I think I upset her. She left."

Kelly looked at her dad right in the eyes and shook her head. "For fuck's sake, Dad."

"I'm sorry. Please give my apologies to Myla."

"You should probably apologise yourself. Look, I'm going to go and find her now. Look after Barley while I'm away."

"Of course."

She had to speak to Myla as soon as possible so Myla didn't get the wrong idea and that this didn't escalate. Myla shouldn't have been made to feel like there was anything untoward taking place and she shouldn't have found out about New York like this either. She wanted to know if Myla was okay. She needed to explain.

Racing through the narrow country roads in the bright sunshine she asked herself some hard questions and thought deeply about her intentions and how it must appear to Myla. She and Myla had a connection right from when they first met. It had nothing to do with Kelly trying to protect the distillery, right? Surely she would know that Kelly's feelings for her were real after everything they'd shared? That they'd got together because of the connection between them and not some hidden agenda. And fuck. The job in New York was now out in the open.

This could be bad.

Kelly pressed the doorbell to Glenbuinidh House and stepped back praying that Myla would answer. After an agonising minute, Myla opened the door with a blank expression. Kelly followed her in and closed the door behind her as Myla walked away towards the sitting room. Myla sat down on a single armchair and Kelly took the seat opposite, sitting on its edge. Myla looked tired. Her demeanour was more sad than angry, though. Kelly would have preferred anger. She wanted so badly to go to her but was receiving major fuck-off vibes amongst the melancholy so did not dare.

"Was what your dad said true?" Myla's tone was cold and lacked its usual feeling.

"No. When you first arrived in Balbuinidh I did tell my parents about you. My dad suggested I keep an eye on you to make sure you didn't sell up, but I told him straight away that I would not be doing that and that he was out of line for even suggesting it. My mum agreed with me. I haven't even thought about it since. It was always your decision what to do with Glenbuinidh. I've always respected that."

Myla shifted her legs up onto the chair and hugged them. She had a faraway look and avoided Kelly's gaze.

"Hey." Kelly spoke softly. "This is me we're talking about here. You know how much I care about you. What we have is real. Never doubt that." Kelly fidgeted with her hands.

"The way your dad talked about me today. It was as if you were all in on some joke at my expense. It really hurt."

"We're not. We care about you. I care about you. I'm sorry my dad spoke like that. I'm so angry with him. I didn't take his advice. We became friends because we wanted to, not because of the distillery. We got together because we really like each other."

Myla nodded and smiled sadly. "I know." Some warmth and feeling returned to her. It was such a relief. "I know it had nothing to do with him. I've never felt safer with a person than I have with you." Her eyes softened.

Kelly breathed properly for the first time since getting here. What they had was special and it was so affirming to know that Myla knew it too. That there was mutual safety in their relationship.

"But we were never just friends. Even if you didn't take your dad's advice and you told him where to go, if you're honest with yourself, there *was* an element of you putting the distillery first at the beginning. It was me who brought up how we'd first met, and it was me who made the first move. You said yourself that my connection to the distillery was a complication for you. You were more concerned with the distillery, and perhaps rightfully so. I was a threat to this place. An outsider. I still am."

"A threat or an outsider?"

There was an intensity in Myla's eyes. "You tell me."

Kelly paused. "You're neither."

"That took too long. I'm an outsider. Always have been, always will be," she murmured, as if on the verge of tears.

"Myla..."

Myla turned away. The sorrow in her voice cut through Kelly. What was really wrong here? Myla was quiet for a few minutes. "I hear you're moving to the US?"

Kelly took a deep breath. There was no way through this other than with the truth. "I'm sorry I haven't said anything about it yet. I'm not definitely going. I got talking to a company while I was in the US, they approached me, and then I had a video call with them recently. I wasn't expecting them to actually offer me a job and I didn't go looking for it. I didn't want to say anything because I'm probably not going to take it and I didn't want to worry you."

"Yeah, well, now I'm pretty worried. You could have told me about it. You could have trusted me."

While Kelly knew they were in a rocky place right now, this admission reassured her, somewhat, as it showed that Myla cared.

"I'm sorry. I'll never keep you in the dark about anything like this again."

"Okay."

Myla was being understanding and Kelly was grateful for such generosity given she hadn't been as upfront as she should have been. Kelly needed to decide about the job. It was becoming stressful not knowing what she was doing next. She'd never been so indecisive.

"Would it be permanent?"

"Yes. Assuming I took it and liked it."

"You should take it."

Ouch. That hurt. "You think so?"

"Yes. If it's what you want to do with your life, then you should go. Definitely don't stay for me. I don't want to be resented for ruining anyone else's life."

Kelly's shoulders slumped. Myla's eyes met hers in a sort of standoff. Her eyes were hurt, and other things Kelly couldn't work out. Kelly had never seen this in her before. Letting out a slow breath, Kelly touched her head, feeling stressed. "I don't think I'm going to take it. I don't think Barley would like New York much. They're not pressurising me to make a decision. Can we just forget about it for now?"

"Okay."

Myla nodded, and some of her defences went down, but she still seemed... off.

"Earlier at the party you didn't seem like yourself. I was worried there was something on your mind, something bothering you even before you overheard my dad being an asshole. Is something wrong?"

Myla rested her face on her hand, over her mouth. She couldn't have looked more closed and disinclined to verbalise her feelings. "Yes."

"What is it?"

Myla sighed. It was such a weary sigh. "I found out some things about my family today." She didn't elaborate.

"Do you want to talk about it?"

She shook her head, gently.

It made sense now. The quietness. The withdrawn behaviour. And to throw a party on top of that, one in which Kelly hadn't yet told her family about them being a couple and then to run into Kelly's dad like that and find out about New York… Kelly marvelled at how well Myla was dealing with it all.

"Anyway." Myla cleared her throat, a bit of normality returning to her voice but still with a hint of distance. "It was good to meet Adam and Nicole."

"I'm glad you enjoyed meeting them."

"Yeah."

Kelly had been debating when to tell her family that she and Myla were together. In the end, she'd left it too late, and didn't want to announce it right at the party. She'd been annoyed at herself when Adam and Christen were so open and relaxed together. She'd been aware of how that must have made Myla feel and worried Myla wasn't okay about it. She had every right not to be.

"You guys are the perfect family." Myla looked down at her hands. "It was difficult for me."

"What do you mean?"

"I've never seen such a loving family up close. It reminded me of things I've never had. Things I didn't even know I'd missed out on."

Kelly absorbed Myla's words. Her heart ached for her. "I'm so sorry to hear that, Myla. What did you find out this morning?"

Myla looked at her squarely in the eyes. "Did you know anything about the reason my mother left?"

"No."

"Did your parents?"

Kelly's stomach knotted. "No. Why do you ask?"

Myla looked down at her hands resting on her knees. "I don't want to talk about it." She seemed small, alone, and upset, underneath that thick wall, like a wounded animal.

It was like Kelly was seeing the real Myla for the first time. "Myla," she ached to go over to her and hold her close but didn't. "Are you okay?"

There was a long silence. "I just feel so alone."

"You're not alone. You have me."

Myla gave her a sceptical look. "No. I don't. Not really."

"Yes you do. We're together. We're a couple." She wasn't finding the right words. She wasn't helping her.

"I'm broken, Kelly. You could do so much better than me. You don't want to be with me. Just admit it now and we can both save ourselves a lot of time and pain in the long run."

"Why would you think that? I do want to be with you."

"I've got issues. I'm fucked up. I'm beginning to realise how much. You said so yourself that I was 'going through something'. Well, I guess I am. In all my glorious twenty-something immaturity."

Kelly had feared as much when she first met Myla at the café that morning a few days after she came to the distillery with Graeme. It was one of Kelly's initial reasons not to get into anything. And Kelly hadn't wanted to be a distraction when Myla was going through something major. She could see that Myla had some growing up to do, didn't everyone in their twenties? Now that she knew Myla better though, she cared for her in ways she hadn't ever cared for anyone else. She wanted to be there for her. In every way that she could. Taking a moment to still her thoughts, she just looked at the young woman across from her, and her heart filled with such affection.

"Myla. How can I help? What do you need?"

"I need to be alone."

"Let me stay with you. I want to know you're okay." Kelly stopped short of arguing her case further and saying the words *because I love you*, as she didn't want *this* to be the first time that she ever said that.

"I just want to be alone."

"Myla…"

Myla closed her eyes and whispered. "Please. Just let me be."

Kelly took Myla's words like a kick in the stomach.

"I can't believe you're moving away."

"I don't know if I am."

"I can't believe you didn't tell me."

"I'm sorry."

Myla's eyes were getting watery. "I'm not in a very good place right now and I would really like to be alone. I just need some space. Can you please give me that?"

It hurt that Myla didn't want Kelly around while she was in pain, and it hurt even more because Kelly was part of the reason she was hurting. She was locked out of that very private space within Myla, one that was increasingly looking like a very wounded place. Would she ever get access to Myla's true inner self? She'd seen glimpses of it. Like when she talked about her childhood and her relationship with her mum. There was a deep sense of grief at Myla's core, Kelly understood, and she'd trodden carefully around it so far. The only thing she could do now was respect Myla's wishes.

"Okay. I'll leave you be." Kelly stood. "Call me when you feel like talking again. I'll be waiting." Kelly squeezed Myla's shoulder on the way out. Myla turned her head away from her as she left.

Kelly sat in the car, rooted to the spot, looking toward the silent house with Myla inside. Myla's happiness *mattered* to her now. Knowing that she was in there hurting all on her own was hard to take. She was worried about her and confused. Kelly suspected that Myla loved her, even if she hadn't told her yet. Myla could say so much without words. So why was Myla pushing her away like this?

Her dad had no business talking to his buddies like that. He had no *official* business with the distillery any more. He had shown such poor judgement. He hadn't been the superhero that she looked up to for a long time, but now he was fast becoming a liability. The realisation that she needed to stand up to him crystallised within her. Kelly blew out a breath, feeling her whole body tense up as if preparing for a fight. Switching the engine on, she left Glenbuinidh House, her thoughts with Myla, to drive back to her parents' house and stand up to her dad once and for all.

By the time Kelly got to back, the party was over, thankfully. She found her parents in the kitchen, tidying up.

"Well done," Kelly said to her dad, with a sharpness in her voice and a need to destroy something.

Malcolm closed the dishwasher, grimacing. Kelly's mum turned around. "Is Myla okay?"

Kelly paused, biting the inside of her cheek to prevent a major rant at her dad. "No. Myla's feeling pretty betrayed right now, thanks to Dad." Kelly's heart ached for the pain that Myla was in, on so many levels. "You really upset her, Dad."

The anger laced in her voice caused Kelly's mum to give her a curious look.

"I'm sorry. I didn't know she was there."

Adam, Christen and Nicole joined them in the kitchen, looking between them as if they were walking into a sensitive situation.

"Why did you feel the need to spread those lies? Why did you even think of it in the first place? No, don't answer that. It was stupid then and it was stupid now, and it doesn't even matter. She's questioning if all I've been doing is trying to manipulate her." While Kelly knew that Myla believed her and they understood the truth between them, it had dropped a seed of doubt into their relationship that didn't need to be there.

"Weren't you, though?"

"What?"

"You became fast friends with her. We thought it was for the distillery's sake."

"We? Leave me out of this. I thought nothing of the sort. Whatever this is it's on you." There was anger in Kelly's mum's voice now, too. "Silly man. You've gone and upset both girls."

"I'm not upset. I'm enraged. You're always trying to get involved with the distillery even though you have nothing official to do with it any more."

"It's part of this community. I'm part of the community."

"You undermine me."

"I mean well."

"Dad, you've got to stop acting like you are involved. You haven't been for a long time. Yes, I've benefitted from your advice in the past but I'm doing it my way now."

"I know you are. I was just having a chat with my old friends. We've all worked at Glenbuinidh at one time or another. We care about Glenbuinidh. Always have and always will. It's in our bones, Kelly. You can't easily separate from something like that."

Kelly took a deep breath. Her dad wasn't a bad man. He did only mean well. But she needed to state her position on this once and for all. She squared her shoulders, assuming the role she played at work, and cleared her throat.

"The distillery is mine now, Dad. I know it can be hard to let go but you've got to stop acting like you're my manager when you're not. I don't want your unsolicited advice. I've humoured you for long enough. I'm sorry if that's hard to hear but it's true. You can talk with your friends about it, I guess I can't stop that, but I'd like you to sever this idea with everyone that you're still in charge and pulling strings." Kelly paused, fully intending to bring up her achievements he kept trying to downplay, once and for all. "I've pushed ahead with Queen of Spirits even though you said it was a bad idea. I then secured a major new distribution deal in the US for it and the signature malt.

The biggest deal the distillery has ever made, and you barely registered it. I'm taking this brand into the twenty-first century whether you like it or not."

Her dad was stunned. A few moments passed in silence.

"And I'm progressing with the Women in Whisky initiative. It's gaining a lot of traction. People seem to want it. I have Myla's full support. I didn't have to manipulate her to get it. She's even agreed to be part of it. Susan is going to interview her and there's talk of an article getting published in The Guardian about it."

"You're joking."

Ignoring her dad's comment, Kelly took a breath. This was it. They needed to know about her and Myla for real. She was done waiting to tell them. They were in a relationship and Kelly was in love with her. She might not say that last part. She hadn't even told Myla that yet. What if Myla was spooked by this whole New York thing? Spurred on by a mixture of fear, anger, and pride, Kelly dropped her final truth. "There's something else you should know." Kelly looked at Adam and Nicole, then her mum, and then her dad. He might as well have had the phrase 'I'm disappointed in you' written across his forehead.

Damn it though, this was important to her.

"Myla and I are in a relationship. I wasn't going to tell you just yet but after today, I don't see why I should wait. So no, we didn't become fast friends because I was trying to manipulate her. We were..." Kelly didn't quite know how to describe their initial friendship with benefits situation. "Dating."

"You're joking. I can't believe you would do something so stupid." Kelly's dad said, quietly, looking graver by the second, shaking his head.

Kelly's mum turned with a disgusted look on her face. "Oh come off it, Malcolm! They can do whatever they want. Kelly," she looked at her. "This is wonderful news. I'm very happy to hear it. She's a lovely girl."

"She's the new owner of Glenbuinidh, for Christ's sake! What are you *thinking*, Kelly?" Kelly's dad's face was bright red.

"I'm choosing to ignore you right now until you have something more constructive to say. I'm done playing by your rules. Done. This is my life and I'm doing things my way from now on."

"You do that."

"Thanks, Mum."

Malcolm shook his head, angrily.

"Congratulations, Kelly," Nicole said. "Myla is super sweet."

"Yeah, congrats. She's cool," Adam said. "Totally called it though."

Kelly smiled, grateful for their support.

Her mum gave Kelly a hug. "How is she?"

Kelly frowned. "She's not in a great place. I'm worried about her."

"I'm sorry to hear that," Eilidh said, letting Kelly go. "She did seem a bit down today. She'll come around though."

Kelly scratched her neck. "I don't know. Dad let it slip about the job offer and I hadn't told her yet."

"It'll work itself out." Her mum's eyes were kind. Knowing. She wished she shared that certainty.

Kelly turned to Adam and Nicole, finding it hard to keep everything together. "I'm sorry this is taking over your party."

"No need to apologise," Adam said, shaking his head. "Um. I'm going to stay in the US after graduation. I'm applying to jobs, and I want to be there for a year or two at least. With Christen."

Kelly's parents shifted all of their attention onto Adam. "You're *what?*" Kelly's mum said.

"I like it there." Adam shrugged. "Kelly might be there too."

"And I'm moving back home to take some time out," Nicole blurted out. "I want to do something less academic, like gardening or working in a bar. I need a break, guys."

Now everyone faced Nicole.

"What? I thought this was confession time?"

Later that night, Kelly couldn't sleep, and still hadn't heard from Myla. Scrolling through the many pictures on her phone, Kelly was looking for signs that Myla wasn't okay earlier on. A look in her eyes. A frown. An unnameable expression. She couldn't find any. Myla was mostly smiling and happy in the pictures. Was Myla being honest about who she was this whole time? Or was she presenting her best side? Didn't everyone do that at the start of relationships? Wasn't Kelly, too, pretending to be younger and cooler than she was?

There was clearly something bad that Myla had found out about her family today. There was ten years between them, and Kelly would be damned if she wasn't going to help Myla in any way that she could, if only Myla would let her. All that extra life experience could go to some good use here, surely.

And that started with honouring Myla's boundaries. However hard it was. She wanted to message her and tell her that she'd told her family and therefore the entire town and distillery that they were a couple and that she'd stood up to her dad about... everything. But the moment to make Myla happy that she'd told her family about them had passed. She'd messed that up. And Myla's wish to be alone was more important. She'd said it with such feeling, numerous times. Kelly had been quite taken aback by her intensity.

If they pulled through this rocky phase, Kelly would know that what she and Myla had was solid and she would turn down New York. She would stay and build a life around Myla and their future together. And that was huge. If they didn't pull through, Kelly would probably go to New York and start fresh. They hadn't set a time limit on this no contact, and she would have to wait for Myla to get back in touch. Kelly switched her bedside lamp off and shifted onto her side, accepting the agonising wait that lay ahead of her.

Twenty-One

I woke up on the sofa at ten on Tuesday morning, having not made it to bed the night before. I'd been up all night in the home cinema room I'd had fitted. Watching films, TV shows and playing video games was pretty much all I'd been doing since Saturday after I'd asked Kelly to leave me alone. That and eating biscuits and pizza. My back ached from sleeping in a funny position and hardly moving in days. I rubbed my eyes and yawned, feeling like shit from sitting around all the time in a haze of sugar and dissociation. It wasn't making me feel emotionally any better either.

To be fair, I didn't want to feel anything. Numbing out on this sofa for days was what I'd needed.

Why had I pushed Kelly away like that? Why did I always ruin my relationships with people? I missed Kelly and I missed Barley. I missed the feeling that had been growing inside of me that I actually belonged somewhere. Finding out the truth about my past, seeing Kelly's perfect family and then overhearing what her dad said had deeply triggered me. Kelly's lack of attention and then finding out she was most likely moving to the US made me feel insignificant. *Unwanted*. So utterly and painfully abandoned.

Kelly hadn't told me the truth about her plans. What else could she be hiding from me? My mother never told me the truth or put me first, so how could I trust that Kelly ever would? She was probably going to move to New York and leave me forever. Kelly had always seemed unsettled here, to an extent, like she wanted something more or something different than Balbuinidh could offer. I wasn't sure if I could give her that excitement either, long-term, because I was waiting for her to realise that I wasn't as interesting as she thought I was and get bored of me too.

All it would take was one decision from Kelly and she'd be gone. And because I wanted her to be happy, there would be nothing I would or could do to stop it. There was no way I would hold her back.

So much for the life changing effects of inheriting a fortune. Was the inheritance a lottery win or a curse? I felt *significantly* worse now than before I found out about it. Before, I was happy in my own little world, blissfully unaware of what I'd been missing out on and what life could be like. And now I'd been broken into a million tiny pieces. This was so not the fun times I thought I'd be having. Money couldn't buy happiness yet the idea of running away and starting over just appealed. I could buy a yacht and sail around some sunny Greek islands to my heart's content. What the hell was I doing wasting my time in this small town anyway?

I got up from my imprint on the sofa and brushed my teeth looking at my messy reflection in the bathroom cabinet mirror. Everything I'd done since moving here seemed stupid now. Like I'd been pretending to live someone else's life.

It was too much.

I needed help.

Later, I sat down at the kitchen table to text Cara and found myself calling her instead. It was too hard to summarise what I was feeling in a text. I didn't normally call out of the blue like this, but well, I hadn't felt this bad since my mother died.

A second later Cara's picture was on my phone for a video call. "Hey you!" Cara said, her face completely filling the screen. "Look at that cooker! It's bigger than my kitchen!"

"Hi."

"To what do I owe this pleasure?"

I tried to smile but all that came out was a grimace.

"Are you okay?" Cara's face grew concerned. "What's wrong?"

I filled her in on everything that had happened: the letters, my talk with Hilary and discovering the origin of who I was. I told her a little bit about Kelly, her family, the distillery, her probable move to New York and her dad treating me like the enemy. I spoke for a long time, longer than I normally did, and said more than I thought I would.

Cara was quiet, her face in a permanent state of concern. "I'm coming up."

***

A day later Cara placed her bags in the hall as I closed the door behind her. "Jesus Christ, you live in a frigging palace! Sarah kept this quiet. Are you sure you're not a duchess or something?"

"I am legally allowed to call myself a Lady. The Scots call large landowners 'lairds' and 'lady' is the female equivalent. I'm not into it."

"You've a good head on your shoulders, Myla. Always have had."

Cara's comment meant a lot, given that she'd seen me lose my head after my mum passed away. It hadn't been pretty. "Let me show you to your room and you can get settled."

"You better draw me a map. My sense of direction is awful, and this place is huge."

I laughed.

A few hours later, Cara and I were two-thirds of the way through a bottle of red wine and had just finished dessert. Despite having an elaborate dining room, I still preferred the kitchen table. It was cosy and warm next to the oven.

"I kid you not. Her camera was on. She was in the bathroom, *sitting down*. Her boss interrupted the presenter to tell her to turn it off. I've never seen someone turn their camera off so fast."

I gasped, and then laughed. "Oh my god! Poor girl!"

"She'll never make that mistake again."

Cara was lifting my mood, telling jokes and generally being her upbeat and charming self. She walked through life so much easier than I did. I'd always been amazed by it, her effortless confidence and positivity. It was comforting to know that it was possible to be like that. That people like her existed. I'd missed her.

"So," Cara took a sip of wine, gearing up for something. "You've been having a bit of a time of it up here."

I nodded. "Yeah. Thank you for coming up. You didn't have to."

Cara tilted her head, and her eyes were soft. "There's no need to do that. I'm here for you, Myla."

I gulped and looked away. I seriously needed to be more grateful for Cara and all the people in my life. Why did I keep painting myself out to be a victim? I blew out a breath, more annoyed at myself than anything. "Thank you. That means a lot."

"You know, after your mum died, I wanted to adopt you."

"You did?"

"Yes. You were young and lost, and in a lot of pain. I wanted to be there for you. To protect you. But you were coming of age and wanting your independence. You were always so self-reliant. You never let anyone in. It took years before you trusted me enough to open up to me. And then when your mum died you shut down again and you shut me out. At nineteen you were technically an adult. You were launching into the world with a broken heart and an understandable desire to escape your pain. It broke me to see you go through that. We were so worried about you."

The memory of that time was blurry. The drugs, the dodgy men, the living out of a bag. It was like someone else, not me. "I didn't know who I was back then. I just wanted to escape."

"It was like you'd completely checked out."

"I was angry at my mum for leaving me. I was angry at everything. I was angry at you. I'm sorry about that."

"You have nothing to apologise for. Nothing. I'd probably have done the same in your shoes."

"Cara, in case I haven't said it clearly before, thank you. Thank you for taking me in and helping me turn my life around. You've always been there for me. Even when my mother was alive. You were my rock."

Cara nodded, as if holding back her emotions.

"I had no idea you wanted to adopt me."

"I wanted to be your godmother in the beginning, but as you know, your mum was against religion and didn't even like the term."

"I didn't know about that either."

"I never told you. Neither did your mum, apparently."

"It was great having you around so much when I was growing up. You were way better than any of her boyfriends."

Cara grew quiet. Her features hardened, and she fixed a stare on the kitchen table. She got up, and walked to the kitchen window, looking out at the warm summer evening. She turned back towards me after a good minute, eyes steadier. "I was in love with your mum for many years. It was a difficult, unrequited situation, that I let go on for too long. Not that you can control who you love," she shrugged. "I knew that your mum was straight, and I knew that she just saw me as a friend. Her best friend. I was okay with that, and now I'm with Kay, who I adore. But before that, I used to feel like we were a little family of our own. Your mum and I were close in every way except one. In time, I learned to live with it. I loved being part of your life when you were younger. I think we got on very well, and still do," she smiled, affectionately. "That's why I wanted to be there for you after your mum died. Adopt you, ideally. It's why I keep asking you to visit. It's why I'm here today. You mean a lot to me, Myla. I'm here for you. Always have been, always will be. Never forget that."

Warm tears bubbled up to my eyes and I blinked them away. I'd never fully understood Cara, but now... I did. That she had stuck around all those years while harbouring feelings that could never be returned was so sad. I'd doubted her. Many times. I'd feared Cara was only checking in on me because she knew my mother, not because she cared for me in my own right or that I mattered to her. I never thought about how Cara felt. That was ignorant and selfish and immature.

I would never be any of those things again.

"I won't forget."

Cara sat back down at table next to me and smiled. She glanced around at the kitchen. "It's understandable you're feeling overwhelmed about all this. It's wonderful, but it's a lot."

"I've bought more musical instruments than I can play, and I've suddenly become focused on home improvement and interior design. I don't know who I am any more."

"It can be good to have something to focus on. You've done exceptionally well dealing with this on your own. So independent. You're a remarkably well-adjusted young woman, Myla."

"I would love to call you my godmother, if that's something you'd still want?"

She smiled warmly. "Deal."

I poured the rest of the wine into each of our glasses.

"She failed you. In many ways." Cara said, taking a sip. "But she loved you. She might not always have been the best at showing it, but I know that she did."

"I feel like that kind of dismisses my experience of her though. It wasn't easy to grow up like that."

"Sorry. I didn't mean to do that."

"No. It's okay. I've learnt so much more about her since being here. It sounds like she had issues before she even left for university. It sounds like my grandfather was very controlling. I can't imagine what she must have gone through when I was young. It must have been overwhelming. And then never to be able to say goodbye to her own mother. It's just sad."

"It is. She had her secrets, your mum."

I told Cara the rest of everything I'd found out since getting to Balbuinidh. I wasn't the only one my mother shut out, as Cara didn't know anything about her life here either. It brought me some comfort, even though I was sorry for Cara, too. "I sometimes think that having secrets was the only way she knew how to cope."

"I agree."

"She wasn't well."

Cara took a deep breath and then gave me a serious look. "No, she wasn't." Her hair was dishevelled and despite the serious conversation, there was still a light-heartedness about her. I loved her for that. "I think your mum had a serious and undiagnosed mental health condition. And untreated postpartum depression by the sounds of it."

"She would never have accepted a diagnosis. She knew better than any doctor, of course."

"I wanted to be there for your mum, but it was hard sometimes. It used to kill me thinking what damage it was doing to you."

"You did your best." In truth, my mother could be downright abusive to Cara. I hated seeing it and wished that it would stop. There was never any reason for her to be like that.

"I just wish she'd sought medical help and treatment. Medication would probably have helped." Cara looked distraught, as if she'd never quite got over it, and never would on some level.

I was quiet for a while. A million tiny memories flashed through my mind. My mother suffered for years when she could have got help and had caused so much suffering to those around her.

"There was a lot of stigma in those days," Cara said. "Things were different than they are now. Shittier."

I nodded, slowly. "Yeah."

"We both have to accept what happened with your mum and move on. She wouldn't want you to be upset about it for the rest of your life."

"I know."

"She'd want you to live your own life. To be happy."

Cara and I had never talked like this about my mother. Granted, in the past I avoided such conversations. But I was ready now. I was sick of running away from it. From myself. I was ready to face my past, accept it for what it was and move on. But even in this deep dive I held back on some things. Yes, I felt safe with Cara, and I was so grateful for her support, but some things were just too private. Our chats stirred up a lot of emotions, and I couldn't allow myself to fully feel them when someone else was around. I didn't know how.

"Well done for opening up like this. I know it's not always easy."

"I don't want to be like my mother, do I?"

"Would you consider seeing a therapist?"

"I don't know. It doesn't sound like something I'd be good at."

"You don't need to be good at it. Talk therapy can help you explore your feelings and come to terms with things. I think it could be good for you. And you could get the best. It's not like you don't have the money to pay for someone who really knows their stuff."

"I'll look into it."

On Cara's last night, I opened up about Kelly. We were sitting by the open fire, with large glasses of Glenbuinidh and the bottle on the coffee table. "I acted terribly at her brother and sister's party and then I pushed her away."

"You were highly triggered that day. Try not to be so hard on yourself. It might be something else to explore in counselling?"

"Yeah. Maybe. Kelly's probably going to take that job and I'll never see her again. There's no way she's going to turn down this opportunity for me after the way I've behaved. I've fucked everything up."

"Yes, you threw a wobbly. But you were rattled that day. She'll understand. It might not be a factor."

"God, I do need therapy. I'm such a mess."

"Kelly sounds wonderful. I think you need to ask yourself if you are pushing her away because there's a problem with the relationship, with her, or if there's a problem," she cleared her throat and gave me her most no-nonsense stare, "with you."

"What do you mean?"

"Are you reacting the way you are because you're afraid of letting her get too close?"

"Possibly." I crossed my arms.

Cara took a drink of whisky, regarding me carefully. "It can be terrifying opening up to people. Especially in the beginning with someone you really like. But how can she ever get to know the real you and love you for who you are if you won't let her in? *Fully* in."

I thought about Cara's words over a few sips of whisky, feeling mildly triggered. "I guess I *might* be afraid that if I let her see the real me... she won't like me."

"Oh Myla, that's the risk we've all got to take. There can be no genuine connection without that true vulnerability."

"It's just so uncomfortable. I don't know how to let her in, even though I want to."

"You reached out to me, didn't you?"

"Yeah."

"And how has that gone?"

"Brilliant. You've been super kind."

"What if you just let yourself trust that Kelly means what she says and does care about you? Let her in. Let her be there for you. If it doesn't work out you'll be okay after a while. You know you're a survivor. Why not take the risk and dare greatly?"

It sounded great but in reality, I wasn't there yet. "I'll think about it."

On Monday morning, I took Cara to the station.

"It's so picturesque here. I'm sorry I never got to see more of the town."

"Come visit with Kay and I'll show you both around. We'll make a holiday of it."

"We'd love that." Cara opened her arms wide and gave me a big hug. "You look after yourself, okay? No more of that 'poor little me' stuff. You're better than that bollocks, yeah?"

My grin turned into a laugh. She was so right. I'd been moping around feeling sorry for myself. I *could* do better than that. I *would* do better than that.

I waved as the train pulled out of the station, Cara waving frantically from her window seat. When all traces of the train had gone, I stood alone on the empty platform staring at the last place I saw the train before it disappeared into the distance, feeling a bit flat.

I took a detour and drove past the house my mother grew up in on my way home. I parked across the street for a bit, just looking at it. I wanted to go back in time and fix whatever was wrong with her. To help her. I cried. The tears that fell from my face were totally annoying, and I couldn't stop them.

I kept busy. I washed sheets, vacuumed, cleaned the windows, scrubbed the bathrooms, even gutted the kitchen and cleaned the oven. I did anything to not have to stop and think about everything I'd talked about with Cara over the last few days and why I was crying outside my mother's old house earlier. As the day wore on, and I'd tired out my body, I finally sat down and sank into the sofa. The house was quiet. Exhaling, I cursed the fact I couldn't hide from myself any longer.

I spent the next week or so holed up in my music room, writing and messing around with my instruments. I hardly left the house. Days blended into nights, and my sleep pattern shifted. I became a night owl. Times like these were usually good for infusing my lyrics with real emotion. Bits of paper lay strewn all over the floor and piano. New lyrics poured out. I had to write fast to keep up and get them all down. For the first time, it was like I was capturing my emotions as I was writing. Instead of avoiding them, I was channelling them into my art. It was the most creative spell I'd ever had.

Kelly was often on my mind. She was respecting my boundaries, even though it must be confusing for her. I needed this space. It wasn't about her. But it also *was* about her.

Getting it all down on paper was cathartic and healing. It wasn't easy but I was compelled to figure it out and face what I hadn't been facing: my relationship with my mother, the truth about my past, how I felt about myself, and how I wanted to show up in a relationship. If writing helped me work through things, then that is what I would do, and keep doing, for as long as it took to feel healthier and happier. I wanted to grow from this experience. Maybe then I would be ready for a real relationship with

Kelly, that is, if she wasn't going to move across the Atlantic.

Did Kelly really want me though? All of me? The messy, and at times ugly side of my personality that could be moody, self-centred, and depressive? *I* didn't even like me when I was like that. Why would Kelly? Was she the real deal? Did I really love her or was I just infatuated with the idea of her?

I found myself looking out of the window at the blooming flowers and the overgrown grass and weeds, longing for some fresh air again. It was summer. The garden beckoned me outside with new colours and plants I hadn't known were there. So I gathered my lyrics into a neat pile, put my guitar on its stand, and shut the piano lid.

I spent the following days with the bees and the soil, getting my hands dirty. I'd need help with the garden in time, but for now, I was content to learn what lay beneath and make it my own. I planted some oak, apple, pine and beech trees. Putting down literal roots at this house seemed fitting.

I began to look outwards past the garden to the land that pieces of paper deemed to be mine and thought of the hills and the mountains nearby. I needed a good walk and a bit of exercise, having got my strength back doing the garden. I bet the sunsets would be magnificent right now with these long and sunny days.

The next evening, I set off on a sunset walk into the mountains, hoping to catch some nice pictures. I chose the hill Kelly and I often walked together. *Our mountain.* I climbed and climbed, reaching the top at about nine-thirty. I'd timed it so I could catch the sunset and make it down quickly before it got completely dark. I knew it was a little bit risky, but the path was well marked, and I knew the way. Life was too short to play it safe all the time.

Deep reds, pinks and purples lit up the sky. I was better at using the camera now and some of the pictures would hopefully warrant blowing up into picture frames I could hang around the house. I took photo after photo trying to capture the sky, the colours, the panoramic mountain views – the moment – but none of them quite did it justice. Not really. They were good, but the *feeling* of it wasn't to be found through a lens. I found a rock to sit on, put down the camera, and looked out at the mountains and the sun going down behind the most northwesterly point.

The sun's descent felt big, important, and stubborn in its own beauty and purpose. The clear night sky enveloped me, and stars began peppering it. I stayed on my little rock for a while, looking up at the sky. It was so vast. I was so insignificant. We all were, in the grand scheme of things.

What if all this time I'd been looking outside of myself for somewhere to belong – trying to fit in at school, feeling like an outsider, clinging onto the café with Michelle long after I should have left and even latching onto this town and the people in it – when all along I just needed to love and belong to myself? I needed to stop walking through the world looking for confirmation that I didn't belong.

My life was now. I was extremely lucky in so many ways, including being able to sit here on top of this mountain and feel this level of peace.

The first time Kelly and I came up here together I was so happy. It was a strange thing, when I was with her, because I felt *more* like myself, in truth. The me I wanted to become. I wished she was here now. Was she okay? Was she going to take that job? I took a deep breath, realising that I was aching for her. Her love, because that's what it felt like, felt like this sunset: all-encompassing, beautiful, and expansive.

I loved her.

I craved emotional connection yet all I did was isolate myself, self-sabotage and push away people that got too close. Like I was pushing Kelly away. What the fuck was I doing? It was *me* getting in the way of us now. My issues were threatening to ruin things between us, if they hadn't already. What sort of girlfriend was I being to her? Shutting her out and not checking in with her? So what if she was weighing up her options about a job offer? It wasn't like she went looking for it. We hadn't even talked about where this was going between us. I hadn't even told her I loved her.

Feeling shaken by these realisations, the beautiful sunset, and missing her, I grabbed my phone and called her, half expecting to hear it ring out.

"Hello?" Kelly answered within seconds.

"How are you?" I blurted out, before steadying myself. There was a lot riding on this call, and I hadn't given it enough thought before launching right into it.

Kelly cleared her throat, sounding unsure. "I'm fine. How are you? It's great to hear from you."

Her voice made me all warm and fuzzy inside. "I...I'm up in the hills watching the sunset, and I was thinking about you." I paused, starting to shiver a bit, from the cold and also the tension. My throat tightened, causing my voice to croak. "I'm sorry for disappearing on you. I would love to see you. To talk. I've missed you."

"You're where?" Her voice was quizzical, and she ignored my latter words.

"I'm on our mountain."

"That's dangerous! It's late. It's getting dark."

"It's okay. I'm just about to start walking back down. I wanted to hear your voice."

"It's so lovely to hear from you, Myla, but I am seriously concerned about your safety right now. Where exactly are you?"

"I'm at the summit. Honestly it was a magnificent sunset."

"Are you warm enough? Do you have a torch?"

"It is a bit chilly, but I'm wearing a fleece. And I have a torch on my phone."

"I'm coming to get you. I think you should start walking back down now. I'll meet you on the path. I'm leaving now."

"That's not necessary. I'll be fine. Please don't put yourself out. It's late. There's something I wanted to tell—"

"Myla get your arse off that mountain, NOW."

Wow. Okay. That just happened. Pissed off Kelly was not to be messed with. "Uh, okay. I'll get going. I can call you back when I'm back in the car."

Kelly didn't answer. Looking at the screen I realised the phone had switched itself off. The battery was dead. Oh shit. I did need to get off this mountain. In the remnants of twilight, I hurried down the single-track path leading directly down from the summit, looking forward to the wider paths to come.

I would be back in the car in an hour. The thought of Kelly coming to check on me made me swoon. But I didn't want her to have to walk up this dark mountain either. I sped up. She was a bit dramatic about me watching the sunset, though. It's not like we have lions or bears in the UK.

After a while, I reached for my camera. It wasn't there. *Fuck. Fuck. Fuck!*

I stopped dead. I patted where it should have been bumping into my chest. I searched my pockets knowing full well that my camera was sitting on a rock at the top. My stomach dropped. How could I forget such a heavy weight around my neck? I had to go back for it. It had too many important photos on it. Photos of my new life up in Balbuinidh. Photos of Kelly. Photos of us together.

I marched back up the path, adrenaline pumping through my body. A breeze rustled the bushes lining the path as my heart pounded. I just needed to nip back up there, find the camera and make it back down as quickly as possible before Kelly got here. I could do that.

Before long, I was back at the top. It was hard to see the ground and I took extra care not to veer too far towards the edge. I rooted around and found it. Turning it to video mode, I used the light on the camera to help me see the path, which was a huge relief, even though it only illuminated about a metre in front of me.

It was eerie up here on my own in the dark. I'd never done anything like this before. My breath and footsteps were the loudest things. I could handle this, right? I made some progress, but after a while, the light on the camera went out. Typical! I froze. I couldn't see my feet. I waited for my eyes to adjust to the darkness.

I knew there were forks in the path, but I now had no way of knowing where they were. Fuck. This was not good. So not good. How would Kelly ever find me now? She would be in danger too.

I shuffled forward, using my foot to feel for the path, stumbling over root branches and stones with every other step. The camera made it hard to balance as I tapped my foot in front of me to feel out the ground. My heart was loud in my ears. I wrapped my arms around myself, willing my fleece to hold more heat and struggling to think clearly. I was lost. I could get stuck out here all night. Fuck. What about Kelly? The wind picked up, rustling the leaves of the trees whose roots slowed my descent. How stupid was I to get lost up here at night? It was June, though, so at least the sun would be up in a few hours. I dropped to the ground and sat. There was no point in getting lost further and I needed to think clearly or I could be in real trouble, and so could Kelly. I crossed my arms over my chest and tucked my freezing hands into my armpits. It was bizarre to think an evening stroll near my new home could result in a mountain rescue search.

Think, think, think!

I was pretty sure I'd come along the wrong fork. I could retrace my steps to the last fork then keep right. Yes, I could do that. I got up and started walking. Stumbling again I stopped. What if I was going in a completely new wrong direction? Deflated, I sat down again.

I started to shiver. It was too cold to be motionless, so I got up and started jogging on the spot. I used to go out dancing later than this and walk home in winter. It was better to keep warm. I'd do jumping jacks all night if I had to.

There was something about being so on your own like this that made you come face to face with yourself. Waving my limbs like a Highland dancer on the side of a mountain in the middle of the night was one way to see that it was me who had got myself into this situation and me who needed to get myself out of it. A familiar gear within me kicked into place.

You've got this.

Feeling warmer, calmer and more confident, I slowly continued along the path, reaching the point where the hill started going up. Yes! That was the main path. Carefully, I turned around and started walking downhill extremely slowly. I made fists with my hands, determined to get myself safely off this mountain before putting Kelly in any danger, hoping I hadn't been faffing about up here in the dark for too long.

I picked up my pace a bit, putting all my weight onto ground that wasn't there. My foot twisted as it hit the ground lower than I expected and I fell. I tumbled down the path, falling for longer than I thought I would, my camera hammering into me. Pain seared all the way up my leg, and through my body, as I came to an abrupt stop against a rock.

I sat there, waiting out the pain soaring through me, unsure what to do next. I tentatively stood up and tested my ankle under my weight, but it was too painful. I leant against the rock.

Fantastic.

I tried to breathe through the pain, but my breath was jagged and shivery. It was so cold. Doing jumping jacks all night was out of the question now.

I sat there for a while. For too long.

Was that my teeth chattering or was there the faintest sound of clanking? In the distance, a beam of light moved side to side. I held my breath, focusing my eyes and ears towards the light.

"MYLA." It was Kelly's voice. "MYLA."

"I'M HERE!"

The light jerked out of its steady sweeping and settled about twenty metres away, in my direction.

"OVER HERE," I called.

I hopped around the rock and waved at the light, doing my best to ignore the pain. A mixture of gratitude, relief and concern took hold inside me. My stupid ankle kept me from running to her. The light grew brighter. Barley's collar clanked louder. When the light reached my body relief washed over me. Kelly had rescued me. Barley brushed against my legs, wagging frantically, it was agony, but I was all relief and joy.

Kelly came right up to me and hugged me tightly, squeezing the camera into my ribs and pressing her heavy-duty torch into my back; it shone up into the sky like a bat-signal as she clung to me. Her breath was ragged. It was *so good* to see her. To hold her. To smell her.

"Are you okay?" She looked me up and down and brushed the hair from my face and searched my eyes. "I was so worried about you."

"I'm fine. I'm fine. Just a little cold. And I hurt my ankle."

"Here," she handed me a fleece from her backpack and a thick beanie. "Put these on."

"Thank you." They were an instant relief.

"What did you do to your ankle?"

"I fell and went over on it. It's a bit sore. I was just waiting for it to calm down and then I was going to hobble back down."

Kelly stepped right back. Even in the darkness I could see that she was angry. Her face was hard and her eyes were unforgiving. "Why did you come up here so late?"

"To see the sunset. It was *so* stunning."

"It's so dangerous up here at night. People have died getting lost on these hills. I was one breath away from calling mountain rescue. I've got Rory on standby."

"It's a well-marked path, I didn't think it would be dangerous. I'm sorry."

"It was reckless."

"I'm sorry I worried you."

"I can't believe you came up here on your own like this, and without any light or safety provisions." She shone the torch up my body, and then back at my feet. "And in those flimsy trainers. No wonder you twisted your ankle."

"I made a bad call. Live and learn?" I hopped towards her, and tentatively put my hands on her waist. I had all my weight on one foot. "Thanks for coming to rescue me." I smiled, close to her face now, and a slight curve appeared at the edge of her lips. I smiled too. "It's so romantic."

"I can think of better ways to be romantic. I'm just glad you're alive. How's your ankle?" She crouched down, moving my trousers up slightly and my sock down carefully. She was very gentle. Even in this situation I tingled at her touch. "It's swollen."

"Shit."

"Right." She stood up. "Let's get you down this hill." She placed my left arm over her shoulders, so she would take my weight. "You might need to go to hospital."

"I don't think that's necessary. It's probably just a sprain. A bit of ice and rest and it'll be fine." Feeling Kelly's body pressed against my side was sending tingles all over me, which in itself acted as the best antidote to the cold and the pain.

"The invulnerability of youth speaks again."

"Will you forgive me?" I didn't just mean about tonight.

"Let's just get off this mountain."

Twenty-Two

Kelly pulled up outside Myla's house. Dawn had broken, and a full chorus of birds was there to welcome the new day. Myla had a minor ankle fracture. Kelly had insisted they go to the hospital because Myla had been in so much pain, despite not using her foot. It had been a struggle to get her to the car. Kelly had given her a piggyback down the mountain, which Barley found highly amusing. Kelly smiled, recalling how funny they'd both found it, too, and how Myla had held onto her so tightly, resting her head over her shoulder, nuzzling into the side of her face.

They were seen quickly, which was a relief after the long drive. Myla had had an x-ray and her lower leg put in a boot and was sent away with a pair of crutches and the bag of ice she'd had on her ankle while in the hospital. Kelly didn't want Myla to be on her own, but she didn't want to presume that she could go in either. A dull throbbing pain had taken root in Kelly's head probably from being up all night in stress mode and the effort to carry Myla down a mountain.

Myla turned to her, the dawn light casting a lovely glow on her face. She put her hand over the back of Kelly's. "Thank you for being there for me tonight. Thank you for rescuing me and then insisting I go to the hospital. Just… thank you." Her eyes were soft but also worried. "I know you must be exhausted, but will you come inside?"

Kelly reached out and touched her cheek. "Of course I'll come in. Let me take care of you."

Myla softened even further.

They went into the house with a sleepy Barley in tow. Kelly turned on the lights.

"I'm so tired," Myla said, balancing on the crutches.

"Me too."

Barley headed straight for his sofa, without a backwards glance. "I think someone's grumpy at being kept up all night."

"I don't blame him. He's such a good dog."

"He is," Kelly murmured.

Myla hesitated. "Would you like to stay over?"

Kelly stepped towards her, resting her hands on Myla's waist. "I'd love that."

In Myla's bedroom, Myla sat on the bed and Kelly helped her get unchanged. She knelt in front of Myla, very aware of their proximity and the gravity of this. "Just let me know if anything hurts." Myla took off her fleeces and t-shirt, and Kelly moved Myla's jeans down, careful to avoid the boot, as Myla winced. "Sorry. It's a shame they cut your nice jeans."

"It's a shame these painkillers haven't fully kicked in yet."

Kelly swallowed hard, getting excited by the sight of Myla in her underwear. That wasn't what this was about. She smiled warmly instead, forcing her eyes up to Myla's face. "Anything else I can help you with?"

Myla's eyes sparkled, narrowing slightly. "Just you, in bed with me."

Kelly bowed her head, trying to think. They hadn't even talked about anything. She couldn't let sex happen again unless they sorted everything out. While she knew Myla needed some space to be alone, where the hell had she gone for the past nearly three weeks? What was wrong? Kelly didn't appreciate being left out in the cold like that, even though she had worked hard to respect Myla's boundary. It had dented some trust in their relationship for Kelly. And now, Myla was acting as if everything was fine.

"Kelly. I know I have no right to ask, and we have a lot to talk about, but could we just get some sleep and hold each other? I can hardly string a coherent sentence together right now let alone have one of the most important conversations of my life."

Kelly's guard went down. Myla was right, and Kelly had a headache. Plus, the bed and sleep looked *so* inviting.

"Sure."

Myla popped her bra off. "Can you grab something for us to wear to bed from that top drawer?" She slid her panties down.

"Yep." Kelly turned away, feeling flustered at Myla's nakedness, and got out some light cotton shorts and tops from the chest of drawers. "Here, let me." She helped Myla get into the clothes and under the covers, feeling so close to her in this moment.

Myla looked so sweet and exhausted, lying on her back with a giant boot sticking out the covers. Kelly had so many questions, though. It hadn't been an easy wait to hear from her again. Kelly had struggled to be in a good mood for Nicole's graduation ceremony, and Georgia had noticed she wasn't as happy at work. The job in the US had seemed ever more appealing the longer Myla shut her out. She wasn't up for this kind of drama, at any age. But there was something deeper to Myla's behaviour the day of the party that Kelly wanted to know more about, if only Myla would tell her. It felt important that she did, before she could really assess what to do next. Because walking away was an option for Kelly, however much it pained her to think about.

Kelly slipped into bed forcing herself not to think about any of this hard stuff, and cuddled into the side of Myla, feeling the heat of her body and the rise and fall of her chest, and just... peace.

***

Kelly woke in the same position to Myla's slow and deep breathing. Kelly was surprisingly refreshed, considering she'd been up all night. Myla was an adorable sleeper. Kelly fought the urge to kiss her awake. Instead, she quietly got up, and went to find Barley and make some coffee.

He was still sleeping on his sofa. "Hey, Barley." His tail thumped the closer she got to him, and he got up to greet her, looking all sleepy too. "I hope you slept well after our adventure last night," she kissed him on the head. After letting him out into the garden, she fed him some breakfast, thinking how thoughtful it was that Myla had got him some food. It was only as she was making the coffee that she realised it was a Friday and she was supposed to be at work right now. She'd forgotten all about it. She was shocked. Forgetting about work had never happened before, especially this close to the launch of Queen of Spirits and the Balbuinidh Highland Games. There was no way she could work today, not with Myla having a broken leg. She needed to shake off the stress of last night and she *needed* to spend some time with Myla today. She got her phone out of her rucksack at the front door and messaged Georgia that she was taking the day off.

Kelly spoke to Barley, who was lying down on the kitchen rug. "Shall we go find Myla?"

At that, he ran off upstairs, and Kelly followed him with the coffee. Barley woke Myla rather abruptly, pretty much headbutting her and nudging the covers off. "Barley, leave. That's too much, pal."

Ignoring Kelly, he caused a huge smile from Myla, who told him he was a very good boy. He then lay down beside the bed, keeping a close eye on them both.

"Good morning," Kelly said, putting Myla's mug and some painkillers next to her on her bedside table.

"Barley, fresh coffee and you all at once? It really is a good morning."

Kelly smiled, sitting on a purple velvet wingback chair next to the bed. "How's your leg?"

"Oh god, *that*." Myla looked down at the giant boot and grimaced. "How could I forget."

"I think we'll both remember last night for a very long time."

Myla sat up and gingerly re-positioned her leg before taking a sip of coffee. She looked gorgeous first thing in the morning. Kelly could only admire Myla's adventurous and romantic spirit, despite how much she disapproved that Myla had gone up there on her own so late at night. "How are you? I brought up some painkillers."

Myla yawned. "I'm okay. Just a bit tired." She picked up a bottle of water and took her painkillers. "Thanks."

"I thought you might be. I can go once I help you get up and settled, if you need space."

"No," Myla found her eyes. "I want you to stay. I'm ready to talk, if you are?"

"I am." Kelly crossed her legs and took another large sip of coffee.

Myla looked away and became quiet.

Kelly's throat tightened.

Myla raised her eyes to meet Kelly's. The intensity was breathtaking.

"Kelly. I don't know where to start."

"It's okay. Just take your time. I'm here."

Myla took a deep breath. "I'm sorry for the way I acted at Adam and Nicole's party. I hope your family will understand?"

"They understood straight away. Even my dad, he apologised. We are all so grateful you decided to keep the distillery. Everyone really likes you. Well, especially me."

"Oh." Myla blushed.

"I went straight home that night and told them all we're dating. I also stood up to my dad about the distillery, too."

Myla's eyes widened. "You did?"

"Yes. I'm sorry I didn't tell people sooner. I'm sorry you had to be there but not as my girlfriend and that I put you in that position."

"I was in a really weird place that day."

Kelly put her coffee down, glad Myla was going there so soon. "What happened?"

Myla hesitated, obviously uncomfortable. "That morning, I found some letters from my grandmother to Margaret about what happened around when I was born. I visited Hilary. I found out that my grandfather was going to force my mother to have an abortion, that he didn't want me to be born. My mother ran away to London and had me all on her own. She was having mental health problems. She really wasn't well my entire life. My grandparents were devastated, and my grandmother died quite young without ever patching things up with my mother. Without ever knowing me. My mother never forgave her dad. Finding the letters brought up a lot of issues around my past and my relationship with my mother. Stuff I haven't dealt with, haven't wanted to deal with before."

"Oh, Myla, I'm so sorry. And then you came to a party with everyone being all happy and heard my dad say that shit."

"On another day, I might have handled it better. I've struggled my whole life feeling like an outsider, feeling like I didn't have the sort of family most people have. That there's something wrong with me. Seeing your happy family and the love between you all was just a lot to take when I was feeling so low. I'd had a bad morning. I shouldn't have come to the party when I wasn't in a good place. I'm sorry."

"It's understandable, darling. You could have talked to me though."

"I know. I was triggered and overwhelmed. I think my default is to handle things on my own. I'm not comfortable sharing that I'm not okay."

Kelly just nodded, feeling such empathy for what Myla must have been going through. What she must *still* be going through, sure that Myla had a lot more to share on the topic of her family and how it had affected her.

"The truth is," Myla tucked some hair behind her ear. "I felt like you were ignoring me at the party. I wanted all of your attention. I'm not used to sharing you with people. It really hurt. I didn't feel like I could trust you any more. It was so fucking childish and I'm super embarrassed about it." Myla looked down.

Kelly furrowed her brow. She had not expected that. Myla had been so quiet and aloof that day. To think she was feeling like Kelly was ignoring her was hard to get her head around. Myla hid her feelings so well, Kelly was fast learning. So she both wanted her attention and pushed her away? It was confusing but this new piece of information about Myla made sense the more she thought about it. "Thank you for telling me. While I do apologise for not being out as a couple at the party, obviously I can't apologise for talking to my family…"

"Absolutely!" Myla said quickly. "These are my issues. You did nothing wrong. Me wanting your attention and being a clingy fuck has nothing to do with them or you. You were perfectly normal. I was being ridiculous."

Kelly wanted to go over and hug and kiss and hold Myla for the rest of the day, no, for the rest of her life at this rate, but Myla didn't seem finished. She seemed to be struggling to verbalise her feelings all through this conversation, but Kelly could tell she was trying her best. So she just sat there and waited patiently for her to continue.

Myla's brow furrowed. "Cara came up from London to visit. We talked. It helped. I did a lot of thinking after she left. I hadn't realised how much the inheritance, this house, and being in Balbuinidh had affected me. I had so much to process. I knew I had issues and I knew I was a bit broken and alone and different from a lot of people, but all this has made me face my past and find out who I really am. Where I came from. I've realised I've got a lot of healing to do. A lot of growing up to do. I used to pride myself on the fact that I didn't have the same problems as my mother, that I didn't have any mental health problems. Part of me always worried that it might be hereditary, so I was glad to have escaped. But now I see that my mental health really isn't that great. I'm going to start therapy and face it head on. Or try to. This is why I didn't get in touch." Myla paused, bit her lip and then found Kelly's eyes and held them. "You've made me feel so supported and so happy these past few months. Being with you has helped me see myself more clearly. The good and the bad. I'm sorry for shutting you out. I won't do that any more." Myla shrugged, as if trying to downplay everything she'd just said. She could be so understated sometimes, and Kelly just found it so beautiful and poignant. Myla's eyes were still uncertain, however. She half-laughed. "If all this emotional baggage doesn't put you off then I'd love it if we could move past this? I, um, really want to see where this goes between us. If you're still up for that?"

Kelly stepped over Barley and sat on the bed. She touched Myla's face. "I'm not put off. I still want to see where this goes, too."

Myla's eyes widened as Kelly tilted her chin upwards and gently kissed her. Kelly lingered as a wave of emotion passed over her, and Myla wrapped her hand around the back of her neck. So much passed between them in that moment, that Kelly had to steady herself on the back of the headboard with her other hand. The sheer strength of her feelings caught her by surprise. Kelly ran her hand through some strands of Myla's smooth hair.

"You have my attention. You've always had it. I think about you all the time. From the moment I first laid eyes on you I couldn't look away. You make me feel like I'm living again. I love seeing the world through your eyes. I really care about you."

Myla's smile was so huge and unguarded and so pure. "I really care about you, too."

Warmth spread through Kelly's chest and outwards to her whole body. "Thank you for opening up to me. I've never had to deal with anything like what you've gone through, but I really respect how you are handling things. I don't know if I would be so strong. So resilient."

A few moments passed in silence before Myla pulled Kelly onto her lap. "Your leg, am I not hurting you?"

Myla pulled her in close, so that their mouths were barely not touching. "My ankle is fine." She brushed her nose against Kelly's then tilted her head and slipped her hands under Kelly's loose t-shirt. "I've missed you." She whispered.

The passion between them was igniting, but Kelly couldn't let that happen right now. Myla was injured and they had said a lot. Kelly pulled back and rested her hands on Myla's shoulders. It had been an excruciatingly long few weeks apart and they shouldn't rush into sleeping together. "I've missed you, too. But…"

"But what?"

"I need to think. A lot has happened."

"What's on your mind?"

Kelly bit down on her lip and took a deep breath. If she didn't say it now, she never would. "If we're to be together, I need you to be open with me like this and tell me how you're feeling. I don't like it when you shut me out. It's happened a few times now."

Myla nodded. "You're right. I understand. I promise to work on it."

That was good enough for Kelly.

A frown passed over Myla's face.

"What is it, darling?"

"Nothing," Myla murmured.

Kelly raised an eyebrow.

Myla found her eyes; her hands had gone limp against Kelly's sides. "Sorry, force of habit. I was thinking about that job in America."

Jeff had given her until after the launch of Queen of Spirits to give them an answer either way, which was just over two more weeks. It was generous of them to wait on her for so long already. That in itself showed her that they were both interested in her wellbeing and not particularly needing her. Her slow response and indecision on the matter was directly related Myla. "They want to know in a couple of weeks, or the offer is off the table."

"What are you going to do?"

Still straddling Myla's lap, Kelly could do nothing but be completely open with her about it. "I'm struggling to decide. Part of me is interested, it's the opportunity of a lifetime, but another part of me really wants to stay here. With you."

Myla inhaled, sharply, and then relaxed her shoulders and her whole face. She caressed the skin on Kelly's waist, sending untimely tingles right to her centre. "I don't *want* you to go." She spoke quietly. "But if it's what you want, I'll understand. I want you to be happy. I want you to follow your dreams. Maybe we could make long distance work? I would love to visit New York. And we do have the money to travel back and forth easily enough."

Kelly closed her eyes. Myla was being so sweet and supportive. She wanted Myla to be happy, too. Kelly wanted to be the one to make her happy. Could she really do that living so far away? It didn't sound like Myla was interested in coming with her. She didn't have to decide right now, though. She still had some time left. Today was about looking after Myla, even if Myla was playing her broken ankle down.

"Maybe. Would it be okay if we don't talk about this any further today? I just want to be with you and look after you."

"Aren't you going into work today?"

"No. I'm all yours. Anything you want, I'm here for you. What with the broken leg and all."

"It's only a minor break. They could hardly see the line on the x-ray."

"You can't walk."

"Hairline fracture. Hairline. The doctor wasn't worried about it not healing well – she even said the boot wasn't essential – so you shouldn't worry."

"But I do worry."

Myla's smile grew and grew, lighting up her whole face. "Because you care about me."

Kelly blushed.

"You know what I really want?" Her eyes twinkling now.

"What?"

"A shower."

"Of course you do."

Myla smirked. "Bless her, dear Margaret, she knew how to have a bathroom fitted. The walk-in shower is big enough for two… The boot comes off. I could really use some help in there. You know, for my health."

Kelly raised an eyebrow and gave Myla a dark look, being flirtier than she'd intended. She held Myla's gaze, which was quickly filling up with desire.

"For your health."

"In case I slip."

"Right."

Kelly helped Myla get out of bed, taking all of her weight as she stood up, which was a bit difficult after last night's powerlifting. Myla's body was warm. There was something so right about being there for Myla like this. Inevitable. Like she'd been waiting her whole life to meet Myla and have her in her life.

Kelly parked Myla against the wall in the shower, on a non-slip mat. Their eyes met as Kelly undressed them both, starting with Myla, and then herself. Kelly turned on the shower but before she could steady herself Myla was kissing her underneath the stream of water that quickly became hot and steamy.

***

Kelly sat with Myla outside Glenbuinidh House by the open fire-pit. The sun had set yet there were still remnants of fading light. The air was still and the garden was so fragrant with summer flowers. The warmth of the firepit was still needed. Barley looked up from his basket, wrapped in a tartan blanket, a few paces away on the patio. The soft orange glow of the flames and steady burning and crackling was hypnotising. Myla stared into the firepit. Since finding her on the mountain, Kelly had been helping Myla with daily tasks and mobility so that her ankle would heal well. Kelly was in such awe of her humility, strength, and courage. Myla shared more about herself and her past. The things Myla had been telling her about her relationship with her mum were heart-breaking. Myla's mum had mental health problems, and it weighed down heavily on Myla, all these years later. Being there for Myla was fast becoming the most all-encompassing and rewarding thing Kelly had ever done. Her life felt bigger now. It had meaning. Coming home to Myla each night was just… everything. She could live very happily like this for the rest of her life. She'd been holding back on further discussions about their relationship and their future because of Myla's need to recover in so many ways. Kelly didn't want to push things too quickly just because she had to make a rather important decision about her career future.

"How are you feeling about Balbuinidh's most *prestigious* Highland Games tomorrow and the launch?" Myla relaxed back in her lounge chair and took a sip of whisky from her chunky glass, and then her eyes settled on Kelly, interested. "Any new feminised whiskies I should know about?"

Kelly smiled. "No. Just the one." It was the launch of Queen of Spirits tomorrow and they were doing it at the games. The games brought out the whole of Balbuinidh and people from towns in the surrounding regions and beyond, including many tourists. Kelly had to liaise with the local community council in the run up to the event each year. The whole thing was a ton of work, but worth it. It was the town's busiest day of the year, and one of the most fun, but also challenging. Since taking over Glenbuinidh she always worked through it, but this year, she planned to loosen the reins a bit and spend some time with Myla in the afternoon. "Everything's ready. It's the calm before the storm."

Myla smiled. "Cool. I can't wait to see it all." She reached across and put her hand on Kelly's knee, causing a warm heat to spread throughout Kelly's body. "I'm sure the launch is going to be great. It's a great bottle. It's an interesting concept."

Kelly took a sip of whisky. She wanted to prove to herself that she could do something really successful while being in this job. Would she get as much satisfaction from the job in New York? From what Jeff had described, she would have full creative control over major drinks labels for some of the biggest brands in the world. But would it compare to the passion she felt at Glenbuinidh?

She glanced over at the young woman who she loved very much but hadn't yet told. Kelly didn't want to pressurise Myla with a declaration of her love so soon in their relationship. It was hard to think they'd only known each other for six months. "What are your plans for when your ankle gets better?"

Myla blew out a breath. "Where to begin. I'm starting therapy next week, as you know. The poor soul is going to have to listen to my life story. I'm going to keep working on my music, and audition for The Light Spectrum – which I'm super excited about. I've also got an architect coming out for a consultation on the animal sanctuary, and…"

Kelly filled the silence. "Those are great plans."

"And I've still got you here with me for now, so I plan on spending as much time with you as you'll allow."

Kelly bit her lip. As new lovers Myla's words were innocent enough but the unspoken issue of Kelly's decision over New York hung in the air between them since their big talk a couple of weeks ago. Myla was a little *too* relaxed about Kelly possibly going away, saying she would support her and being positive about a long-distance relationship. Myla was playing it cool, even after everything they'd shared. It was confusing.

So Kelly had taken her time to make sense of what was going on before she made her final decision.

Things had been going *very* well. Kelly had never dreamed she could be this happy with someone, especially not someone who was ten years younger. She smiled more. Pleasure and joy were a priority once again. Life was good. Like waking up next to Myla and having coffee together. Like talking with Myla about the flowers that were blooming in the garden and the inter-connectedness of everything in nature. Conversations that sparked off in different directions and had depth. She was no longer bored in Balbuinidh. Her career was taking off. She'd finally stood up to her dad.

Kelly had changed.

The fear of staying in Balbuinidh and one day regretting not taking the opportunity diminished more and more with each day she spent loving life with Myla. Kelly gazed into the fire along with Myla, enjoying the quietness between them and the fire's heat on her shins and face. Was she going to leave everything behind and return to her old fast-paced city lifestyle in probably the most exciting city in the world? Or would she stay in Balbuinidh and build a life with Myla, assuming that was what she wanted too?

Twenty-Three

I'd heard of Highland Games, but I'd never been to one before. I walked as fast as my boot and crutches would allow into the thick of things, after showing my VIP pass to enter. I'd been looking forward to this. My ankle was still healing and I wasn't able to stay on my feet for long given the weight going through my arms. But I wanted to come to this and support Kelly. It was in a field at the edge of town. The car parking was like going to a music festival, with attendants directing cars this way and that. It was packed with people walking around, spending time together and watching the games amidst bunting and banners and marquees.

The main arena consisted of large men in kilts throwing tree trunks into the air. Caber tossing, according to the loudspeaker. I couldn't believe they were able to pick up them up and throw them. I passed what appeared to be medieval versions of shot putt, hammer throw, and throw-a-kettle-bell-over-a-high-jump-without-it-landing-on-your-head. Jenny from the visitor centre café had a food stall. She was busy serving customers but smiled over at me and waved. I was probably hard to miss shuffling by on my crutches. The next minute I was drifting into a tent selling locally made things – ceramics, cheeses, ciders – there were even some authors selling paperbacks, too. I loved looking around places like this and visited most stalls.

"Myla, pet. Hello."

I looked up. "Hi, Hilary! How are you?"

"I'm good, thank you, sweetheart. This is one of my daughters, Alice."

For a split second I pictured my own grandmother and mother, together, here today at these games, happy and spending time together. But they were gone. It was okay. There was peace in my acceptance. This loss would always be a part of me, but I was determined to live my life to the fullest, taking comfort in the fact that at least I knew my full story now.

"Hi, Alice, nice to meet you," I smiled, warmly, glad to know Hilary and see her with her daughter.

"And you," Alice said. "Thanks for visiting my mum, she's spoken fondly of you."

Hilary gestured to my boot. "What happened here?"

"I managed to break my ankle but it's fine. I'll be walking normally in a few weeks."

"You didn't." Hilary put her hand on my arm holding the crutch. "You look after yourself now, dear. There's nothing more important."

I hadn't spoken to Hilary since the day of the party. Thinking back, I was so full of anger and pain and confusion that day, but today, I felt none of those things. I was happy. I knew who I was. Being here and finding those letters and talking to Hilary was exactly what I'd needed.

"I will. I know. And thank you for your honesty that day. I needed to hear it."

Hilary's smile was knowing and kind. "You're a good girl, Myla. Keep it up. Pop in again soon, if you have time."

We said our goodbyes and I promised to call to arrange another visit for tea. I wanted to enjoy Hilary's company for as long as possible and spend as much time with her as I could.

I found Glenbuinidh's area and *wow*, was it something. We had a large and fully branded up marquee fronted by an archway to enter. There was a whisky bar and a central area for the launch of Queen of Spirits. The branding was based around the Scottish folklore and looked good. The goddess was fierce. And hot, but that was naughty thinking that. Bottles of it were elegantly stacked in cabinets scattered around the marquee. Customers or drinkers – the lines were a bit blurred today – milled around. There were long queues at the tills. Anna was behind the bar, rushed off her feet by the looks of it.

"There you are." I heard Kelly's smooth and sexy voice before I saw her. She wrapped her arms around me from behind and rested them around my waist.

"As if you could miss me with these monstrosities?" I turned around and kissed her. I inhaled her citrusy smell, and her hair tickled the side of my face. "This is incredible. You've done so well putting this together."

"It was the team's hard work. I can't take credit."

"So humble. I love that suit, by the way. You look amazing. But I was kind of hoping you'd be dressed up as our Gaelic warrior goddess." I nodded at the pop-up. "What was her name, knock-kneed Anne?"

Kelly laughed. "Neachneohain. If only you hadn't broken your leg, you could have been the Queen of Spirits yourself, enticing new customers over to the tent."

"Finally worked out how I can be useful to the distillery, have you? Or I could herd people over with my crutches?"

"Don't demonstrate, you'll fall! How is your ankle?"

"It's fine. It's more my arms. How has it gone today?"

Kelly put her hands on her hips in a sexy power pose. I don't think she was aware she was doing it, which made it all the more attractive. "Queen of Spirits is landing well. We've had queues snaking back outside the tent all day. Socials are going crazy, and the TV advert is getting lots of attention already. It went out last night."

"A success! Yay!"

Kelly grinned. "I think it's my proudest moment at Glenbuinidh. My parents have just been in."

"What did your dad say?"

"He said he was really impressed and he apologised. Said he was wrong to hold Glenbuinidh back. To hold me back."

"I'm glad he admitted that." Everything was going so well for Kelly here. I still couldn't understand why she was even considering leaving.

"He also asked if I would consider creating a new single malt, given how well received Queen of Spirits has been."

I inhaled sharply. Perhaps her dad was trying to keep Kelly in Glenbuinidh too? "Will you?"

Kelly folded her arms over her chest. "No. I don't think so."

A wave of disappointment washed over me. Maybe she really was going to leave town?

Kelly inhaled, nodding, something having caught her attention elsewhere, and clenched her jaw. "I still have some work to do but I promise I'll be yours in like ten minutes. Can you wait for me?"

"Sure. I'll wait."

Kelly kissed me quickly on the cheek before going off. That word: *wait*. I felt like I'd been waiting ages for her to decide about this job in New York. I'd had to wait for her to tell everyone about us and I was waiting for her to see how good we were together. When was Kelly going to finally see that what we had was worth it? There had been many times this past week when I'd wanted to tell Kelly that I loved her with every inch of my being, that I was so *in love* with her I could hardly breathe. The life we could have together came gloriously into view this past couple of weeks since my mountain escapades. It could be so special. It could be everything I'd ever dreamed of and then some. If only Kelly could see it too.

Even though our bond had deepened since she rescued me from the mountain and we'd been making love every night as if our very lives depended on it, Kelly was still holding back a little. It was starting to seriously get to me. This not knowing about what our future held, it was hard. And after everything I'd just been through with facing my past, my nerves were becoming more frayed each day.

I found a bench, in front of a History of Glenbuinidh pop-up stand. I sat down heavily and scanned the display again, despite having read the same information at the distillery when I came in for the tour and at the tourism summit. I smiled at the memory of Kelly giving me the tour. She'd been nervous that day. From what I knew of her now, that was quite unlike her. I got out my phone and went over my lyrics again. I knew the song inside and out, but it couldn't hurt to be extra prepared. A message from Rebecca flashed up on my screen.

Rebecca: *Hey dude, I'm pregnant!!*

Rebecca: *Sorry for the random text out of nowhere and for not telling you f2f. I'm claiming baby brain at thirteen weeks ;)*

Myla: *OMG that's amazing!!!!!!!! I'm so happy for you and Josh this is such lovely news, congratulations!!! How are you feeling?*

Rebecca: *Euphoric, nauseated, terrified. Josh is being great.*

Myla: *You guys are going to make the best parents. So so happy for you both.*

Rebecca: *Thanks dude. You're so sweet. I'm a bit worried he's going to make a better mother than I am, lol.*

I messaged Rebecca for a bit longer and arranged a time to chat properly on the phone. I loved it when good things happened to the people I cared about. Out of the corner of my eye I noticed someone walking towards me. I lifted my head and was struck by how stunningly gorgeous Kelly was. She really rocked that power suit. She was so hot. A slow smile appeared on her lips as she came to a stop in front of me. Was I really in a relationship with this stunning woman? Was this for real?

"That's me done. I'm all yours."

Was there a hidden meaning in that? Had she decided to tell that guy in New York to fuck off in the short amount of time I'd been waiting here? I put my phone back in my pocket and tried to silence my anxious thoughts. "About time."

Kelly undid the top three buttons of her shirt. I forgot where we were and stared at her as she did it.

"Feels so great to be finished work early. I haven't not worked the games since I took over. I just want to hang out with you this afternoon. Here," she entwined her fingers in mine. That fluttery feeling came over me as she kissed my hand. "Let's go explore."

Kelly rested her hand on my lower back, steadying me as I got my crutches ready. Kelly didn't seem to mind the public displays of affection. She had got over her issue about my connection to the distillery, which was wonderful. But if she was so comfortable with me, why was she about to up and move to another part of the world? How could she leave me when we were so… *happy*?

Kelly wanted to watch Rory toss the caber, so we stayed there for a bit, and then moved onto the tug-o-war, which was exciting. The crowd cheered and laughed as the tuggers did their best. Eventually, one side won the battle, and celebrated as if wining the World Cup. I suggested that the distillery should enter next year, and Kelly thought it was a good idea. An open-air highland dancing competition was underway, and we drifted over to it. Alana from the pub was participating. Kelly pointed out people she knew and stopped to speak to some as we meandered through the gathering. I even bumped into the guy at the community council I'd spoke to, once, about the local park. I was flattered that he remembered me. We had lunch at a picnic table in the food area while watching the world go by. I recognised more people than I thought I would. It was nice. I was beginning to feel like I belonged here, especially with Kelly by my side. But I now knew that real belonging began with myself, and there was a calming sense of freedom in that.

I didn't want today to end. Kelly kept smiling at me, which was charming and a little unnerving. My future happiness felt completely at the mercy of her job decision on Monday. I would support her if she went, but I was worried everything was going to change if she left. Not seeing her everyday would be just sad.

Louder Than Words

I needed something special that would make her smile and give her a reason to stay. I needed a big gesture, a *moment*, where I made Kelly see how much she meant to me. So I was going to perform on stage in the music tent and sing her a song. I'd arranged it with Grant from The Light Spectrum during the week. He was organising the bands playing at the games. I'd asked if there were any cancellations or free spots, because I wanted to sing a song for my girlfriend, who he knew. He'd said I could jump on in between two bands, instead of the filler music, which was so kind. He'd even picked up my guitar from the house ahead of time. I checked my watch. It was time to head over to the music tent and pray for a small miracle.

It was an intimate venue, and not as large a marquee as some of the others. It was perfect.

"They're really good," Kelly said, getting into it, swaying a little to the music.

We'd listened to two songs. I held onto her waist, needing her by my side, as close as possible while I still had her. The band, led by a girl in her early twenties, was exceptional. Outwardly, I was having fun and smiling but inwardly I was getting so nervous about my performance and her impending departure.

"I've never been to the music at the games before. This is so cool."

"There's a first for everything, right?"

Kelly tilted her head towards me and raised an eyebrow. She smiled, knowingly, with sparkling eyes. The other night, we'd had sex outside which was a first for me. We'd made a small fire and lain down on a blanket in the woods near the river on the estate. She'd been teasing me about popping my al fresco cherry ever since. "Like fucking your girlfriend in the woods?"

"Kelly," I hissed. "There are people right here."

Kelly laughed. "Oh yeah."

Many of our conversations ended up veering towards sexual innuendo and outright filth. I secretly loved it but wasn't letting on. I kept my voice low. "I'd prefer it if we could keep our sex life private. Half the town already know we're dating."

"I like dating you."

"Oh, that's a relief. I thought we were just hanging out as gal-pals for a second there."

"I like how private you are. And how only I get to see that part of you."

"Interesting. You like me because I'm private? Otherwise known as introverted?"

Kelly laughed. "No. There are other things, too." She held my hand and found my eyes, turning sincere. "Like how creative you are. The depth you have. The way you see the world and how we have similar values. Like how you trust me with your deepest truths and fears. You're a complicated woman, Myla Murray, and I like trying to understand you. I like being there for you. I don't know… When I'm with you, I can't think of anywhere else I'd rather be."

Before I could fully comprehend what Kelly had said her lips were on mine and her hands were in my hair. There was such feeling in Kelly's embrace and all I could do was sink into it and kiss her back. I was getting breathless and horny and emotional and didn't care that we were kissing like this in public – another first for me, I would tell her later. Kelly broke away from the kiss, pressing her cheek against my cheek, now holding my lower back.

"Would you like a drink?" Kelly asked, doe-eyed and flushed, and slightly out of breath.

I held her eyes, still moved by what she'd said and the passion in her kiss. "Sure."

"What would you like? I know you have good taste so you might be disappointed with the selection at this bar."

Kelly's question reminded me of the first time we met. Kelly, so confident and warm, had been just as mesmerising then as she was now. I grinned. "Still talking nonsense to random girls at gigs, I see?"

She smiled. "Maybe."

"I'll take some Queen of Spirits, if there's any going? Feels only right given that it's its birthday and all."

She kissed me on the lips again, this time just a peck. There was a strange look in her eyes now, one that I couldn't quite place. "I'll be right back."

Kelly weaved her way through the small crowd out of the tent. I already mourned her absence. If ten minutes was a lot, how was I going to handle long-distance? Turning back to the stage, avoiding some curious glances from the people next to me, I let myself breathe and just enjoy the moment. Kelly was in me now. Her life, her energy, her heart – I'd never felt like this before. The band hit their chorus as I decided to focus on that feeling, that *love* feeling, and channel it into my one song. Because in, I checked my wrist, thirty minutes I was going to be up there, singing my heart out for Kelly, hoping to convince her to stay by impressing the hell out of her with the song I was most proud of.

But was I doing the right thing here? If I truly loved Kelly, wouldn't I want her to go wherever she wanted to go and be happy? I mulled this over as more songs were played. If she didn't want to stay in Balbuinidh any more, and only stayed for me, I wouldn't want that either. She would resent me. Maybe our time together was going to be short, and maybe that was okay? Or maybe I *could* get used to living apart? New York did seem exciting, and I could afford to fly there as often as I wanted. As often as Kelly wanted. It *could* work. We could make it work.

And then it struck me. Why would we go to all this effort for someone we were just dating? I *loved* her. But I hadn't said it yet. Wasn't that the most important thing to come out of today? I hadn't planned on singing the song with the lyrics *I'm in love with you* basically on repeat, but perhaps I should? Another flutter of anxiety rang through me. Despite my nerves, I got this *knowing*, and realised that a love song was what I needed to play in order to put my heart out there for Kelly and this whole tent to see. It would be easier than trying to verbalise my love for her from a standing start conversation in any case.

Yes. She was getting a sappy love song whether she liked it or not. My complex and technically challenging song could wait for another time.

Oh god.

In fact, where was Kelly? It had been ages since she'd left. Twenty minutes to be precise. What if she missed my love song? I wanted us to have this moment. I stared at the entrance, dying to see Kelly come back through.

Five minutes until I was due up there. The singer announced this would be their last song and applause filled the tent. My heart rate skyrocketed, and my palms were sweaty. I wiped them against my thighs – sweaty palms were not conducive to playing the guitar.

Where is she?

Time ran out. She was going to miss it.

My whole body deflated, like I'd missed a life changing moment.

"Hey you," Kelly said, behind me.

I spun around. "You were ages!"

"Sorry. I had to deal with some stuff." Kelly handed me a small plastic cup with whisky in it, with a funny look in her eyes. I took it from her and downed it in one, feeling it burn my throat and bolster me for this performance. Kelly raised her eyebrows.

I handed her the cup back as the band finished their song and my stress levels went through the roof. "Stay here. This is for you." I kissed her softly on her cheek, just beside her mouth. I hobbled away towards the stage with my crutches. A dishevelled looking guy in a black t-shirt put a chair in the centre of the stage. I would do this without any sound checking and just go for it. I took a tentative seat and placed my crutches on the floor. He handed me my guitar, lowered the microphone and plugged me in. He did this so quickly, as if a whole tent of people weren't behind him watching his every move.

"That's you good to go." He gave me a quick nod and then briskly walked offstage.

I blinked at the faces in front of me, and then found Kelly, who had moved to the front. Her eyes were a mixture of confusion, excitement and... love. She was often like this, with her actions speaking louder than words. *Surely* she felt this too?

I took a deep breath and centred myself, taking a quick moment to get in the right position and start, no longer able to look Kelly in the eyes. I started playing and changing chords surprisingly easily considering how nervous I was. The lyrics came easy to me, too. They were right there, waiting to come out, and waiting to be said. It was more emotion than lyrics, anyway. Sometimes a song was like that. There was no way Kelly could misinterpret its meaning: *I loved her.*

I sang and sang, feeling every chord and every second of this heartfelt song during this short stint on a small stage and when I finally found her eyes, they were intensely focused on me and so soft.

By the time I got to the chorus, my nerves were gone and I was just going for it. Music had that effect on me. I felt free when I was playing.

With a level of professionalism I barely felt inside, after letting go like that, I politely thanked the crowd as they clapped and cheered, and did I hear a few whistles? What was that about? The guy was back straight away and took my guitar and helped me up.

"That was awesome by the way," he said. "Like, really good. Thanks for playing today."

I wanted to squeal but held it together. "Cheers."

"Seriously, you just played one song and you're by far the best act we've had on stage all day."

"She is amazing," Kelly said, appearing out of nowhere just to the side of the stage as we were leaving it. He acknowledged Kelly and gave me a final nod and moved off to help the next band set up. I rested my eyes on Kelly feeling so vulnerable and so happy to see her all at once. Now she knew how I felt about her under no uncertain terms. There was no taking that song back, and I wouldn't want to.

"You," she said, stepping in close to me. "That song. What you said. The way you sang it. It means so much to me. I can't believe how beautiful that was. How beautiful you are. I had no idea you were going to do that. You're so brave."

"I haven't sung onstage since school. I was so nervous. It was a bit of a gamble."

"It didn't show. Your song was incredibly moving. You moved me."

"I wanted to surprise you."

"Come with me."

Kelly led us out of the tent to where it was quieter. The fresh air was a relief. The crutches were a pain but at least they held me up. We looked into each other's eyes, with the last bricks of the wall between us lying in a rubble at our feet.

Kelly smiled. "Myla," she searched my eyes. "I love you, too."

Could someone's whole body smile? That was what happened the moment Kelly said those three words to me.

"And I'm not moving to the US."

"You're not? Since when?"

Kelly put her hands on my waist. "Since I've come to my senses. Since I realised how worried I was about you when you were lost on our mountain. I called Jeff while I was away getting us drinks, that's what took me so long. I told him I don't want the job. I can't leave this place. I can't leave Glenbuinidh." She paused. "I can't leave you." She tucked some of my hair behind my ear, still searching my eyes. Sincerity and sheer strength of emotion poured out of her. "What we have is too special to risk living apart. To risk not giving it a chance and seeing where it goes. I love you. I'm in love with you and I want to see you every day. Moving away is nuts."

"But if it's what you really want—"

"I want *you*."

"Don't stay here just for me. You'll resent me."

"I won't. I used to think that the big city lights would make me happy, that everything I needed was *out there*. But you've shown me that there's more meaning to be found inside myself, living a life I'm passionate about with the people I love. There's nowhere else I can go to cultivate that level of meaning. I have a great life here. All I need is right here. I realise that now because of you. When I went back to the marquee, Anna told me that Queen of Spirits is going *viral*. I'm enjoying the distillery again. I'm enjoying this town again. My life is here, with you."

Her words reverberated around my mind. It was everything I wanted to hear and more. Her actions were clear. She was staying. She wanted to be here. The truth in her words was louder than ever.

"You're my Queen of Spirits, Myla. You protected this place when you didn't have to. You walk your own path and you are the bravest person I've ever met."

"I don't know about that—"

"The article was published in The Guardian today for Women in Whisky. What you said… it was so beautiful."

"Ah yes. The interview." After speaking with Susan, I spoke to a journalist. He reminded me of my mother's friends and colleagues, full of charm and intrigue, like they were planning their next move on the chessboard. He was engrossed in what I had to say, which was thrilling. I wanted to do something good for Glenbuinidh and let everyone know just how special it was here. I'd been handed my role here on a plate, so it was the least I could do ahead of the big day. He hadn't promised it would be published by the launch date, so this was a lovely surprise.

Kelly got her phone out. Her eyes danced and smiled over the words as she read out the article. "Glenbuinidh is the epitome of the independent, family-run business that's been going for generations. But family in Glenbuinidh means so much more than just ancestry. Everyone who works here and the local community are part and parcel of the fabric of this distillery. They make it what it is, and they always have." Kelly stopped, pride bouncing off her, and then her face softened even further. "Coming here and finding these people has been like coming home. I've never felt like I truly belonged anywhere until I got here. It's a very special place and I'm so happy I get to be part of it. I feel like the luckiest girl in the world."

"I was waxing lyrical that day."

"And that song you sang." Kelly leant in close. "That was the most romantic thing anyone's ever done for me." Her lips hovered next to mine. "Thank you."

I leant further on my crutches, clumsily wrapping my arms around her waist, and lightly gripping the fabric of her shirt. "Well, that's because I'm in love with you."

Kelly laughed, gently. "Yep, I got that."

"I'm so happy you're not going. Is it okay to say that yet?"

Kelly smiled, a full beam taking over her face, her lips still right next to mine. "It is."

"Are you going to kiss me yet or what?"

I was grateful for the crutches because our kiss made me dizzy. I tightened my grip on her shirt. Kelly fucking MacGregor loved me back.

Twenty-Four

"Who wants to play Monopoly?" Malcolm said.

We'd decamped to the sitting room for the much-anticipated annual post-Christmas-dinner MacGregor family board game. The sitting room in Glenbuinidh House had been transformed into a cosy Christmas den with fairy lights and tinsel and a Christmas tree in the centre of the window adorned with tasteful lights and baubles. There were Christmas cards everywhere. I was touched by how many I'd received from people in the local area, including from Caroline and Bob, the new cleaner and gardener I'd taken on. They were fast becoming like family, with Caroline's steady presence in the house and Bob's willingness to impart his knowledge of gardening onto me. I'd spend hours with him in the garden while he worked, listening to him and helping a bit.

We huddled around the coffee table. Barley swished his tail nearly knocking a drink over the board game which had been laid out across the table.

"I'll take the Scottie dog." I reached for the small metal piece.

"Good choice." Malcolm said.

"Let's roll for who's to go first." Adam said.

I rolled a six.

Adam nodded. "Myla it is."

The game began in earnest. Kelly's family were super serious about this, except Eilidh who was reading a book on her new kindle in between her goes. I quite fancied doing that too, but this was becoming highly entertaining. Kelly and I held hands when it wasn't one of our turns.

"Oh come on, I wanted that one." Malcolm scoffed.

Nicole had snapped up Mayfair. "If you're not fast, you're last." Nicole smirked.

"Dad, you always win, you can at least give one of us a chance this year." Kelly said.

"Pass Go. Collect two hundred. Here please," Nicole gestured to Malcolm, who was always in charge of the bank, apparently.

Malcolm handed her the note, pausing briefly before letting her take it. "How does this feel so familiar?"

Nicole sighed, loudly, like a moody teenager. "That joke was old ten years ago, Dad."

Kelly squeezed my hand as I laughed.

I rolled another six. My fourth of the game.

"That's not fair. Myla, you always roll sixes!" Adam said, looking actually a bit pissed off.

"I'm just lucky."

"It's not luck. She gets what is rightfully hers." Malcolm glanced at me. There was a look in his eye and a tone in his voice that spoke of something else. Was it acceptance? Since the graduation party, Malcolm had become like a father figure to me. He'd apologised profusely about the incident with his friends, and I believed him. Kelly had seen a big change in him since then, too. He'd backed off and was more supportive of Kelly. Life was too short to hold grudges.

I watched Kelly's family get more and more competitive about the game as the night went on.

It was soothing.

"We'd better call it a night. Come on, you lot," Eilidh said.

Cold air rushed into the warm house as I held the door open for our guests. Barley stayed by Kelly's legs, gently wagging as his humans said goodbye. As Christmases went, this had already been the best one I'd had in a very long time and very different.

"Thanks very much for hosting us today, you two, and thanks again for inviting us into your lovely home, Myla. You really have done a great job with it." Malcolm paused, as if searching for the right words. "I know your family would be proud."

I gulped. "Thank you."

I'd insisted on hosting Kelly's family for Christmas dinner. I wanted to make the effort and do something nice for them as they had been so welcoming and lovely to me and had accepted me into their family since Kelly told them we were a couple in the summer. Also, the massive dining room was built for occasions like this, and Kelly had moved in, so it seemed like a no-brainer. I relished the challenge of catering for so many people. I'd never done that before.

"It was a pleasure. Plus, it was highly entertaining watching the MacGregors get so competitive playing board games."

"Yes, we do get ridiculous with that," Eilidh said, shaking her head. "Thank you for cooking, Myla. It was a real treat to put my feet up like this. Let me know when you want to talk about how the practice can assist your animal sanctuary." She gave me a big hug and another warm look. "Merry Christmas, sweetheart."

"My tummy feels like the size of a house and I'm going to go home and collapse into a food coma, which I think must be the biggest compliment of all." Nicole ran her hands over her tummy, which didn't look much different in my opinion.

"You say that," Adam said, standing beside her. "But we all know you'll be demolishing the rest of the Christmas chocolates as soon as we get in."

Nicole turned to her mother. "Mum. Gonna not let me touch any more food tonight."

Eilidh shook her head. "Taking responsibility for yourself again, I see?"

"Right, you lot," Malcolm said. "Let's leave these two be."

As Kelly's family piled out of the house, I smiled at the feeling of being part of their family, and how nice it was. I was getting used to it. My initial uneasiness and feelings of being triggered around Kelly's family had thankfully disappeared, most likely as a result of a lot of work in therapy over the last few months.

My therapist, a no-nonsense Northern Irish woman called Irene, believed I needed to grieve the loss of the family and life I never had, separately to how I handled the long-term actual loss of my mother. That the loss I had even before my mother died needed to be dealt with. That they were two different and equally valid things. She thought that I'd missed out on a stage of development because my mother passed away before I had processed what it was like when she was alive, and her dying forced me to focus on that.

She also thought I had developed a disorganised or anxious avoidant attachment style because of the trauma of growing up with my mum. It explained why I both craved connection but also feared anyone getting too close. Why I had a chronic fear of abandonment and clung to people, yet also shut people out, didn't believe people loved me, and didn't like confiding in anyone or asking for help.

I had no idea how she came to any of her conclusions, but her insights had been helping me a lot. She was challenging me, in a way. It wasn't easy but I was giving it a chance.

Plus, Kelly had been so patient and supportive about me being in therapy, which helped. She understood me and it meant the world to me.

Kelly turned to me and smiled; her eyes were soft. "Thank you for today." She wrapped her arms around me and gave me a peck on the lips. Hosting today was going to mean serious brownie points. "It means a lot."

"I'm glad everyone enjoyed themselves. I like doing the cooking."

"You didn't have to. You don't have to perform like that. However, you are, objectively speaking, a wonderful human being and the best girlfriend in the world."

I narrowed my eyes, but playfully. "You flirt."

She kissed me quickly again. "Right. I'll do the tidying up and you can go and chill if you want." She slid her hands off my waist and headed towards the kitchen. Barley trotted behind her, as usual, probably hoping to score some more leftovers.

I went back into the sitting room and stood by the Christmas tree. Kelly and I had got the tree from a local farm. We went shopping for it together. There was something so committed about the outing and had set the tone for our first Christmas together. I touched the spiky needles, feeling a mixture of emotions about today, and sat down by the log fire.

There was something I needed to do. I fetched Hazel's letters from the study. They had to go. I no longer wanted to hold onto this story. I no longer wanted these in my life. In my house. I wanted to move on. I held the letters to the top of the flames and watched as the flames took hold. I let them fall into the fire, watching the paper burn. There was something so healing about seeing the words disappear. That part of my life no longer defined me.

I picked up my laptop and played the video of my mother's last Christmas, watching as she ripped open the self-help book I got her and laughed hysterically at it. There were some things I would never let go of. Her blonde hair was wild and her eyes were so full of fire and intensity. She looked so *young*. She finally composed herself. "Oh, Myla. My sweet and sensitive girl. Thank you. I'm sure this will come in very handy when I need a good laugh one day."

My favourite cinnamon Christmas candle from my old flat flickered on the mantlepiece, scenting the room. I let the video play on to my favourite bit, a rare show of affection from her. "This is for you." My mother handed me a present from under the fake tree we'd put up last-minute and turned my phone filming the video onto me. The video rustled and blacked out for a second before it settled. My face as I opened the present was so innocent and not unlike a delighted child's. It was a box with two tickets in it to go and see my favourite band at the time. The sheer joy on my face when I realised what it was was more from the fact that my mother had remembered they were my favourite band. "Will you come and see them with me?" I'd asked. I remembered how she'd shrugged and nodded in agreement that she would. And then, she turned the camera around and spoke into it and said, "Of course I will, my sweet Myla. I'd do anything for you." Her eyes were bright and full of life. I knew now that she'd meant what she'd said, in her own unique way.

We never did get to go and see that band. She died a few weeks before the gig. The years of pain and suffering that stood between that moment on video and me sitting here now, in her ancestral home and hometown, collapsed into nothing. If she were here now, she would probably be opening another bottle of wine ready to keep the party going. She was who she was, and she never apologised for it. She was larger than life. I'd always been in her shadow, but now, after finding out everything I had and after being in this place that had raised her, I finally understood her. I was seeing that I was her great love. She did her best with me, and I would be forever grateful for having known the wonderful and complicated person that she was, even if only for such a short time.

"Hey," Kelly said, coming into the room with Barley and holding two small glasses. "The kitchen's done. Barley helped. I brought us some Baileys." She sat next to me. Barley lay in front of the fire. "What are you watching?"

I was tempted to shut the lid but stopped. Kelly knew a lot about my mother by now, although I'd never shown her any videos or photos of her.

"Is that your mum?"

I took the glass that she passed me. "Yes."

"Can I see?"

I replayed the video and tried not to look at her as she watched it. I'd never shared this with anyone before.

Kelly spoke softly as it ended. "What a beautiful moment to catch on video. She clearly loved you very much."

"I just miss her sometimes, you know?"

Kelly pulled me closer, and I inhaled her familiar scent. "Of course you do."

I nuzzled into her chest and neck, grateful that Kelly was so understanding but also wanting to change the subject. This had been such a happy day overall and I didn't want it to end on a downer. From where I was last year, I already had my happy ever after. "I had a great day. Happy Christmas, my love."

"Me too. Happy Christmas, Myla." Kelly kissed the side of my head. "I love you."

Epilogue

I leant over my violin and sang into the microphone, watching Susie for the next cue. The pub was hot, with people packed in to see the gig and stove fires burning all evening. And it was noisy as hell. I was rocking out with The Light Spectrum in my new hometown surrounded by friends and the love of my life.

Kelly sat with Anna and Nicole to the left of the small stage, and Rory and his nephew were at the bar in their usual spot. There was a lot of love for the band tonight. I could feel it. A few people were singing along to the chorus now. Lots of people were clapping to the music, Susie's gravelly voice never missing a note.

I loved playing in this band, I realised as another song dropped and the pub erupted. They were a quality act, and the songs were well written. The music was a joy to play. Susie was a great performer and my backing vocals blended nicely with hers when performing live. Although one day I would like to be performing my own material, being a part of this local band was amazing.

We'd been playing for ages, and I didn't want us to stop. The energy from the crowd and the connectedness with the music was intoxicating. Ritchie swung an elaborate air shot and messed up his section for a few beats. Grant laughed. I smiled. Susie didn't break a note through her smirk, and Ritchie continued as if he had meant it, giving us a quick wink. Grant gave me a nod as we neared the end of our set.

I could get used to this.

My fingers did what they did as I pushed and pulled the bow up and down. I caught Kelly staring at me and we held eye contact. She looked so hot tonight in her skinny jeans and heels, and loose checked shirt. The way her smouldering eyes were raking over me was seriously making my pulse race. I would see those eyes dance with ecstasy later and I *could not wait.*

I hit my solo. Ignoring the fluttering in my stomach, I could feel Kelly's gaze on me.

I was exactly where I needed to be.

After we finished playing, a pint of beer was placed in my hand. In the swell of the pub, it was impossible to thank each person who patted me on the back and congratulated me. I didn't get very far from the stage area. Everyone wanted to talk to the band.

"So, Myla." Ritchie the drummer called out over the noise. "You want to join our band officially?"

My eyes flicked towards Grant and then Susie.

"We'd love to have you, honey." Susie said. Her speaking voice was so charismatic, too. "You're a natural."

Grant nodded his head. He was the leader of the band, but in a quiet, sensible and methodical way. "That just clicked. We knew straight away tonight. We'd love you to join The Light Spectrum."

I grinned at my new band mates. It was exactly what I wanted right now.

I found Kelly after a little chat with the band. The sense of new opportunities and possibilities with my music career was making me buzz with glee. She was still at the side with Anna and Nicole, sitting on a stool. She watched me wade through the people towards her. The slow smile that spread across her face as I approached was everything.

She was like a homing beacon. Beaming. *She* was what home felt like to me now – warm, happy, and loving.

"Hello there, Mozart." Kelly reached out for me. "You were stunning."

Our hands entwined, almost unconsciously. Her skin was soft and warm. I grinned, uncontrollably, leaning into the side of her leg. "They want me to join. I've said yes."

"Well done, darling. You deserve it." Kelly planted a soft kiss on my lips.

My lips tingled. Every time she touched me my body still went into overdrive.

"No way, that's amazing!" Nicole said, mouth wide open.

"Congratulations, Myla. That's very cool." Anna leant across and hugged me lightly around the shoulders.

I couldn't stop grinning. "They're talking about starting to write the next album. They want me to have an input."

Kelly squeezed my hand. "I'm so happy for you. I'm so happy for them, too. They're so lucky to have you. You guys will be selling out stadiums around the world before you know it. The Light Spectrum were already going places, and with you involved now too, they won't know what has hit them."

"You might be a little biased, but I'll take it."

"I know it's a bit early to ask but can you like wangle us VIP tickets to your gigs and stuff?" Nicole said. She was serious.

"Since you asked so discreetly, yes."

"Yaaaas. Thank you."

Kelly laughed.

"Sweet." Anna smiled, and then picked up her vibrating phone to take a call. "Sorry. It's Hayley. I'd better take this." She disappeared through the pub doors.

Nicole started talking to some friends from school. She picked up her pint of beer and joined them.

Kelly and I faced each other. Her cheeks were flushed, and she had a few strands of hair loose. I still couldn't get over the fact that we were together, and how lucky I was.

"Excellent bow strokes by the way. I was getting jealous of your violin, the way you were playing her so passionately. Amazing fingering."

I laughed. "Do you want to go home?"

"You don't want to stay and hang out with your new band mates?"

"There will be plenty of time for that." I rested my hand on her knee and bit down on my lip, knowing that it turned her on. "I want you."

Kelly pulled me into the fire exit.

"I believe someone got caught in one of these once." She slid her hand around my waist. "I wanted to check out their story. See if they were telling the truth."

I rolled my eyes. "The front door would have been perfectly fine." Once the door was closed, the noise from the pub muted. "You still don't believe me?"

She laughed. "Of course I do. I just plan on teasing you about it forever."

Forever. I loved the sound of that. "If you must."

Kelly put her hands in my hair and tilted her head. She kissed me so slowly that I forgot where we were. My heart was about to burst. Kissing Kelly was essential to me now. I couldn't imagine my life without her.

As we stepped out into the chilly winter night together, I knew that forever might be a possibility, although it would never be long enough.

~ The End ~

Author's Note

Hi! Thank you *so much* for reading my book! I am so grateful you decided to spend your precious time in my world.

If you want to spend more time in Louder Than Words, please find a free soundtrack on Spotify via: tinyurl.com/yb3926zn.

If you'd like to know more about me and my writing, you can go to www.lisaelliotauthor.com and sign up to my newsletter or find me on social media.

And lastly, if you enjoyed this book, please leave a quick rating or review! I live for them!

Thank you.

About The Author

Lisa Elliot is a Scottish author of sapphic fiction.

She loves reading and writing romance novels and enjoys nothing more than getting lost in a good story.

Lisa used to be a personal trainer and still loves trying to lift heavy things in the gym. Her guilty pleasure is techno and house music. Has cried at every episode of Grey's Anatomy.

She lives for coffee and cake and long walks in the hills. Is task-managed by her dog.

www.lisaelliotauthor.com

Other Books by Lisa Elliot

Up Against Her (2021)

Skye, Head of Qualitative Research, loves her job exploring what makes people tick and generating insights for her clients. She's worked her way up and is on the brink of a promotion at her top market research consultancy. But when she's forced to merge her department and compete for the job she thought was hers, she's seriously displeased.

Brianna, Head of Quantitative Research, prefers numbers and statistics over people. Confident and successful, she never shows any vulnerability at work and keeps her personal and professional lives strictly separate. She's only been at the consultancy for six months, so when she's offered the chance to go for the top job, she doesn't hesitate.

They have two months to work together, jointly leading a single research team, to prove they should be the next Director of Research. As rivals going for the same job, their opposing styles clash as they try to lead their team into a new future.

They don't get on. But as they spend more time together, prior assumptions give way to pleasant surprises. Will they keep it professional and ignore the electricity between them? Or will they find their way to each other against the odds?

~~~

The Light in You (2020)

Yoga teacher Angela Forbes has fulfilled her dream of opening her very own studio, Heart Yoga, on the outskirts of Edinburgh, Scotland. Passionate and principled, she believes in yoga and wants to make a difference. Unfortunately, her studio is hanging by a thread after a slow start. She doesn't have time for love, and isn't attachment the root of all suffering anyway?

Life isn't going the way Emily Mackenzie had planned. She's lost her high-powered corporate job and isn't coping well. She's spent her twenties sacrificing her personal life for her career and now she has nothing to show for it. Stressed and struggling, she might just be at her rock bottom. When Emily joins Heart Yoga she finds a lot more than just a good stretch.

An unexpected kiss forces Angela to question everything she holds dear, and as Emily gets back on her feet is it wise for her to risk getting involved with someone who's not looking for love?

~~~

Dancing It Out (2018)

Kate has moved to London and is embarking on a new life. She has become an independent, high-achieving young lawyer, who still hasn't figured out who she really is yet.

But when she moves into a house-share in north London and meets Lorraine, an enigmatic filmmaker, whose room is next to hers, an intense bond quickly develops. After an epic night-out clubbing, Kate's crush on Lorraine leads Kate to question and discover her true sexuality.

A slow-burn romance about awakening desire and finding the courage to follow your heart.

~~~

Printed in Great Britain
by Amazon